Raven's Children

Sabrina Chase

ISBN-13: 978-1-940006-16-1

CONTENTS

Also by Sabrina Chase

Firehearted
The Last Mage Guardian

THE SEQUOYAH TRILOGY:
The Long Way Home
Raven's Children
Queen of Chaos

ACKNOWLEDGMENTS

Many thanks to the long-suffering members of STEW, my editor Deb Taber, proofreader Roger Ivie, and all the enthusiastic readers who cheer me on. You make this so fun it should be illegal.

S.Chase

PROLOGUE

It's a trap.

Harrington froze. There were people already at the Kulvar dock, waiting for him. He had expected that, but he really ought to have anticipated they would be armed. Especially since he'd recently toured Kulvar's extensive criminal areas while chasing one of them—the ordinary-looking woman standing before the docking hatch. The young man who so strongly resembled her was aiming a rifle at Harrington's head.

Ennis had known Moire Cameron was dangerous; they'd been on the same Fleet ship when she'd mutinied. What had happened to him?

You really have no one to blame but yourself for all this. He'd sketched Cameron unawares while waiting for a ship off of a refueling station. He hadn't even known her name at that point. Ennis had seen the sketch, and then the rest came out. That she was wanted for her part in a Fleet mutiny, and had been presumed dead in the escape. And that was only the beginning.

He still didn't know what had drawn his attention in the first place. To a casual observer Moire Cameron was completely unremarkable in appearance: brown hair, a medium build, neither tall nor short. If he had been searching for an explorer archetype to draw, he would not have chosen someone like her. No striking features, no aura of adventure or daring deeds. It was only if you looked more closely that you saw the focused, observant gaze of hazel eyes under straight black brows, hinting at the intelligence behind them. Things had a way of happening around her. Dangerous things. Did she know that he had shown the sketch to Fleet? Was that why she had tricked him with a false message from "Commander Ennis?"

That should have alerted him right there. Ennis had made a point of not mentioning his Fleet rank in public on this mission. He drew a sharp breath. Ennis was lying on a crate just outside the hatch, in front of Cameron. Dead, or merely unconscious?

It was a bad situation, but he hadn't been shot yet. He forced himself to relax and made sure his empty hands were in view. They must want something. He saw Ennis's fingers curl slightly once, twice, and he felt a wash of relief. Ennis was alive, and awake.

"How would you prefer me to address you?" Harrington asked. He knew Cameron would not be pleased if he said her real name out loud.

The hazel eyes narrowed slightly. "I'm known here as Captain Roberts."

"I trust you have not done away with him, Captain?" When she stepped away from the crate, he approached cautiously. "His indisposition...."

"Temporary. If you're impatient, use one of these." She tossed him a clear plastic packet, moving stiffly, and he caught it midair. He saw a dark stain on her side that could be blood. So, Ennis hadn't gone down without a fight. A quick glance at Ennis showed no obvious injuries. How had Cameron gotten the upper hand?

He glanced at the packet. In addition to a few stimulants, it contained a datatab. "What is this for?" He held it up.

"I hear you're curious about me. It has some answers."

"I cannot imagine why you would have the slightest interest in helping me."

She smiled. "My enemies don't want that information out. They will be your enemies too, if you publish it." This seemed to please her. "Exclusives don't come cheap."

She certainly knew how to bribe a reporter. Harrington looked at the datatab, knowing that if Ennis had told him the truth it was equal parts treasure and explosives. He knew from experience Toren was willing to kill to keep that information secret. They had already put him to considerable personal inconvenience, and he very much wanted to know why. He also wanted to know why Ennis was as determined to find her as Cameron was to escape him. Even if it meant getting shot at again.

When he looked up again, Moire Cameron was standing in the open hatch door and the young man was behind her, inside the ship.

"Don't be looking for me, Mr. Harrington. I'm going to be very hard to find for a while." The hatch closed with finality.

CHAPTER 1
EVERYTHING IS PERFECTLY FINE

The voices slowly percolated through her perception until they became noticeable. Moire rubbed her eyes, hoping whoever it was would go away. The transit to the sargasso wasn't fun even with a second pilot, and she hadn't been sleeping well, either. She should be trying to sleep now. Instead, she was sitting in her cramped office off of *Raven*'s bridge listening to two of her crew argue, because Alan was in her cabin and seeing him would be enough to start it all off again.

Her son was finally starting to tell her what Toren had done to him.

The argument was getting louder, and now she recognized Kilberton's voice. Maybe she should see what the problem was. She hadn't realized he even knew *how* to argue.

Opening the door, she caught his last few words. "...the captain will not like it!"

Yolanda Menehune was facing him, hands on her hips and dark brows furrowed over narrowed eyes.

"What won't I like?" From their startled reactions, they hadn't known she was in the office.

"It's just some cargo," Yolanda said, smiling weakly. "Nothin' we want. But I can get real *dos* price for it. I just wanna take one of the scooters and..."

"She wants to sell morgatane," Kilberton said, each word clipped and sharp. His dark face was austere and cold. Moire had never seen him this angry before.

She had to ask. "What's morgatane?"

Kilberton's entire body sagged in disbelief, while Yolanda blinked and struggled for words. "They din' have it back then, eh?" she said finally. Both Kilberton and Yolanda knew about her lack of contemporary knowledge.

Moire shook her head. "Never heard of it. It's a drug?"

"It is poison." Kilberton's lips were drawn back from his teeth.

"Yeah, like the rest of 'em aren't," Yolanda snapped. "It's hard to make, see? Real sparse to the load." She paused, looking at Moire's face, and translated, "only few runners got it, right? You got that, you big mover."

Kilberton folded his arms. "The other drugs can kill, it is true. This one *always* kills. If you take it you must take more, or you die. If you keep taking it, you die. In the station where I was born there was one who had it. The morgatane leaked when the police fought with him. Sixteen people died."

Yolanda rubbed her chin, her eyes darting from side to side. "It's bad, yeshure. You let me sell that other stuff, though. Thought it was OK."

It was true Moire had carried on the established tradition that let Yolanda handle illegal cargo, especially now that they were doing salvage. It was quite profitable to the ship, but more importantly it kept up their cover as pirates and their contacts to the criminal underworld. Moire gazed at her cargo master, noticing the way she was playing with her kink-curled hair and other little signs that she was uncomfortable. Yolanda knew morgatane was dangerous, all right, and she had guessed Moire wouldn't allow it if she knew.

"This may be more trouble than it's worth," Moire said. "We don't need the money that badly. Besides, if it's that hard to get it will be noticed if we sell it—especially when we can't get more."

"There are only two combines that deal in morgatane," Kilberton said, nodding. "They fight wars. If they hear we have sold any, both will attack us."

"Hey, how come you straight-up know so much about morgatane, hah?" Yolanda said, sticking out her jaw, eyes narrowed with suspicion.

He was silent for a moment, looking down at the deck. "My friend from childhood, he was the policeman who found the runner. He had been hunting him for a long time," he said softly. He looked up again. "Slavers use it."

Yolanda didn't say anything. Her light brown face was getting red.

"No morgatane," Moire said, and Yolanda just nodded. "Are we having money problems?"

"Nah, we're good for now. Harvey'd better be there with the money from the sale when we get back to Kulvar, though. Better be there anyway. Tired of doing his work as well as mine. Took me a week to figure out how he kept the ship books."

If Harvey Felden didn't show up they would have a whole new set of worries. The old steward had left to get the money from a ship sale on Cullen, where Moire didn't dare show up again. He'd left before the incident with Ennis. Moire rubbed her fingertips lightly over the pale, still-shiny scars on her palms. More unfinished business.

Gren Forrest's distinctive clomping steps entering the bridge made her look up. The engineer had his long black hair back in a folded queue, indicating he was planning on working in an EVA suit. His shaggy brows went up in surprise when he saw her. "You're up early," he grunted.

"She's up late," Yolanda said sourly. "She never left."

"What?!" All three of them, Gren, Kilberton, and Yolanda, turned to face her. Moire felt a sudden urge to back into her office and shut the door.

Gren peered at her. "You haven't been looking good lately. Maybe Fortin should make sure everything's healing OK."

"Don't wake her up just for that," Moire objected as he headed for the wall comm. "She got shot up a lot worse than I did. I'm fine, really. I hardly notice it anymore."

Gren hesitated, then sighed. "So which one are we starting with? The cargo hauler with the hull breach?"

Moire nodded, relieved. "You know where it is, right?" she asked Kilberton.

"In the cluster next to the ship we worked on last time," he said, and moved to the realspace controls.

"You coming with us?" Gren asked Yolanda.

"Yeah, I'm comin'. Got some personal cargo space to fill," she grumbled.

"Don't leave just yet," Moire said, going back to her office and rummaging through the datatab rack on the desk. Since Yolanda would be outside *Raven*'s network on the salvage ship, she wouldn't be able to access any of the data there. Moire found the tab she wanted and went back to the bridge. "While you're out there, see if you can find any of this."

Yolanda slotted the tab in her hand-size datapad and quickly scanned it, starting to look interested despite her sulky expression. She loved searching the wrecked ships out in the sargasso. Moire hoped it would take her mind off the forbidden morgatane.

"OK. You got food fabrication equipment, water recyclers...? That's for stations, not a ship crew. We're salvaging plenty of supplies."

"We'll need the equipment on Sequoyah once we start living there. There'll be more people, too." There'd have to be, if they were going to defend the planet. A *lot* more people.

Yolanda nodded. "Makes sense. Now this other one. 'Any and all weapons and explosives found.' What's that about? You think Toren is gonna come in shooting?"

"They will find out where we are eventually, and when they do they'll want to take the planet from us." Moire rubbed her face with her hands and walked back to her office, feeling a wave of tiredness wash over her. "Oh yeah, and make sure you find any guns before Alan does. He gets upset when I keep taking them away from him." Just like any kid would with a shiny new toy. Once again she wondered why Toren had done such a thorough job of teaching him how to kill. Weren't they afraid their created workers would turn on them? Of course, they had the control bracelets...

"Are you going to tell me what's wrong?"

Moire turned sharply. Gren had followed her inside. He shut the door and stood in front of it, his arms folded across his chest.

"I'm tired." She collapsed into the big chair. "Dammit, Gren, why can't you be captain for a change? Everything I do just seems to get us in more trouble."

His face showed no reaction. "It was the right choice at the time, and it's still the right choice. Not only is the crew making three times the usual salary, we've got first claim on an Earthlike planet. Even with the good pay none of us would be able to afford to live on either of the other two they've discovered. You're doing fine."

Moire slouched in her chair, feeling uncomfortable. She needed to tell somebody, and if there was anybody on the ship she could trust, it was Gren. "I'm not focused on my job," she said reluctantly. "You know how Alan...came about, right?" Gren nodded, looking serious. "When I first met up with him I knew somebody had done some awful things to him, but he wouldn't talk about it. Now he's telling me more. Two days ago he told me just enough for all the pieces to come together." She took a deep breath. "Toren has this facility somewhere. They're making more accelerated-growth kids, just like him, and I'm pretty sure they are using stolen genetic material from the NASA protective storage project to do it. Alan escaped, but the rest are still there and I keep..." she closed her eyes, swallowing around the tightness in her throat. "I keep thinking about them."

She'd solved the problem of how to report the discovery of Sequoyah by essentially giving it to *Raven*'s crew, even if they still had to keep it from being taken by Toren. But she had an obligation to the other explorers too, to the children they never knew they had. She was the only one left who could help them.

"Where is it?" Gren was watching her closely, his face hard.

"I don't know. I don't think Alan can tell me. He didn't even know what planets were when I met him." Only eight years old and he'd never been anywhere else before he escaped the facility.

"We need more information," Gren said, stabbing a finger at her. "Figure out how he got free. Then we can decide if there is anything we can do."

It was tempting, so tempting... "We're going to have enough to do defending Sequoyah," Moire managed, finally. "I don't see how we can do anything."

Gren grunted. "If the others are like Alan, they can help us with that."

That hadn't occurred to her, but it made sense. "Good idea. I'll see if Alan remembers anything useful." She stood up, wavering a little until her balance steadied.

"First you are going to get some sleep," Gren said, frowning. "If you don't head for your cabin, now, I *will* wake up Fortin. I hope she gets well enough to start cooking again," he grumped as he followed Moire out of the bridge. "Pico tries, but you can tell he's never had anything that wasn't processed to death."

"Are you quite sure you're all right?"

Ennis cracked one eye open. Harrington was leaning over his bunk. The reporter's melancholy, aquiline face was outwardly calm, but something in his voice told Ennis he was more concerned than he was letting on.

"What did she do to you? Perhaps a visit to the medical station is in order."

He had to reassure him. Then he could go back to feeling miserable in peace.

"Muscle relaxant in some coffee." Harrington's skeptical expression made him add, "She drank it too. Took something to counteract it beforehand, made me think it was a painkiller."

Harrington gave him a long look. Ennis couldn't tell if he'd convinced him or not, but after a moment Harrington left the tiny cabin. They were on a ship bound for Shipman Point, a station with a Fleet base where he could find a military courier to FarCom. Every second brought him closer to the moment when he would have to explain himself and what he had done—or failed to do.

How could he make it sound like anything other than "I let her get away"?

Every time he tried to figure out a reasonable explanation he'd remember what had happened on the dock on Kulvar. Reliving the feel of the gun recoiling in his hand, the sick feeling as he realized an energy blast shouldn't *have* a recoil, and then seeing Moire's shocked expression as she fell, clutching her side, the blood leaking through her fingers.

He didn't like to think how close she'd come to dying. It was all Namur's fault for wanting him to take that stupid gun in the first place. Was it just because it was scan resistant, or because they had stolen it from Toren and wanted the corporation to know their secret had been compromised? Namur was the head of Umbra, the most secretive of the Intelligence groups. He probably had any number of underhanded plots going on.

Once Moire was wounded he'd had to patch her up as soon as he could. She'd managed to take the gun away then, but she hadn't shot him with it. When it seemed like she was cooperating and would go back to Fleet with him, he had been willing to believe it.

Perhaps he hadn't been as suspicious as he should have been. She'd been devious enough in getting the gun, pretending to collapse. Of course he'd had to catch her. He'd gotten distracted, that's all.

Very distracted. Ennis got up and paced, restless and irritable. He'd failed because he'd *wanted* to believe her. He still couldn't decide if he'd been wrong. She had taken the gun, but then she'd given it back. She'd drugged him to escape, and then found Harrington to take care of him until he recovered.

And she had promised to return to Fleet. He felt his pocket, seeking the reassuring shape of the NASA pin she'd given as a pledge of that promise. She'd said it belonged to someone she knew, which meant it was at least eighty years old and probably more. She'd taken a long trip through time and space, leaving all she'd known behind. Mementos of her past would be extremely rare and precious to her.

The pin was there, but so was something else. A datatab. He frowned. A fuzzy memory floated into his consciousness, of a voice–Moire's voice–arguing with someone who wanted to kill him. He'd felt fingers opening his shirt pocket, and had been suddenly and irrationally terrified that Moire would see the sketch he still kept there. Then he heard her voice, close to his ear. "It isn't much, but it might help." The rest was a blur of images and echoing sounds he could not resolve, gradually clearing to reveal the empty dock where her ship had been.

The door to the cabin opened, and Harrington stepped in again. He shut the door quickly when he saw the tab in Ennis's hand.

"If that is from our mutual acquaintance I suggest you keep it hidden. Have you had a chance to look at it yet?" Ennis shook his head. "It is well worth your time. I've already sent encrypted copies to several locations, with a few on time-delay just for luck. Her adversaries have shown their ruthless nature before."

Ennis managed a faint smile at this. Harrington was still put out at nearly being incinerated by Toren on Bone. He fingered the datatab thoughtfully. This was the first good news he'd had in a long time. Maybe the information would be enough to at least keep him from getting discharged.

She'd put the data together in a hurry. Misspellings, missing words, and incomplete sentences–but then she'd been doing it with both hands scraped raw after climbing the air shaft on Kulvar to get away from him. First there was a terse, choppy report of the events leading to the discovery of Sequoyah, and an even more terse summary of what Cameron remembered of events afterward. She hadn't wanted to remember; he could feel it. Another report, this of her actions in the mutiny on *Canaveral*. And then a few rough sketches of Sequoyah's surface with a brief description of the planet's characteristics and biosphere.

One small knot of tension vanished. She was trying to help him, even after he'd nearly killed her. He hoped there had been someone on the ship to take care of her. Perhaps her son, the son she hadn't known about. He wondered if he would ever find out the rest of that story.

He wondered why he wanted to know so badly.

They arrived at Shipman Point two days later. Ennis felt no remaining effects from the drugs, just impatience to report in and get it over with. He wanted to know what Fleet was going to decide to do with him. Was there any chance they would keep him in a combat post, even for a little while? He had no right to expect it. His promotion cutoff date had already passed. The choices now were a desk job or exile to life as a civilian. He shuddered.

"I suppose I shall have to muddle on by myself," Harrington said as they left the ship. "Unless you have changed your mind about reporting in immediately?"

Ennis gritted his teeth. Why would the reporter be trying to find Cameron again? "I seem to recall someone saying you shouldn't go looking for her," he said.

"I do have other lines of investigation," Harrington said, with a touch of frost. "No doubt she will show up in her own good time."

"No doubt." Ennis looked gloomily at the station map. The Fleet outpost was near the commercial freight area of the docks some distance away. "Perhaps you'll have better luck without me."

He picked up his bag and walked away, but Harrington was still beside him. "Permit me to accompany you. I remain unconvinced of your good health after your latest adventures. Your melancholy silence is unusual."

Ennis took a deep breath. "I'm in a lot of trouble," he said finally. Harrington could take that any way he wanted. "If I..."

Something wasn't right. It took him a moment to figure it out. There were a number of toughs and dockworkers hanging out at this level, and he'd paid them only cursory attention. But one had snagged his eye—a man who looked remarkably clean for a dockworker. He also looked familiar. There hadn't been enough time for news of what had happened at Kulvar to get back to Toren. These must still be the original set of thugs looking for him. Another thing he could thank Namur for.

He glanced out of the corner of his eye, saw Harrington looking at him with concern. "They're here," Ennis said softly. "The ones with the flamethrowers." Not a good idea to name Toren out loud now.

"Where?"

"Up ahead." The operatives were not moving. Yet. Ennis stopped and looked at his chrono, as if planning a rendezvous. "Between us and the number forty-five cargo hatch."

Harrington rubbed his chin and looked at his own chrono, for all the world like someone wondering if it was time for lunch. "How inconvenient."

That's probably how he'd describe his own death. "Maybe we should go back and admire the cross-corridor," Ennis suggested.

"Why not?"

They turned and walked casually in the other direction. Ennis looked up at a reflective display on one wall. The operatives were coming closer.

"It must be our magnetic personalities," he said dryly. "Got your weapon ready?"

"Yes, but I don't quite–"

Ennis spun around. The Toren operatives weren't even bothering to conceal their weapons. "Cover!" he yelled, ducking behind a big crate loader. Harrington was on the other side in a niche in the wall, his little snub-nosed gun in his hand.

One of the Toren ops fired, a blast of heat and energy that seared through the open gaps in the crate loader. Ennis looked around desperately for inspiration. The bright orange stripes of a pressure zone caught his eye, and he smiled grimly.

It took a few seconds to find the sensor, tucked behind some utility cables on the ceiling. Taking careful aim, he shot it out. Sirens blaring, pressure doors descended with a clang between them and the Toren operatives. Unfortunately, other pressure doors were blocking the exit. He hadn't noticed those before.

Ennis swore. "We have about fifteen minutes before someone comes to check and open the doors. Hopefully they'll be friendly, because we can't go anywhere."

"I wouldn't be so quick to say that," Harrington said thoughtfully.

"Why?"

"The builders of this particular station had a tendency to cut corners during construction. I wrote a bit of an exposé some time ago. I suppose you didn't read it," he said mournfully, looking like a disappointed Caesar.

Ennis sighed. "Skip to the pertinent piece of golden prose."

"The maintenance accessway for the pressure doors is one continuous corridor, and the corridor hatches seal on positive pressure only."

"You're joking." Ennis stared at him, appalled. "If the access corridor is compromised, then..."

"Precisely. The entire sector of the station is perforated." Harrington pointed to a hatch on the wall, near the ceiling. "If they haven't fixed it, I can live to write another scathing exposé." He smiled gently.

Ennis jumped and caught the lowest rung of the ladder to the hatch. Harrington followed.

"I hope those goons don't subscribe to your wireservice," Ennis muttered as he climbed.

"Quite."

At the top, Ennis propped his shoulder against the hatch door and shoved. One foot slipped from the rung, and he scrambled to regain his position. It took three tries to overcome the hatch seal.

Harrington peered over Ennis's shoulder. "Oh, good. Another article to write."

The corridor was narrow, but Ennis could see it went the entire length of the docking area. He put the hatch cover back in place as soon as they were both inside. When they found the hatch nearest the Fleet outpost, the sirens were still sounding in the distance but the pressure doors had been reopened.

"Nobody there," Ennis reported after a careful look through a crack. "Just a worried-looking noncom poking her head out to look every now and then."

"Right. I'll give you cover, then, shall I?" Harrington checked his gun and nodded, satisfied. He already had his finger on the trigger and was pointing it down the ladder that Ennis would be using. Judging from his technique Harrington had gotten most of his ideas of gun tactics from bad trid shows. Ennis winced. Harrington *was* trying to be helpful.

"If you point it *that* way, down the corridor, you'll be more likely to hit the bad guys than me. Up to you." Ennis hesitated on his way out the hatch. "How are you going to get out? They'll be hunting you too, now."

"Yes, I think a period of quiet is in order. Somewhere else. Don't worry about me; I know this station rather well. Now off with you, before they come back."

"Good luck. And thank you." Ennis quickly dropped down the rungs to the corridor.

🦅

Moire stood at the cave mouth and looked out over the rocky bay and the forest of pseudotrees looming in the shallows. It was a view she never tired of. Sequoyah's sun was just thinking about setting, and if you knew what to look for you could see one of the moons on the far horizon.

I suppose we're going to have to come up with some names if we're going to live here.

The sound of footsteps made her turn back to the cave entrance, full of gear and people moving it. Gren Forrest was coming toward her. The engineer was looking grumpy, but that was normal for him. He was also peering up at the sky with a suspicious expression. Like most of her station-raised crew, he was having some trouble getting used to the concept of "outside" as a place where you didn't need protective gear.

"Everything OK? Having trouble with the equipment?" They'd found a lot of useful stuff in the sargasso this time; enough that she'd wanted to bring it back to Sequoyah before selling the salvaged ships. They needed to get the base camp set up as soon as possible.

He stopped, staring out at the bay as she had done. "How long ago were you here again?"

"Over eighty years by the calendar. Only two years for me, since we had a bad case of Einstein's Revenge coming back." Moire carefully didn't think about *how* she'd come back. The only one alive, in a ship that was more holes than structure.

"And Toren doesn't know about it?" He sounded completely

incredulous.

"They know it exists. They don't know where it is or how to get to it. Why do you think they're so hot to find me? There's a tricky bit of piloting to get around that gravitational anomaly; that's why it takes so long to get here. They need someone who knows how to do it."

Gren sighed, his brown face gloomy. "They aren't going to let us keep it. There's going to be a hell of a fight."

Moire tilted her head back toward the cave. "Hence the equipment."

"Won't do us much good if we don't have the people to run it. Or we aren't even here, because we're doing something else." He gave her a look. "Alan tell you anything useful about the place he came from?"

She nodded. "I've got a mock-up of the section of the Kerezin dock from his description of how he got to *Shintai*. We should be able to find out what ships were there at that time from the stationmaster, and then we just need to find the one that shows up there on a regular basis. *Shintai* was on the cargo row, so Alan's ship wasn't there for a quick stop. Then we just need to find out where the ship is going. I'll need your help for that part. Ever heard of a drop-dead loop?"

He stared at her for a moment. "What? They stopped using those fifty years...oh. Sorry." After a bit of thinking, he asked, "What would you want one of them for?"

"I want something that will tell us how long the drive is engaged, and maybe the heading of the ship. If you've got something better than a drop-dead, that's great. But it's the only thing I know of that will cut out when the gravity bubble pops."

He ran a hand over his head, face wrinkling in thought. "I guess it would work...our fabricator is limited, but a drop-dead isn't that complicated. Sure, I can do it. So, you're gonna smuggle it on board or something, then get it back?"

Moire nodded. "Then I'll probably have to sneak on the ship and take a look at the place, to see what there is to work with and what I'll need to bring."

"You? What are you going to be doing there?" Gren was compressing his lips and his face was rigid, both signs he was about to lose his temper. "Ignoring for the moment that Toren isn't going to hand these people over for the asking, what about you keeping a low profile? Toren is hunting you, right? And what about us?" He was yelling now, his hands sweeping in sharp, expansive gestures. "You're the only one who knows how to get here! Or to the salvage field!"

People in the cave were glancing their direction now. Moire made calming motions. "Look, I'm not planning on leaving a note saying I did it. Besides, how can I ask one of the crew to do something that dangerous?" She grimaced, belatedly realizing that was not a good argument to use. "It's not something they signed on for. I've got my own reasons for doing this."

"We're stuck if you get captured. Or killed. I still think this is a good idea, and we sure need the people, but if you want to do that part by yourself you need to get everybody to agree to it."

Moire turned back to face the bay, thinking hard. Gren had made some good points. She had to consider the crew of *Raven* as well as the Created she planned to rescue. There was also the issue of the crew's willingness to bend, if not break, the law for her. They were not entirely law-abiding individuals, but this might be more trouble than they were willing to risk.

"All right, let's ask them."

They walked back together, under the furtive and curious glances of the others. Moire sent one of the repair team to gather everybody together. The crew had grown considerably since they'd quit using *Ayesha* and switched to *Raven*. She couldn't immediately recall all their names; the new crewmembers hadn't been with the ship long. The senior crew from *Ayesha*–Fortin, Gren, Montero–knew about her time jump and the exploration ship that found Sequoyah, but the rest of the crew didn't.

They were watching her now, seated on the cave floor and crates or perched on the hydraulic struts of the landing craft.

She told them how *Bon Accord* had landed in the cave they were in now, all those years ago, to try to repair damage sustained on the way in. How the repairs hadn't quite worked, and how Toren had found her in the wreckage of the ship and tried to get the location of Sequoyah from her.

"Turns out there's something else they've been doing in their spare time," she continued. "When the exploration teams left Earth, they left reproductive tissue behind in storage. Toren found it, and they are doing things with it we never planned." She pointed at Alan. "I didn't have a son when I left Earth eighty years ago. I do now. Toren used my tissue to make him, and they're making others, in secret. I only know this because Alan escaped. I want to find the place they are doing this and stop them. Rescue the others that Alan left behind and get them to join us. Alan has already been a big help, and if we are going to keep this place we will need even more."

A repair crewman stirred. "So what's the problem?" he asked, indicating Gren.

Gren scowled. "She wants to do it on her own. She's too valuable to risk." Gren was probably thinking of the last flight of *Ayesha*, where Moire had been the only surviving pilot and their last hope of survival. He wouldn't forget that in a hurry.

"We have another pilot," Moire pointed out. "I can show Kilberton how to get here and to the sargasso." They should do that anyway, just in case. Kilberton had already shown he could be trusted, and then they could get multiple ships carrying cargo to Sequoyah.

"But how could they even think to attempt such a thing?" Kilberton asked, perplexed. "What you describe is gene theft. The Index will show it."

"She's not in the Index." Yolanda stood, her dark eyes snapping. "Those bastards thought about it real careful. Remember? She left Earth before the Index was even started. To prove gene theft you go to the Index and match the person's genes, and she ain't there."

The repair crewman nodded. "That'd explain it. They're desperate for workers, and you can't steal that many without people noticing."

Moire turned to Gren, puzzled. "There aren't enough people in the Fringe for all the work," he said quietly. "It's not just web pilots. Sometimes people can't hire anybody, so they...steal them. And there are slavers to do it."

She'd heard that term before, and thought it was a joke. Now she understood why her crew was starting to look angry. They knew better than she did what Toren had been doing, and why.

"If you don't want to be involved, just say so. I will be breaking the law to get these kids out, and it could get violent."

"Comes to that, Toren's breaking the law even worse," said the repair crewman over the general muttering of the crew. "Slavery's same as murder, and gene theft is almost as bad. Can't always call for the heavies out in the Fringe–sometimes you have to do it yourself. "

She looked at the faces of her crew and saw only agreement there.

Nooreen Meniran narrowed her eyes. Something was up, and she was going to find out what it was. She could smell the fear. The silence in the conference room deepened, until the muted thrum of the jammer was the loudest noise she could hear.

"So, we have no further information on Cameron. This cannot be allowed to continue. When she was on that Fleet ship we at least had her pinned down, but now she could be anywhere. Not only did she steal one of our ships to escape, the next representative we sent managed to screw up so monumentally even those monkeys in uniform noticed!" She took a deep breath, trying to control her temper. "What of the officer?"

Viello adjusted his vest to lie more smoothly. "Unconfirmed sightings. Our people are still looking. We have to be careful; Fleet suspects something. There are indications Umbra might be involved."

Meniran mulled this over for a moment, then made a decision. They couldn't afford any more wasted time. Cameron could be anywhere, doing anything by now. And if Umbra even began to suspect the existence of the Long Range Plan, they might ask other, more awkward questions. "Send out Kolpe Anders."

The others around the conference table blinked or rocked back in their seats, shocked.

"He's expensive."

"That's not why we don't like to use him. We have the budget for this. The problem is he insists on complete information." This was a source of resentment even at her level in Toren's organization, that a contractor could demand and get information that was jealously guarded. He produced results, and he had never compromised that information. They had to trust him.

She smiled coldly at their uncomfortable expressions. They thought the worst was over for this meeting. "Now. What other disasters haven't you told me about?" This should never have escalated so far. Cameron was one person, and their entire organization could not find her?

Viello shifted in his seat. "Um. Got a strange report from Cullen, probably nothing. The source is not very reliable. Small-office manager. He claims he saw a generated worker there. Free."

Yes, that was a disaster. "And?"

Her subordinate looked around the table, licked his lips, and swallowed. "He tried to do something about it."

Meniran closed her eyes. "Did he succeed?" The only hope was this idiot manager had not seen what he thought he had.

"The police somehow messed up the ID test and—"

"The *police* were involved?" She didn't even bother to hide her anger this time. "Take steps. Immediately. This must be contained, do you understand? If the generation project is affected..." If the project was detected, they would be in a lot of trouble. The Long Range Plan required those workers.

She'd have to prepare the lawyers for possible legal defenses. At least the generated workers wouldn't show up in the Index; that was one buffer she was glad she'd insisted on, even if it had restricted the project at first and greatly increased the budget. Now her superiors would see why it had been necessary. "Did he say why he didn't just grab the...individual?" It had to be a mistake. They would have told her if one was missing. At least, they *should* have. As bad as it would be if one got loose, it would be worse if anybody found out about it.

"Said he didn't have enough people. This guy was sent there because he didn't make the cut for the project, but he was in on some of the initial planning. Keeps applying for transfers to the project, probably thought this would look good. That's why I didn't pay much attention to it."

Meniran felt a cold chill. This could be bad. Two disasters on her watch. Why now? Didn't they have any preventive procedures? The Long Range Plan was too important, and Toren had placed all of the company's efforts toward it. It had to work. The rewards for success were commensurate with the consequences of failure. Sometimes she wondered if they were risking too much, but she couldn't back out now. She would simply have to make sure Fleet never knew until it was too late.

CHAPTER 2
TRAVEL BROADENS THE MIND

Within minutes of Ennis's arrival at FarCom, a marine escort was taking him on the familiar route to Namur's office. The quick response had him worried. He'd gotten to FarCom sooner than he'd expected, because the giant station/supercarrier had moved since the last time he'd been on board. It was closer to the Inner Systems now.

That wasn't reassuring either. Fleet wouldn't move FarCom on a whim, and they wouldn't move it back from the Fringe and the front lines unless they had to. The war must not be going well.

If Namur wanted to see him he couldn't be in complete disgrace. Then again, maybe he just wanted to get all the information before the court-martial.

Namur, and his office, were unchanged. He was seated behind the desk, a dim island of light in the shadows. Little golden glowballs were still scattered in odd corners, providing the only other light. It occurred to Ennis he had never seen Namur anywhere else. Perhaps he lived there.

He couldn't tell anything from Namur's gaunt face, but that was nothing new. The head of Umbra was accustomed to learning secrets, not telling them.

Let's get this over with. He straightened, forcing himself to look Namur in the eyes. "I failed," he said curtly.

Namur raised an eyebrow, but that was his only reaction. "I am afraid you will have to be more explicit, Commander Ennis. Precisely how did you fail?"

Ennis hesitated. *Shouldn't I be getting yelled at by now?* "I was able to find Moire Cameron. But when I attempted to capture her, the gun..." *The gun you made me take, damn you,* "did not function as anticipated. Instead of stunning, it nearly killed her. She recovered while I was dealing with her injuries, and escaped again. It's all detailed in my report." He could hear his voice tightening. He placed the datatab with the report on Namur's desk.

"Is that all?"

Ennis looked narrowly at Namur, but his thin, drawn face revealed nothing. It was possible Namur just had superhuman self-control. He shrugged. *Figure it out later, soldier.*

Ennis reached into his shirt pocket. "She gave me some information." He produced the second datatab. Namur reached for the tab just as Ennis reluctantly placed the NASA pin beside it. "And this."

If Ennis hadn't already been suspicious he would have missed it. Namur's eyes widened infinitesimally with surprise, and the taut mouth relaxed. Namur hadn't expected the pin. The logical conclusion that followed was that he had been expecting everything else. How was that even possible? Ennis had used the fastest means of transportation available to get to FarCom, and who else would know about the datatab? Cameron's crew might, but they wouldn't tell Fleet. Somebody had, but who?

Ennis concentrated on breathing and showing no sign of his shock. He shouldn't be surprised; he'd suspected from the start of this operation that he was going to be shadowed. *Pay attention, idiot. This isn't over yet.*

Namur had found an offline tab scanner in a drawer and was putting Moire's datatab in the slot. "Considering the source, we can't be too careful. That's how she got in trouble in the first place."

Under the impression he'd missed something, Ennis blinked. "Sir?"

"Cameron's record, if you recall, mentioned illegal computer activities. That could include deliberately corrupted data." A green pinlight flashed on the device, and Namur smiled. "But not this time."

He put the tab in the regular data port and started reading. Ennis knew the contents by heart now. Instead of giving him the answers he wanted, it just created more questions. "Why did she give you this?" Namur's voice was soft.

Ennis closed his eyes. "I don't know, sir. She said...she thought it might help." His eyes snapped open as he remembered something else. "She gave another tab to Harrington. I don't know if it had the same material or not."

The pause was perfectly timed. Namur was good. "Harrington?"

Of course. Harrington. "He was with me at the time. It's in my report." Harrington who had on two separate occasions shown up very conveniently with information about Cameron, and had insisted on joining the search. If his guess was correct, he might at least dodge a reprimand for working with a reporter. Who, apparently, wasn't always just a reporter. He wondered if Shabata knew.

"And what was this for?" Namur lightly tapped the NASA pin with one finger.

Ennis stared at the little metal and enamel pin with the crumpled corner, and wondered how to explain. "She said she would come back for it," he said finally. "When she could."

He braced for more questions, but Namur merely said, "I see." Leaning back in his chair, he continued, "I confess I had hoped you would produce Cameron herself, but you are not a trained agent. All things considered, you did quite well."

Oh, boy. Here it comes. "Am I being sent back to regular duty, sir?" If he wasn't sunk in disgrace, at least he'd shown he wasn't suited for the work. He'd never asked to be handed off to the most dubious of all the dubious intelligence organizations. Captain Kushstan's primary motivation in sending him to report to FarCom in the first place was to get him off her ship. She'd seen firsthand how ruthless Toren could be when they wanted information.

Namur shook his head. "The same reasons to detach you exist. If we had Cameron..." his gentle voice trailed off, and Ennis felt his heart sink. It was true. Toren would still be hunting him even if he'd brought her back, and thus endangering any Fleet ship he served on. In the middle of a war. That wouldn't have changed if he *had* brought Cameron back. He couldn't really blame Fleet for acting cautious, even if it was personally inconvenient. He hadn't wanted to end up in Intelligence, even if he had developed profound respect for Namur, and now it looked like Intelligence didn't want him either. But where could they post him where he wouldn't be a liability?

It was suddenly an effort to breathe. Maybe they weren't going to post him anywhere. They could solve their problem simply by making him leave. *What will I do without Fleet?* "Am I...will I be discharged, then?"

Namur's eyebrows lifted in his thin face, and one hand made a dismissive gesture. The faint light of the glowballs reflected off the clear prosthetic webbing on that arm. "That would be completely unnecessary," he murmured. "Not to mention shortsighted. But I will need to think about what to do with you."

"You are worried, Captain." Kilberton's voice came from the realspace console.

Moire didn't look up from her board. They were getting close to Kulvar, and she had to nail the dropout. "I'm worried about that crate. Maybe they found out and changed the reading. It just doesn't make any sense. And then there's Harvey. He's had plenty of time to get the money and get here from Cullen, but no sign of him."

Everything had seemed so promising at first. They'd found only one ship that matched all the parameters Moire had set, culled from Alan's memories of escaping. *Speedi-Web III*, allegedly a transport ship for the Speedi-Web delivery company, not only matched but showed up at Kerezin at least once every four weeks. Nobody had ever heard of *Speedi-Web I* or *II*, which made her suspect that the ships never existed and the Speedi-Web delivery company was just a front for Toren.

Nobody on Kerezin shipped with them, either, which meant they'd had to smuggle in Gren's drop-dead circuit by putting it inside the frame of a crate of standard shipboard supplies. She'd worried about that, but the empty crate was returned to the station just as Gren had predicted, and he'd been able to get the drop-dead circuit out right on the supplier's dock without detection.

Then Gren had shown her the results. Something must have gone wrong somewhere, because the coordinates didn't match up with any system. They were going to have to think of something else. Maybe this was too much for her small band of scavengers. But who would believe her?

Ennis would. He would understand the need to rescue the Created; he'd been trapped on the icy prison planet Fimbul until Fleet rescued him. He knew about Toren, too. How could she get a message to him? Would he be glad if she did?

Moire grimaced. She'd gotten him in a lot of trouble, even if she hadn't done it on purpose. He wouldn't thank her for sending him more.

The proximity alert bleeped. She turned it off.

"Captain? Aren't you going to drop out?" Kilberton was looking over the edge of the pit at her, his hands gripping the edge tightly.

"Few more seconds." Moire watched the readout, then hit the dropout control with a snap.

Kilberton shook his head, frowning, and turned back to the realspace controls. "That would get your license pulled in the Inner Systems," he said.

Moire sighed, stretching in her seat. "This is the Fringe, not the Inner Systems," she said, standing and pulling her ID from the console. "Relax. Max-prox limits are just safety rules, mostly for stations with a lot of traffic. I knew exactly where I was going to drop out. It's all timing."

She stopped short on the stair out of the pilot's pit. Timing. Timing was location. What if Gren's drop-dead circuit had been right? Toren would want to keep the location of the Created site as secret as possible. Any star system had the possibility of an accidental visit, but there was an awful lot of empty space between stars that nobody would have any reason to drop out for.

She had to tell Gren before the ship docked. Before she could get to the wall comm, Yolanda Menehune entered the bridge.

"Crew's going out, right?" she asked.

Moire nodded. "It's been a while; they need a break." She paused. Yolanda had a serious look on her face. "What's up?"

"I think maybe I should go out first and kinda check on things, ya know? I got the bad wire last time. Think something's goin' on." She jerked her shoulders up, sharply. "Maybe nothin'. Heard some talk about the ceeyo making space; if that's it we don't need to worry. Local power struggle."

The ceeyo was the Kulvar crime boss. Moire wasn't sure that they would be immune from any local fights, but Yolanda could tell her if things were too dangerous for the crew. "I'll get your gun from the locker," Moire said. "Ask Gren to come see me, Kilberton." He nodded acknowledgment.

Kilberton had docked the ship by the time she returned to the bridge, and Gren was waiting. He listened to her explanation of the strange drop-dead results with a thoughtful scowl.

"You think you could fly like that?"

Moire smiled. "Any pilot could, if they knew the location."

Gren scowled even more. "How does this help us? If we fly there ourselves we can't just blend in with local traffic, or pretend to be lost or something. They probably have long-range guns."

"I hope so. I've been wondering how we were going to get some."

Gren sighed loudly. "You have to get there, *and* not get shot, in order to steal them."

Moire shrugged. "There's one ship that can show up and they won't blink an eye. We'll use that."

"What, *Speedi-Ship?*"

"*Speedi-Web III*," Kilberton said, joining them. "Not only are they likely to have guns, they will have more than simple visual identification for any ship that arrives there. They are doing very, very illegal things, and they will take...extreme precautions."

It was a valid point, although Moire didn't want to admit it. "OK, so we do it this way. Sneak in, figure out their procedures, and take over the ship on the way back to Kerezin. Then we come back with a surprise."

"Yeah, and take a look at their setup on the ground, too." Gren nodded. "Have a better chance of coming up with a workable plan." He gave Moire a look. "I suppose you're thinking of going yourself."

That question she had been expecting. "Who else were you thinking of? Whoever goes has to be a pilot."

Kilberton lifted his chin, but before he could say anything the captain's earring chirped in Moire's ear.

"Yes?" Yolanda must have gotten back early.

"Pico here, Captain. There's someone at the hatch. Says his name is Felden."

Moire sagged with relief. "Harvey! Tell him..." she paused. What if it wasn't really Felden? Pico had never met him. "Hold on a sec." She went to the communications console and fiddled with it until it got her the hatch vid. It was Harvey all right, and he was by himself. "Let him in."

In a few minutes the hunched, wiry form of Harvey Felden was hovering uncertainly at the entrance to the bridge. He looked worried, even for Harvey.

"What took you so long?" Gren said, his bushy eyebrows colliding fiercely. "We thought something had happened to you."

"I thought something was going to happen to me if I wasn't careful," Harvey snapped. "I got the money, all right. But I wasn't sure they were going to let me keep it if I stayed. They were saying you're...that we're pirates. They were asking how we found the ships we've been selling. They want to talk to you."

At this rate, I'm going to have to hire a lecture hall. "These people have names, Harvey?" Moire asked.

"Station police, of course. Some that weren't, too. Maybe hoping it was true and wanting to join up. They looked dangerous. Anyway, I started getting real worried, especially after what you said. I didn't even want to go straight to Kulvar, so I took a ship to Criminy and quick got on the next ship to Kulvar. I made sure nobody on the first ship was following me, see."

A number of people were showing up now, both crew waiting for the all-clear to leave the ship and others who had heard of Felden's return. Moire noticed Alan was now standing beside her, waving shyly at Harvey. Carlos Montero had also wandered over, smiling vaguely at everyone. He didn't seem surprised to see Harvey again. Perhaps he hadn't noticed he'd been gone.

"How's Madele doing?" Harvey asked, giving Alan a friendly pat on the arm.

"Much better. Still not up to a full schedule, but it won't be long."

"She got shot too," Alan added, indicating Moire.

Moire winced. "It was just an accident," she said quickly, interrupting Harvey's question. "One of the...oh, Fortin will tell you all about it. It wasn't serious."

Harvey gave Alan a look. "There was blood," Alan said solemnly. "And she wouldn't let me shoot him."

"Harvey, good to have you back. We've got lots of work for you, if you still want to associate with this madhouse," Moire babbled. Her earring chirped again, and this time it was Yolanda Menehune. She listened for a moment, then snapped her fingers for attention. Everyone went silent on the bridge and looked at her. "Yolanda says things have calmed down, but stay out of Level Four if you can. OK, head out and be careful."

The first shift of crew on leave headed quickly for the door. Gren waved Yolanda over when she showed up. "We need to discuss something," he said, when the bridge was empty except for the senior crew. "She wants to go in by herself."

Yolanda blinked, then jerked her thumb over her shoulder. "What, in there?"

"No. His place." Moire pointed at Alan, who stared at her.

"I thought we don't know where it is," Yolanda said.

Moire took a breath. "I think those coordinates are correct. Wouldn't you put a place like that in the middle of nowhere?"

"Yeah, but..."

Moire recited her reasons why a pilot was needed to steal the ship after the initial reconnaissance. "I think Kilberton would be willing, but I know more about the place from what Alan told me. Besides, he's not my first choice for any job that involves sneaking around."

Yolanda snorted and nodded. "What about everything else, though? You gonna shut down the rest of the operation?"

"We *can* trust Kilberton with that," Moire said. "He's gotten us this far. I'll teach him what he needs to know before I leave."

Moire felt Alan grab her wrist with painful strength. "If you are going away I want to go with you," he said. His face was pale, his eyes worried.

"I'm going back to the place you escaped from," Moire pointed out gently. "Are you sure you want to go there?"

"I don't want to go *there*," he said, impatient with her lack of understanding. "I want to go with *you*."

"You don't like it, and I can't blame you," Gren said. "But it makes sense. He's the only one of us that has even been there. He'll protect you, too. I don't like the idea of your going any, but if you do, take him."

A long silence followed. Harvey broke it. "How are they going to get on this ship, if it is so secure and all?"

"They can go in a crate. We know that works," Gren said dryly. Everybody else nodded, grim. That was how the pirates had gotten aboard *Ayesha*.

"*They* got working scanners, though," Yolanda said. "How are we gonna shield the crate?"

Argument swirled about. In a lull, Montero asked calmly, "Why don't we fix the scanner?"

Moire looked at him with approval. Every now and then Montero came up with a really good idea. The trick was remembering that the rest of the time when he was being a foggy idiot.

"OK—who wants to figure out how we diddle their scanner?"

Ennis leaned his full weight on the corner of the printout unit until the signal pinlight changed from amber to green. Everything on Lambert Station seemed to have some idiosyncratic requirement to work and he was disturbed at how quickly he was starting to accept it as normal. In the three weeks since his arrival from FarCom he had learned about the printout unit's sensitivity to artificial gravity fields, how to deal with the data grid's habit of occasionally sending open files to random destinations, and the correct method to shut off the heat regulator in his quarters when it thought the temperature was fifty degrees lower than its set point. He still didn't feel ready to operate the drink dispenser in the mess hall, though.

The printout unit whined and pitched out a handful of sheets, and Ennis let go. Taking the printout without looking at it, he left his office with a feeling of doom and despair. Judging from his new posting, Namur had been furious but determined to make him useful if at all possible. He'd murmured something about making it easier for Cameron to contact Ennis by posting him in the Fringe, but that must have just been an excuse.

He went down the main corridor, detouring around a crew pulling cables out of a hole in the decking. He hoped they were pulling the right ones, and they would know what to do if they did. It was a gamble.

Maybe finding Cameron was Namur's condition for returning him to his real Fleet post. At least he was still *in* Fleet. Other than that, he couldn't find any positives to his situation.

The commanding officer of Lambert Station, Colonel Garner, was hardly ever sober off-duty. The second-in-command, Voss, alternated between fits of arrogance and petty vindictiveness. The noncoms were at best only borderline competent, but that hardly mattered since they were never called on to do anything more complicated than routine maintenance of the two Fleet ships and rescue of inebriated barge pilots. And of course, there was no library.

He reached his destination too soon. Standing rigidly at attention, Ennis took the printout and fastened it with exactness in the proper section. More proof that the base on Lambert Station was a low-priority backwater–it had an old-fashioned bulletin board. Not a display wall, not even a cheap textsheet–an actual, physical surface you pinned things to. This was one of his most important duties so far, at least the one that would be noticed if he didn't do it. Posting the base pookball schedule.

Ennis shuddered. Pookball was the deranged creation of Vyasandran, the station sergeant, who was definitely the brains of the operation. It was played in one of the hangars with a range of implements scavenged, or, in some cases, liberated. None of them were the same, which made the rules extremely complex. Most of the game seemed to involve deciding which set of rules to apply. Turning away, he glanced at the text and sighed deeply. His worst fear had been realized. His name was on the schedule.

Everybody on base played pookball. There was nothing else to do. The books he'd ordered wouldn't come in for at least another three weeks, and that was if he was lucky. There must be some other form of entertainment in the civilian part of the station, judging from the amount of trouble the noncoms got into, but he'd decided that was too dangerous. Toren was still trying to find him and there was no reason to make that any easier.

Walking back, he saw that the colonel's office was still dark. He shook his head, wondering if he should risk a comm call. She must have had another bad night.

It didn't matter. There wasn't anything that needed her attention, and it was better if she didn't come on duty until she'd recovered. Still, it set a bad example. Garner was a good officer when she was sober. So why couldn't she stay that way?

He entered the main room and headed for his desk.

"Hey, Commander! They got a new circular out." Sergeant Vyasandran waved him over. "Must have come in on that ore freighter."

The sergeant had introduced him to the Fringe "circulars," a curious kind of patchwork news service added on to at every stop. The writing was breathless, the vids rough in quality, and the reliability of the reporting dubious.

"Seems like they got some pirates around Cullen," Vyasandran said, pointing to the section in question.

"What happened? That area has been safe for years."

The sergeant shrugged. "Maybe it isn't true. I thought maybe you might know, eh?" He grinned.

"Sorry, they haven't told me anything." They must think it strange Lambert had been sent an intelligence officer when there was nothing even remotely connected to Intelligence for him to do. By default, he had inherited Communications–hence the pookball schedule. He could justify his data research as intelligence-related, but he really did it for a sense of contact with the outside world when so much was changing. His former commanding officer, Shabata, had been promoted and was no longer on *Canaveral*. He hadn't seen where she'd been posted yet.

Of course, the courier didn't show up very often, and when it did the Fleet data was short and to the point, and never had enough information about the war with the crabs. Even that was happening somewhere else.

Sitting at his desk, he checked his old mail-link out of habit and was surprised to see a message waiting. He kept forgetting all ships carried mail out here. It was from Harrington.

Continued survival astounds self and others. Advise avoiding seedy docks and friendly strangers. H.

The origin code said it came from a public kiosk at Criminy. You could get a ship almost anywhere from Criminy; he was probably on his way somewhere else. On a job for Namur? If he had been right about Harrington's second occupation then Namur should have someone shadowing him here, but everyone on Lambert had been there for at least three months. He'd still been on *Canaveral* then. Unless he'd been wrong, and nobody had followed him at all. *No. Somebody told Namur about that datatab before I did.* It had to be Harrington. Nobody else knew.

Ennis reread the message, smiling grimly. He carried the scan-resistant gun everywhere he went, and he never left the base alone. That should lower the chances Toren would be able to get him.

He glanced at the clear polyacrylate block on his desk. Inside it was the ceramic needle he'd shot Moire Cameron with. Sometimes he thought he could still see the blood. Ennis sighed. Wherever Cameron was, she had to be having a better time than he was.

"How many days is it again?"

I should have put him in a separate crate. Sedated. "Got at least another day and a half, kid." Moire shifted position carefully so the crate wouldn't rock. How had the pirates survived five days like this?

They must have used drugs. But Moire had wanted to be alert to scope out the ship and spy on the crew, and Madele Fortin had convinced her that drugging Alan was potentially dangerous. They hadn't quite figured out all his physiological weirdnesses, like the synthetic hormone implant he had, or whether his brain chemistry was that of an adult or a child.

Yet another reason to crack Toren's secret facility. They would have documentation of what they were doing to the Created, and why. Then she could find a way to fix it.

"What's a garden?"

It took her a moment to even make sense of the question. Then she saw the reader in his hand and understood. He'd been reading one of his books.

"Didn't you look at the pictures?"

He shrugged, looking confused. "They don't move, or say anything. Are they finished? The pictures in the dictionary move."

"Those are vid clips. They are supposed to move." She shifted again until she was sitting beside him, back against the narrow end of the crate. She took the reader and called up one of the illustrations of *The Secret Garden*.

"See? It looks like that because it's a painting. Not a vid still. Those green things are plants, and the colored bits are flowers. That's what a garden looks like."

"Oh." He thought for a moment. "In the book, they have to get dirt and seeds to have a garden. Can we get some?"

"You want to have a garden?" Moire asked, wondering.

"Yes!"

Moire winced, making shushing motions, and Alan put a hand over his mouth. He looked frightened. She put on the viewgoggles and picked up the control for the spycrawlers, switching to the one she'd left in the hold for backup. Nothing was visible; the hatch was still closed. She played back the audio recording, and was relieved to find that Alan's outburst had been barely audible outside the crate.

"Montero did some good sound insulation, kid. Looks like nobody heard us."

His eyes squeezed shut. "I'm sorry," he whispered.

"It's OK. Try to be careful. We can't tell when the crew will come down here, you know. What else did you read about in that book?" she asked, trying to distract him. If only they could take the risk of getting out of the crate now and then it would be a lot easier. She'd only dared to stay out long enough to get the spycrawlers in position.

He scrunched down, stretching his legs. The crate had just enough room for the two of them, supplies, and a tiny sanitation station. The crate was small for Moire, but for Alan it was downright cramped. His face screwed up with thought.

"Sometimes they...when someone says they don't have a mother, it makes people sad. Can't they get another one?"

Hoo-boy. This is going to get interesting. She took a deep breath, thinking furiously. "You only get one. That's all." She waited, tense, for his next question. The trick was to only answer what he was actually asking, not what she *thought* he was asking.

He scrunched down even farther. He didn't look at her. "How did they get that one, then?"

"They were there from the beginning," Moire said carefully.

"You weren't there from the beginning," he said in a very small voice. Suddenly Moire understood, and she couldn't explain without hopelessly confusing him. *Just answer what he asked.*

"I didn't know where you were," she said finally. Truthfully. She hadn't even known he existed. If he had been a normal child, he would know that wasn't a real answer.

"I thought it was part of the Game," he said. The Game, otherwise known as Pretending to be Normal. "You really are my mother?"

It took her a moment before she could trust her voice. "Yes. Really." The fact still had the power to panic her. Sometimes she wished she could forget, could hand over the crushing weight of responsibility she had done nothing to deserve. Other times she wondered how she could ever live without him. That frightened her too.

Alan clutched the reader tightly in his arms, then suddenly pressed his face against her shoulder. Just as suddenly, he turned away and curled up on his side.

Moire blinked. He'd done something like this before. A quick nudge with his shoulder, then away. As if he was afraid he'd be seen.

She took a deep breath and let it out slowly. Toren's doing, no doubt. Well, she was doing what she could to fix that. That's why she was sitting in a crate full of gear for three days. Maybe she wasn't the best mother in the world, but she was the only mother he had. She would just have to figure it out as she went.

One thing she was sure of was kids needed love. Moire sat up carefully and found one of the blankets. She tucked it all around him, ignoring the way he stiffened when he first felt her touch. He'd done that before, too, and she didn't want to think about why. But then his tension slowly left him, and he turned back toward her and smiled.

She cupped the side of his face with one hand, marveling at the deep color of his gold-brown eyes. "Get some sleep, kid. I'll wake you before we get there." He just nodded and closed his eyes, oblivious to her joke. She still had never seen him laugh.

Better get back to work. It will take my mind off things. She put the viewgoggles on and switched back to the first spycrawler. She'd gotten it up to the crew level, but now she wanted to place it inside the bridge. It took forever. The spycrawler was small, which meant it didn't have much in the way of speedy movement. It hadn't been intended for covert ops, either. Montero used them for tracing connector problems in tight areas.

Good thing they hadn't had to rely on Montero for the scanner fix. That had taken too much delicate work, from the long-range focused EMP gun she'd gotten Gren to make, to bribing the station comm operator to allow a temporary reroute of the repair company code. Then all they needed to do was aim the gun in the open hatch of *Speedi-Web III*, fry the scanner inside, and wait for them to call for a repair. They did let Montero do that part, in a borrowed uniform. Nobody would suspect him of something as complex as an ulterior motive when he seemed barely awake.

It had worked. The newly desensitized scanner let them through without a problem. Now she just had to get as much information as she could before the ship arrived at its secret destination.

She made the spycrawler pick up a scrap of plastic with its grabber arms to hide under as it moved. It hadn't been very fast to begin with and that slowed it down even more, but she had more than a day to work with. The first priority was to not be caught.

She saw motion through the eyes of the spycrawler, and stopped it. Something in the corridor ahead...but not a human. Something low and compact, moving with slow sweeps side-to-side as it came closer.

Cleaning bot! Why can't they run a messy ship like everybody else in the Fringe? Quickly, she released the shred of plastic and made the spycrawler shove it out in the corridor then back away. The plastic would delay the cleaning bot, but not for long.

The cleaning bot reached the plastic, whirred angrily, and sucked it up. She swiveled the optical sensor and saw a mesh screen over a vent at the base of the wall.

She trundled the spycrawler as fast as it could go toward the screen. The audio pickup was getting louder with the sound of the cleaning bot, coming in for the kill. There was the mesh, right in front of her. With skill born of desperation she forced the spycrawler to climb the mesh, using its grabbers in sequence. It wasn't designed to do that, and she fought to make it release the grabbers to reach the next wire up.

Suddenly the video signal was vibrating wildly, and the audio nearly deafened her. She quickly turned it down. *Dammit, if I have to start from scratch with a new crawler...* But when the shaking stopped, she could still see the mesh. The spycrawler had hung on.

She rotated the optical sensor again and saw the retreating form of the cleaning bot. Waiting until it had turned a corner, she started the spycrawler back on its way. An hour later it had reached the entrance to the bridge, which was occupied by one of the two-person crew. She parked the spycrawler in a narrow space between two consoles near the pilot's chair. Remembering the cleaning bot, she made sure to have the spycrawler firmly clamped onto something.

Setting the audio to record and save, she shut down the controls. Alan was asleep beside her, still curled up. *Good idea.* She slid down beside him and closed her eyes.

"Um, sir?"

Ennis looked up from his gloomy contemplation of the data on his screen. Wernicki's round face was peering around the door to his office, as if she could use the flimsy wall as a shield.

"Yes, what is it?" Of course his one and only direct subordinate would be terrified of him. She was frightened of everybody. He'd tried everything he could think of to get her to show some spine, but it only made things worse.

"The, uh, signal. And I...the manual says to report immediately, but there's no form reference and *all* the other report procedures have a form and the *general* regulations specify a—"

"What signal?" Ennis asked, as gently as he could, considering his growing irritation. *At least she's trying,* he reminded himself for the tenth time that day.

Wernicki blinked, visibly restarting her thought process. "Um. I don't know, sir."

She wasn't being insubordinate. She didn't have enough intelligence to be insubordinate.

"Then what are you trying to report?"

She blinked again. "Signals. Um. The manual says signals from ammlom...anomalous locations should be reported immediately and investigated. But it's just noise, sir. It doesn't mean anything."

"Show me." She whisked herself from view, and he got up wearily to follow her. Wernicki was one of the few at Lambert Base who knew she wasn't up to standard. Unfortunately, the way she made up for it was by blind devotion to manuals and regulations. He was continually amazed at her ability to quote reams of text and remain completely ignorant of the meaning.

At her console, Wernicki pointed at a display. "That's where it's coming from. But nobody goes there. This scow got in the debris field by mistake and the core went critical when they got hit and...um, they can still detect the radiation here at the station."

Ennis turned his attention to the signal analysis. Short, compressed bursts, with too much regularity in the components to be natural. He leaned over the control board and tried out a set of standard algorithms. Nothing useful happened. The signal remained incomprehensible.

"Probably just a comm call." Ennis turned his head. The second-in-command, Commander Voss, was observing them with a scornful expression on his face. "She's found them before, since she doesn't know how to filter out station noise."

Wernicki was hunched in her seat, looking scared and miserable.

"It's coming from a rock debris field three thousand kilometers from here. The signal is clearly artificial, compressed, but not using any of the standard methods," Ennis said blandly, keeping his voice neutral. Voss would take even the hint of contradiction as an excuse to do something unpleasant to both himself and Wernicki.

"So, you think it is criminal activity? You would know."

Voss had wasted no time in finding his connection to the prison planet Fimbul, and mentioned it whenever he could. Ennis fought to keep control of his temper, and failed.

"I defer to your judgment. You would know better than I would."

Voss recoiled, and his eyes narrowed.

"Oh...it's pirates!" Wernicki blurted, completely oblivious to the undertones of the conversation. It succeeded in diverting Voss's attention to her.

"Pirates need ships to steal. There's nothing there except radioactive scrap. Get back to work."

Wernicki cringed and turned back to her board. Her eyes bulged.

"Sir! There's another one! But it's not in the same place."

The signal was different, too. Simple, choppy, and brief. *Locator pulse. Something's going on out there.*

Voss stared at the display, then glanced back at Ennis. "Since you think it's so important, check it out. Take the twenty-three."

Thanks for the vote of confidence. The OPSIC-23 was an old sublight patrol boat, mostly famous for never having enough room for the required crew. It did, however, have guns. If you could get to them.

"Come on. You're running the comm board," Ennis said to Wernicki.

"But sir, I...ship, no manual..."

"Your other option is to stay here and update Voss on our progress."

She paled. "Um."

Ennis picked up a commlink and started to jog toward the hangers. He felt the first swing of optimism since he'd been posted here. "Attention! Twenty-three crew, report on the double!"

CHAPTER 3
UNSCHEDULED ARRIVALS

Ennis alternated between watching the comm board over Wernicki's shoulder and the scanner console. It wasn't that hard on the tiny flight deck.

They were getting close to the location of the second signal. He'd ordered the ship as silent as possible, in the hopes of catching whoever it was by surprise.

"I got something, sir!" the pilot said suddenly. "Two of 'em, though. Funny, I'm not getting any profile match."

Ennis had been expecting at least two ships—why else would there be signals? But the profile matching ought to be working. "Maybe you have the match percentage too high, Pereira. Are you getting anything at all, or is the match cycling?"

"No sir. Comes up 'No match, enter manufacturer to add profile.'"

Even a new model of ship should pull up *something*. All the profiles for existing ships were in the system. A horrible thought occurred to him.

"Do you have the crab profiles loaded on this ship?" He shouldn't even have to ask, but on Lambert Base a lot got left out.

"We got the basic set, but it takes too long to run. Besides, they never show up here." Pereira caught Ennis's fulminating glare and gulped. "Running now, sir." He paused while the data ran, then relaxed. "No match this time either."

Suspicious, Ennis looked over his shoulder at the scan display. Now it read "No exact match—add supplemental data?"

Not an exact match, but enough of one the scanner thought it belonged in the crab profile data. *Those aren't our ships.*

"Guns live," he snapped at the pilot. "Yoshi, damn you, wake up! Get to your position!"

The gunner started up from his slouch, looking bewildered, then scrambled to bring his weapons online. Ennis was already halfway out of his seat and reaching for the handholds to swing up to the top gun console.

"Sir! But..."

"Assume the unknown ships are crabs until you get proof otherwise. Wernicki, get ready to send a burst back to base telling them we are engaging one or possibly two crab ships, but wait for my order to send, got that?"

"Visual on scope, sir!" called Pereira.

Ennis pulled up the visual feed on the tiny display, cursing under his breath at the grainy picture. They got closer and he cursed again, louder, seeing the dark, spiny hull of the ship ahead of them. He wasn't surprised the scanner hadn't made a match; the ship wasn't like any configuration he'd seen before. But he could still tell who it was. *Crabs. Why here, why now?*

"Enemy ship," he said tersely. He heard sounds of fear and consternation below. "Full acceleration to engage. Yoshi, Pereira–wait for my command to fire." There was no need to waste ammunition this far out. The big crab ship apparently hadn't detected them yet.

Ennis frowned. The crabs should have seen them by now; at least they always had before when human ships were this close. Maybe his silent measures had worked, or maybe they were just lucky. The second, smaller ship was still out of visual range, headed away from the station and toward the big ship. The big ship was large enough to be web-capable, which meant he *had* to prevent it from going into drive or they could get more uninvited guests.

"It's changing course! And accelerating!" Pereira shouted. "They've seen us!"

"Keep the intercept!"

On the visual feed, Ennis saw the big ship move straight for the smaller one, a course that cut directly in front of the OPSIC-23. Ennis fumbled for the arming switch. *It's trying to pick up the scout before going into drive!*

"Gun one!" he yelled, and fired. The range was extreme, but he didn't have much choice. The crab ship was going to run rather than fight, and he couldn't let it get away. "Wernicki, send that message!"

His first few shots were wide, as he'd expected. The crab ship jerked and swerved erratically, but remained on course. When it returned fire, the targeting was nowhere near the OPSIC-23.

Something wasn't right They could shoot better than that. What if it was a trap?

"Close in ten kilometers and hold," he ordered.

"Confirm hold at one zero k?" Pereira replied, sounding confused.

"One zero, and watch your board for more ships! Wernicki, keep sending updates." He checked the range, grimaced. "Yoshi, fire at will."

"All *right!*" came an enthusiastic yell.

"Get a lock first!" Ennis shouted as the ship shuddered with recoil. *If we only had some missiles on this tub...*

He was firing steadily now, every time he got a lock. One shot connected, solid. Yoshi clipped part of the outer structure, then he and Ennis both got major hits. The big crab ship was no longer able to maneuver, and the small ship was barely half a kilometer away.

No sign of a trap. The threat to Lambert Station had been dealt with. The realization dawned on him that now he had a damaged crab ship, a ship that could be captured. Much more useful to Fleet than a destroyed one.

"Hold your fire!" Ennis shouted, but it was too late. Yoshi had already let loose a salvo that ripped into the wounded crab ship. A moment later a flash blazed over the video feed, followed by a second explosion as the smaller ship was caught in the blast.

"I got 'em, sir! I got 'em!"

Ennis sighed, running a hand over his face and trying to keep his frustration and disappointment from showing. He didn't want to take the victory away from his substandard crew; it was amazing they had pulled it off at all. It wasn't to be expected they could handle a sudden change in objectives, especially since this had probably been their first live fight. "Yes. You certainly did."

The celebration slowed to a halt.

"Um. Sir. I...thought we wanted to get them?" Wernicki ventured. Her forehead wrinkled with confusion, rapidly changing to distress.

"Absolutely," Ennis said, before she asked if the crabs were still the enemy. "We had to protect the station, but if we could have done that without destroying the crab ship it would have been even better. We've blown up a lot of crab ships in this war, but we've never captured one intact." And they'd come so close...

He didn't mention his attempt at capture to Voss, who was panicked and imagining the crab fleet arriving any minute when they got him on the comm. Voss ordered the 23 to remain on patrol as well as sending the OPSIC-98 to join them. They searched for hours, assisted by some local craft, but nobody found any sign of more crabs. Only wreckage.

At least the 98 had enough crew for shifts. Pereira was getting so tired Ennis wasn't sure he could dock safely.

None of it made sense. In all his time fighting the crabs, Ennis never heard of an encounter like this one. Stupid tactics, lousy gunnery, and a suicidal attempt to rescue the scout ship. If the crab ship hadn't turned back, it could have easily escaped into webspace. It seemed...amateur.

"That scow driver wants to talk to you, sir," Wernicki said drowsily.

"Yeah, go ahead."

"So whaddya want's ta do wit all these junks, eh? I not keeping them nothing, you gotta say where they go." The scow driver sounded peeved. "What'sa pay, pickin' up crab scraps?"

"Eternal glory and the praise of all humanity," Ennis snapped before he could stop himself. Yes, he was tired. Wernicki spluttered with astonished laughter. "Take it in to one of the hangars." By the time both ships were docked again he'd figure out somewhere else to keep it. He brightened.

They wouldn't be able to play pookball if he kept it there. "Submit a time bill to the quartermaster; we'll get you paid somehow."

The driver muttered something that might have been thanks but probably wasn't, and closed the connection.

"What are you going to do with all the pieces, sir? Do you think they'll have anything useful?" Wernicki asked.

"I hope so." He wasn't sure what he was going to do; wasn't sure why he'd commandeered the scow to pick up the wreckage of the crab ship. Maybe he was just trying to annoy Voss.

His mind drifted, tired, reliving the brief combat. Noting all the anomalous actions. Hours later, Garner's voice came on his earclip. She must have sobered up enough to take charge.

"Ennis. Bring your people in and get them rested. Those damn crabs aren't going to show up now."

When he finally got back to the base hangar, he made his way over to the pile of fragments the scow had unloaded. Even though he was so tired he could barely move he spent an hour poring over them—some pieces no longer than his arm, one almost the length of a fighter. They'd only recovered a portion of the whole ship.

One piece he recognized as a part of the hull. The texture of the skin was almost organic in appearance, the spines and struts fractal in pattern. Like branches.

A violation of that pattern snagged his gaze and he frowned, looking closer. The structure looked like a gun, but it didn't fit. He stood stiffly and moved to the far end of the piece of wreckage, sighting down the length of it. The gun was out of true, possibly because of the explosion—but why was it in the wrong place?

He looked more carefully at the gun itself, and found the answer at the very base where it mounted to the hull. The material there was subtly different in appearance from the hull—coarse, and lighter in color.

They added those guns later. And not very well. Ennis suddenly wondered if the crew had likewise been a bodge job. Remembering the crab ship's strange behavior, he was convinced of it. They'd been fighting the crab equivalent of Wernicki. No wonder it had been so easy. These crabs hadn't understood about the harsh realities of battle. They'd tried to rescue a comrade even though it had ended up getting all of them killed.

They hadn't been like that before, and he hadn't heard of any fights like this one either. Did that mean the crabs were running out of real troops? It had been easier killing them when they were vicious, competent, and dangerous. This just made him feel depressed.

The memory was sudden and vivid. Moire Cameron sitting on a crate in the mercenaries' launch bay after she had singlehandedly destroyed a crab carrier. Her eyes deep with a sadness that had surprised him at the time, but now he felt the same. Why were the crabs attacking them with such suicidal desperation? Why were they attacking at all? After all these years, they still didn't even know how the war had started. Was killing every last crab the only way to stop it?

I wonder who it is we're really fighting.

Moire held Alan close as something slammed into their crate. "Almost over now," she whispered into his ear, holding him tight. Now she'd find out if she'd been right to trust Montero's work. She could never be sure when his mind was in the same dimension as his body.

They had fixed the scanner. Now they just had to fool the autoloader, and they didn't have the luxury of doing it at a distance. They'd guessed the existence of the autoloader from the digital tags on the crates. It made sense; Toren would prefer that the crew not know what they were shipping *out*. Then there was the curious ease with which Alan had escaped. She'd gambled nobody had been there to see him. Only automatic machinery that wouldn't notice anything wrong. And now, the automatic machinery didn't care that one crate still remained on the ship.

The sounds echoed and died. She checked with the second spycrawler, wedged near the cargo door. It was dark, and nothing was moving.

"Right. Looks like we're alone. Get your gear on, kid. We don't have a lot of time." The spycrawler that she'd parked on the bridge had captured some useful information. The two pilots were the only people on board. One of them, a woman, was not happy about that since they had to do everything. More importantly, *Speedi-Web III* would be leaving eighteen hours after arriving at the deep space facility, a completely isolated station. Three hours had already elapsed with the unloading, but now they could finally get moving.

It had been awkward living in the crate. It was even more awkward for two full-grown people to put on heat-mask gear at the same time, in a hurry. As soon as she could, Moire popped the cover of the crate and slid out stiffly, luxuriating in the space and freedom. The air, too. It wasn't quite as...thick as it had been in the crate. She started pulling out equipment, wincing when her sore muscles made themselves felt. Alan stepped out and stood close beside her.

"If I give you the pistol now, do you promise not to shoot unless I say so?" she whispered.

He nodded, a sharp, jerky motion. She couldn't see his whole face through the heat-mask hood but his eyes were wide, staring out the open door to the station beyond.

"What's wrong?"

"Bad place." He was vibrating with fear. If she'd had any doubts about this being the right place, they were gone. Alan clearly recognized it.

He was also petrified with fright. "Maybe you should stay here for a little while," she said finally, turning away to the door. They didn't have enough time for her to wait for him to calm down. "I'll come back."

"No." In a flash, he had a tight hold on her arm. Whatever he was frightened of, he was more afraid of being alone.

"It isn't like before," she said softly, her mouth by his ear. "You aren't wearing the cuff anymore. You have a gun. Besides, we are going to do everything so they don't know we're here. Right?"

He looked down. He wasn't shaking so much. "Leave soon," he whispered.

"That's the idea," Moire whispered back, prying his hand away with effort. She picked up the little spycrawler from its hiding place and scootched it across the threshold into the station.

As she had feared, there were vid pickups. Two of them, keeping watch on the cargo door. The corridor was bare and sterile; no people, no signs or even equipment. Just the track overhead for the cargo hauler.

She heard a faint hum and looked up. The track was vibrating. Moire gestured Alan back, and they crouched down in the shadows of the hold. Through the spycrawler's eyes she saw something large coming down the corridor. As the thing got closer, she could see it was some sort of large crate.

Of course. Now that the hold was empty, they could load new cargo. The crate came closer, swaying heavily. It followed the track into the cargo bay and the autoloader clicked and whirred, dropping the crate with a clang in a far corner.

Where were they coming from? Moire snatched the spycrawler from the doorway. There was a direct road, if she could get to it.

"When the hook comes by, lift me up!" she whispered to Alan, who looked puzzled but willing.

The cargo hook carriage disengaged and headed back on the return track. As it came by she nodded at Alan. He grasped her waist and propelled her up in the air so fast her head banged against a strut supporting the cargo track. The pain made her eyes water, but she managed to place the spycrawler on the top of the hook carriage.

She tapped Alan's hand, and he lowered her down. Another crate was coming through the hatch now, and they backed away to a less crowded area. Flipping the viewgoggles back down, Moire watched from the spycrawler's eyes as it was taken along the cargo hauler track. The track wasn't very long, but there were vid pickups at regular intervals for the entire length.

How on earth did Alan get out of this place without setting off fifteen alarms? More to the point, how were they going to get in?

The track turned from the main corridor to a branching one, and then into a large room with a number of the big crates. For the first time, Moire saw people. People being loaded into the crates.

Shock paralyzed her, stopping the breath in her lungs, then fire-hot anger took over. That horrible woodcut that every history book had, the diagram of how to pack a ship with human bodies, stacked like bales. Back like a bad dream. For a moment she started thinking of how she could rescue them all, now, but the cold reality of the situation forced her back to the original plan. She couldn't do it by herself, not without risking the only chance they had. She should have tried to send a message to Ennis anyway, just in case something happened to their plan. What if they were caught?

She moved the spycrawler closer to the edge of the hook carriage. The people being loaded had the same stiff, fearful, and yet open expression that reminded her painfully of her first encounter with Alan. They were wearing the same flimsy clothing, too.

So those were the Created. That must mean the people in bright-colored uniforms were the Controllers. They were injecting the Created with something before making them climb into the narrow slots in the crate. One crate held eight people.

She felt her fingers tighten and took a deep breath, trying to suppress her anger. At least they could rescue these right away. But if she wanted to get the rest, she was going to have to find a way in.

A crate was attached to the hook carriage, making the spycrawler's video output sway. Moire moved the spycrawler off the hook carriage and onto the crate top as the crate left the room. When the crate turned the corner into the main corridor, she moved the spycrawler off the edge.

It landed with a jarring thud on the corridor floor, scrambling the video output for a second. She moved it, testing the controls. It seemed to be intact. The crawlers were built to be tough. She moved it down the main corridor, away from the cargo hatch. The corridor ended a few hundred meters from the branch corridor. The area only had emergency lighting, so she could just barely make out the signs on the doors. It seemed to be primarily storage.

Moire pushed back the goggles and looked around the hold. The second crate of Created was just being dropped off, making the floor shake. There was about half a meter between the bottom of the crate and the floor when they were on the cargo hook. Just enough space to crawl under.

"Think you can crawl fast?" she whispered to Alan. "We need to hide from the vids, under the crates as they go by. Just to the end of this corridor. Nobody there."

He nodded. They waited, tense and nervous, by the cargo hatch. The next crate was moving slowly down the corridor. Moire glanced at Alan, and her gaze snagged on the pack of gear on his back. "Take that off!" she hissed. "It won't fit. Push it ahead of you." He struggled with the pack, working it free just as the crate began to block the view of the vid in front of the hatch.

Moire pushed Alan forward, and he dived under the crate. She followed so fast behind him his boot hit her in the chin. She squirmed ahead as quickly as she could, trying to ignore the glancing blows of the crate as it swayed above them.

The crate moved on, and Moire grabbed Alan's ankle. "We have to wait for the next one!" she whispered. She felt dreadfully exposed, but they were between vids–they'd find out soon enough if anyone could see them.

It was an eternity. From the way Alan was hunched on the floor, he wasn't enjoying it either. As soon as the crate came, they were both scrambling. They kept going even when it had turned the corner, heading for the safety of the shadows. Moire collapsed against a wall, realizing she had no idea what to do next.

She scanned the corridor quickly, hoping for inspiration. The spycrawler was waiting patiently for further instructions; she picked it up and stashed it away for later use. "Anything look familiar?" she asked Alan.

He was crouched down, his entire body posture speaking of fear. "It says I should not be here."

Following his pointing finger, she saw a half-blue, half-red circle on the wall. The same symbol was repeated at regular intervals all along the corridor. She frowned and peered into the gloom. She could just make out the surface of a door that had a different symbol on it.

She glanced at the intersection they had just left. No sign of any activity. Alan followed her closely as she sprinted across to the door.

"So what does this mean?" The symbol on the door was a red circle on a black triangle.

"If you go in, you become broken." Alan rubbed his wrist where the control bracelet had been. "The other ones, you can go if a Controller is there and they say to."

If it was forbidden, then maybe it had something useful in it. "OK, kid. Time to start breaking and entering."

"But it says..."

Moire sighed. "We are here to do things we aren't supposed to do. Right?" She looked at the door. A standard sliding panel, with a square plate on the wall for entry. But instead of a pressure switch, or even a key slot, there was a single round hole and a thumbprint plate.

"It doesn't look like our doors," Alan said, watching over her shoulder.

"The lock is different. Hopefully the door is the same." At least it wasn't a bulkhead door. Those were designed to seal for pressure, with bottom edges several centimeters below floor level. This was just a security door, and not even a heavy-duty one.

Even with Alan's help, she couldn't get it open enough to get Montero's clever electronic doorcracker in. They had better luck with the second door, which also had the "forbidden" symbol on it. With the doorcracker in the narrow gap where the edge of the door fit into the wall, it was simply a matter of finding the wall switch controls.

It took longer than it had when they'd practiced on *Raven*, and Alan was getting nervous and impatient. Moire didn't like the exposed feeling either, wondering if there were some concealed vids they hadn't noticed. Then the door opened, and they darted quickly inside.

Closing the door, Moire carefully toggled the lights, sagging with disappointment when she saw what the small room contained. *I hope we didn't do all that work just to break into a broom closet.* Racks up and down the walls held pieces of equipment, piles of cables, and tattered fiberboard boxes. Moire walked slowly down the aisle, wondering why Toren had bothered to secure it at all.

Picking up a disposable cup half-hidden behind a burnt-out readout panel lying on a rack, she saw a thick, scummy film of dried-up gunk. Everything had a thin layer of dust.

"Is this a book?" Alan held something out to her. It was a textcard. Some of the pixels, or whatever they called them these days, had reversed from their original color making the text difficult to read. She tabbed through the whole thing, but it was scrambled and useless.

They had to find a way to get to the upper levels. They didn't have a lot of time to do it, either. "How did you get to this level, when you escaped?"

Alan looked at her and shrugged. "I just went through doors."

Well. He had done it, so it must be possible. She doubted they would have the same luck twice, though. They needed something a bit more subtle than that.

Leaving the storage room, Moire carefully examined all the doors in the corridor. No sign of any upper level access, and there hadn't been anything in the section near the dock, either. That left the loading area, which had too many people in it right now, and there was no guarantee it would be empty when the loading was done.

Desperate for ideas, she retrieved the doorcracker and opened more doors. The first two were merely storage. The third, however, had two desk terminals and a multiplex data copier. Moire followed the cables up to the ceiling and felt a small glimmer of hope. Since the levels were expected to stay isolated in the event of an accident, the cables were connected to a feedthrough panel, connectors on either side of a metal plate. The panel itself, however, was not completely sealed to the ceiling–and it looked just wide enough for them to get through.

Piled data storage boxes made a wobbly stair to the panel, allowing Alan to remove the two remaining bolts with a rivet cutter as silently as he could. Moire popped her head up quickly to make sure the room above was clear.

It was dark, and when she flashed her palmlight around, small and unoccupied. Just what they needed. Grasping the edge of the hole, she pulled herself up.

Kolpe Anders blinked at the fresh-faced receptionist, fumbling with his briefcase to produce his ID. He mumbled something deliberately incoherent about an appointment, knowing his face looked red and flustered. The receptionist scanned his ID and gave him an empty smile.

"If you would wait over there, sir?"

He nodded hastily and took a seat in an area off to the side of the main entrance. It wasn't the general waiting area, meaning his ID had pulled up a scheduled appointment. At least that much had worked.

From the corner of his eye, he saw that the receptionist was scanning the entire lobby in careful, regular sweeps camouflaged by fussing with her earclip or some other distraction. He smiled inwardly. Toren had not had such thorough concealed security the last time he was here. Was his business in any way related?

Running a hand quickly through his hair, he wondered if it was too thick. He always strove for the full effect in his impressions, and the best ones were never dependent on one or two things but layer upon layer of little details. The carefully tailored pants, for example, that always appeared just a fraction too short. Or the facial mods that produced a tiny, nervous twitch at the corner of one eye.

His voice was harder to change; another reason he worked so hard on the visuals. He shifted in his seat, wondering how many scanning devices were active in the room. The frosted, pale-green glass panels in bentwood frames, ostensibly for privacy, were rather obvious. Perhaps the chairs themselves...

He looked up as someone approached, and froze, momentarily uncertain. Nooreen Meniran was standing just inside the entrance. She was wearing full formal business trousers, but instead of the fitted tunic that usually completed the ensemble, she had a long vest made of woven scarves over a thin silk shell top. Only upper management would be allowed to dress that way, and he felt his mouth thin. If anyone saw her with him it would be noticed. *He* would be noticed.

"This way." She tilted her head. At least she had retained the sense not to use his name. Any damage had already been done, so he got up and followed her down the hallway.

After the first security point he allowed himself to talk. "I was told secrecy was a priority for this project." He made no attempt to conceal his annoyance.

"It is." Her clipped, sharp words conveyed her own irritation. "You will need access to very sensitive information. By taking you in myself, I avoid being summoned to give you clearance. This project is not the only one I have to deal with."

"I will need all connected information."

"You shall have it." She smiled without warmth. "The officer is being dealt with by someone else, but you will be given all the details." They went through another, more thorough checkpoint. "There is one important piece of new data that you may not yet be aware of. Umbra is aware of the planet. Not the location, just its existence. But that's bad enough."

Anders blinked, assessing the information. "And the target's last known location?"

"A backwater Fringe planet called Bone. She has already left." Meniran stopped before a secured door. She used the palmprint and retina scan station, and the door opened. "George will be able to access any information you need," she said, indicating the astonished tech seated at one of the consoles. "You may also call up the detailed contract, with all of the pertinent specifications. Do you have any questions?"

"You are certain this...other problem is not connected?" He was rarely called in, except for the gravest emergencies. He knew Toren did not like his conditions, and would do a great deal to circumvent them.

Meniran shook her head. "There is no connection whatsoever."

CHAPTER 4
LONG AND VENGEFUL MEMORIES

Moire carefully stood up in the darkness, then flashed the palmlight around again.

"I want to see too," Alan whispered, his heat-masked head rising through the hole in the floor.

"Wait a bit. There's not much room." The room was tiny and cramped, a cable and switching room, but it had a regular door switch. Moire quickly cracked open the door and let the spycrawler out to investigate. The corridor was empty, and the symbols on the wall outside were all red circles on black triangles.

"You could turn on the lights," Alan said hopefully.

Covert ops with an eight-year-old had problems all its own. "We don't have time."

She hadn't found anything that would be useful yet, and her window of opportunity was vanishing. She glanced at her chrono. A little over ten hours left, and she had to get everything done without detection *and* get back to the ship before it left. Feeling suddenly paranoid, she switched the viewgoggles to pick up the first spycrawler, still on the bridge of *Speedi-Web III*. The signal was poor, which nearly gave her a heart attack until she realized they had gone far enough from the dock that they were almost out of range. The ship was still there, and the bridge was empty.

Moire sighed and switched back to the other spycrawler. There had to be *something* she could do. She soon realized it wouldn't be using the spycrawler, though. The floor of the corridor was covered in a soft, textured material that caught on the crawler legs. By the time it got to the end of the corridor the ship would have left.

"I'm hungry." Before that, though, Alan would be terminally bored.

"Take a drybar from your pack," Moire said, scanning the visual feed in the viewgoggles. "Don't forget to put the wrapper back."

"Why?"

"If somebody sees it they will know we were here." They had to get out of the cable closet. It was risky, but at least this corridor seemed fairly quiet. It was strange, though. Not like the usual station environment. Besides the carpetlike floor, the walls were a smooth, uniform surface with shaded coloring that matched, and there were clear sidelight panels beside each door. It looked like an office building, not a station.

She shook her head, annoyed with herself. As far as Toren was concerned, it *was* an office building.

The nearest office was dark. Taking one more glance up and down the corridor, she opened the cable closet door.

"Come on!" she whispered to Alan. He tossed his pack up and pulled himself into the tiny closet with agility. Moire led the way to the office, remembering to note the door code on the cable closet for their return.

"Here," she said, taking off the viewgoggles and handing them to Alan. "Stay in the back and watch the corridor. If you see anybody, let me know but don't move, OK? People notice movement."

Alan nodded and sat cross-legged with the spycrawler controls. He seemed pleased to be given something to do. Moire scanned the palmlight over the desk. It wasn't hard to figure out the office belonged to someone named Marga Toos, and from the formidably bare and organized desktop this did not look like a promising place to start. Sure enough, the desk was secured. She didn't feel confident enough to attempt picking the electronic lock; better to try somewhere else.

It was a pity wastepaper baskets had gone out of fashion. Those could be very useful.

A small rectangular shape caught her eye as she knelt on the floor, searching. She picked it up. The datatab had been hidden out of sight near one of the legs of the desk, from where it had evidently fallen. Moire fumbled for her datapad and slotted it in.

She skimmed the contents as quickly as she could. It appeared to be draft files of whatever the current equivalent of memos was.

"People!" Alan whispered, and she ducked under the desk. Her heart hammered as she wondered what she would do if the missing Marga Toos showed up. She risked a glance around the edge of the desk and caught a glimpse of someone in the corridor. They walked past.

Moire picked up the datapad shakily and started reading again. Marga had many problems she wished to bring to the attention of her superiors. It appeared she was somehow involved in the day-to-day operations of the facility. She also seemed to have less than harmonious relations with the leader of the maintenance team, who didn't file reports properly and was not responsive to her requests.

Marga wanted him relocated closer to her, so she could keep an eye on him. Moire grinned. The maintenance leader sounded like someone she needed to meet—at least, his office. She noted the office code mentioned in the file, then darted across the room to the emergency map on the wall by the door. It was just a simple map with no numbers, and she frowned.

Their current location was marked by a red circle. She put her finger on it, intending to trace the way back to the cable closet, then blinked when the map suddenly displayed text with the office code and Marga Toos's name. She tapped other locations, and the corresponding information displayed.

The maintenance guy was several corridors away. Moire frowned. It would have been much more convenient if he had moved already.

"Anybody else out there?" Alan shook his head. "OK, we're going to try another place."

"What are we looking for?" he asked.

"I don't know." That was the good thing about having a junior assistant. An adult would be getting upset right about now, but Alan just accepted it and went on. She took out her pocket vid and captured the map for future reference.

It took a lot of time to get to maintenance, and more than once Moire considered giving up and trying somewhere else. The shortest route was too busy, so they had to take a longer, more nerve-wracking path that went past several occupied offices. They were both tired and jumpy by the time they reached it.

It was empty, as she had hoped. If his boss was out chances were he would be too, which was one reason she had kept going. She also suspected the head of maintenance would have some very useful information, if she could get to it.

Alan took up a position behind the door, watching out the clear sidelight as she went to the desk. Of course the viewscreen didn't come up when she tried to activate it; she was expecting that. She started searching.

This desk was not locked. Nothing obvious was visible, however, and she stared at the viewscreen hoping for inspiration. The frame was smudged on one side. She glanced at the wall beside the desk, which had a rack of tools and equipment. Did he really need to adjust his screen position all the time?

She felt along the edge of the screen frame, her fingers finding a small, round hole on the back surface near where the support connected. She smiled. Physical security. Someone like the maintenance guy was a hacker's friend, too. Careless and resentful of rules.

Moire examined the desk again. Besides the screen, there was a dock with a small datapad; a pile of textsheets; a small handmade and vaguely obscene sculpture of old grommets and link fasteners; and a tangle of cable. She narrowed her eyes. Part of the sculpture had a thin layer of dust on it, but not the base. She picked it up. In a few moments she had figured out the catch and a short, slender clear blue rod dropped into her hand.

It fit the hole in the viewscreen frame perfectly. The screen blinked and came alive, and she grinned madly. Finally, they had a break. *Ah, security. Doesn't matter how good the tech is if an idiot is using it.* She was definitely getting the feeling the ordinary folk of the station had no real fear of a security breach and had gotten very sloppy in consequence. This would make everything easier.

She glanced at her chrono and swore. How had they managed to use up so much time? She would just have to grab as much information as possible. She started searching through everything on the screen. There were a lot of diagrams and repair requests.

Then she found a systems plan of the station. It took her a moment to realize exactly what it was, then she studied it carefully. Locating the dock gave her their current location. The station was separated into two distinct areas, the one they were in and a very secure section labeled "Production."

She could see that getting in there was not going to happen this trip. She would just have to do what she could to prepare for the next time. The map had filters, and she selected the one that said "monitors." It showed the vid monitors on the level they were on and several others. The main control was in a room on the next level up.

She had to copy the map. Moire pulled open the desk drawers, rummaging through the contents. She finally found an open package of datatabs and pulled one out. Hesitating, she wondered if there would be some means of recording the copying of the map, then shrugged. It would look like the station maintenance chief wanted the map, and he obviously had the clearances to look at it.

Alan had not changed position at the door, still alert. She copied the map, then a collection of items from a "general information" node that included a station comm code listing and emergency procedures. It would have to do.

Moire plugged the tab in her own datapad, just to make sure they could read it. It showed up fine. Then she hurriedly removed the blue code rod from the screen and replaced it in its hiding place.

"Come on, kid," she said to Alan as she opened the door. "Let me show you how to have fun with sabotage."

Once she got inside the control room for the vid monitors, Moire no longer wondered how Alan had managed to escape. All the active security was in the Created section–the vids in the cargo area were on storage loop. Nobody was watching them.

"It would have been nice to know earlier," she muttered. But there was no guarantee they *wouldn't* be watched, just when most inconvenient.

"What are you doing?" Alan hovered over her shoulder.

"Telling lies to a machine," Moire said absently. "For when we come back." The storage loops could be loaded for viewing. With some experimentation, she had them set now to show the same empty loop, forever. A cleanup routine then stored the real loop somewhere unexpected. She'd tried to get it to delete the loop, but it wasn't working and she didn't have the time to figure it out. They had less than an hour before the ship left.

She blanked the cargo area vids, and a few on the upper levels. The risk was too great to mess with any of the others; that might get noticed.

"All right, let's get out of here." She took the viewgoggles and the spycrawler controls back from Alan.

He looked at her hopefully. "Going home?"

"Yes."

They ran for the cable room and the hole to the lower level, sparing precious minutes to return the feedthrough plate and the boxes to their earlier positions. The lower level was empty, too, the cargo track silent and motionless. Moire rummaged in her vest pocket for two flatbombs as they ran for the cargo hold. The vid monitors were happily replaying an empty loop, so they didn't have to worry about that anymore.

"Go back to the ship! Get inside the hold!" Moire said, pushing Alan ahead as she ran. She dodged down the branch corridor, where the cargo loading area was. Feeling for the spycrawler goggles, she groaned as she realized she'd forgotten to get the spycrawler from the upper level. It was too late now; they couldn't take the time to go get it.

The loading area was empty, just as the monitors had shown. She ran across the room to the heavily secured doors. They had a separate control panel on one side, and she peeled off the adhesive cover on one flatbomb and stuck it to the underside of the console. The other she put on the back surface of a green tower with the label "Control repeater."

She turned to leave. Alan was standing in the doorway, terror in his face. "The door is closed!"

Oh, terrific. She felt suddenly cold. Had she mistaken the time? Had they left early? How the hell were they going to hide out for a month without getting caught? She took a deep breath and put the viewgoggles on, switching to the first spycrawler on the bridge of the ship. It took her a moment to reorient herself, but when she saw nobody was sitting at the pilot's seat, she forced herself to relax. They hadn't left yet, just shut the cargo doors.

She had to get the doors open, and only the ship could do that. They'd find out, and...

Who were they going to tell? This ship was scheduled for a violent crew change in the very near future. Moire pulled out her datapad, which still had the tab with the stolen data, and called up the comm listing. It had a directory of divisions, as well as one listed "outside dock."

There was a comm panel on the wall by the entrance. She punched in the outside code.

"Yeah?" said a puzzled voice after a moment's delay. Alan was looking at her in horror. She just grinned and put a finger over her lips.

"Oh great, you guys are still there. This is Marga Toos. Look, can you do me a big favor? Maintenance needs to check the interlocks to the bay. If you could just open your doors for five minutes they could do it without EVA suits, but if you have to leave right away, never mind." She held her breath, hoping and praying.

"Um, sure, we can do that." Moire sagged with relief. "Why didn't they do this earlier, though?" *Good question.*

"They were supposed to, the dumbshits, but I just started my shift now and saw they forgot."

"Good thing you caught us, then. OK, opening the doors..."

"They'll shut the dock doors when they're done."

"Sure thing."

The pilot cut the link, and Moire and Alan ran for the cargo hatch. Moire slammed the hatch manual override as soon as she heard the vibration of the ship hold opening. Alan dashed in as soon as he could fit through. Moire waited for the doors to both fully open. Reaching around the edge, she hit the manual switch again and pulled herself in as the station hatch began to close.

A few minutes later, the ship hatch doors closed as well, and then they heard the sounds of the dock connections releasing. Moire leaned against the wall, suddenly very tired. The hold was crowded now with crates, she couldn't even see theirs. It didn't matter. They weren't going back in that damn thing ever again.

They rested in the little space they could find near the hold door. When she felt the bone-itch that told her the ship had made the transition to webspace, Moire slowly got up and pulled the pistol from her side pocket. Alan looked at her, his eyes solemn.

"You ready?" He nodded. Moire took one last look at the spycrawler view—the bridge had just the first pilot, nobody else. The door was open.

They moved silently through the ship, up to the bridge level. No sign of the other pilot, who was probably in her quarters sleeping. When they reached the bridge entrance, Alan swung around with his weapon drawn, guarding the way they had come. Moire aimed at the pilot and fired, missing the first two times she tried but hitting him the third time. The tranquilizer dart was visible in his neck as he fell. He'd seen her, but it didn't matter now. She sat down at the controls, preparing to drop out and take *Speedi-Web III* to a new location. The ship was theirs.

Ennis stood at attention in Colonel Garner's office and attempted to make one last argument. "Those fragments are still useful, sir. The only analysis we've done is what I was able to do personally. Fleet has experts that could get even more information."

Garner gave him a weary look. The skin was loose on her face, making her seem even older than she was. "Then someone needs to come and get them, because the experts are not coming here. Besides, you knew enough to make a good report. This is a war, Ennis. We will never have enough resources to do everything we want to do the way it should be done. I'm sorry, but the hangar needs to be cleared."

"Yes sir." He tried not to sound bitter. Maybe Garner had a real reason, but he suspected pookball had played a more important role than ship maintenance in influencing her decision.

"You did an excellent job with the means at your disposal. You know, I begin to think someone has been setting the base code wrong for transfers," she said, apparently at random. "At first I thought you were just an anomaly. Now here's another, apparently competent and in no obvious disgrace. It's baffling." She shrugged her thin shoulders, once. "But I'm not complaining. With reliable people on duty I can rinse my brain with chemicals without concern."

It was stated so calmly he almost misunderstood, then he couldn't think of anything he could safely say. Then he realized she was looking at him with sad understanding in her red-rimmed eyes.

"Sir, I..."

"Blank send, Ennis. I don't impair myself on duty, you know that."

"Yes sir. I know."

"You have my permission to report me, if you think it will help." She sighed. "For a year or so I even reported myself. They didn't care. Or they didn't have anyone else who had screwed up enough to punish with this post. Knowing oblivion awaits at the end of the day is the only thing that keeps me alive, sometimes. I just want you to know that having good people to count on when I'm...not available eases my conscience. What there is of it."

She turned back to her screen. "So, we now have Junior Weapons Technician Sendali Oberst, late of Alpha Centauri Training Center. I hope she's not expecting much in the way of action. We can't count on the crabs getting lost here again."

When Ennis finally met Technician Oberst, he had a suspicion why Lambert Base had been given the honor of her presence. She was certainly competent. However, she was also so new she squeaked and credulous beyond the dreams of the station pranksters. Sergeant Vyasandran started off by sending her to get ten meters of flight line. The cook gave her hell about using oxygen dihydride without filling out the dangerous chemical report. When she finally figured out it was a trick, she would give a little whinnying laugh and carry on as if nothing had happened. He had to give her credit.

Still no word back on the report he'd sent on the crab ship fragments and his analysis. He'd sent a reference link to the report to Namur, just in case Umbra might find it useful. And, he admitted to himself, to remind

Namur he was still alive.

If Cameron was out there she wasn't looking for him. He couldn't think of any reason why she should. She would be avoiding any Fleet station by a wide margin.

He picked up the block of polyacrylate on his desk with the ceramic needle he'd removed after shooting her. He'd have to be careful not to think about that too much, or he'd end up like Garner. Taking a chemical vacation in his off-hours.

At least his books had arrived. They helped, but his mind would still wander in the midst of a passage and he would suddenly remember the scent of bloodglue and antiseptic bandages, strands of straight brown hair scattered over a too-pale face, hair that was soft against his cheek when she leaned against him...

To steal my gun. And I let her do it.

A noise made him look up quickly. Technician Oberst was standing in the doorway, looking uncertain.

"Excuse me, sir," she stammered. "I was looking for the sergeant."

"He's out. Won't be back until tomorrow, late, probably hungover. Is it urgent?"

She shook her head sharply, her eyes wide. "Oh no, sir. I just thought he could tell me where people go for fun around here." Oberst smiled, a little uncertain. "I guess there isn't much, huh, sir?"

"I don't go out." It sounded curt, and he relented when he saw her look away. He remembered what it was like being new and ignorant. That was why he had refused to take part in the pranks. "You're right, there isn't much. Ask Yoshi. He manages to get himself in trouble on a regular basis, not that I'm recommending you follow his example."

She grinned and took a tentative step closer. "Is that a souvenir from a fight, sir?" she asked, pointing.

Ennis looked down at his hands. He was still holding the polyacrylate block. He could feel his face harden.

"A reminder. Of a mistake."

When he looked up again, Oberst had gone.

✺

"How many are there?" Gren asked, joining Moire at the galley table.

"Thirty-four. Madele says they're starting to wake up now. The ones she gave stimulants to." She swallowed another gulp of cold coffee. At least now that they had rendezvoused with *Raven* she could get some rest. "Alan's down there helping out. He knows how to talk to them."

"This Enver—think you can trust him?" The main pilot of the cargo ship had turned cooperative. Mengai, the woman, still refused to talk.

Moire shrugged. "Now that he's seen what he's been shipping all this time, he's more afraid of Toren than the law. He knows enough to guess his life isn't worth much if they find out he's been caught. They won't want him telling the world about their secret facility in the middle of nowhere."

Gren grunted thoughtfully and drank from his mug. Enver had given them a lot of useful information.

"He knows the locations of previous shipments," Moire added.

"You're thinking of going after them?" Gren gave her a sharp look. "How long before Toren figures out something's wrong?"

She hesitated. "Worst case, six weeks if they have someone expecting that ship at Kerezin. Enver says they don't always, but there's no way to know for sure."

Gren took out his datapad and arranged it carefully on the table. "You can't rescue the ones at the main site and the ones that were shipped. You have to choose. There isn't time for both."

"How can you say that?" Moire snapped. "They're *children*, Gren! Nobody else is going to help them! I looked up some of Enver's drop-off coordinates. No listed stations. More secret facilities. If I tell Fleet, are they going to go off and look just on Enver's testimony?"

Gren looked at her, puzzled. "Why Fleet?"

"They got ships, they got guns," Moire said, hoping her face wasn't too red. "Toren isn't going to just hand the Created over for a search warrant."

"Fleet's busy fighting the crabs. I know you want to save them all, but you can't," Gren said bluntly. He pointed a finger at her face. "You have a hard choice and I don't envy you. But isn't saving some better than saving none?"

Moire stared into her coffee mug, hoping for inspiration. She knew Gren was right, but it still hurt. How could she choose? Was there anything she could do to protect the ones she couldn't rescue?

They had to go after the main facility. It was the source, and as far as she knew the only one. They wouldn't kill the other Created if they didn't feel threatened by them, which meant they had to conceal the fact the facility had been attacked by outsiders.

"We go after the main site," she said finally, feeling sick. "And we don't leave any evidence. Blow it up, make it look like an accident." She was going to get Enver's information to someone, though. She wouldn't be able to sleep if she didn't.

Gren nodded solemnly. "That map you got is real useful," he said after a moment. "Think we can get that lower level secure, the one with the dock?"

"I've diddled the monitors, assuming anybody's looking at them. Nobody much there. Why?"

"We can access a lot from there, or the next level up. Air circulation."

"Don't they have scrubbers? Anything we put in will get cleaned out."

Gren gave a grim smile. "Not if we turn the scrubbers off."

Alan gripped his gun tighter, wondering why he felt excited and scared at the same time. He didn't want to go back to the Place again. They didn't have to stay in a box this time, though, and that was good. Also there were more people, so it was almost like *Raven* except nobody was smiling. Everyone used small, hard words to each other. It wasn't like they were angry, but like they were planning to be.

Moire was busy talking for hours with Gren and Yolanda and the others. They didn't want to go to the Place either, but they were going anyway. To get the rest of the Created. He wondered if the ones they'd left behind on Sequoyah knew they were free now, or if they were still frightened. He'd *told* them it was OK, but they weren't listening.

Now they were docking the ship to the Place. Moire had told him they would tell lots of lies, so the Controllers would think it was the people who belonged with the ship when they stole it. They wouldn't let him help with that part, but Gren gave him his gun. It was the same one he'd taken from the pirates.

Were Controllers pirates? He wanted to ask Moire, but she was wearing the goggles that let her see through the eyes of the metal crawler things.

"Oh good. It's still there. Looks like it got wedged in a corner," she said. "Are you guys at the loading area yet? Is it clear?"

She was talking to the ones in the crate, who were pretending to be cargo to unload. They were going to make sure nobody was there.

Her commlink buzzed and whispered with voices he couldn't hear, but she looked up at the others and nodded, and they all moved quickly out the cargo door. Everyone had guns like him.

"Put on your mask!" Moire whispered to him, and he pulled it up awkwardly with one hand. They were going to put something in the air to make people sleep.

He ran as close as he could to Moire, watching for Controllers. Now they were in the loading area, and Moire was holding something with buttons. It looked like a big commlink.

"Flatbombs are going off on the door," she said, and her voice sounded squashed through her mask. "They give off a lot of heat, so watch out. Neriyov, take out that broadcast unit. We don't want them trying to activate the cuffs."

He almost looked at his arm, but remembered. His cuff had been taken off. They couldn't hurt him with that anymore.

There was smoke and a few small flames at the big heavy doors, and soon they were sagging open. They used hooks to pull the doors away, and then they were in the corridors he remembered from the very first, when all he knew was his nenner and the other Created in his group.

It was very confusing for a while. They found Created and woke them up and told them to follow the loading track to the ship. The Created did it without any questions. He wanted to tell them it was a good thing, and they could talk about it and even touch if they wanted to, but there was no time. They had to rescue everybody as fast as they could.

Someone came in to tell Moire the first ship was full, and they were bringing in the big ship they'd found in the sargasso. They would have to wait before sending more of the Created out.

"Yeah, the bad guys are all zapped upstairs," the one called Neriyov said. "Sleeping like babies. They won't notice a thing."

"Get some float-pallets and start collecting them," Moire told him. "We're not leaving them here."

He didn't like that. Why would Moire want to take the Controllers too? He went up to ask her. Yolanda was already there.

"You gonna take all the cargo, right? We can get that started up and ready for when it docks."

Moire nodded. "Sounds good. Alan, you want to help?"

Cargo loading was interesting, especially with the big cranes, and he almost said yes. He didn't see any pirates to shoot, but this was still a bad place. If he stayed with Moire it wouldn't be so bad.

The broken doors were still smoking. When he looked at them, there were parts that looked like water or tears, but they were metal, flowing down the door. They'd stopped moving. He reached out his hand to touch, but the heat felt like a wall when his fingers got too close. Other parts were burning, and the smoke made his eyes sting.

He heard shouting and turned his head to find it. It was coming from the Created section.

"What the hell are you creatures doing? Get back in your pens!"

It was a Controller! Alan waved his arm until Moire looked his way. Now she could hear it too. She took her gun out, and some of the others came with her to the door.

They snuck back inside. Now he heard yelling, and other noises that made him feel afraid. He was close to the sounds, and he looked carefully around the corner the way he'd learned in the special training.

There were two Controllers, wearing the blue clothes of the medicals. They were very angry. A third one was standing in the doorway of the stairs to the upper level.

"Get back, get back!" The Controller in front had a rod, the kind that would make your cuff hurt if they pointed at you. Alan saw the fear in the Created's faces, then surprise. He could almost hear the words in their heads when they figured out the rod didn't work anymore.

The Controller lashed out with the rod at the Created nearest to him. She put up her hands to stop it. He struck again, cursing. This time she hit back, on purpose. It wasn't a very good hit, but it was enough. Created didn't hit Controllers, ever. Now the Controller was the one who looked afraid.

"I thought you said everybody was gassed!" he heard Moire whisper. She sounded angry. Gren mumbled something he couldn't hear.

Alan shifted to move forward, but Moire had put a hand on his shoulder.

"Wait. Where's the third one?"

The Controller in the doorway wasn't there anymore. He must have gone up the stairs. Now the Created were looking at the Controller with the rod, and they moved all at once, as if someone had told them to. He was hitting them with the rod, but it didn't stop them. They were pulling at him, clawing at his face, and he was screaming. The other Controller tried to run away, but the Created grabbed her and she fell.

There were horrible screams now, screams that went on and on and made his stomach hurt.

He moved away from the wall. Moire was running toward the cluster of struggling bodies. He saw shadows on the wall of the stair entrance and yelled a warning just as two more Controllers came out, firing.

More screams now, from the Created too. Alan pulled Moire back, away from the guns, and then started firing back. He killed one of them, but the other ran back up the stairs.

"Let's go!" Moire yelled, and ran after them.

Alan followed her. There was blood on the floor, and bodies lying still. One of them was a Controller, he could tell by the clothing, but the face was missing, it was all red and messy. Some of the Created were broken. *Not broken. Dead.*

Voss stuck his head into the common area, looked around with narrowed eyes, then left abruptly without saying a word. Ennis caught Sergeant Vyasandran's eye, and he shrugged. Garner had been late coming on duty before, but never this late. This was getting to the point Fleet would have to take action even if they didn't want to.

The sergeant left, leaving Ennis alone with his troubled thoughts for a while. Then Yoshi came in, followed by Oberst. They both looked very worried.

"Sir, about the colonel..." Oberst began.

"That is *none* of your business, is that clear?"

Yoshi waved his hands in agitation. "She's not in her quarters, sir! Michelson just checked."

OK, this was not good. "Does Voss know?"

"Not yet," Oberst said eagerly. "I think I know where she is. Will you help us, sir?"

"What do you need me for? Why haven't you gone to your superior?"

Yoshi's face fell. "It's off base, sir. And...well, it's not..."

"Not the kind of place you want your superior officer to know you know about. I see."

"Yes sir." Yoshi sighed with relief.

If they acted quickly, they might be able to get Garner back on base without Voss knowing. Nobody wanted Voss in charge, which was the most likely outcome if Garner was cashiered. Ennis struggled with his conscience for a moment, then gave up.

"All right, let's move. One of you stay behind and deal with any questions."

"I'll do it, sir," Yoshi said immediately. "I'll tell Voss you are trying to store some of the crab pieces. Besides, I'm in enough trouble off base already," he said with a sheepish grin.

Ennis and Oberst left as soon as the main gate was clear. The guard was studiously looking the other direction, so Yoshi must have already passed the word. They passed the commercial levels and continued up to the residential section. Oberst was walking quickly. Ennis had never been this far in the station; his only other excursions had been in groups, to the few food shops.

"Are you sure this is the right place?" he asked, going past yet another corridor of living quarters. The place was empty.

Oberst was walking even faster, almost running. "Off-record business. They try to keep it quiet so nobody reports them. I hope she's still there...left at the corner!"

He turned, and skidded to a halt when he realized the corridor was a dead end. Only a utility closet. The next thing he felt was a sudden burning sensation in his arm. Glancing up at Oberst, he glimpsed an injector in her hand.

Ennis grabbed for the scan-resistant gun, but it was too late. The blackness was sudden and overwhelming.

CHAPTER 5
THE BEGINNING OF WISDOM

I should have been more careful, Ennis thought as light filtered through his lashes. At least he was still alive. If he wanted to stay that way he should get moving. He tried to sit up and discovered he couldn't move at all. He was still slouched against the corridor wall in an uncomfortable position. His jaw was clenched shut, locked. He could breathe, but all he could consciously move were his eyes.

He wasn't alone in the corridor. The door to the utility closet was open, and Oberst was taking out a small plastic packet that had cheap, colorful lettering on it. She had exchanged her uniform for some grimy work gear, and her hair was now short and black. He squinted down as much as he could. He was in civilian clothes too now.

Oberst turned away from the utility closet and came toward him, carrying a duffel bag along with the plastic packet. With a sinking feeling, he saw the small translucent gun tucked in her waistband. Now he was really in trouble. He spared a brief second to wonder how Toren had managed to infiltrate an agent into the ranks. He hadn't even suspected.

She looked him over, a hard, scornful expression on her face as she opened the packet. She was now someone very different from the wide-eyed, green recruit he'd felt sorry for. Reaching out, she yanked his head down with a painful jerk and started spreading a thick paste over his hair. It smelled like a mixture of plastic solvent and rancid protein brick. After a few moments she took out a small metal comb and pulled it through the mess. Now there were thin filaments falling over his eyes. The fumes made his eyes sting.

Stranding compound. I never did like that fashion. It was a quick and effective disguise, though. She must be planning to keep him alive a little longer—but if he couldn't get away, it didn't matter how much time he had. He tried desperately to force his legs to move. He could feel his muscles tensing, but nothing happened. His joints were locked.

Oberst put the stranding compound away and took something out of her bag. Grabbing his arm, she closed a narrow green plastic cuff over his wrist. It looked like a medical monitor.

She grabbed his now-long hair and pulled until he looked at her.

"Listen up," she said in cold and even tones. "This is a control bracelet. It works like this." She held up a small rod and made an adjustment with one finger.

If Ennis could have screamed, he would have. Waves of pain washed through him, again and again. All he could manage was a small moan through his clenched teeth. Eventually the agony stopped and he could hear her voice again over his harsh breathing.

"You will do exactly as I say, when I say it, or I'll activate the bracelet. Don't try to draw attention, either. If anyone asks questions, I have documentation to prove you are a victim of partial paralysis and seizures caused by grin dust addiction." She took out her injector and inserted a new cartridge. She applied it to his hips, knees, and ankles. At first all he felt was a gentle, spreading warmth, but it grew to an excruciating burn.

She yanked him upright. His feet were clumsy and he still couldn't stand straight or talk, but he could move. It was a relief, even though he knew his situation really hadn't improved. Oberst pulled him impatiently out of the corridor, bag of gear over her shoulder, and headed down through the station. One hand had a strong grip on his arm; the other was tucked in a pocket with the scan-resistant gun.

He had to get away, but how? She had the gun and the control rod, and he could barely walk. He couldn't expect any outside help; nobody else was off base and the station people wouldn't recognize him now.

They were heading for the dock area. *She's taking me on a ship. Why?* Lambert Base was in a small station, and the sudden disappearance of two Fleet personnel was going to create a commotion. Maybe that was it. She had to get him away to have enough time to interrogate him. And then dispose of him safely.

He started dragging his feet and stumbling, even when she used small jolts of the control rod to hurry him up. If she thought he was weaker than he really was, maybe he could escape before it was too late.

Moire ran up the stairs two at a time, flinching when she heard a sudden whumping noise that shuddered through her feet. How had those Controllers avoided the gas? The one that escaped must have sounded an alarm. Or were they trying to blow up the facility?

Someone was tugging at her belt–Alan.

"I want to go first," he said urgently, trying to get past her. "I can help!" She kept running. Another whumping sound, louder. Did everyone have shipsuits on? She couldn't remember.

The door at the top was blocked, and they wasted precious seconds breaking it open. The whumping sounds were closer together now. Alan shoved past her the instant the door was clear.

"No! Alan!" Moire screamed. He fired as he ran for cover, and one of the blue-uniformed Controllers crumpled and fell.

He learned that from you, you bastards. Serves you right.

Had he been hit? She pulled back as a bullet whined by her head. She couldn't see him anymore, and panic threatened to overwhelm her. The room was huge; an upper and lower level with banks of equipment and catwalks. There was a wide open space between her and the nearest cover. Alan had made it across, but Moire doubted she or any of the others could do the same. They'd have to use more of the gas. Alan had his mask, he should be OK. God, she hoped he was all right. Why had he run off like that?

She could see some of the Controllers, apparently unarmed, running from bank to bank of equipment. They were paying no attention at all to the fighting below. One was close enough for her to see him grab a red-handled lever at one end of the large, opaque cylinder each bank had. The cylinder started to empty, revealing a small human figure in the tank, about the size of a ten-year-old child. The figure flailed and gave a wordless cry as it was dumped into a large opening, making the whumping noise they had been hearing all this time.

For an instant Moire froze with horror. *Dear God. They are getting rid of the evidence.* No time to wait for gas now. She fumbled at her equipment belt for a flash grenade, armed it, and hurled it into the room.

It went off with a harsh crack and poured acrid smoke, intended to stun and confuse. "Don't let them at the equipment!" she yelled as she ran into the room. "They're killing the Created in there!"

The others followed her. She heard another flash grenade go off as she rounded the corner of a row of equipment. Where was Alan? There was someone tall standing in the shadows, but it was a Controller—and she was reaching for the red lever of another cylinder. "Back off!" Moire shouted, aiming her pistol. The Controller put her hand on the lever and Moire fired, killing her.

The sound of a flash grenade was followed by a larger explosion, and the lights went out. Emergency lighting flickered on, making pools of murky light in the smoke. Moire ran past rows and rows of cylinders. Red pinlights were flashing on some of them now, and a slow chorus of alarms drowned out the sound of gunfire.

Where was Alan? Had they gotten all of the Controllers? She hadn't seen any for a while now, just her crew. She had lost track of where she was. Maybe she should go down to the lower level. At the top of the stairs the body of a Controller was lying slumped against the railing, a single gunshot wound in his chest. Typical Alan center-of-the-target shooting. She flipped the body over with one foot. The exit wound was higher, meaning he'd been shot from below.

She ran down the stairs. Sweat was pooling inside her face mask but she didn't dare take it off with all the smoke. More bodies on the lower level, and dim shapes running in the gloom. One just ahead of her seemed to be attacking one of the cylinders with a long pipe.

"Stop, or I'll shoot!" He was too close to the cylinder, though—and he wasn't wearing a Controller uniform. He turned his head, and she saw just enough of his face to recognize Gren Forrest. His face and mask were streaked with soot, and his eyes were wild.

"What the hell are you doing?" Moire yelled.

He kept swinging the heavy piece of metal with massive blows. The container began to shatter. "Gestators have lost power! Got to get them out or they'll die!" he gasped.

Fluid gushed out, leaving a writhing Created in the bottom of the broken container. He looked full-grown, but a snakelike umbilical cord was still connected to a disc of placenta at one end of the cylinder. After a short burst of coughing the Created started to cry.

Gren reached in, but Moire pulled him back. "He'll be safer there for now. Get the rest out!"

The fighting seemed to have stopped. Moire tried smashing a cylinder on her own, but whatever material it was made of was too strong for her. She rounded up everyone she could find, but that took precious time, time they didn't have.

In the end, they were only able to save three of the hundred or so left in the gestators. Some had been killed by stray bullets, but most had died from lack of oxygen when the power went out. Even the ones they rescued sometimes didn't survive more than a few minutes, apparently not developed enough to survive outside the gestators. Nobody knew what to do to keep them alive. Even the few medtechs captured alive didn't know.

She finally found Alan when the lights were restored. He was crouched by Gren, who was holding the body of one of the premature Created. Tears left tracks through the soot on his face as sobs shook his body.

"My fault, my fault..." he choked out.

Alan looked up as she approached, the fear in his eyes as he watched Gren changing to relief. He tugged on her hand as he held it, silently begging her to do something. He appeared unharmed, so she forced herself to focus on Gren.

"This is all Toren's fault," Moire said. "None of this would have happened without them." That was only partly true, and the realization made her numb. These Created would not have died if they hadn't tried to rescue them.

"My fault," Gren said harshly. He bent his head over the childlike body, holding it even closer. "Medical section had its own scrubber. Gas never got to them." His face twisted, tears flowing even faster. "Should have thought it through. Looked at the plan. It must have been there."

"It was my idea," she said, feeling her throat tighten. "I gave the orders. My responsibility."

"We wanted those orders," one of her crew said in a soft voice. Others had gathered around them, somber and sad.

Gren was making keening noises now, and Alan pressed close. She felt like screaming herself. This was not how it was supposed to happen, but it had, and now she had to deal with the consequences. She was the captain, and that meant she was responsible for all of them. She couldn't let him grieve now. They had to keep going or it could get much, much worse.

"Gren." He wiped his hand over his face, but he kept gazing at the little Created. "I still need you. *They* need you. All the ones that are still alive." He looked up. "We can't leave this place intact. If Toren knows somebody found it, all the other Created they shipped will be tidily done away with before anybody can get to them. They'll come hunting, too. How long will it take you to rig a remote for the reactor?" she asked.

Gren sighed. "I'll have to get around the safety interlocks. Two hours. We'll want some sort of feedback to make sure it's working, too." He got up slowly, carefully laying the Created back in the shattered gestator. "I just wish..."

"I'll get someone in here with a vid," Moire said softly, putting a hand on his shoulder. "Take one of the tanks as evidence. Yolanda should be getting all the files, too. We'll get them justice, Gren. Somehow." He nodded heavily and trudged off.

Moire turned to Alan, who was standing nearby looking at her uncertainly. All of her fear exploded full force. "Don't...you...*ever* run off like that again!" she yelled. He flinched. She took a gasping breath, trying desperately to get back in control. "I was frightened for you," she said, more calmly. "You didn't know how many people were there, or whether they had guns."

"I can shoot," he mumbled.

How could she explain? How many other mothers had to give their young children combat strategy lessons? Moire narrowed her eyes. Alan wasn't acting like he usually did when he didn't understand something. He knew why she was angry. He'd run away on purpose, so she couldn't stop him from taking dangerous risks.

If there was an afterlife, her parents were probably laughing themselves sick. She had one advantage over them, though. She knew what a risk-taker would consider a threat.

"If you can't follow orders I won't let you have a gun."

He stared at her, shocked and horrified, and he clutched his gun in both hands. Yes, that seemed to reach him. Her sudden fear was replaced by a flood of relief, and before he could move she hugged him fiercely. He could have been killed. "You have to be more careful," she whispered. "I would be so sad if you were hurt..." She couldn't speak for a moment, and hugged him even tighter.

Alan ducked his head beside hers. "Gren was sad." He said it as if he had only now understood. "All of him."

"I would be more sad than that."

He pulled back and looked at her with a worried frown, his gold-brown eyes searching her face. "You would?" She nodded. "I won't get hurt, then."

She couldn't help smiling. If it were only that easy... "Come on, kid. Let's get out of here."

They headed for the stair out of the medical section. Moire stopped before one of the gestators that was still intact. Leaning her face against the clear surface, she could just make out the floating body in the cloudy amniotic fluid. Even though power had been restored, the instrument readout on the gestator was dark.

I'm sorry, kid. We tried.

Moire pulled out her commlink and called Yolanda as they descended. "How's the loading going?"

"You wanna wait a day or so? Lots of good stuff here, least the equipment."

Moire shook her head. "Too dangerous. We need to leave as soon as Gren gets the reactor rigged. Get as much as you can, OK? And any data files you find."

"Yeah, right," Yolanda sounded unenthusiastic. "Is it worth our time?"

"If we're lucky, we can find out things that will nail Toren's ears to the wall," Moire said, irritated. "How valuable is that?"

"Enough for me, Captain." Yolanda cleared her throat. "I'm on it."

Fortin was still working in the lower section when Moire got there.

"Found this, thought it might be useful." Madele indicated a small case, open and full of tools and electronic readout panels. "One of the medtechs said you can use it to take those cuffs off." She smiled grimly. "Thought I'd try it on him, first."

"Good idea."

Moire waited on the ship for Gren to finish. She kept seeing the bodies and the blood smeared on the walls, smelling the residue of the flash grenades and the pale, salty smell of the spilled amniotic fluid. Alan stayed beside her, and she was glad. He reminded her that they had saved something, that it hadn't been a total failure.

At last the signal came. When everyone was on board, she undocked the ship from the station and pulled away, stopping at a distance that was safe but still close enough for the vid they'd left in the reactor control room.

Gren pushed the switch on his remote on her command, and a brief moment later a blinding light flashed and faded on the visual feed. The remote vid signal went dead, and the bridge scanner showed only a drifting cloud of debris where the station had been.

"All right," Moire said into the silence. "Let's go home."

Ennis had feared his interrogation would begin as soon as the ship undocked. Oberst had certainly planned it that way. When she opened the cabin door and found one of the crew inside setting up a temporary he saw the ugly gleam in her eye, but she didn't lose control.

"Hey, this the wrong one?" She held out the billet slip. "Says here two-berth cabin, and we got both."

The woman didn't even look up. "Got an extra passenger coming in. Sorry, but you gotta share."

As soon as they had the cabin to themselves, Oberst shoved him down on the lower bunk and secured him to the bunk with some strips of memory plastic.

"We'll have our little chat soon enough," she said in a low, threatening voice. "We're getting on one of our ships at the next station." She tugged on the memory plastic strips, making sure they were secure, then draped a blanket over him so they were no longer visible.

The trip was unrelenting misery. Oberst kept a careful eye on him whenever the other passenger was in the cabin, giving him occasional jolts from the control rod if he even attempted to make eye contact. When the injection started to wear off, he was only able to tense against the restraints–and Oberst seemed to know exactly when she needed to give him another dose. He didn't even have a way of telling how much time had passed.

He counted injections. The third one was just starting to wear off when there was a break in the routine. Oberst had left for the messroom, apparently thinking the other passenger had also gone there, but instead he showed up in the cabin a few minutes later. He was a heavyset man with a silent manner, and generally ignored both of them.

Ennis struggled to speak, wondering how much help he could ask. First he had to know how close he was to ending up on a Toren ship.

"Dock. When." he managed through his clenched jaw.

The man looked at him, startled. "Huh?"

"When ship dock. Station."

Comprehension cleared the man's face. "Oh. Six hours."

No time. He couldn't count on Oberst being careless again. "Tell captain. Kidnap!"

The man stepped back, looking apprehensive. "Hey, your sister's just trying to take care of you."

"Not sister!"

The door shot open and Oberst came in, breathing deeply. She'd probably run all the way back from the messroom. Her gaze darted between the two of them.

"Anything wrong?" Her voice revealed nothing but innocent concern, but Ennis felt his heart sink.

The man shook his head, appearing glad he could hand the situation off to someone else. "He's not making sense. Time for his meds?"

"Yeah." Oberst took out the injector. "I'm sorry he bothered you. He gets crazy sometimes, thinks everyone's out to get him. Even me!" She laughed in the brainless way she had at Lambert Station. Ennis felt his last hope evaporate as the injection took hold.

She fussed over Ennis until the man left, and then her face changed from concern to steely fury. She held the control rod in front of his face. "Remember this?" She smiled at his indrawn breath, and activated it. Ennis spasmed. The agony was intense, but all he could do was moan through his clenched teeth. She hit it again, and again. His vision started to darken.

Gradually he became aware that the pain was ebbing. She was in the top bunk now. He doubted she would leave even for an instant until the ship was docked. He breathed deeply, trying to relax in the aftermath. Sweat was dripping off his face. Involuntarily he moved to wipe it off, then felt the restraints holding his arm.

He blinked. His arm had moved. He tried moving his other arm. It moved too, slightly and painfully. So. Somehow forcing the joints to move broke the lock of the injection. She'd never used the control rod for that long at full strength. The restraints must have held him rigid enough that the muscle spasms were enough to do the job.

She'd just given him an injection, though. He needed to keep the joints moving, or they'd lock up again. Slowly, carefully, he shifted as much as he could without making any sound that would alert her.

It felt like knives when he moved, but he kept on. This was his last chance at escape. If Oberst got him on a Toren ship he was dead.

When the ship docked Oberst pulled him up from the bunk, and he fought to keep his joints rigid, as she would expect them to be. With a quick glance to make sure they were unobserved, she used the injector with the local antidote so he could walk.

He tried moving slowly and stiffly, to see if she would use more, but she just pulled him along.

Every step sent sharp, jabbing jolts of agony through his joints. Somehow he stumbled his way out of the ship, unable to focus because of the pain. It was a little better out in the station. He had a brief respite when Oberst stopped at an information kiosk. As she searched, he surreptitiously moved his arms, judging the range of motion, looking about desperately for inspiration.

It was a poor, beat-up station, and not very crowded. He wondered where it was. Definitely in the Fringe; they hadn't been traveling that long.

Oberst dragged him along with a jerk, muttering. "Three levels down. This piece of crap station has four levels?"

The dropdowns were located in the center of the station. Oberst held him close, alert for any attempt on his part to get away, especially at the first level security station. Slowly the big box of the dropdown rose from the level below. Instead of a metal door, yellow and black plastic safety strips hung from the top of the dropdown to the ceiling. He'd only seen that in construction sites, but this appeared to have been in place from the beginning.

Still nothing he could use. They got on, exiting at the next level and waiting for the dropdown going to the next lower level.

The dropdown they had left moved up again in its shaft. The safety strips on the bottom were not in very good shape. Several were missing, others were broken. It wasn't much, but he didn't have a choice.

Ennis tensed. If he could just time it right...

He watched the dropdown shaft carefully, waiting for the first sign of movement. As soon as the dropdown began to descend, he groaned and began to collapse, shifting closer to the edge.

Oberst cursed and yanked at him, but by now he had fallen to his knees. The bottom of dropdown was halfway to the floor of the shaft. He fell farther, twitching and making more noises as if he were in pain. Which he was.

"Dammit, get on your feet!" She went to one knee beside him, holding the control rod. Ennis snatched it away and shoved suddenly with all his strength. Oberst fell back through the safety straps, flailing, and he twisted and kicked her leg out from under her. She yelled as she saw the dropdown descending, a yell that was abruptly cut off with a crunching, grinding sound.

Ennis scrabbled to stand up again, casting about for the bag she had been carrying. He had to crouch down to pick it up, and he could barely grasp the handle. He ended up sliding the grip over his hand and lifting his arm. It hurt so much...he must have done some serious damage breaking his joints free, and using them made it worse.

Everything had happened so fast nobody had noticed anything was wrong yet, but they would. He had to get away. Oberst might not be dead, and in any case Toren probably had other people on station who might recognize him.

The dropdown to the upper level was waiting patiently, and he stumbled on. The sudden exertion brought on a wave of sharp, debilitating cramps, and he braced himself against the wall to stay standing.

Where should he go? The first level had a security station. Maybe they could help him. He'd have to be careful, though. He had to get there before

Toren did.

Moire looked back and sighed. The others were still standing inside the cave. Near the edge, which was progress, but Harvey was peering up at the sky looking even more hunched than usual, and Madele started whenever something moved in the breeze.

It was peaceful on Sequoyah; the sun starting to go down in glorious color reflected in the sea between the islands. At least, it would be peaceful except for the strenuous discussion they were having.

"Is it supposed to look like that?" Gren asked suspiciously, pointing at the sky.

"It's a sunset, Gren. A really nice one. Earth has one every day." Sometimes she could get them to accept the newness of planetary living by saying it happened on Earth.

"We gotta do something," Harvey said, stubbornly returning to the argument in progress. "We can't leave them alone. Well, they aren't alone now; they're all asleep. Together." He shrugged, raising his hands in an eloquent gesture indicating he was just reporting the facts.

"Why?" Gren shrieked in a whisper. "It isn't decent!"

Moire snuck a quick glance to make sure Alan was out of earshot. "They have the minds of children," she pointed out. "Even if their bodies are adult, they haven't figured out, um, anything yet."

"That's the hormone suppressant," Madele Fortin added in an acid undertone.

"Hallelujah." Harvey agreed.

"Besides, it's what they are used to," Moire said. "We've changed everything else, and it frightens them. It's not like they're *doing* anything, Gren!"

Just sleeping, that was all. Together. In piles. She had to admit, it did look like the aftermath of an orgy. Except everybody had their clothes on.

She had two nightmares now. One featured blood and body parts. The other involved explaining the facts of life to over two hundred Created, including her son. *Maybe I can bribe Madele when the time comes.* It would probably have to be a pretty large bribe, though.

"We can't keep them here," Harvey said. "Montero found the white-haired one playing with the power wrench today. If he doesn't pull his own ears off, he'll be disassembling equipment."

They had enough food, thanks to the sargasso and Toren's supplies for the station. What they didn't have were babysitters, and it was becoming a problem. When the Created stopped being frightened, they started being curious. The ones they had rescued from the ship had been on Sequoyah longer than the others and were becoming more confident. It wouldn't take the rest much time to catch up.

"OK, the cave is a bad idea. We're going to have to build shelters elsewhere–maybe that island north of the bay." That should keep them out of trouble, mostly. Until they learned how to swim, or build boats.

The prisoners from the Toren facility were already on islands halfway around the planet. The weather was warm enough that tarps were sufficient shelter for them, but she wanted something more for the kids. Besides, they were going to have to get serious about digging in for defense.

"We won't be able to do it ourselves. Anybody know some decent construction firms?"

Yolanda shrugged. Gren frowned, rubbing his chin. "Kind of thing you're thinking of? Bunch at Jessack, some that do surface and station work."

"We don't wanna go there," Yolanda said abruptly. "I see that name mentioned a lot in that stuff of Toren's we took. They got a depot there or somethin'."

Moire sighed. "They might tell us to get lost anyway, if they've heard about us."

"I think we can convince them," Gren said. "We can pay 'em, and nobody knows for sure we're pirates. They may not have heard the rumors."

"What about me?" Moire asked. "What about the kids? Jessack could be crawling with Toren people. It's too risky."

"No more than usual," Yolanda said. "Their station is in pieces, but they don't know why. They don't know who."

Moire spent a restless night alternately dozing and admiring the Sequoyah night sky, which blazed with stars, trying to figure out what needed to be built first, and how.

The cave was perfect–the pseudotrees sheltered the entrance, and the rock was deep enough to mask most heat signals. Underground, or at least hidden, she decided. They could build visibly once they won.

If they won. She'd have to build well; well enough they could carry on without her. She'd made a promise to Fleet to turn herself in when it was safe.

Be honest. You made a promise to Ennis. That's what you really care about.

She squirmed on the thin padding and discovered she wasn't alone. Alan was crouched beside her sleeping pad, just visible in the dawn light. Behind him, not quite brave enough to follow, was a group of Created.

"Urm?" she asked, blinking her eyes clear. "'s something up?"

"They wanted to know how I have a name now. I said you gave me one," Alan said earnestly. "I thought maybe you have names for them too."

"Ah." She got up, feeling stiff, and folded her pad and blanket. "Breakfast first. No names on an empty stomach."

How long had they been waiting for her to wake up? She puttered with the galley equipment that had been placed on long tables along the side wall of the cave. They had a lot of people to feed now.

Juice and a drybar would do until somebody started cooking. She handed out the same for the others. There were three: the boy with white hair Harvey had mentioned, a pale girl with grey eyes, and another boy who looked like his gene mix had some Japanese.

Moire found a seat near the mouth of the cave, in front of the transport ship. "So you want names, huh? Let's take a look at you." She noticed the Created didn't seem to mind being outside the cave. She'd have to watch that. If they decided they wanted to explore, her crew might not notice they had gone.

First in line was the white-headed one. That was easy. "You're George." As in Curious. The others took more thought. As she looked at them, she thought she could see slight resemblances to people she'd known in NASA. It made sense; the kids had gotten their DNA from the NASA tissue storage facility.

The girl she named Ash, and the other boy Hideo. *Bon Accord*'s biologist, Michiko, had a brother named Hideo.

They're all going to want names. I'll never keep two hundred plus of them straight. Finding a paint pen and roll of plastic strapping, she made up some dog tags.

They hadn't gotten brave enough to talk to her yet, but from the way they held the tags, carefully examining their own and each other's, the names were quite satisfactory.

It felt strange, having a name. He wondered what a George was, if it did anything special. *She* had said it, so that's what he was. He wondered how she knew.

The sleeping space here only had little places, so they couldn't all be together. They sat on the floor, close, and then it was almost the same. Alan didn't. He stayed on his sleeping space–he called it a *bunk*–and looked at his square thing with words in it.

They all had names now. He pulled out the piece of plastic with the marks on it. The one with all the fun tools had made a hole in it so he could wear it around his neck.

He spelled out the letters in his head. *George.* The others had tags too, with their names. Ash and Hideo.

"Do you have a tag?" George asked Alan.

Alan shook his head. "She didn't give me one."

"Why not?" Hideo wanted to know. He did that a lot. Now they could ask any questions they wanted to, and they wouldn't be punished.

"I don't know, she just didn't." Alan thought for a moment. "She gave me this, though. Maybe it's the same thing." He tugged the ends of the beautiful red thing tied to his arm. It had small sparkles inside, like the metal shavings in Carlos Montero's workshop, but it was bendable all over. If there were any letters on it, they were too small for George to see.

"What's her name?" Everybody looked at Ash, and she tried to make herself small. Ash hardly ever talked. She looked at things a lot, and thought about them.

"It's Captain!" Hideo said, excited. "I heard the one with the long black hair say it. Grrrenn."

George rolled his eyes. "No it isn't. That's just a...it's a what you do. Like Carlosmontero, that's his name, and Maintenance is what he *is*."

They all considered that for a moment.

"I thought Maintenance was the place he works," Hideo said.

"It's sort of both," Alan said. "All together."

George looked at him. "Do *you* know her name?" Alan had been with her the longest–months and months. He knew more than any of the other Created.

Alan ducked his head. "Sometimes it's Ren Roberts, but that isn't the real one," he said slowly.

"What is the real one?"

"She doesn't want me to say it where people can hear."

"Why?"

"Because she said, that's why," Alan said, scowling. "Somehow it's bad."

Nobody said anything for a while. Then Ash wiggled restlessly. "I wonder what names the others got."

Hideo lifted his head off her shoulder. "Go ask them?"

"The big door doesn't work. I tried. The little picture on it is all black. I can't see the cave or anything."

"We aren't in the cave," Alan said, shaking his head. "We're going somewhere else."

"Before, the cave was outside. We went in the room full of seats, and if you looked in the little picture in the big door the cave was there," George said doggedly.

Alan sighed. "We aren't *there* anymore. That was the shuttle. The ship is...is like a box, and we're in it. The box moves, and when we get out it's someplace different."

George frowned. If they could find it, the door should open to the same place it had before. All the other doors in the ship stayed the same.

Ash opened her mouth as if she was going to ask something, but then the comm on the wall buzzed. Alan got up and listened for a while. George just heard a small voice, but no words.

Alan looked at them. "She says we are at Jessack. Nobody is supposed to leave the ship, because it is dangerous. There are Toren people here!"

"Toren is what?" George asked. Alan seemed worried, and that made him scared.

"Toren is Controllers," Alan answered quietly. "I'm going to find her."

He left, and they all huddled closer. "She's not going to give us back, is she?" Ash whispered, shaking. George nudged her with his shoulder.

"She doesn't like them. Remember? Alan said she *killed* one. Maybe she's going to kill the ones here."

Her mouth quivered. "I don't want to be in a box," she said, her voice going squeaky at the end. "They could get us."

George looked about their room. It wasn't big; it just had the sleeping spaces on the walls and the empty space between. Nowhere to hide.

"Let's find a better place," he said, getting up and pulling Ash with him. "Where they won't see us."

The others moved with him out the door. If Alan was there they could ask him a good place, but George didn't know where he'd gone.

George saw someone in the hallway and started. "Ooh! People!" He turned to run, but Hideo stopped him.

"We know those ones. Remember?"

Even the familiar faces made him want to run now that he was scared, and he knew the others felt the same way. When they saw Gren walking down the corridor they did run. None of them could figure out Gren. He was one of the good people, but he had a fierce face and he yelled at them when George was trying to figure out the interesting tools. Then sometimes he would give them good things to eat and just look at them sad, not saying anything.

"We should go where he is," Ash said in her soft voice, almost too soft to hear. George stopped.

"Why? He would say mad words at us again."

She swallowed, struggling to say her thoughts. "He is...he would be that way to the Controllers, if they came. He could make them go away. If we are where he is, but he doesn't see us, it would be safer."

When she said it, he could see how it would happen. It was a good idea. They carefully retraced their way, keeping out of sight of their target. George could still hear him. He was half-saying words to himself, like he sometimes did after yelling.

"Go and get them, she says. At least McNaulty will talk to us. And what do we do if they turn us down? Build it ourselves? Can't leave those children like that..."

Hideo stumbled into Ash, who made a startled noise. Gren turned, frowning, and they quickly darted into a side passage before he saw them. George scowled at them, then peeked around the corner. Gren was walking away again, sighing and shaking his head.

"Quick! He's going through a door!" Hideo whispered. They ran up, just as the door almost closed. George held it open just a little.

"I didn't know that room was there," Ash said, surprised. "It's really big."

"Lots of places to hide," Hideo added.

There were ladders to places high up, in shadow, and stacks of boxes and big machines. George moved out carefully, looking for Gren. He didn't see him.

The room was very big. Maybe too big. George frowned, feeling scared. He wanted to find Gren now. Maybe he yelled, but he belonged to them.

Nobody had seen which way he went. They walked down one way, but it was just a wall. The other direction went on and on, and still no sign of Gren. Somebody else was walking toward them. She was almost as tall as the nice Madele but with the same kind of warm brown skin as Kilberton, the pilot. She smiled as she went by.

George had never seen her before. He was all of a sudden cold, and his stomach squeezed itself.

"We gotta hide!" he said, and ran for the nearest area of shadow, behind and under a big metal thing with legs. There was room for all of them, just. The others were breathing hard now too. They knew, just like he did.

He didn't understand how it had happened, but they were Outside. Where the Controllers were. And he didn't know how to get back in.

CHAPTER 6
WAYFARING STRANGER

George carefully watched the people walking by the hiding place. The people didn't look like Controllers. Maybe they were safe for right now, but when the Controllers came they wouldn't be. How were they going to get back? There were lots of doors along the wall and they were all the same.

Ash and Hideo were pressed close to him and they were shaking. He was shaking too. There should be someone to tell him what to do. Not a Controller, but one of the rescuing people. "Find Gren," he said, and felt a little better. He could tell *himself* what to do.

"How?" Hideo asked. "We looked and he wasn't there. Maybe he went in one of the doors!"

They all contemplated the many doors.

"We could open them and look in," George said. They waited until nobody was in sight, and scrambled out from under the machine. There was a door directly ahead of them. Hideo pulled the long handle, but it didn't move. When they tried pushing on the little pad by the door, it flashed the message "Authorization Failed."

"We walked and walked before we came here," Ash said after they looked at each other, worried. She squeezed her eyes closed for a minute, then blinked them open. "When we came out of the door there was a small box, and it had some yellow stripes on it. We should go back and look for that box, maybe..." her voice trailed off, and she looked frightened again.

"That box has yellow on it," Hideo pointed.

George shook his head. "It isn't stripes, though."

"Hey! What are you doing?" George spun around. The door was open now, and a man was standing in it. He looked angry. "That's ours. Were you messing with the door?"

George was to terrified to speak or move.

"We're looking for a box we can't find," Hideo said in a fast, gasping voice.

"Oh." The man didn't look so angry now. He glanced at Ash. Her face was all white and her eyes were big. "Sorry if I startled you. Yeah, stuff can relocate here. You're gonna get yourselves shot if you look for it that way, though. Go to the security station." He pointed, and glared at them until George grabbed Hideo's arm and pulled him away. Ash was already walking quickly in the direction the man had pointed.

George knew why. The man had said go, and when you were Created you did what someone said to you. He glanced back over his shoulder as he followed Ash. The door was closed now.

"Wait," he said. "What's a security station?"

They stopped and looked at each other. "There's a sign," Ash said in a whisper. She nodded her head forward with a small twitch. "But *people* are there!"

George bumped her with his shoulder to make her feel better. "This place is different. We can go look and they won't say we are wrong." Even the angry man hadn't said they were wrong, he just told them to go away.

He could see lots of people up ahead. They were in an even bigger room. Now they were close enough to see the sign on the wall, and it said, "Jessack Station Security Post." It was next to some windows in the wall, and he could see inside to the room there.

"Controllers!" Hideo pushed George and Ash hard, away from the place with windows. George scrambled for somewhere to hide, but the only thing near was a wheeled machine. They hid behind it, gasping.

Nothing happened. George peeked around the corner of the machine. He saw what had made Hideo want to hide. Inside the window place the people were wearing clothes that were all one color, like the Controllers did, and they had belts with things on them. He frowned. Controllers wore bright colors, but these people were wearing a green that was dark. He almost hadn't seen it as green.

He wrinkled his nose. The machine didn't smell very good. "I think it's OK," he said slowly. "They just look like Controllers." He shifted forward.

"No!" Ash had a wet face from crying. "D-don't! I don't want to be b-broken..."

Something moved in the darkness, just a little shifting noise, but it hadn't come from them. George went closer to see what it was. It looked like a pile at first, but then he saw it was a person. The bad smell was stronger there. He remembered a smell like that from the Place. The ones who were punished smelled like that before they were cleaned again.

The man shifted again. "Look!" Hideo pointed. "A Created! He has a hurt bracelet!"

Two eyes blinked open. Deep blue eyes. George froze, frightened again. The man was breathing hoarsely now, and his face looked like pain when he moved the arm with the green plastic bracelet away. George blinked. The man was trying to get away from them. Maybe he wouldn't hurt them.

Hideo came closer, cautiously. "Why do you still have that?" he asked. "*She* took all of them off!"

The man stared at them, and gasped. "Medic...need medic." His mouth hardly moved, and it was hard to hear all of the word when he said it. "Hide me..."

If they found the way back in again, they could take him to Madele. She was a medic. *She* could take the cuff off too. Maybe they wouldn't be mad at them for leaving the ship if they rescued someone.

Ash was hovering behind them, nervously watching as people walked by their hiding place. George heard her gasp, and he quickly looked her way.

"Gren!" Ash pointed. George put his arms behind the hurting man and lifted. The man made a horrible sound, but he kept his mouth closed so it was quiet.

"Help me lift him," George whispered. He didn't want to hurt him anymore, but they had to get back and find Gren.

Ash flapped her hands. "Hurry! He's going away!"

Hideo took the other side, and they quickly darted out from behind the wheeled machine. They moved as fast as they could, but there were more people now. He wasn't scared of them, though. Maybe if he thought about it he would be, but he was thinking too hard about finding Gren.

Ash was ahead, looking from side to side. She didn't see the man stopped in front of her until she ran into him. She made a small sound in her throat and backed away when he turned.

It was Gren. George didn't care if he was going to be yelled at, he was so glad to see him again. Then he saw a small box with yellow stripes outside a door, and felt even happier. They'd found the way back!

Gren's mouth went open, all the way. His face started to change color. "You were told to stay on the ship!" Then he saw who they were carrying. "What did you...where the hell did you get him?"

"He's hurt!" Hideo protested. "Can't we even take this off?" He held up the man's arm, showing the bracelet.

Gren's eyes widened. "Get in the ship! Quick!" he whispered harshly, opening the door and shooing them inside.

❦

Kolpe Anders adjusted his ID before entering the office, simultaneously standing a fraction taller and lifting his chin. He'd be a regional inspector this time. Ordinarily he wouldn't have made contact so soon, but Meniran had stressed speed and accuracy. He needed the most current information they had.

The staff was properly deferential, making a private office available. Anders accessed the main system, via an account that did not match any of his assumed identities, and made a minor change to a file. He then accessed a new account that had just been created.

The new account had access to certain files that had accumulated, files that were only readable on his personal datapad. He frowned as he read. The information was two weeks old, which was very recent if it came from Earth. The suspicions of Fleet Intelligence involvement had been confirmed. The officer in question had been located and an operative in place to bring him in for investigation. They were sending Anders an assistant.

He compressed his lips. That was clumsy work. A missing intelligence officer was bound to attract notice. Toren felt they were powerful enough to avoid the consequences, but Kolpe preferred to leave as few traces as possible. And why burden him with an assistant, when speed had been given top priority?

He smiled thinly. He wasn't going to wait for this assistant. If they could find him the way he moved, they would have to be good.

Kolpe removed the files from the main system, and returned the security switch to its original setting. He left the office silently. Hearing faint voices, he stopped and looked about.

No one was in the hallway. He took out his earboost and activated it. His implant picked up the signal, and the faint voices became louder and more clear.

How did they find out so fast? We only knew for sure six days ago.

He could be here for something else. We've been inspected before.

You want to take that chance? They have to blame someone. A whole damn station in small bits? And that one in particular? I tell you, it's time to fade out and not come back.

Maybe we can make it look like the delivery ship caused it. It's missing too.

Kolpe left the office, wondering what they had been talking about. It wasn't connected to his task, but he was always looking for information Toren didn't want him to know. It could be useful later on.

Moire squinted at the display on the control bracelet for the captain's earring as she walked down the corridor to Medical. The display was supposed to give her readouts from the captain's earring, but it was getting harder and harder to read. She'd have to get a new one soon. No, she hadn't imagined it. That was Gren's code, and he had asked her to come to Medical immediately. He would have told her if one of the crew was hurt, so it couldn't be that. But what else would require her to go to Medical?

He was waiting for her in the corridor outside, glowering at high intensity. "The Created got out!" Gren yelled. "I found them wandering around outside!"

"Uh-oh. How far did they get?" she asked, feeling a spike of fear. "I just had station control asking if any of my crew were near the second/third-level dropdowns. Seems there was a fatal accident and they are looking for witnesses."

Gren muttered something profane. "Who can tell with them? They were terrified, though, I'll say that. I'll believe they stayed right there once they realized they were lost. You can't leave the docking area without going past a staffed security office. They wouldn't do that."

That was good news. The last thing they needed was more fallout from the kids' little adventure.

"Anything could have happened to them!" Gren moaned, pulling his long hair. "Why couldn't we have just left them on the planet?"

Moire winced and made quieting motions with her hands. "Careful, Gren. We've got strangers showing up soon, remember? No mentioning you-know-what."

"Oh. Sorry." He lowered his voice one notch. "Er, actually, that's the other problem. They found somebody and insisted on bringing him back, and...I think you'd better take a look."

She rounded the corner to the medical station. The area was crowded and noisy; Alan and the other Created were arguing with each other while Madele Fortin was doing something to someone lying on the exam table.

As far as she could tell none of the kids were hurt. Gren was grumbling to himself again, and the Created glanced at him nervously. They were both fascinated and terrified by Gren, whose irritability was frequently interrupted by flashes of guilt when he dealt with them. It sounded like they'd managed to persuade him into letting someone on the ship.

The stranger on the exam table was ragged, dirty, and bruised. Lank brown hair obscured his face. He appeared to be unconscious.

"Look, kids. I know he looks bad but we can't help everybody–"

"See?" Alan glared at George. "I *told* you she'd be mad. You shouldn't have gone Outside."

"Why didn't you stop them?" Moire asked.

"I wasn't there," Alan said. "I told them to stay."

She sighed, feeling suddenly tired. "Next time you stay with them, OK?"

"Why can't we rescue someone?" George asked, sticking his chin out at Alan. "You got to go back to the Place and do that, and it wasn't wrong. We want to help too. We rescued him so you could take this off, like you did for us," he continued, looking up at Moire pleadingly. He had pulled back the stranger's sleeve to show the same green plastic cuff the Created had worn.

Moire stared at it, momentarily stunned. What had George gotten into?

"Madele. Have you tried to remove it?"

Fortin turned away from the medical diagnostic equipment stiffly and raised her eyebrows when she saw the cuff. "What, another?" She bent with a grunt to reach a low cabinet and brought out the kit they'd stolen from the Toren site. She took out a slim metal rod tipped with tiny, jewel-like datachip inserts, and gently threaded it into the access hole near the cuff hinge.

The cuff popped open.

"Huh. Guess we have confirmation," Moire said glumly. More

problems. "OK, kids, where did you find this guy?"

"He was behind the thing with wheels," Hideo said with enthusiasm. "He was hiding too!"

"What's wrong with him?" Moire asked Madele.

The medic shook her head, looking puzzled. "No broken bones or internal bleeding, but the physical stress markers are what I'd expect for major trauma. Some traces of drugs, but I can't tell what they are." She scowled at the medical scanner, then said slowly, "and this thing says he's sprained every major joint in his body." She made a humphing noise. "I'll set it for a longer scan."

Madele took a disinfectant pad and started cleaning the cuts on the stranger's face as Moire wondered what to do. If Toren had put a cuff on the guy...they'd taken it off, but from what Fortin was saying it sounded like he needed medical attention. They couldn't just dump him out the hatch and leave.

There was a small duffel bag on the floor next to the exam table. "That bag is his?" Gren nodded.

Moire rummaged through the contents. There wasn't much. A small case had a space for a medical injector, which was missing. It also had several injector cartridges.

Remembering some of Yolanda's tricks for contraband, she patted the sides of the bag between her hands. The fabric of the bag was thicker than it should have been in one place. With a little searching, she found the seal for the opening. Reaching inside, she pulled out a handful of fabric. It was purple-blue. The color of a Fleet uniform.

"We're in trouble," she said grimly, and held it up.

Gren snatched it from her, staring at it and then at the stranger.

Moire stood up, a horrible sinking feeling in her gut. It couldn't be. This man had long brown hair. She looked more closely. Madele had cleaned up some of the grime, and a cut near his hairline. Near where Madele had been cleaning the color of the man's hair had changed from mottled brown to black. Moire took another disinfectant pad and rubbed hard. A long strand pulled loose, leaving short black hair behind.

It took a moment for her to see past the bruises and the dried blood. Then she took a sudden deep breath, her heart hammering.

"I know who he is." Had Ennis been looking for her? What had happened to him? She didn't think this had been part of any plan of his. More importantly, what was she going to do about it?

They all looked at her. "He's one of us. Right?" George asked.

Moire shook her head. "He's a Fleet officer. We need to get him off this ship."

"Not the..." Fortin stopped. The horrified look in her eyes told Moire she had recognized Ennis too. Now if they could just get him away before

Alan figured it out. "He's in bad shape. I don't know if he can even walk."

"Can't he stay? We just found him!" George said plaintively.

"You did a good job," Moire assured him, and he cheered up a little. Hideo looked confused. "He, uh, doesn't want to stay. In fact—"

A signal from the captain's earring chimed in her ear, and Moire tapped a control on the bracelet to respond. "Madele. Do what you can for him. Keep the door to medical closed, and don't mention him to anybody. Alan, you and the others go back to your room and stay there until I say you can come out, OK? Our guests just arrived." Maybe she could get Ennis out somewhere safe when the contractors left. Why was everything happening at once?

The discussions were agonizingly slow. The contractors were conscientious and thorough, and she had to fight to pay close attention. She kept wondering about Ennis. There were a few difficult moments when she had to deflect their questions about location by invoking security. Their contract matrix had an option for confidentiality protection, so perhaps it wasn't that uncommon.

After they left, Gren picked up the reader with the contract and looked it over again.

"Their estimate assumes a vacuum site," he pointed out. "When they find out it's atmosphere, and a planet, it will be cheaper just from the fittings alone. Building leakproof is expensive."

"Yeah, but shipping to a gravity well isn't going to be cheap, either." Moire sighed. "We're gonna have to salvage some more ships. We still need to figure out where we want them to build. We'll need a lunar station eventually, even if it's tiny."

Gren got up from the table stiffly. "Got what, six weeks to figure it out? That's not very long to wait. Usually contractors are booked up more."

Moire frowned. "Yeah. Notice they weren't asking any hard questions? Something going on there?"

"They must need the work." Gren shrugged and left.

Moire picked up her datapad and the contract tab and left for the bridge. The contract should go in the safe, and she wanted to find a way to get Ennis off the ship. Without damaging or endangering him any further.

Kilberton was already there when she reached the bridge. "Got a job for you on station," she said, and he looked up expectantly. "Need passage for one to the nearest Fleet station, the sooner the better. Don't use the kiosk."

He raised his eyebrows, but only said, "You are being cautious, Captain?"

"The traveler has already attracted the wrong kind of attention." Somebody had it in for Ennis, and she wondered who. Why had he been by himself? How had he known where she would be?

"Ah. Our unexpected guest." Kilberton inclined his head in

acknowledgment. "I will be most careful."

He left, and it occurred to Moire she should check with Madele. Maybe he had regained consciousness. If he was too sick to travel immediately they would have to make other plans, perhaps find a safe place for him on station.

"He's still out," reported Fortin on the comm. "The residual drug levels are going down, though. I can't really tell how much damage he has until he wakes up."

Moire grimaced. This was going to be awkward. Maybe they would have to keep him, just for a while. They could probably stay a few more days at Jessack. She could keep out of sight. Ennis wouldn't have recognized the other kids, or Gren. He might remember Madele, though.

A comm signal broke in suddenly, with a priority code. "They're all over the docking level," Kilberton's voice came in, breathing in short, quick gasps. "Guns. They're all armed."

"Who? Cops?" *Nope, wrong century.* "I mean, police?"

"I don't know who they are. No uniforms."

This was not good. "Where are you?"

"In the ship. They shot at me just as I was leaving the hatch."

Sounds like a declaration of war to me. Moire changed the broadcast setting of the captain's earring to shipwide. "Attention! Ship is under attack. Anybody on station?"

After a few confused moments it became clear all the crew were present, meaning one less thing to worry about. Then Kilberton came back on line. "Captain, I think they are trying to force the hatch."

Moire spun the chair she was sitting in and launched herself at the docking controls. She slapped the undock sequence, yelling into the comm. "Kilberton, get back on deck!"

The undock wasn't working. The indicators for all the mechanicals showed them still engaged. Moire swore. Somebody wasn't playing nice. "Time for a bigger hammer," she muttered, and reached for the trim engine controls. The mechanicals were all exterior, so when she pulled the ship free the damage wouldn't endanger the people on the station.

Alarms flashed and bleeped; she ignored them. As soon as the ship separated she called up an external line to the station police. It took longer since they were no longer hooked up to the dock, but even when she got the connection the response was slow.

"What is it?"

Moire blinked, wondering if she'd gotten the wrong comm code. The voice sounded harassed and very unpolicelike.

"This is Ren Roberts, of *Raven*. Somebody's trying to shoot up our dock hatch. Can we get some help down here?"

"Look, I'm just the desk clerk, OK? " the voice said, ragged and losing control. "Everybody's out already. I'll tell 'em when someone calls in free but that's all I can do." He cut the connection, and Moire stared at the commlink blankly. *What the hell?*

She heard pounding feet in the corridor, and Kilberton burst in. "Station has gone insane," she said in response to his inquiring look. "I don't know what's going on but we need to get away from it. Take us out a bit, so we don't have to worry about traffic."

He moved to the realspace controls and got to work. Moire went to the scanner and turned it on. What had gone wrong? Had Toren figured out she was on the ship, or had the kids managed to blow something up without telling her? No, the cops weren't calling them. This was unofficial–organized crime, or Toren.

Another ship undocked from the station, and she watched with a growing coldness as it matched their trajectory. "We've got company," she said grimly. "Change in plans. Get us to drive point as quick as you can."

"Where?" Kilberton started entering data in the web console.

"Doesn't matter! Anywhere but here!" She started running for the gun controls. They were up a ladder from the bridge, and she flipped the guns live before she had even landed in the chair. "Talk to me, Kilberton! Where are they?"

"Port aft high, closing fast. *Santé!* They are firing!" Now her instruments were on line, and she could see it was a deliberate warning shot. A tiny bleep sounded insistently in her ear–an outside comm signal. *I don't think they want to sell me life insurance.* She took aim and fired, once, twice. The oncoming ship was quick, and dodged. They fired back, and Moire felt the ship shake.

"Are we there yet?" she yelled. "What got hit?"

"Almost ready," Kilberton said faintly. "Cargo three has lost pressure. Close, close...got it!"

Moire felt the itchy ripple of the gravity transition and sagged against the gun chair with relief.

CHAPTER 7
OLD FAMILIAR ADVERSARIES

Reality faded in slowly, and in pieces. Ennis stared, puzzled, at the empty bunk on the opposite wall. He ought to be worried, but a heavy, warm tingling pervaded his body and made it hard for him to be concerned about anything. The pain was gone.

What had happened? He'd gotten away from Oberst and tried to get help. He frowned, struggling to remember. It was all confused and blurred in his mind. Had he found the security station?

The memory came back, sharp and clear. Someone was already at the security station. He watched from hiding, trying to decide if he should risk contact. Then he had discovered he couldn't move. His muscles simply wouldn't obey him anymore. What had happened after that?

Had Toren found him? He struggled to look around the room, but he had no energy. He caught a glimpse of a display sheet on one wall showing an image of some trid star, and tacked to the underside of the bunk above him was a string of red and gold plasglas beads.

He sighed, feeling slightly relieved. He doubted this was Toren's idea of prisoner accommodations.

A small sound of surprise, and then a young woman was leaning over him with open-eyed concern. She looked vaguely familiar. Before he could speak she had darted away, calling "Madele! Madele!"

He was so tired...Ennis drifted back into unconsciousness again. Voices filtered through the darkness.

His eyes are shut now.

That's all right, Ash. He'll wake up again.

There was something he had to tell them; something he had to do. What was it? He struggled to open his eyes. What was he forgetting?

There were two people in the room now. The pale, grey-eyed young woman he'd seen before, and a huge older woman who was looking at him with friendly concern.

"I'm Madele Fortin, ship's medtech," she said. "Are you feeling better?" Ennis managed a nod. "This is Ash."

Now he remembered where he had seen her. "You...found me," he grated.

Ash tilted her head, brow furrowed with thought. "George found you first. I was there, too, though." She peered at him. "You slept a long time."

He tried to ask how long, but it was too much effort. He was vaguely aware that Madele Fortin was doing something with a portable diagnostic, and then he felt the cool weight of a fluid pack being attached to one arm. Even though she moved his arm, it didn't hurt.

They left, and he fell asleep again wondering where he was.

He slept a lot. Once, he woke to find Ash with the two others that had found him on the station, watching him with the same look as an eager new recruit. As soon as they saw his eyes open they began peppering him with questions. Why was he hurt? Did he have a name yet? Had he been lost like them? Why had he made his hair look funny?

Fortin came in then and shooed them off before he could gather the strength to answer. Now he had questions of his own. Ash and her friends were rather peculiar.

The next time he woke up, it was because he felt an injector activate against his shoulder. Without thinking, he jerked away and grabbed at the hand holding the injector.

"Ah, very good!" Madele Fortin was smiling at him, making no attempt to pull away. "You should be careful not to overdo, however. The new tendon tissue is not so strong."

Ennis let go. "I'm sorry. I was..."

Madele held up a hand to stop him. "I saw the cartridge case in that bag you were carrying. I hope it wasn't yours, because none of those cartridges had legitimate medical uses." He shook his head vehemently, stopping when he noticed. He could move again! Madele popped the cartridge out of the injector and showed him the label. It was a standard anti-inflammatory.

"They used drugs to keep me under control," Ennis said as she continued to give him injections.

"Now, who would take the risk of doing that to a Fleet officer?" Madele wondered.

"They weren't planning on leaving any evidence," he said dryly. "How do you know I'm Fleet?"

She seemed to hesitate for a moment. "We found your uniform in that bag. Two, in fact." Yes, Oberst would have taken her own as well. "Do you feel up for a small walk? You'll recover faster if you keep your joints flexible. We can get some food in you as well."

Food. That was a wonderful idea. Fluid packs did nothing for the hollow feeling in his stomach. When he tried to stand up, he realized he was too dizzy to walk.

Fortin took hold of his arm. His progress was painful and slow, but as he kept moving the pain decreased and his balance improved. His mind was working better, too. He had to contact Fleet.

"I need to send a message," he said. It was hard to think what to do after that, though. He couldn't go to the station police, not with Oberst's body to explain. By the time they understood what had happened, the other Toren people would have found him.

"That's a bit difficult," Fortin said, turning him toward the galley. "We've been in drive for six days now."

He collapsed into a seat, numb with shock. Six days? No wonder he was hungry. "Where are you going?"

Fortin hesitated. "I believe the captain should answer that question." She got stiffly to her feet and went to a wall comm and spoke a few words into it. "I'm sorry if this presents a difficulty for you. We had to leave, and you were in no condition to be left on your own."

He nodded, sighing. "Yes. Thank you for getting me out of that."

"Thank the children. They were the ones that rescued you," Fortin said, opening a cupboard. "I wouldn't have thought they'd even talk to strangers."

Children? His memories of his rescue were blurred, but he didn't remember any children. Then he lost interest in anything except the food in front of him. He was almost too tired to eat.

He had to make contact with Fleet as soon as possible. Or, he temporized, Umbra. Somebody needed to know about Lambert Base, and how Toren had gotten an agent into Fleet. He didn't even know if Garner was still alive. It could be months before any of the other lot got a message back to FarCom that something was wrong.

"Madele feeding you well?"

He started, and turned in his seat. Moire Cameron was standing there, watching him with a faintly rueful expression. He was suddenly aware of how small the galley was, and how difficult it would be for him to move quickly, even if he had the strength to do it. He was trapped.

She looked exactly as he had remembered her: trim, alert, and deceptively ordinary in appearance. Only the strange hazel eyes gave her away, and he thought he saw a hint of shadow there that hadn't been there before. Was it because of him? He hadn't *planned* on escaping on her ship.

"He wants to know where we are going, Captain," Fortin said, tilting her head as if curious to see Moire's reaction.

He was in even more trouble than he thought. "You're the captain?" he asked, incredulous.

She sighed. "It was their idea."

"How?"

Moire turned away and picked up a mug. "The crew picked me when Captain Davies died in the pirate attack. It was supposed to just be an emergency measure," she said, glaring at Madele Fortin, who gave her a bland smile.

Now he remembered. He and Harrington had been on Bone, waiting to hear of *Ayesha*, and word had come that the captain had died. At the time all he had cared about was it hadn't been Moire.

Everybody gets promoted but me.

"The ship was badly damaged, but she got us back," Fortin said.

"You're good at that," Ennis said before he could stop himself.

Moire gazed down at the contents of her mug. He knew she was remembering the less-successful return of *Bon Accord*, and he could have kicked himself. "Yes. I am." She sat down opposite him at the table, looking at him intently. "The kids told me their version of what happened, but it didn't make much sense. Who did this to you?"

Ennis felt a twinge of annoyance. She'd done much the same thing to him the last time he'd seen her, only in her case she had not tried to make him a prisoner. And, he acknowledged, she hadn't hurt him. "Toren got someone in where I was posted. She drugged me and was taking me to a Toren ship at that station. The injection she used kept my joints locked, so the only way I could get rid of her was by shoving her under a dropdown. I tried to get to security, but it looked like Toren had got there ahead of me—and then I was too injured to move. That's when your people found me."

"Where did they find you?"

"Same corridor your ship was on, near the entrance to the main causeway. Why?"

Moire smiled crookedly. "They weren't supposed to leave the ship. We had to leave Jessack in a hurry, with you on board, because someone started shooting at us. We barely made it in to webspace. Something happened to make us a target, and I want to know what. The kids *say* they didn't do anything wrong, but they don't always know what that is."

Ennis frowned, suddenly worried. "Shooting at you?"

She leaned back in her seat, sighing. "Armed people on the dock level, trying to pry the hatch. Had to undock the hard way, and when we did, a ship came after us. They knew exactly which ship to attack. Did anybody follow you?"

Ennis was sure nobody had seen him at the dropdown, or they would have raised the alarm then. Oberst was probably dead, and who else would have known he was on the station? "I don't think so. Nobody who would have known what ship I got on, anyway."

He rested his arm on the table, noticing as he did so the green plastic cuff was gone. That had to have happened while he was on this ship. Yes, that would make sense. Toren would want to be able to find him wherever he was.

"It was that cuff. It must have had a locator chip." The timing was right, too. Just enough for someone in Toren to learn about Oberst and her prisoner and start looking.

"Damn, you're right. Should have thought of that." Moire shook her head and took a drink from her mug. "This is a refreshing change. You've gotten *us* into trouble. I wonder where I can take this ship without getting shot at now?"

Ennis gritted his teeth. *None* of this would have happened without her, but it wouldn't be a good idea to point that out. He needed her help.

"What about McNaulty?" Fortin asked. "They'll be waiting at..." she trailed off, and Ennis caught Moire giving her a faint twitch of her head, with a glance his direction.

He pretended not to notice. "I have to get back to Fleet as soon as possible. Or someplace I can send a message."

"Saying here she is, come and get her?" Moire asked, unenthusiastic. "Do you really think I'd put myself anywhere near a Fleet station right now? Don't tell me any fairy tales about how they can keep Toren away. Fleet didn't do a very good job protecting you." She put the mug down with a clang, scowling.

It was the truth, and galling. What was even more annoying was he hadn't been thinking of her mutiny. How could he possibly forget something like that? She certainly hadn't.

An amiable-looking older man wandered in the galley, nodded vaguely in their direction, and headed for the storage area. He started rummaging through the bulk food bins.

"I wasn't expecting you to go with me," Ennis snapped. "Fleet needs to know what happened to me, and I have a duty to get back as soon as I can. You understand that much, I hope."

"You don't have a duty to get shot by Toren, and if I show up anywhere in this ship, that's what will happen. Relax. You'll get back eventually." She drank deeply from her mug, apparently unconcerned. "We just have to find another ship, that's all."

He raised a skeptical eyebrow. "How are you going to do that, if you can't show up at any ports?"

"I have a very good source." She grinned, and Fortin suppressed a smile. "I think you'll find it interesting."

His temper snapped. It had always hurt when people joked about his background, but it hurt even worse coming from her. "I am in enough trouble already, thanks to you. Don't drag me into your criminal network." She blinked, looking confused, and he struggled to regain his calm. "You have survival shells, don't you? All you would have to do is a quick drop at a Fleet station."

She shook her head. "No. I need them. Besides, do you really want to be a helpless target like that?"

A crunching sound made Ennis glance aside. The older man was sitting on a nearby bench, facing them and munching on a bowl of fresh flavored starch puffs as if he were watching a show.

Ennis looked back at Moire, questioning. Her eyes were dancing. "Another member of my desperate criminal crew. Carlos Montero, in charge of maintenance. Carlos, meet Fleet Commander Ennis. He's going to be visiting us for a while."

Montero dusted off a hand and offered it to him. His gentle, foggy expression was the antithesis of criminal, and Ennis felt ashamed. He didn't know anything about the crew, just Moire Cameron, and he had done the same thing others had done to him—judge Carlos by his associations. He glanced at Moire. Her expression had changed from mocking amusement to affectionate exasperation looking at her crewman.

In the end, did it really matter how soon he returned? She wasn't going to come back with him, which meant he would still be in trouble with Umbra. Fleet might decide they'd had enough and kick him out as soon as he reported in. Besides, he didn't have a choice. He was stuck on her ship until she found him a way out. He had no right to complain. Anything was better than what Toren had planned for him.

Moire got up to leave, and he felt a twinge of disappointment even though he was starting to feel exhausted. "I'll get you back as soon as I can, but it won't be this week, or the next. We have a long way to go."

"Where are we going?" Ennis asked.

She grinned, and he couldn't help smiling back. "My secret base, of course. I think you'll like it. You can tell Fleet all about it, too."

"Really." Now he was suspicious.

Moire nodded. "In fact, I insist."

The data bouncebacks were expensive, but effective. Since he had no way of knowing where he might be next, Kolpe Anders did not hesitate to include all the databot nodes. Every place he had set a databot received data from all the other locations.

That was how he found one of the former crew of *Ayesha*. Her name was Tenna Ondolai, now crewing on a passenger/cargo ship running the Fringe. Her dialogue was rapid and inconsequential, making it difficult at first for him to find out anything useful.

"S-so, no p-positions?" he asked timidly. He was posing as an Inner Systems dockworker wanting a ship job, but with no real skills.

She smiled with regretful sympathy. "Sorry. Not for what you're looking for. Now on *Ayesha*—my last ship—they would have hired you right off but we don't have the room, you know?"

Kolpe pricked up his ears. "M-maybe your old ship would h-hire me?"

"Oh no, it isn't flying anymore. There were pirates, see, and when they tried to take over the drive..." Wearing an expression of calculated shock and wonder, Kolpe let her voice wash over him. He wondered when he could steer the conversation back in a more interesting direction. "...and

Ren got us to Mullery OK, but the drive was shot. *Ayesha* was falling apart anyway."

"H-how did you get out of Mullery, then?"

"Oh, they got the new ship and..." for the first time, Tenna's artless flow of talk faltered. "And I didn't want to go."

"M-maybe your old captain is hiring?" Kolpe asked hopefully.

"He's dead, but they picked Ren...I don't know. I haven't seen them since." Tenna looked over her shoulder, back into the ship. "Look, I have to go now. Good luck. Try down with the ore haulers, they usually need help."

"T-thanks anyway," Kolpe extended a hand, and she shook it. It felt dry, he knew. It was dry because it had been sealed to protect him from the thin film of dermal drugs that would make her short-term memory unreliable.

He made sure to leave looking dejected, just in case anyone else had observed them, but he was feeling elated. Ren Roberts had been the name his target had been using on the planet Bone, when she hired onto *Ayesha* as pilot. It looked like she now had a ship, and a loyal crew. Even the former crew weren't willing to talk about her to outsiders. They must know something.

He needed to get to Mullery, or somewhere close by where they might have heard about the pirated ship that almost didn't make it in. He could pick up the trail there.

Arranging his next trip took longer than he expected, irritating him. When he found the ship a muscular woman moving with a trace of a swagger followed him in to his cabin.

"Occupied," he snapped.

She flashed a grin. "Yeah, I know." She shut the door and offered him an ID chip with a blue T in a circle marked on the surface, looking him over as she did. "Sure hope you don't always look like that, if we're bunking together."

Kolpe had to take a deep breath to contain his temper. The ID checked out. Plymson was a security enforcer. His helper.

"How did you find me?" he grated. If this muscle-bound idiot had done it herself, he would quit.

"Sent a whole bunch of us out. Stationed us at all the places you'd been seen last, and nearby. I got sent here. Soon as you activated your expense account here, they added me to the ticket."

Well. He had not expected Toren to be so profligate, or determined. He would have to find a way around that in future, perhaps carrying a larger amount of cash. Meanwhile, he had to get rid of Plymson.

"Get off the ship. You will just be in my way."

She ignored the dangerous tone in his voice and handed him a datatab. "They said you'd get huffy. Message from the boss."

He read through with a growing feeling of coldness. It was even worse than he'd thought. The Fleet officer had killed the agent sent to bring him in, and escaped. The ship he had left on had not been seen since.

They could have blown the whole operation with their stupidity. That officer was probably at a Fleet station at this moment. For the first time in many years, Kolpe swore.

Their landing site was on the dark side of the planet when they arrived, but Ennis still caught some glimpses of the scattered islands that made up the land surface of Sequoyah from his viewport in the scout.

The trip to Sequoyah had been a long one, but Ennis had still not met many of the crew. He'd spent most of his time either sleeping or doing physical therapy with Madele Fortin. He'd learned a little more about the three who had rescued him–Ash, George, and Hideo. They were Created, children that had been artificially accelerated to full adult size. He wasn't clear on who had done this or why, and his questions were ignored.

Moire's son, Alan, was Created too. He had been very upset when he found out Ennis was on the ship. He wondered how many of the crew, like Alan, resented his presence. They certainly hadn't gone out of their way to talk to him. He hadn't seen much of Moire, either–busy piloting the ship, in what he understood was a difficult transit–and when he did Alan was always there, glaring at him.

Strangely, he did not feel the tension he had always experienced before on a new ship. Perhaps the crew avoided him simply because he was an outsider. Understandable, and it had nothing to do with his past. Ennis suspected they would treat any stranger the same way.

He heard the sound of the landing hydraulics vibrate through the ship, which slowed and angled toward a patch of light that showed like an open door in the darkness. If it was a door, it was huge–larger by far than the scout–and he strained to see more. He'd gotten the impression that they hadn't built anything on the planet yet.

The ship landed, and the others quickly popped the hatch and exited the ship. The ship hadn't docked, but the crew weren't using any protective equipment, either. Ennis hesitated at the threshold of the open hatch. A cool breeze carried scents of salt and musty spice. Moire walked by him and stepped out, and he followed.

A hunched, wiry man came hurrying up. "It's about time you showed up. I thought they were going to go crazy, waiting for you." He got a good look at Ennis and his Fleet uniform and backed up a step. "What's *he* doing here?"

Moire sighed. "It's a long story, Harvey. How are the kids?"

Harvey rolled his eyes. "Still won't sleep in the bunks. And some of them heard how you gave George and his bunch names yourself, and now they *all* want that."

Moire frowned. "I thought you gave them names already."

"They want it from *you*." Harvey shrugged. "Not to mention they were getting frightened you were never coming back. Month's a long time to them."

"I'll go see them, then. Or are they asleep?"

"Better see them anyway. Oh, and that Enver fellow–he says he wants to help."

"Later, Harvey." There was an edge to Moire's voice.

"Who are these people that need names?" Ennis asked, curiosity overcoming caution.

Harvey threw a quick, anguished glance at Moire, who looked amused. "Can't hide two-hundred-plus Created very easily, Harvey. More to the point, we couldn't hide him from them. Find Commander Ennis a bunk, and I'll take him to see the kids."

Harvey walked off, throwing up his hands in resignation. Ennis followed Moire. As his eyes adapted to the low light he could see rock walls on either side, curving as they rose. They were in a cave. In the very back, past crates and boxes of supplies and gear, were several room-sized structures of fabric over open frames. A faint blue light glowed inside each one.

Moire parted the opening of one of the tents and stepped inside. He wasn't prepared for what he saw–a tumbled clot of people on a pile of crate padding, asleep in the dim light of a jury-rigged safety light hanging from the top of the metal frame. Moire motioned him to stay at the door, and she moved inside.

They sensed her immediately. One gasped and stirred, waking those around her. "It's only me," Moire said, soft and gentle. "I've come back." The woman subsided and mumbled something sleepy. "In the morning. Go back to sleep. I'll be there when you wake up."

The woman nodded, but reached out her hand. Moire touched it, and the woman smiled sleepily and tucked it under her head again. More hands raised, trying to reach Moire, and she touched each one lightly before leaving.

"Who did this? Why?" Ennis asked in an urgent whisper. The air of unreality about the Created disturbed him.

Moire took a deep breath. "There's a bad labor shortage in the Fringe. Toren doesn't like that. People can refuse the dangerous, scut-work jobs because they can find something better. Toren evidently got the bright idea of growing their own. Figured out a way to grow them faster, stronger. And they just happened to have a whole bunch of genetic material on storage from the NASA exploration teams. None of it in the Index."

It took a moment to sink in, and then his mind refused to comprehend. It was too many horrible things combined. Slavery, gene theft. Probably gene engineering, too. "Your son...you said you didn't know about him, and I thought you..."

"Yes." Her face was hard, and her hazel eyes burned with anger. "My son. They created him when I was still in the webspace bubble with *Bon Accord.*"

"They aren't normal. Are they?"

She closed her eyes, looking tired. "I'm not sure if they'll turn out normal or not. They're young, no more than seven years old, and Toren controlled everything they learned. Alan escaped from their facility and found me. When I was able to, I found *them.*"

She entered another of the tents, and the same scene played out. The hands reaching out for comfort; Moire soothing them with calm words.

They walked back to the cave entrance in silence. Finally Ennis burst out, "Why didn't you tell someone? You could have left an anonymous message, or..."

"I thought about that. If Toren even suspected anybody else knew, they would have killed them to cover up." When she spoke again her voice was rough. "I wasn't able to rescue them all. Sometimes I think I recognize who their parents were."

Moire was leaving out some crucial details, like how she'd done it, but he was reluctant to ask more. Toren hadn't handed their captives over voluntarily, he was sure. It wasn't important. She'd known someone needed rescuing, desperately, and she had rescued them. Probably using desperate measures.

He should ask, but he wasn't going to. She'd refuse to answer, but that wasn't the reason.

It had taken a year for the rescue ships to arrive at Fimbul. A year when people had to expose themselves to the radiation, the roving gangs, the damaged systems. That was why Penderhest had built their shelter on the surface. That was why he had only rarely allowed Ennis to go with him to the interior tunnels, and that was what had killed him in the end.

If Moire Cameron had known about the disaster on Fimbul it would not have taken her a year to get there. And Penderhest would still be alive.

CHAPTER 8
STANDING ON THE EDGE

The insistent beeping finally woke her. Moire searched by her bedroll, bleary-eyed, for the commlink. "Mmm?"

"We are ready to leave, Captain." Kilberton's voice came through, faint and scratchy. *Long-range communication equipment*, Moire added to her expanding list. "I will act with greatest caution, and remember all you have told me of the transit."

Moire got up, groaning and stretching, and moved away to the edge of the cave, closer to the scout. The transmission would be better, and there was less danger of anyone hearing who shouldn't. "I'm not worried about your flying, Kilberton. You've done the transit twice now with no problems. Just remember there's some nasty people out there looking for us, and don't take any risks. Listen to Menehune; she'll know if it's dangerous. Get the crew and gear from McNaulty and head back."

"Yes, Captain." Kilberton ended the transmission, and Moire clipped the comm on her belt with a sigh. She didn't like splitting up the crew like this, but she didn't have much choice. They had to pick up the construction crew and equipment, and *Dunkirk*, the cargo ship they had used to rescue the Created, was both big enough and not yet connected with her.

It should be safe enough. Yolanda was going with him, and she had all the street smarts Kilberton lacked. She hoped he'd listen to her. Maybe it hadn't been the best idea to send her law-abiding copilot off with their resident expert on the criminal underworld. The two of them had had some heated arguments on the subject. No, they both knew this was important. They'd have to save the ethics discussions for later.

Now she had to figure out a way to get Ennis back where he belonged before *Dunkirk* returned.

The sun was just starting to think about coming up. She was the only one awake in the cave, and it was blessedly silent. It wouldn't stay that way long, and she had a lot of thinking to do.

She stuffed some drybars and a drink bulb in the pocket of her jacket and strapped on a pistol. They still didn't know all the surprises Sequoyah had for them, and she made sure everyone went armed when they left the camp. Besides, it was a good habit to get into for later.

She took the path down to the bay, jumping carefully from rock to rock.

The gravity was just a tad over earth-normal, and she didn't want to break an ankle. The trail split just before it reached the water, where thick, rubbery reeds filled in between the huge bases of the pseudotrees. Moire took the path up the hillside, to the cliff top.

The sun had not yet reached this side, and the moonballs were still floating about. A large one drifted past her as she climbed, and the tiny insects suddenly started to life, dispersing in a cloud. A moment later, they coalesced back into a handful of smaller balls, which merged back to the larger ball again. It was still too cool for them to scatter for the day.

After she got the guns, maybe they should shop for a good xenobiologist, too. The moonball insects weren't the only creatures they'd seen. There was something that looked like a flying mop and sounded like a foghorn in a blender, and the giant whatsits in the oceans. They'd probably have to wait for large, armored submarines before they could investigate those.

Seeing the telltale round orange balls of a splatter plant ahead, Moire made a careful detour. The balls were full of some caustic, noisome substance, and the slightest touch made them burst. After a few of the more adventurous Created had run afoul of the splatter plants, they had developed a profound respect for them. Very much like a vegetable skunk. Maybe they could use that, if they could figure out a way to move them without setting them off. Or could they grow them from scratch? How could they tell what the seeds were, if they had any?

We need a xenobiologist.

The top of the cliff was rocky and mostly bare, with large boulders scattered about the surface. She could see all the way to the next island, still wreathed in morning mist. The rocks were chilly and slightly damp, so she broke off a mat of wiry tanglegrass to sit on in a sheltered spot, out of the wind.

They needed more medics. They needed more everything, but especially medics. The new Created—you couldn't really call them born—decanted? Unplugged? Hatched? required constant attention, just like a real newborn. Then there were the Toren prisoners. She couldn't keep them stuck on their islands forever, though sometimes when she had the dreams of blood and screaming it seemed like a good idea.

The sun rose higher, and she still hadn't found a solution. She closed her eyes against the light, letting the warmth soak in. The flying mop things (they *had* to start getting some real names) were making their "oooOOgh-whhhhrg" noise. What did that mean? Watch out, there's a nasty predator? Hello, attractive mop thing? Hey, that's my splatter plant you're eating?

A moment later she heard the faint scuff of footsteps, and she sighed. It was surprising they hadn't tried to reach her on the comm first if they needed her for something. Her station-born crew didn't like moving around in the open.

Moire opened her eyes. Ennis was standing near the cliff edge, shading his view with one hand as he looked out over the water. After a moment he stepped back and walked over to her. He sat down cross-legged and picked up a stray strand of tanglegrass that had fallen to the ground, running his fingers lightly over it.

"I was on Irukyn-Riu twice, for shore leave," he said eventually, breaking the silence. "It's supposed to be the most beautiful habitable planet. It isn't half as beautiful as this." The bruises had mostly faded from his face, but he still looked gaunt to her. He was frowning against the light.

"Ever been to Earth?"

He twisted the tanglegrass into a loop. "Once. It rained the whole time." He glanced up, then looked down again, frowning. "I don't understand why people want to live there, even when it doesn't rain."

Moire suppressed a smile. "Where did you go?"

"Cornwall. England."

"Why?"

He sighed and rolled the loop of grass on the ground. "My foster father was born there. The one thing he wanted was to go back. When he was dying, he made me promise...anyway, I carried his ashes in my kit for three years before I could go. And then all I saw was rain, and cliffs, and huge crashing waves..." He stared out into the distance, then looked up at her. A piercing, intent look.

Moire took a deep breath. *I had forgotten how blue his eyes are.* "Are they looking for me down there?"

Ennis shook his head. "Just starting to wake up." He hesitated, then said, "What's wrong?"

She'd have to be careful. He'd been annoyingly observant back on *Canaveral,* too, when she only had a mutiny to hide. "It isn't as easy as it looks, running a criminal enterprise. I had no idea the overhead costs were so high."

He grinned, a sudden flash. "Less paperwork, though."

"True." He was still looking at her with a thoughtful expression. Unconvinced. "And I need about fifty babysitters with combat experience."

"Babysitters?" Ennis said, pronouncing the word slowly.

Moire felt a sudden chill. She drew her knees up and wrapped her arms around them. He didn't know what the word meant. The tech had changed, but tech had always changed rapidly. That didn't bother her. But the language had also changed in eighty years, and every time she was reminded of it she felt lost in a strange world. And she could never go home again.

"It means...someone paid to look after kids," she said when she felt she could trust her voice again. "I don't know what they call them now." A little ragged at the end. Perhaps he wouldn't notice.

"I'm not the person to ask." He wasn't sounding completely calm himself.

No, he wouldn't be. Not when he grew up on a prison colony, leaving only to join Fleet. Not a lot of structured child care either place. She glanced at him. He was looking at her with an uncertain expression, one that changed as soon as their eyes met.

She cleared her throat. "Anyway—we need help with the Created. Can't leave them alone or they're liable to blow themselves up. I also have to find a way to get you back without getting anybody arrested or shot."

He looked down at his hands, frowning. "I don't know where to go. Lambert has already been infiltrated, and few ships go there anyway."

"What were you doing at Lambert?" Moire asked. It seemed a very boring post for him.

"Being punished for not bringing you in," he said in a very even tone.

Careful... "They don't have dangerous combat postings where you could still be useful, as well as punished? The crab war is still on, isn't it?"

"Oh yes. But since I'm targeted by Toren, Fleet doesn't want me on their ships. One of their agents got rather destructive on *Canaveral* trying to find out more about you, and now Toren infiltrated Lambert looking for me. If only...we had some crab ships show up at Lambert, but those boneheads blew them up before we could capture them. That might have been enough to at least keep me in Fleet."

Moire grimaced. How was she supposed to know Toren would cause him so much trouble? "I'm sorry you got involved. I was desperate. You were captured by them just like I was, you know what it's like."

"Yes," he said quietly. He sighed. "It doesn't matter. My career wasn't...Fleet is all I've ever known. It's not like I can go back to Fimbul." Then he reddened, glancing at her. "I shouldn't complain. You've been through worse."

Moire shifted, uncomfortable. Ennis had never had much, and now he was going to lose what he did have. Because of her. The problem was, even if Fleet did cut him loose, Toren would hunt him as long as they thought he knew something useful. There had to be something she could do to help him. Maybe then Fleet would value him enough not to stick him out in the middle of nowhere for Toren to grab.

What he had said finally registered, and she blinked. "What was that about capturing crab ships?"

"We haven't. Oh, we've picked up lots of wreckage, but nothing intact. No, there was one, but Fleet doesn't have it."

"Who does?"

He gave her a sardonic look. "Toren."

And why the hell are they so interested in the crabs? Well, that was one thing she could do to help Ennis, help Fleet, and annoy Toren in the bargain. "I know where to find a crab ship. Probably not flyable, but it's in one piece."

He stared at her for a long moment, doubting and incredulous. "Where? Is it far from here?"

She stood and held out a hand to help him up. "It's on our way."

Ennis followed Moire down the steep path from the cliff top, trying to decide which question to ask first. Wondering if she would answer any of them.

"Does anybody else know about the crab ship? How did you find it?"

She looked back over her shoulder at him. Her expression was worried, even more than before. "Besides me, Gren. It's in the sargasso—a bunch of wrecked ships. We go there to salvage them. I haven't told the rest of the crew about it yet."

An intact crab ship. Maybe this wasn't a complete disaster after all. He heard the thrumming of engines, and a shadow passed over them. Moire glanced up.

"Good. The unloading is underway."

"When can we leave?"

Moire scratched her head and sighed. "Tomorrow. Maybe. I have to make sure the kids will be OK here for a while, and...and stuff like that." She tilted a look at him. "I was serious about the babysitters, you know. If Fleet kicks you out, you can always come back here."

He stumbled and stared at her, his first impression that she was mocking him fading with uncertainty. Her expression was unrevealing; just a hint of something in her eyes that was soon gone. "I'll keep it in mind," Ennis said lightly. "Combat would be easier, though."

She grinned. "I know. That's why we need the help." They'd reached the base of the trail, and Moire headed for the cave. Ennis hesitated, then took the other branch that skirted the bay. He didn't want to encounter anybody until he was calm again.

He was a Fleet officer. There was a war on, and he had a job to do. He shouldn't be thinking of how he might like to stay here. It wouldn't do any good to wonder about the end of the crab war, either. At the rate things were going he probably wouldn't be around to see it.

The local sun was bright, but filtered through the broad planes that projected from the huge things Moire had called pseudotrees. Not real branches, but close enough. He walked along the water's edge, where the pseudotrees thinned out and he could see the open water. A rocky beach faced the cliff across the bay; he could just make out the cave entrance through the broad trunks. Small waves lapped and gurgled in the rocks and pebbles underfoot.

It was peaceful here, but it wouldn't last. Cameron had her own war coming. Maybe it would be better if he did stay here. He wouldn't be endangering any Fleet ships, he could find out whatever Namur wanted from Cameron, and she wouldn't have to leave.

Except Namur wasn't the only one with questions. There was still the mutiny investigation. She'd promised to go back for that, and if she did, what were the chances of her returning? He stood motionless, suddenly feeling cold.

He didn't want to stay on Sequoyah. He wanted to stay with Moire.

Ennis shoved the thought away, furious with himself. She was a mutineer. If he stayed, he became one too.

Alan moved the controls, and the world below shifted in the viewer. Not quite in the right place, so he nudged the controls again. Now the numbers in the readout were the same, and he looked at his mother for confirmation.

"Good job," Moire said. "Remember how to do the re-entry?"

Alan nodded slowly. Re-entry was bumpy and rough, and it felt like you were doing it wrong even when it was right. It was getting better, though. He used to not like docking, but this time he had done it all by himself without any mistakes. Maybe re-entry would be easy someday.

"Don't worry, I'll be watching." Moire smiled and patted his shoulder.

It was even bumpier closer in. Moire said it was because they were coming in on the daylight side, so the atmosphere was turbulent. He didn't understand how something you couldn't see felt like falling over rocks.

Moire took over the controls for the approach and landing, and he was glad. The scout seemed bigger in the cave. In orbit there was more room to move.

"What do we do next?" he asked when the ship had settled and Moire was unstrapping from her seat.

"We let the others unload. Jim or Ulrike will drop supplies to the prisoner islands, and then somebody will go up for the final load. You want to ride with them?"

Alan shook his head. Flying was fun, but he didn't want to be that far away from her. Especially if he would be going to the places where the Toren people were kept.

Moire stretched and yawned. "I'm racking out for a bit." She looked around, moving her lips but not saying words. She started to look worried. "I don't see George, or his friends. Find them and make sure they aren't getting in trouble, OK?"

The cave was getting more crates and boxes. Alan wondered how much more they could unload before it was full. What would happen if they couldn't land the scout inside? He looked all through the cave. Madele was with the rescued Created that didn't know how to walk yet. Some others were helping, but they weren't the ones he was looking for.

Alan went all the way to the back of the cave and then to the opening again. Then he heard Hideo's voice, outside, and he ran to the edge to look. They were down at the bay, below the cave. Was that getting in trouble? He jumped from rock to rock down the hill. It was more fun than the trail, and he could pretend he was flying. Planets were much more interesting than stations or ships.

"This one has sparkles!" shouted Hideo, holding something up. Ash was sitting on the ground, a pile of small rocks beside her.

George turned at the sound of his footsteps. "Alan is back! Look, we're finding neat rocks. I had the best one, but it ran away," he said mournfully. "It was blue, and round."

"Ran away?"

George nodded. "I picked it up, and when I put it in my pile it moved away really fast."

"Maybe it wasn't a rock, then. Rocks don't move unless you push them yourself." Alan started looking for his own rocks. The ones in the water looked best, at least for a while. When they got dry they looked just like the rocks on the beach.

"Someone is coming from the other side," said Hideo, looking over the bay. "Oh! It's the commander guy."

Alan looked up, worried. Then he remembered Moire was in the cave. Ennis was coming from the other direction.

"You aren't supposed to go there by yourself," George informed him as he came closer. "One of the olders has to be with you, and they have to have a gun!"

"He *is* an older," whispered Ash. She peered at Ennis. "Are you still sick?"

Alan could see why she asked. Ennis moved tired, and his eyes were made small with pain. "I'm better now," he said, but it was like he had to think about it first. "I didn't know it was dangerous out there. I'll stay in the cave."

"No!" Alan scrambled to his feet. Ennis stepped back, surprised. "She's there. You stay away!"

Ennis closed his eyes for a moment, looking even sicker. He held out his empty hands. "I don't have a gun," he said quietly.

"If you ever hurt her again, I don't care what she says! I'll shoot you!" Alan felt himself shaking.

"I understand."

Alan blinked. Ennis didn't seem very frightened. Sad, maybe. "You do?" Ennis must not believe him.

"If I had...if someone had hurt my mother, I'd do the same thing."

"Oh." Alan thought for a moment. "Then...then why did you do it?"

Ennis sat on one of the large rocks at the edge of the beach. "It was a mistake," he said finally. "The gun didn't act like I thought it would. I don't have it anymore."

"Why?" asked George.

Ennis smiled with half his face, as if he was thinking of something funny and painful at the same time. "Toren—the people who put the cuff on me—took it away," he said, tapping his wrist.

Ash drew in her breath, looking afraid. Alan was confused. Toren was bad, because they hurt people. But taking away Ennis's gun was a good thing. Wasn't it?

"She took my gun away too," he muttered. "How can I kill pirates without a gun?"

Ennis smiled again, but it was a real smile this time. "Are pirates a problem?"

"They came on the first ship. *Ayesha*. They hurt her. I shot five of them and they stayed dead." Alan picked up one of his rocks, then put it down, frowning. "But I had a gun."

He looked up. Ennis was staring at him, and his face was frozen. "I see. And where..." He stopped, and shook his head. "Who taught you this? Who showed you how to kill?" His voice sounded squeezed down.

"The Controllers. At the place we came from." Alan waved his hand at George and Ash and Hideo. "Where they made the Created."

Ennis was silent for a long time. The others were still, watching him. When he stood up they started, jumping to their feet and ready to run. They could tell, like Alan could, that Ennis was angry. "You don't need a gun to fight," Ennis said, standing in front of Alan. "You can be a weapon all by yourself. I can show you."

Alan scowled. He wanted to look away, but something about Ennis didn't make that possible. It was like his eyes were holding onto him. "Why would you show me? I could fight you then. And I would!"

Ennis didn't even blink. "I'm not her enemy. If you can defend yourself, that's one less thing for her to worry about. And you can defend her. All of you," he said, looking about.

Alan hesitated, wary of trusting Ennis. But if he could fight without a gun...he could learn, and then decide if he should fight him.

"Sounds like fun," said George. "What do we do?"

When they left the ship, Plymson insisted on going first, as always. Kolpe had to admit she took her job seriously and did it well, which irritated him. It prevented him from indulging in complete contempt.

"We gonna get some action here?" she asked, looking carefully about Jessack's main passageway.

"*I* am going to the main office. If you wish to use the people there for target practice it would undoubtedly benefit our employer," he said, biting the words off. He had never been so angry before. Now he had to fix the mess they had created in order to get his own job done. "You probably had some other kind of action in mind, however. I assume this station has a sex industry section; all the others do. Go get it out of your system."

Plymson shook her head, grinning. "I swear you take drive dampers. Or maybe you're dead and don't know it yet. You spent the whole trip messing with your datapad; ain't good for you. You don't even watch trid on it."

The office was in a back section of the station, without much traffic. Kolpe turned down the side corridor that led to it, breathing heavily. "That is how I do my job. I don't shoot people, torture them, blow them up, or anything else that draws attention. In my field, boring is good." And now, courtesy of Toren, he was followed by someone who looked and moved like she was five minutes out of shocktrooper training. Even the local drunks could tell she was a heavy.

He had to get rid of her. But first he was going to deal with the inbred incompetents at the local office.

The room visible through the first door was a front, of course. Two dockworker-lookalikes started toward him when he entered, protests sputtering to a halt when he flashed his ID. One pointed to the concealed entrance then. They both looked terrified, and Kolpe looked them over just long enough to see them start to sweat and shake. It felt good.

"Stay here," he told Plymson curtly, and scanned in. The manager in charge, Bronsen, was not as easy to intimidate. Kolpe had to produce his encrypted contract to get him to talk.

"We found her underneath a dropdown," Bronsen said reluctantly. "She had a control rod, an injector with a cartridge of counteractant for antitrib, and a gun. He must have surprised her somehow—but I don't see how he could have escaped when he was shot up with antitrib. He would barely be able to move."

"He moved enough to kill one of your trained agents," Kolpe reminded him acidly. Their so-called trained agents.

Bronsen's face hardened. "We pulled the tracer code from the control rod as soon as we found it. We found and isolated the ship he was on, got a diversion going to draw the local law enforcement away, and attempted an extraction. However, the ship managed to pull free and escape, and evaded pursuit." He spread his hands. "The ship, *Raven*, had been docked before the agent even arrived. We don't know anything more about it. It's possible he took a chance and got on board without their knowledge."

Well. They hadn't put out a random floating holo-ad, but that was about the only thing they hadn't done to draw attention. Kolpe raised an eyebrow, his mind working furiously. Maybe they should.

"I want all the details on this officer. I believe I can help you with your problem."

Ennis walked slowly past the crates and boxes in the hold. They were getting better; he could hardly hear them moving. His plan was working well. The Created were enthusiastic about what they thought was learning to hunt pirates; the crew, especially Gren Forrest, were happy the Created had something to keep them out of trouble, and he and Moire were relieved to see them, even Alan, learn to follow orders. They would need that once they got to the sargasso.

He spun, the high-beam flashlight in his hand flickering over the boxes.

"Your elbow is showing, George." George was ahead of the others, like usual, and had forgotten some details in his enthusiasm. Like usual.

"There's no room," George complained. "I can't go in any more."

"A pirate won't tell you, they'll shoot. You need to find better cover," Ennis said firmly. "OK, turn on your lights."

The Created rustled and mumbled, and an array of high-beams converged on him. "Hideo, you're too close to Ash. If you aren't careful or she moves, you could hit her." One beam was coming from up high, and was centered on his chest. Alan had climbed on top of the crates. "See where Alan is? That's good. I might not see him up there, and if I did see him and fire back I'd have to take my eyes off of the rest of you." Alan was always very motivated to make him a target.

"Did we win?" shouted Hideo from the back.

Ennis rubbed his chin. "You got me, but George and Ash are hurt. Try it again, and this time remember to watch for each other as well as..."

The door to the cargo area opened. Carlos Montero peered in. "Oh, are you busy? I just want to borrow Alan for a bit, if that's all right."

Alan jumped lightly down from the crates. "Can't we kill the commander one more time?"

Montero's foggy expression turned to one of distress. "Oh dear. I don't think so. It really isn't nice, you know."

Ennis struggled with himself, trying not to grin. The crew had warmed up to him over the last few weeks, at least as long as the conversation stayed away from dangerous topics. They'd even loaned him some clothing to extend his limited supply. Montero had never even questioned his presence, but sometimes Ennis suspected he had confused him with a regular crewmember.

"It isn't *real*," George said reassuringly. "He's being a pirate, and we're sneaking up on him. He killed me twice."

"Oh, that's all right, then." Montero looked relieved.

"What did you want Alan for?" Ennis asked, dragging the conversation back to its original starting point. Carlos Montero and the Created operated on much the same level of distraction.

"Just getting some things ready for when we arrive. Captain said we should be there tomorrow...at least, I think that's what she said." Montero stared abstractedly at the hold door control panel.

"You haven't asked her?"

Montero shook his head. "I didn't want to wake her with a comm signal if she's asleep. It's a long run for one pilot."

Looking at his chrono, Ennis saw it was late, ship time. "I think we're done here for now. Go help him out, Alan, and I'll think up more things to do for later on."

The Created trooped out the door after Montero, chattering happily as they told him all about what they'd been doing. Even Alan didn't spare him a backward glance. His earlier hostility and suspicion were still present but not as open or obvious. Even so, Ennis was careful during the hand-to-hand sessions and at the earliest opportunity had the Created spar with each other instead of with him. They were very strong, and frighteningly quick. All they lacked was training to be very, very dangerous.

Out in the corridor, he hesitated, then headed for the bridge. He could see if Moire was there and check the arrival time. There had been another pilot on the ship the last time. What had happened to him?

Standing in the bridge entrance, he saw Moire slouched in the pilot's chair, staring tiredly at the display. She picked up a drink bulb, took a gulp, then set it down, her arm dangling over the side of the chair.

"Montero is saying we'll arrive sometime tomorrow?" he said finally.

She stirred and lifted her head to look back at him, then sat up with a groan and tapped a control.

"Yeah. Should be at the sargasso just after Prime ends." She slouched down again, silent.

Ennis went up to the communication station nearby and took a seat.

"How did you find this place? It seems...well, out of the way."

"Yeah. No kidding." Moire snorted, without humor. She closed her eyes. "We found it when *Ayesha* had her little accident. Helped by the pirates, of course. They didn't know what a dancy ship she was to fly."

"This is where Alan got his five kills?"

She opened her eyes at this, fully awake now. "Told you about that, did he?"

"Yes. He was regretting not being able to make me number six at the time."

A smile flickered across her face and disappeared. "He's good, you know. Best I've seen. Makes me wonder what Toren was up to, trying to train a supersoldier. Don't need them in mines." She subsided in a dark silence.

Ennis persevered. "The pirates flew the ship here?"

"Ship flew itself. Pirates got the drive oscillating, and then it latched on to the strongest gravitational anomaly I've ever heard of. I couldn't get..."

She stopped, covering her face with her hands. "If the drive hadn't fried itself we would have died."

"Where's your relief pilot?" he asked. "You look exhausted."

"He's busy," she said curtly. Montero had been right. She was doing all the piloting herself. Moire jerked a thumb at the wall, where a hammocklike sling had been mounted. "Got a temporary set up, but I can't stop checking. We should be hours away from the danger point, but what if the damn thing moved, or changed strength?" Her voice was ragged now.

"Let me help," Ennis said without thinking.

"Can you fly web?" Moire snapped.

"I can read instruments. Show me what to look for, and I'll watch. If anything happens I'll wake you."

Moire turned away. "It's not much longer. I'll sleep when we get there."

"Why do you have to do everything yourself? If it's dangerous you need to be able to deal with it, and you look shredded. Get some sleep, dammit! If you don't trust me, get somebody else up here."

She looked at him for a long moment, then sighed, sinking into the chair as if deflating. She waved him over to the board. "That's the coupling readout," Moire said quietly, pointing to a display. "If it ever gets above fifteen, yell. And if it reads eighteen, even for a second, hit the dropout." She tapped the protective cover of a red scram button.

"Coupling readout fifteen, yell; eighteen, dropout," he repeated.

Moire stood, stretching stiffly. "Don't take your eyes off that display, even for a second. It happens so fast..." her voice shook, and she turned back, as if having second thoughts about leaving.

"Go sleep. I'll watch the readout," Ennis said. He searched her face, seeing fatigue, irritation, and the same disquieting shadow in her eyes that he'd seen earlier. A painful shadow that shouldn't be there. Suddenly realizing what he was doing, he snatched his hand away just before it touched her.

"You're not looking at it now," Moire said, giving him an enigmatic look as she left. Ennis sat down hard in the pilot's chair, jaw clenched and heart pounding, staring fixedly at the readout. It read a nice, safe 9.73.

You need to keep your mind on your job, soldier. Whatever had just happened wasn't part of it. He glanced briefly away from the board. Moire was already sound asleep in the temporary, and he let out a pent-up breath, feeling better.

CHAPTER 9
ONE OWNER FROM NEW

Moire looked over at the suited Created and suppressed a shudder. They'd done fine on the drills. She had to remember that. The trouble was they didn't understand why the suits were needed. She toyed with the idea of leaving them on *Raven*, but regretfully discarded it. She might be able to trust Alan not to get into trouble, but the other three needed constant supervision and all her crew were busy with other jobs.

She might have felt a little better if they were wearing the tougher work suits, like the rest of the crew. Trouble was they were damned expensive and hard to find in the salvage ships, so they didn't have extras. Only construction workers needed them.

"Everybody ready? Gren, are the tools loaded?"

He nodded. "I just hope there isn't damage forward. This is a tight cluster, so it could have hit one of the others coming in."

"All we need is something that runs this time. Kids, stay together and be careful. OK, let's go."

They filled up the scout completely, even with Gren sitting in the copilot chair. Ennis was with the crew, silent and subdued. Something had happened on the bridge, but she'd been too tired to figure it out then and now she wasn't sure she wanted to know. He probably didn't know himself.

I don't need this. Not now. The longer he stayed, the more it seemed like he had always been with them. He was even helping with the kids. *He's not staying. Get used to it.* What she needed was to get a new working ship as soon as possible so she could send him back to Fleet. That's what he really wanted, and she had other important work to do. She had to get Sequoyah defensible before Toren showed up.

When the scout had docked and the crew began to file out, she tilted her head at Ennis to stay.

"We're going to take a look at the crab ship," she told Gren softly, under the noise. "Tell the others we're looking at other salvage possibilities, if they ask."

Gren gave her a morose look. "You're sure it's dead?"

"Hasn't moved since the first time I saw it. If it's a trap, it's been in place for a long time. They aren't that patient." He nodded, unhappy but resigned.

As soon as the gear was unloaded, she undocked the scout and moved away. Ennis, in the copilot seat, pulled up the scope and was looking at the sargasso.

"This is incredible. How many ships are there?" he said finally. "How did they get here?"

"Accidents in drive," Moire said, shrugging. "The anomaly doesn't have much effect in realspace. Most of our time is spent finding the ones where the core didn't blow, or something like that."

"How many have you salvaged?"

She chewed her lip, wondering how to answer, then caught a glimpse of the crab ship. "Look, there it is. At the end of this loose cluster." There was a line of ships, like a string of islands, and the crab ship was at the very end. Partially hidden by a big cargo ship, just like she remembered.

Ennis was staring at the scope, scanning and zooming in for the closest view he could get. "That's strange. I haven't seen that configuration before, have you? Not their usual size. Too big for a fighter. It's almost like the one we shot down at Lambert, but this one is definitely military. Plenty of guns."

Pity we can't steal them. She still hadn't found much in the way of armaments in the sargasso, and with Ennis around she wasn't going to be looking for them. Moire flew the scout out and around the end of the string of ships, turning on the floodlight at the bow to get a better look.

"Huh. No gaping holes. I wonder what happened to them."

Ennis shook his head, still engrossed by the view on the scanner. "This is perfect. Can we get inside?"

"Let's see how the others are doing." She punched up Gren's comm code. "Any luck?"

"It's a good one. I think we can fix it, but we'll need some of the stuff I packed," Gren's voice said. "Pick me up and we'll get started."

"On my way," Moire replied, and spun the scout around. "That was quick."

"Mm." Ennis looked up. "Some of these ships have cables snagged everywhere. I hope the crab ship isn't tangled up like that."

"I didn't see anything, but with those black hulls it's hard to tell." Moire brought the scout in to the salvage ship and docked it. "Let's take a look and see what else Gren needs." She pulled on her helmet and sealed it, and Ennis did the same.

The scout was docked to a midlevel port. Someone had already paint-penned arrows with directions, and put clip lights along the corridor. Moire pushed off and floated away.

"I hate zero-g. I hope Gren can fix the power soon," she muttered.

Ennis smiled. "This is fun. Although I can see it would be hard to work like this."

"Yeah, it's fun the first few times. After that it's pure annoyance."

Gren was down in Engineering, in a bad mood. "I don't know what the hell happened to this ship, but I think they were too cheap to replace things that broke. See that space? Should be a secondary readout there. Just ripped it out and didn't put anything back. That's not the only thing that's missing. Nothing critical, but it's a bad sign." He sighed, looking gloomy. "Maybe we better look around for another one, just in case."

"Maybe." Moire glanced around the room. "Where are the kids?"

Gren looked up, alarmed. "Hey, they've been real quiet..."

They found Alan and the others in a section near the hull, gathered around something.

George pointed. "Look, it *is* moving! It's alive!"

"It can't be. There's no air and it isn't in a suit," Alan protested.

Moire pulled her way along the wall. The kids were watching a chunk of jagged metal. It was slowly drifting toward the hull. She did a quick scan, relieved that none of them appeared to have damaged their suits or found explosives to play with.

"What's going on?"

Alan spun around and had to grab onto George to stop spinning. "We followed it here. Why is it moving?"

It was an ordinary chunk of metal. It looked like a cable conduit brace. Moire shrugged. "Somebody must have pushed it loose when they started working. There's nothing to make it stop."

"But we stopped it, and it started again," Ash said quietly.

Moire reached out to the chunk of metal and held it in her hand until she was sure it had come to a stop. She let go.

Slowly, it began to move again. Toward the hull.

"Magnet?" Ennis guessed.

Moire shook her head and pointed at the wall. Now she could see there were lots of little pieces of junk lining the hull side; crumpled pieces of flimsy plastic, a broken stylus, even a glass rod.

"That's why there's a cluster here. One of these ships still has gravity." She pushed away from the wall toward the door. "Let's find a viewport. Hey, Gren!"

She impatiently worked her way down the corridor, searching. An emergency airlock sign was visible ahead, and she aimed for that. A lot of those had some kind of viewport.

Sure enough, there was a ship outside. It was so close she couldn't see the whole thing. "Gren, look! That ship still has power!"

Gren pulled himself in to the airlock hatch. "That would save us a lot of time–and if it's running, it has all the pieces. Can we get the scout in?"

Moire screwed up her face, thinking. "It's tight. Get some line. We're close enough we can freewalk out to it."

Data was always the key. If he had enough, if it was the right kind, everything worked together like a complex piece of music. Kolpe considered his next move. He had been too direct before, trying to satisfy Toren's need for a quick resolution. That hadn't been very successful.

So. The trick to seeing a faint target was to look ever so slightly away from it. If he couldn't find Cameron, perhaps he could find her crew instead. He had the listing of the original crew of *Ayesha*. He debated leaving out Tenna, but decided to keep her in. The others might contact her.

He started assembling the data he needed, thinking about what he'd learned so far about *why* Toren was so determined to find Cameron. They'd been desperate enough to call him in, which meant they thought she was a threat to the company or had something they wanted very, very badly. The first option he discarded almost immediately. Toren hadn't even existed when her exploration ship took its final flight, and she'd spent the intervening time either in Toren's custody or on the run.

Toren was very careful about information leaking out, which was why he was so intent on finding out what he could. He'd learned some interesting things in the course of working with them. Sometimes he could almost see the overall plan. Their control over their colonies, and shipping, and the industries they were running in the Fringe that were never listed in their public holdings. If the crabs didn't exist it would form the base for an audacious, dangerous plan, but as long as the war continued the colonies needed Fleet for defense. Toren would not be able to build up the necessary military force to counter it in secret.

He knew they had some plan for the future of their colonies. One that probably did not have much to do with the laws currently set on Earth and enforced by Fleet. Cameron must have found something they needed for that plan.

With a few hours of work, Kolpe had a new set of databots crafted and sent to the bounceback addresses all over the Fringe. If any of the listed people activated anything with a standard ID key, he would know. The data service he had paid for didn't know he was getting that information, but he had added procedures to ghost-echo the information download and capture it. Illegal, of course, but a carefully calculated risk.

The scan for Jessack came back immediately. To his surprise, there was a match. Gren Forrest had used a public kiosk to send an on-station message with an account key on the same day the Fleet officer had escaped.

Kolpe raised his eyebrows. A remarkable coincidence, and worth further inquiry. He started more searches, using even more illegal procedures and slowscans. The message had been sent to a construction firm, and merely requested a meeting. Nothing useful.

He called in Bronsen. "I need access to the local security database."

The manager thinned his lips. "It's too risky right now. They are suspicious."

"Not as risky as a new link. I require that access to do my job." Realizing his annoyance was only making Bronsen more stubborn, he changed tactics. "How did the article work?"

Bronsen's expression thawed slightly. "Three calls to verify the amount of the reward already. I think we'll add additional details after a few days. Make it more realistic."

Kolpe nodded and forced himself to smile. "Good idea."

Bronsen still refused to allow him direct access to the security data, and had enough good reasons that Kolpe reluctantly agreed to stored searches.

They took two days, but they were worth the wait. Matches to the still of Gren Forrest had been found on several security tapes. Kolpe looked at them all, returning to the one from the docking level. Forrest was leaving from the hatch of a ship.

When he ran the dock number to find the ship, he stared at the screen in disbelief, feeling a tightness in his gut he rarely experienced anymore. "*Raven,*" he whispered. It was too neat. Surely even these blithering idiots had done their own search?

Then again, they hadn't been looking for the same thing he was. They had only been interested in the escaped Fleet officer. The search they had run was saved, however. Everything related to the brief visit of the ship *Raven*, including the emergency services call from *Raven*'s captain.

This is Ren Roberts.

At the sound of her voice he could feel the vein throbbing in his throat, his heart pounding. For an instant he was furious, thinking Toren had withheld information, but the local office had attached no importance to *Raven*. They didn't know who Ren Roberts really was.

Kolpe licked his lips. How had she known? How could she *possibly* have known? He played the recording again, listening to the cadence of her voice. She had been here less than three weeks ago, to rescue someone before Toren even knew he had been captured. It wasn't possible.

He felt a slow smile spread over his face. This one would be interesting. He would have to use every trick he knew to complete his assignment successfully. Quickly, he sent another wave of databots, this time with the ship name.

Gren Forrest had visited a construction firm. Why? Kolpe paused, thinking. He should find out more. It might be best to wait here for the databots' return. If the visit was business, someone from her crew would come back.

He leaned back in his chair, feeling satisfied with the day's work, but then a disturbing thought crossed his mind. If Cameron had known about the officer, did she know about Kolpe, too?

It was easier to freewalk to the gravity ship than Ennis had thought it would be. There was something to grab onto the entire distance from one ship to the next. There was even a long segment of beam that was conveniently wedged near the outer hatch door of the ship.

"Huh. I wonder why they did that," Montero said, one hand holding on to the access rung beside the hatch.

"Can't you get in?" Moire asked.

"Oh, I can get in no problem. That's the strange thing. See?" He pushed one of the outside controls. Now Ennis could see what he was referring to. The hatch looked like a regular maintenance access hatch, not a cargo or docking hatch, but it had a full panel of outside controls instead of the basic emergency set. "It's taking longer than I...there it goes."

The door pushed in and slid to one side. Montero held onto the rung and swung his feet in, letting the gravity pull him down. The rest followed, imitating him. Ennis felt the effort of standing with relief. Moire was right; zero-g did get annoying after a while.

Montero's helmet was almost touching the controls and readouts inside the airlock. "So that's why it was so slow. Still got pressure."

"You're kidding." Moire peered over his shoulder at the readouts, and Ennis craned his head to see, too. It looked like there was a full atmosphere. "That's a first. Well, let's pretend the readouts aren't lying completely. We'll cycle through like good spacers. If there are any survivors they won't want us dumping their air."

The airlock controls worked as smoothly as the hatch door had. The readouts were correct. Ennis checked his suit indicators again, incredulous— one atmosphere, breathable.

The corridor they were in was clean, intact, and empty.

Moire surveyed it with a satisfied expression. "Right. What luck! Let's get Gren and the rest of the team in and go exploring." She made some adjustments to the comm controls on the arm of her suit.

Ennis turned to shut the interior door of the airlock and froze. At the base of the latch was a lump of grey-black, grainy material he'd seen once before, on a fragment of wreckage from a repaired crab ship. A broad metal plate was sticking out of the lump. A handle, perhaps, for someone that couldn't use the original lever.

"We've got a problem," Ennis said, as soon as his shock wore off.

"Yeah? What?"

"That's crab work. Somebody's been in this ship, and they weren't human."

Moire's head snapped up. She looked at him, then at the thing he was pointing at. Her breath hissed in.

"Gren! Get everyone back in the scout, now!" she yelled into the comm. "We got trouble!"

She grabbed a bewildered Montero and shoved him in the airlock. Ennis followed close behind and slammed the inner lock shut, using the emergency cycle to open the outer door a few seconds later.

There was no way for him to move quickly between ships, even though all his instincts screamed for speed. If he moved too fast and lost hold, he'd float free. He also had to help Montero, who still didn't seem to understand what had happened. More slowness in the salvage ship, still without gravity and now clogged with the rest of Moire's crew.

After the scout docked to *Raven* and the crew scrambled out, Moire ordered the scout out on patrol and ran for the bridge. Ennis followed. They used every detection device the ship possessed, but nothing unusual showed up. As the minutes progressed and still nothing was found, the tension decreased a notch.

"At least we know they are stuck here. That crab ship hasn't budged since the first time," Moire said, slumped in her chair.

"I'm not picking up any signals, either." Ennis glanced at the communications station again, just to be sure.

Gren shifted. "You know what to look for?"

The signal Wernicki had found at Lambert was unique enough he should be able to recognize anything similar, but there was nothing to analyze. "To a degree. It doesn't matter—I'm not picking up anything at all except our comm chatter."

Moire sat up, a crease between her brows. "I hope they didn't hear us. We've been making plenty of noise. Where's the scout?" She went over to the communications board. "Ulrike, see any sign of activity?"

The voice from the comm sounded shaky. "No, Captain. Nothing is moving. But the ship with gravity? I could see through the other ships a little. Most of the midsection is missing, big hole. It would take us very long to fix."

This was good, since there would be no reason to go to the powered ship now. Ennis frowned, remembering the too-convenient path between it and the ship they'd picked to salvage. What if a crab had made that?

Moire drummed her fingers on the console, eyes narrowed. "All right," she said finally. "Get that little float-pallet, Gren."

"All right what?" Gren said, irritably. "How's the float pallet going to help?"

She tilted her head at Gren as she left the bridge. "Meet me at the weapons locker."

"Are you sure this is a good idea?" Gren muttered under his breath, hauling out a box of ammo. "Let's just find another ship."

Moire shook her head sharply. "Same problem, Gren. We don't know how mobile they are. The ship with gravity is in the same general area as the crab ship, but it's a long way if you are going on foot. Or flipper, or whatever they use. We're almost done here. Let's finish, and when we come back next time we'll bring more firepower."

Adult firepower, that is. She hadn't missed the gleam in Alan's eyes when she first mentioned getting the guns. At least they had some vacuum-capable weapons, thanks to the raid on the Created site.

She rummaged through the rack of weapons, pulling out the ones that would be most useful. "Huh. Only three magnetics? I thought we had more."

Gren shifted the weapons to the pallet, along with the boxes of needle ammo. "Remember? Boris lost his down that gestator chute in the fight, and the other got fried. Why are you taking out the Gemers?"

Moire smiled grimly. "The energy pulse won't be as effective in vacuum, but not completely useless. I'll give 'em to the kids. They aren't ready for projectile weapons yet."

"Them! What about us? They're dangerous enough without weapons. Always getting into things, messing with my equipment...we should have left them with the others. They'd be bored, but safer." Gren shoved the float-pallet out into the corridor. Moire keyed the weapons locker shut.

"You're forgetting the only way we convinced Harvey to stay with the others is if we took these three with us," Moire pointed out.

"Ash isn't that bad. Why'd she get on the list?"

"She's quiet, but she's real smart. She was the one who figured out how to defeat the safety lock on your hull borer." Moire grinned as Gren paled in horror. "Good thing we found out before they actually used it."

He shook his head sadly. "Still...it seems wrong to give them weapons. They are too young for this."

She tried not to think about it herself, since she agreed with him. "This will give them something to do. Everybody who isn't working on the repairs gets guard duty, so nobody will be free to watch them. Commander Ennis has done a good job training them. I think they can handle this."

Gren thought for a while as they walked back to the bridge. "Don't think we can do shifts. Not enough people."

"How much more work do you have?" It was getting close to when they would have to leave to get to the rendezvous point in time. If they didn't, they'd have to wait here for Kilberton to show up.

"If we're lucky, it won't be much longer. Less than two days."

Alan bounded to his feet as soon as he saw them enter the bridge. When he grabbed a weapon, Gren held up a hand to stop him.

"I need you working on the hull, Alan."

"But..." Alan glanced at Ennis, scowling. "Does he get one?"

Oh boy. This could get difficult. "Everybody who isn't working on the ship gets one. They need to guard us."

"Why can't I have one, then?"

"I don't know how to fix ships," Ennis said. He hesitated, then looked at Moire. "What will you be doing?"

"Keeping an eye on the comm, running supplies and equipment back and forth with the scout, and making sure we don't get unexpected visitors," she replied, feeling a surge of gratitude for his diplomatic question. "I won't be on that ship much. I can't fix it either."

"Oh." Alan's face screwed up with thought, and his hands clenched the gun. What was she going to do if he refused? She hadn't had to get tough with him yet. "I'll go with you, then."

She shook her head. "Gren needs your help. We need everybody who can do the work on the repair team, and the rest of the crew is counting on you to join in. Besides, I'd like you to help watch the other kids. They don't have your experience, and I'd feel better about leaving them alone if you are there too." Alan didn't look convinced. "Commander Ennis knows how to fight crabs, and what to watch for. Even if he'd rather do something else, that's what would be most useful to us now."

Alan glanced at Ennis for a long moment, then back at her. He held the weapon out. "He can have it." It was said grudgingly, but Moire was astonished he'd said it at all. She quietly let out the breath she had been holding.

"Why don't you keep it until we get there?" Ennis suggested, and Alan nodded silently.

Feeling like she'd just survived a battle, Moire led the way off the bridge. Alan's face was still troubled. "Don't worry. I'll be on the comm to let you know I'm OK," she said to him quietly.

"You aren't mad at us?"

The question puzzled her, but she answered anyway. "I'm not mad at anybody. You're doing good."

He looked at her searchingly. "I'll fix the ship really fast. Then we can go away and the crabs can't get us." He seemed satisfied with his plan.

"There's one thing I still don't understand," Gren said as they boarded the scout.

"What's that?"

"They went to the bother of rigging the door, so they probably went there more than once. Why would a crab want to get to a human ship?"

Kolpe knew he had to be cautious. The temptation was to infiltrate the construction firm or plant some devices, especially when he discovered that a different crewmember, Yolanda Menehune, had shown up mere hours before he made his discovery. He had a better idea of who he was dealing with now, and it was too dangerous to risk Cameron discovering his existence.

He had not been able to find the ship. *Raven* had not docked at Jessack since the officer escaped; as he expected. Cameron would know better than that. This Menehune must have come on a different ship. She had visited several different dock hatches, perhaps looking for transport back to a rendezvous. Either she knew the tricks to hide from the security vids or the stills he had were incomplete—he was not able to trace her with the same ease as Gren Forrest. He had not found out where she had gone.

The construction firm had yielded some data; enough for him to suspect Cameron would be dealing with them again. No crew or equipment had moved. That would be the best way to find her. When they did leave, he would follow them.

The bounceback data was trickling in. Already he had a node of intersecting data at Kulvar, famous for its criminal underworld. A dangerous place if you didn't know the rules, but an excellent location for someone like Cameron to hide out. If the construction firm didn't work out, he'd try that next.

The door to his workspace opened and Plymson came in, the suggestion of a swagger in her walk. Kolpe studiously ignored her.

"You haven't been out of this place since we got here," she said, swinging a chair over and sitting down, ostensibly to watch what he was doing on his datapad. He changed the screen.

"I have been out three times," Kolpe answered curtly.

"Yeah, but that was for work. You even eat here." Plymson stretched, looking slyly at him from the corner of her eye. "Had a real good one last night," she said, grinning.

Kolpe grimaced despite his determination not to show any reaction. He knew she did it just to annoy him, to get a response. It still made him feel physically ill to listen to her sexual exploits. She knew that too. "Then go back for more."

Plymson laughed. "Oh, I think I will, when I'm off duty. One or two things I haven't tried on him. But for now, I'm all yours."

She started in on a lurid description of her activities. Kolpe shuddered, tasting bile at the back of his throat. It was impossible to think, to concentrate on his work. Why had Toren thought Plymson would be helpful? He was in more danger of detection because of her, not less. They had made it very clear, however, that she was a nonnegotiable requirement for his continued employment so he could not demand her removal.

Now he had to share space with her and listen to her describe her disgusting, animal behavior. Why did she do it? Was it possible she was thinking of doing such things with *him*?

A wave of fury swept over him. His hands lifted from the datapad as he suddenly rose from his seat, every muscle taut. "Be...silent!" he said through clenched teeth.

Plymson stared at him for a moment, then gave an uncertain laugh. Kolpe sat down and arranged his datapad so the screen was not visible from her location, annoyed with himself. He had shown too much. She would be more alert and cautious around him now.

He smiled inwardly. He would have to appear calm from now on, no matter what she said or did, to lull her suspicions. But not for long. At the earliest opportunity, he was going to get rid of Plymson.

Moire yawned and brought the scout in to dock, her motions automatic by now. One more quick glance at the comm, scanning away for anything unusual, but it was blank. Gren's estimate had been too optimistic. By the second day they had managed to get the environmental gravity working, but the hull still wasn't sealed and more work needed to be done on the drive gravitics.

"Hey Gren. It's me, got the gear."

His voice on the commlink sounded as tired as she felt. "OK, just a minute. Nobody's here to move equipment."

"I'm coming down to take a look."

"Right. Bring the box of high-field components, willya?"

"Sure thing."

Moire rummaged through the supplies and found the box he wanted and hefted it on her shoulder. Gravity all the way now, and the box was heavy. She pulled down the faceplate on her helmet and tapped it to make sure the seal was good, and cycled through the airlock.

At least they'd cleared out all the remains of the former crew. That was the part everybody hated. Ennis had suggested they sweep the ship bow to stern before starting again, to make sure there weren't any surprises, and she had agreed.

She took the stairs down to the engineering level. A suited figure spun and leveled a weapon. Moire stopped in her tracks, feeling stupid. She'd forgotten to do a general broadcast. Fatigue was making her sloppy.

"Oh, it's you!" The voice and face belonged to Ash, the quietest of the Created. The hand holding the weapon was shaking, from exhaustion or fear.

Gren's bulky form emerged from Engineering. "Dammit, Ash, don't shoot the captain! I'll take that," he said, reaching for the box of components. "Why don't you go get some sleep, child? You're about to fall over."

"If I sleep, something could come," Ash said softly. "Nobody else is here to watch, they are all at the engines or guarding other places."

"I'll watch for you," Moire said, changing her comm settings before she forgot again. "Why don't you go back to the scout? You can take your helmet off, and there's food in the locker—"

"No!" Ash shook her head violently. "I want to stay here with you."

Moire sighed. "All right, rack out here if you can. It won't be comfortable, though. Give me your gun. I'll stand watch until the others come back."

Ash complied, and promptly curled up in a heap on the floor. Gren looked down at her sadly, shook his head, and stomped back into Engineering.

"I thought you were staying on the scout." Ennis's voice sounded in her ear. She looked at her suit's comm panel, on her wrist. A single line channel, not broadcast. She set her comm to single line too.

"Gren needed some components, and Ash was about ready to collapse. Where are you?"

"Down with the heavy-mechs. They're shifting a beam for the drive node support. See anything?"

"Nope. I'm wondering if those survivors died. How recent was that repair job?"

He sighed. "I have no idea. Could have been years ago."

A pause grew and lengthened. "From what Gren was telling me earlier, we could be ready to go in a few days."

"Yes."

Moire took a deep breath. Why was she having to do all the work with this conversation? "Figured out where you want to go?"

Another long silence.

"What's near here?" he asked finally.

"Nothing. Closest Fleet station I know of is on Fivemoons."

He whistled softly. "That's a long way from anything else. How about—"

An attention signal interrupted, followed by a voice. "Something is outside the ship. I'm picking up hull vibration from the outside detectors." Another idea from Ennis, after they'd swept the ship. If anything was going to get them, it would be from outside. They didn't have enough people to watch all the hatches.

Moire slapped her comm to general broadcast. "Where are you? Can you locate it?"

"It's up, and I think...it's near the airlock on three!"

The airlock on Level 3 was the one they'd used to go to the gravity ship. It was the level above where she was now.

"Everybody move!" she yelled into the comm. "Drop what you're doing and go! Get to the scout, and check your ammo!" She yanked Ash to her feet and started running. If the crabs got between them and the scout, they would have to shoot their way out.

Moire pounded up the stairs, hastily checking her weapon. Not one of the magnetics, of course. She made sure that the toggle was still set to energy blast and did a quick scan of the corridor at the top of the stairs. Nothing so far.

Now she could feel vibration on the stairs. Ash, followed by Gren. From the comm, she could tell the others were not far behind.

"Keep behind me. We have to get past that airlock to get to the scout. Ready?"

"Yes," Gren said, breathing heavily. Ash just gulped and nodded.

Moire moved sideways along the wall as quickly as she could, weapon in front.

"Lights on the airlock controls—they're coming in!" Gren shouted.

"Get down the stairs!" Moire said, jerking her head back. The door mechanism was starting to move. She pulled herself into a cross-corridor and took aim at the door. Maybe there was only one. Maybe she could hit it.

The door was opening. More people were behind her and in the corridor, weapons up and ready.

Something grimy and ragged emerged. Just as someone shouted "Hey, they're human!" an energy burst flashed beside her.

The door slammed shut. A minute later it opened again, slowly, and two empty, gauntleted hands emerged from the crack. They were shaking.

Moire slung her weapon and started cycling through frequencies on her comm.

"Oh god, oh god...you came, after so long–please, don't shoot me, just...please!" A man's voice, cracked and agonized. Moire patched the frequency in with theirs, so the others could hear without changing their comms.

"Who are you?"

"I'm...I'm Jim. Jim Perwaty. Support systems engineer on *Helios*. At least I was, and what's left of her..."

He sounded human, anyway. "Come out slow, and keep your hands in sight, OK? We weren't expecting you."

"I know, I thought nobody would ever..." The door opened farther, and he stepped out into the corridor. "Hey, the gravity is back!"

The man's suit was filthy and patched in several places. He was tall and thin, and from what she could see through the faceplate, had pale eyes and light tan skin. He wasn't carrying any weapons.

"Stay there, please." Moire switched to her team's frequency. "Do we have any more hull vibration readings?"

"All quiet."

She glanced beside her. Ennis was standing there, his eyes steady on Perwaty. "What do you think?"

Ennis shrugged. "Not a crab, obviously. He was as surprised to see us as we were to see him."

"Good point." Moire changed the frequency back. "Sorry about the blast there," she said. "Are you hurt?"

Perwaty shook his head. "No, not even singed. Door got most of it, I think. How did you...are you..."

"We came here to salvage. We'll be going home soon."

He sagged in relief, and almost fell. "I almost gave up, so many times..." He smiled a little. "I've been salvaging too. This ship showed up after mine did, and it had parts I needed."

Gren popped his head out of the stairwell. "So that was you taking the displays!"

"Seen any sign of other survivors?" Ennis asked, lowering his weapon.

"Only from my ship, and Bethalis died soon after we got here. At least she lived long enough to get the reactor going again, or I wouldn't be here now."

"How long have you been here?" Moire asked.

"Oh, I think it must be around three years now. Yes, that's right." He nodded. "Three years. I can't wait to see the last of this death trap."

Moire looked over her crew, thinking. They were tired before, and now they would be tired and twitchy. "OK, everybody. We're going back to *Raven* for some rest. Perwaty, you want to get anything from your ship?"

Perwaty froze, his eyes wide. He shook his head sharply. "Nah, nothing worth the trouble of getting. Don't have any reason to go back now."

Gren wandered up. "You said your reactor was working. *Helios* is the one in the center of the cluster?"

Perwaty gave him a quick glance. "Yep, that's the one."

"Like to take a quick look at it."

"What for? Got a lot of damage. Too much work to salvage," Perwaty said. "It's almost split in half."

"It is not that bad," protested Ulrike, who had come up to join the conversation. "The superstructure is mostly there."

"Yeah, well, you haven't been inside. It's a mess. You don't have to go there, I can tell you all about it."

It probably would look impossible to someone who didn't have experience in salvage. "We'd like to see for ourselves. Ulrike, take the first group back to the ship. Who else wants to take a look?"

Alan didn't say anything, he just shouldered his way through the crowd. He had a magnetic in his hands. She wondered if he'd taken it from someone, or if they'd handed it to him at the first sign of trouble.

"Gren, I know you're coming. Montero, will you make sure Perwaty gets settled on board?"

"I'll come with you, if you insist on going," Perwaty said grudgingly. "Least I can show you where the dangerous parts are so you can keep away."

Moire nodded. In the bustle and confusion of the corridor, she felt a tap at her wrist. Ennis was looking at her, holding up one finger close to his chest, where it could not be seen by anybody else.

She glanced down at her wrist and casually switched to single channel, turning her head away from the others. "What is it?"

"He doesn't want us on that ship, and he hasn't said anything about crabs."

"True. If he's been here that long and not seen them, then they're long gone. It sounds like he's been scrounging the entire cluster. He's suspicious, but then he doesn't know who we are. Lots of nasty people in the Fringe and we could be some of them."

Ennis looked skeptical. "What's he protecting?"

"Maybe other survivors. He knows we aren't leaving right away, that will give him a chance to check us out and make sure we're legit. I'm told there are slavers around."

"Perhaps." He didn't look convinced, and she couldn't blame him. Something was definitely going on with Perwaty. He'd acted normal until they wanted to go to his ship. Ennis looked at Perwaty, then back at her. "I don't think he's frightened of us, though. If I were you, I'd keep my weapon ready."

"I intend to. Let's find out what he's hiding, hmm?"

Ennis nodded, his eyes narrowing intently. "I'll ask him about the door. In three years he must have noticed *something*."

They followed Gren and Perwaty back out of the airlock and over the clutter of debris between the ships. Moire shook her head. Now that she knew what to look for, there were signs the beams and cables had been deliberately arranged. Had Perwaty done all this himself? Some of the beams were rather large.

Inside *Helios*, Perwaty opened his helmet. Hesitating a moment, Moire did the same, then nodded to Alan when he looked at her questioningly. The air smelled more than a little of unwashed human, but that was to be expected after three years.

"I was wondering if you could explain something to me," Ennis said in a deceptively calm voice. Moire wandered casually to the other side of the corridor, where she wouldn't block anybody's line of fire.

"Eh? What's that?" With his helmet off, Perwaty's stiff brown hair made him look like a bottle brush.

Ennis pointed. "This, on the door. What is it?"

Perwaty moistened his lips. "I dunno. Always like that. Um, I mean I found it like that. Original one broke so I found some parts on another ship. I forget which one."

"You've never seen anything else like this?"

"No, never." Perwaty was emphatic. "So, what did you want to see here?"

"Engines and gravitics," Gren said. Perwaty led them down the corridor and down two levels. He didn't seem happy. Moire kept a close eye on their surroundings, letting the others talk and distract Perwaty. Everything seemed normal, if a bit worn and dirty. No other crab additions that she could see.

"Engineering," Perwaty said, and stopped. He was standing so he blocked the corridor heading toward the stern.

Moire turned, looking over his shoulder. "What's down there?"

He shrugged, a quick twitch. "Storage, smaller cargo area. It got damaged. Nothing there now."

Now she saw something different. The deck was worn and scratched along the corridor behind Perwaty. One gouge was recent, judging from the fresh surface of the metal, and deep. Something heavy had been moved to the supposedly empty, unused space. Moire caught Ennis's eye, and nodded briefly at the floor.

"Let's check it out. May as well know what we need to fix, right?" she said brightly, dodging around him and heading down the forbidden corridor. Perwaty started sputtering protests; fragments of incredible reasons why she shouldn't go there. When she stopped at the door to a cargo area, he became even more frantic.

"And...and there's radiation! One of the cargoes was..."

Moire punched the door controls and blinked in puzzlement. It was the smallest cargo area she'd ever seen—and where was the outer hatch?

"If it's radioactive, why do you bunk here?" Ennis asked dryly, pointing to the bedding in one corner of the room. Against one wall was a workbench with several gutted pieces of equipment and a pile of salvaged components. Tools were ranged neatly in a rack. An output panel displayed a page from an equipment manual.

Moire moved to the wall next to the workbench. It looked like a section of outer hull with a square-meter viewport and an airlock door. It couldn't have ever been a part of the original ship. The actual hull was at least ten meters from the wall, so what was the airlock for? She peered through the viewport. The space behind it was dim, but she could tell it was not empty.

"No! Don't...get away!" Perwaty grabbed her arm and yanked. "It's dangerou–" Moire twisted away, and saw that Alan and Ennis had their weapons pointed directly at him.

"Hands off the captain," Ennis said in a gentle, dangerous tone.

Perwaty let go and stumbled away. "You don't understand. This ship has–has a lot of problems. I had to fix them my own way, all right? There...there was a leak. Needed a hull section." He turned to the workbench. "I guess since I'm here, I'll take some of my things." He snatched something that looked like a large datapad with wires and components attached to it. One of the cables ran along the wall with the viewport and seemed to go through to the other side. He yanked the datapad loose and stuffed it in a ripped duffel.

"Let's go. Please. All this ship has is bad memories of dead friends. I want to go away and never come back." His voice cracked. "Now." He pulled a few more things off the bench, apparently at random, and put them in the bag, too.

Maybe there was just something wrong with Perwaty. Had he really moved all the pieces of the hull section by himself? He'd had three years to do it, if he'd been telling the truth.

"All right. Let's take a look at Engineering, then we'll leave," Moire said, taking another look around the room. He probably was a little off edge after being stuck here for so long. Gren was already out in the corridor, and Perwaty was waiting impatiently at the doorway for them to follow. Moire turned to go. A sudden loud bang made her start.

Perwaty had gone as pale as his tan skin would allow. "We gotta go now," he said hoarsely. "I heard this before. Ship's breaking up." He made no attempt to put on his helmet.

Two more heavy knocks. Gren ran back in the room. Tears were falling down Perwaty's face now. Three knocks. Perwaty suddenly ran to the wall, pushing against it with his hands as if he could mask the sound that way.

"Stop it! They have guns! *They have guns!* Do you want to die?"

A deep moaning voice came from behind the viewport, and a barrage of pounding.

"Something's moving in there," Gren said tensely, pointing at the viewport. He picked up a heavy wrench from the workbench and moved back toward the entrance.

"What the hell is it?" snarled Ennis, moving back with Gren and waving at Moire to do the same while aiming his weapon at the wall.

She stared at the viewport. The banging had stopped, but the deep voice continued. Gren was right, something was moving. Something with a strange shape, emerging from the shadows. Something that seemed to be looking at Perwaty's sobbing face, but without human eyes. Something that was touching the surface of the viewport, but without hands.

So I was right. There was another survivor.

Perwaty turned and stood straight, a certain desperate courage in his eyes. His arms spread protectively across the viewport.

"Don't shoot. He's my friend."

Ennis kept his weapon trained on the creature. It had to be a crab. Realizing that he actually was looking at one of the enemy made a chill shudder through his body. His fingers tightened on his weapon, and he fought to relax them. Killing one more crab wasn't going to make a difference in the war. It would be more valuable alive.

How strange it looked...it was bigger than he was expecting. Only the upper part was visible through the viewport; a long, narrow head with curving ridges along the length of it. The skin had a subtle pattern in shades of grey, with occasional black marks that didn't seem to match the pattern. Long tendrils sprang from the area between the head and what seemed to be the neck. They were pressed up against the surface of the viewport behind where Perwaty was standing, writhing as if the crab was trying to grab him. The eerie noise seemed to be coming from the crab, too.

"Are you sure he's your friend?" Ennis asked, suspicious.

Perwaty swallowed. "He saved my life. We help each other."

"You do know there's a war on, right?"

"We ain't fighting!" Perwaty snapped. "Coulda killed me any number of times if he wanted. I coulda killed him. Sure, I know there's a war. But here it's him an' me against the Universe."

"If he's your friend, why did you try to leave him here?" Moire asked. Ennis risked a glance her way. Her face had a grim, dangerous look he'd never seen before. Alan, beside her, had his weapon aimed like the rest of them but was gaping at the crab in astonishment.

"You shot at *me*." Perwaty snapped. "I'm human. Think I'd just tell ya he's here an' hope for the best? I'd never do that to him." His face twisted. "He'd be stuck here, but...at least he'd still be alive," he said in a small voice. He turned his head, looking back at the crab. He put his hand against the viewport. "I'm sorry...I didn't know what ta do."

The crab shifted. His tendrils moved, still pressed against the viewport but now opposite Perwaty's hand.

The ship. Moire had said she'd only seen one, and that one was huge. "Where are the others?"

Perwaty shook his head. "He's the only one. I didn't even see any bodies."

Moire snorted. "Oh, come on. He didn't get here by himself. Did you look in his ship?"

"Been out with him a couple times, get supplies and such. Nobody there. Besides, why would he want to move in with me if any of his own kind was still around?"

"Why would he want to share quarters with an enemy?" Ennis wondered. Something strange was going on, because all the indications were that the crab did. He was starting to think Perwaty was telling the truth about the crab being alone.

"I keep tellin' ya, we don't fight. 'Sides, he says there's something wrong with the war."

"What?" Moire asked.

"I dunno, that's where it gets confusing. He keeps saying we aren't the right ones, or something."

"Wait a minute. You can *communicate*?" Ennis said, incredulous.

"Not much else to do around here. We worked something out, but it ain't up to anything fancy. I'll show you."

Perwaty scrambled through his bag and brought out one of the items he'd tossed in from the bench. It looked like some kind of scanner. He plugged it into a cable that ran along the bench and into the bulkhead between them and the crab. Perwaty held up the scanner so the crab could see it. The crab's long, narrow head lifted up, and the tendrils along his neck slowly uncurled. The noise stopped.

Moire drifted closer. "What do you think?" she said in a barely audible voice.

Ennis gave a quick shake of his head. "The crab? I'm not sure. I *do* know we have to get him to Fleet. This is more important than the ship."

She scowled. "We're already late. Why are they called crabs? He doesn't look anything like one."

"They got the name from the ships. The hulls looked like crab shells," Ennis said. "All the spines."

"How do you talk with a scanner?" Alan asked Perwaty, peering around Moire.

Perwaty started, dropping the device and cursing. "Don't sneak up on me like that. You a mercenary?" Alan stared at him, then shook his head uncertainly. "You wear that thing on your arm, like they do," he said, pointing to the red metalmesh scarf Alan had tied on his suit.

"He got it from a mercenary," Moire said, the corner of her mouth twitching. "So how does it work?"

"Me an' him, we have something we want to talk about. Like this," Perwaty nudged a loose pinlight on the workbench. "I point to it, he calls it something and puts that in his device. So I get his signal pattern from his device, scanner reads it, and I set it in memory and call it 'pinlight.' I send him that pattern, he gets his word for it."

Ennis glanced over at the viewport. The crab was gone. No, he had moved back to a treelike structure he could barely make out in the gloom. He could see more of it now. Two thick, powerful-looking hind legs, two thinner, articulated limbs springing from a common point in what would be a human's chest, and an overall body structure that was pyramidal and bottom-heavy. Crabs didn't seem to need much light to see with. He was manipulating something with his tendrils on the tree-thing.

The scanner display flashed text. Perwaty looked at it and scratched his head. "I think he doesn't want me to leave," he said finally.

Ennis got closer, so he could see what Perwaty was doing. He was tapping out something that showed as JIM GO TO HUMANS. Well, he'd said it was a simple system.

After a moment the display blinked and displayed JIM GO TO HUMANS. RADERSENT NO ALONE. (JIM, RADERSENT) GO TO

HUMANS.

"He wants to come with me," Perwaty said slowly. "What the hell?"

"We want him to come with us too," Ennis said, feeling numb with shock. Communication. He'd seen it himself. Communication with a crab.

Moire grimaced. "You want him. How are we going to do this? Looks like he doesn't breathe our kind of air, and I'm damn sure he can't eat our food. Not much use dead, is he?" she asked dryly. "Crew might not like it either. Ulrike lost a brother in the Zamaia raid, and I'm sure there are others. Why can't you come back and talk to him here?"

Before Perwaty could answer, Alan spoke. "He doesn't want to be alone." He pointed at the scanner. "He says so."

Yes, that made sense. If the crab was terrified of being alone, he would be willing to risk being a prisoner. Which would make him more likely to cooperate, if he was afraid they'd leave him here. "He wants to go with Perwaty, and I'm sure Perwaty doesn't want to stay here. The crab comes with us."

Moire held up a hand. "Now wait a minute. This crab doesn't have all the facts. You." She pointed at Perwaty. "Tell him we've personally fought and killed his people." She indicated herself and Ennis. "Tell him if he comes with us, chances are good he'll never go home again."

Perwaty sighed. "I'll try. How about some names, so I can keep you straight?"

A silence, then Moire said, "Call me Ren Roberts. That's my son, Alan, and Gren," she said, jerking her thumb back toward the doorway. Then she looked him with an amused expression.

Ennis hesitated, finally saying, "Byron." He'd always tried to avoid giving his first name if he could. He felt it was the only thing truly his. On Fimbul, you didn't show things you valued. Even though he knew his name could not be taken away, old habits died hard.

They were introduced to the crab, which involved a great deal of waving and pointing from Perwaty. The crab seemed to take this in without comment until Alan was introduced.

[QUERY]ROBERTS SHE read the crab's message.

Perwaty tapped out. MORE SEND.

"What does that mean?" Ennis asked.

"Oh, that's a general 'huh?' Means I need more info," Perwaty said.

The response came almost immediately. ALAN CHILD ROBERTS. [QUERY]ROBERTS SHE.

Perwaty rubbed his chin. "Hmm. Now that I think about it, we had a real long talk when I showed him the vid of my wife and daughter. Damn persistent he was. Took a long time before I figured out what he wanted to know. Seems they got females too, and it's real important to know about 'em. Still don't know *why* it's so important," he said, shrugging, and typed in his reply.

The crab suddenly pulled his head down and pulled his tendrils in until they were no longer visible.

"What's he doing?" Alan asked.

"He's not happy," Perwaty said slowly.

"I thought he'd have second thoughts," Moire said, nodding.

Perwaty snorted. "I haven't told him anything yet, 'cept your names. He asked if you were female, and I said yes, and that's what set him off."

"He's afraid of females?"

The crab moved very slowly back to his communication device. His tendrils extended only as far as necessary to manipulate it.

RADERSENT GO WITH JIM. RADERSENT GO WITH ROBERTS.

Perwaty tapped out a rapid sequence, then peered at the response. "I told him you've killed crabs. He wants to know if you're going to kill him."

Moire shook her head. "Not unless he tries to kill us."

RADERSENT NOT DEAD HUMANS -> HUMANS NOT DEAD RADERSENT was the message Perwaty sent. Ennis was starting to see how the communications worked. It was crude but effective.

The tendrils went out a little more. RADERSENT GO WITH ROBERTS, the crab sent.

So. The crab was willing. He just had to convince Moire.

Moire stumbled in the doorway of the scout. Damn, she was tired. Too much excitement.

"You were in *Helios* a long time," commented Ulrike from the pilot's seat.

"There was a lot to see," Moire said eventually. "It's an...interesting ship."

You could sense the intelligence in the crab, that was the disturbing thing. Alien, and intelligent. She hoped they could ask it the one question she'd wanted an answer for since she'd found out they were fighting the crabs–what was this war about?

She couldn't make sense of how it moved. Sometimes it just used its stubby legs, but now and then it used the set of limbs that seemed to function as rudimentary arms and secondary legs as needed. She frowned, remembering. Maybe the forelimbs didn't grow symmetrically, but she suspected this crab had been injured. One forelimb was bent and awkward, and the crab never moved it much.

Alan twisted in his seat, and Moire cracked an eye open watchfully. He was facing Ennis. She tensed, but when he spoke his tone was not angry or confrontational, but resentfully curious.

"How did you know?"

Ennis glanced at Ulrike, piloting the scout, and made a slight gesture for him to lower his voice. They hadn't told the rest of the crew about their discovery yet.

"I guessed. From something I saw."

"What?" Alan persisted. Moire blinked in amazement. This was the most civil conversation they'd ever had. "I want to know, so I can guess too. If there is another...another Secret, maybe it is dangerous."

"I'll show you when we go back."

Alan nodded, seeming satisfied. Soon the scout was docking to *Raven* and Moire forced herself to move.

"All right, everybody. Rack out. Six hours, and we'll get back to work. You too, Alan." Alan muttered something, then shouldered his gun and went in the direction of the cabin he shared with the other Created.

Gren sighed. "What are we going to do about the whatsit?"

I suppose I can't pretend it isn't there. "The commander and I are going to discuss that right now," Moire said shortly. "After I set the security systems."

Gren just gave her a look and grunted, but Ennis asked, "You still think there are others out there?"

She shrugged. "I'm not trusting the ship on the word of one guy and his trained crab. There have been too many surprises lately."

When they got to the bridge, Moire checked the status of all the hatches and then activated the security systems. If anything tried to get in now, they'd know about it. She headed to the small captain's office, Ennis following her. When he stepped inside she shut the door and turned to face him. He was watching her warily.

"We need him," he said intensely, his voice low. "Do you have any idea how badly we...he's communicating with us! He could have all kinds of useful data."

"He's probably a Bottle-Washer third class and can't tell you anything important. Or won't. The only communication system we've got is hardwired, has the vocabulary of a two-year-old child, and is generally not suited to convincing a crab carrier to hold their fire. I thought you wanted to get back as soon as possible. If we try to take him along now it could take almost a month to get something set up."

More importantly, her crew might start complaining. They knew they didn't have a lot of time to prepare Sequoyah's defenses, and this current trip was really only justifiable since they could sell the ship they were fixing after Ennis was back at Fleet. They wouldn't get anything from towing a crab ship or a prisoner.

She sat down, suddenly feeling tired. Why was she coming up with these half-assed objections? Of course Fleet needed any information the crab had. Even a crab janitor would be tremendously useful, and this crab seemed willing to go with them. And she would do it anyway, because Ennis wanted it so badly. She sighed.

"Look. How about taking lots of vid shots of the crab and the ship? We can't move it yet anyway; it's too large. He can go with the ship once we get it figured out."

Ennis looked down at the deck, frowning. "Better if they're kept separate. That way if anything happens, we don't lose them both."

Moire leaned back in her chair. "We'll go out after we unload everybody tomorrow. Maybe we can convince the crab to come with us, and Perwaty—they must have some way to communicate without that scanner thing."

"No." His head jerked up; his eyes were fierce. "Not you."

"But—"

"It's too dangerous. You keep putting yourself at risk when you have everybody here depending on you. Your other pilot isn't here, remember? What if the crab ship has traps? Or more crabs?"

Moire closed her eyes and took a deep breath, deliberately unclenching her fists. "Kilberton knows where we are. He knows how to get here. If we don't leave soon, he's going to be coming here anyway to see what's wrong. Don't tell me how to look after my crew! If they have a problem with the way I do things, they'll tell me." They probably would, too, once they found out about this.

Ennis spun around and leaned closer, breathing hard. "Your crew would follow you into a black hole just to see how you would get them out," he said, each word bitten off. "If you told them they could breathe vacuum, they'd try it. Don't go by their judgment."

"What are you worried about?" Moire asked, trying to hang on to the tattered shreds of her temper. "Everybody here, including the crab, can survive without me. You can get your ship. They can get home. Or are you afraid I'll miss the mutiny inquiry? Does Fleet really care if I die here instead of in front of their firing squad?" She was standing now, shaking with anger.

His face went white. "Don't. Don't say that!" Ennis grabbed her shoulders with painful strength. "They won't, they can't..." Just as suddenly he let go.

Moire stared at him, frozen with shock. His eyes were anguished. She felt like she had wandered into a minefield, and she wasn't sure she could get out again even if she wanted to.

Ennis reached out and just touched the side of her face. "Moire, if you say it I have to listen," he said in a low, rough voice. "I can pretend it isn't there, but if you say it..." He swallowed.

She knew what she wanted to do, but the small voice of conscience was shrieking in the back of her mind, what about him? She should tell him to get lost. She should say it was none of his damn business. But it was too late for that, and had been for some time. She'd just refused to acknowledge it. The signs had been there. The way she was always aware of his presence. The way the bleak look in his eyes made her do everything she could to make it go away when she saw it. Now it looked like it wasn't just her.

"Byron Ennis," she said finally, "are you sure you know which side you're on?"

His face twisted and he turned his head away. Without conscious thought she found herself reaching for him, torn by his pain. "It's all right, it's all right...it will be our own private war, we'll figure it out somehow," she whispered, holding him close. "Nobody else needs to know."

He was clutching her as if he were drowning, and she could feel his rapid, gasping breaths. "I don't want to have to choose," he said, so softly she could barely hear him. "Please don't make me choose..." His face turned to hers, and his kiss tasted of tears and desperation.

CHAPTER 11
A LITTLE FIXER-UPPER

Moire sat at *Raven*'s realspace controls, alternately watching the approaching hull of the salvage ship through the main viewport and Ennis out of the corner of her eye. He looked haggard and pale. She doubted he'd gotten any sleep. She hadn't slept much herself, but she didn't have to worry about inappropriate involvement with the object of a mutiny investigation. She just had to ignore various bodily impulses that said their encounter had been far too short and unsatisfactory.

They both had to do some thinking–with their brains–and decide what they were going to do. Neither of them had room on their schedules for more trouble. She had to get the construction of Sequoyah's defenses going. He had to get back to Fleet with the crab data without getting killed. And if they pulled all *that* off, they were then going to find themselves on opposite sides of a court-martial. Not much chance of a happy ending for them there.

Gren came clumping in, and at her sign, shut the door to the bridge.

"How soon do you think you can get the ship pressurized?" Moire asked, her eyes back on the docking readouts.

"A few hours for the hull, then I'll start testing. If we don't have too many leaks, living quarters should be ready tomorrow," Gren said.

Moire nodded without looking up, her fingers floating over the control board. She felt a faint shudder through the ship as the docking apparatus engaged. She flipped the switches for the interlocks, then spun her chair around. "Gren. We're going to take the scout out to the crab ship for a while and investigate."

Gren scowled. "Who's 'we'? And how am I going to get hold of you if I need to?"

"Me, Ennis, Perwaty, and his little friend. I'll set the comm board to route any calls to *Raven* to the scout and then to our suit comms."

Ennis drew in his breath. "Shouldn't you stay..." He paused when she glared at him, then continued, hands spread before him to stop her objections. "We don't know what's on that ship. It would be a good idea to have someone as backup in case of trouble. You don't need to go inside."

"But I want to." Moire scowled. "You don't have much choice, if we still want to keep this quiet. Besides the three of us, the only other member of the crew who knows is Alan. Gren needs to work on the salvage ship. You really want to go in there by yourself with Perwaty and the crab?"

"You should take Alan anyway, and stay on the scout," Gren said in a growl, leaning over Moire with his hands on his hips. "Dammit, why do you always have to be the first into trouble?"

"She used to be a test pilot," Ennis said quietly. "'First into trouble' is the job description. They don't think about risk like normal people."

Gren glanced at her for confirmation, and Moire nodded. "Before I joined NASA. Before...everything happened." She grinned. "It was fun."

Ennis and Gren exchanged resigned looks. Gren sighed. "Try and think of the rest of us, OK? You've convinced us to join this impossible crusade of yours, so you'd better stick around to help out."

"All right, all right! What a bunch of wet blankets." She muttered a curse under her breath. She knew they were right, which made it even more irritating. It wasn't fair. Didn't she get to have *any* fun? "Come on, let's get going."

She remained silent and annoyed as everyone suited up and filed out to the salvage ship. When Alan hesitated, looking at her and then at the departing crew, she motioned him over.

"You're staying with me."

He nodded, then glanced at her uncertainly. "You look mad. Did I do something wrong?"

Moire winced. "No, kid, you didn't do anything wrong. I'm sorry. We're going to look at...at some other ships, and I want your help."

"Oh." Alan bent to get a better view of her face through her helmet. She managed a smile for him, and he straightened and gave her a nudge with his shoulder.

"Let's go tell Perwaty we're going for a ride," Moire said, and headed for the airlock. Alan was going to see the crab ship. Well, one thing was certain. She was going to see it for herself before they handed it over to Fleet, responsibility be damned.

They made their way to the connecting airlock to *Helios* and over the jury-rigged bridge. Alan punched the entry panel and they cycled through.

"At least he hasn't bolted the door," Moire commented. Inside, she opened her faceplate and shouted. "Hey, Perwaty! You awake?"

They started down the corridor. Perwaty was waiting for them at the bottom of the stairs, looking rumpled but remarkably cheerful.

"Good, you're back! Radersent had a lot of questions about you. Every ten minutes, it's 'where Roberts, where Roberts.'"

"We've got some questions for him, too," Moire said, following Perwaty. "You call him Radersent?"

"That's what it sounds like to me when he said his name. Maybe it's something else, but it works for now."

The crab was visible at the viewport when they entered the room. He tucked his long head down as soon as he saw them.

"So when can we leave?" Perwaty asked, his pale eyes eager. "Need to get something set up for Radersent. He's pretty clever that way. Didn't take him long to get this place all working."

Moire glanced at the viewport and the crab watching them. "That's what we need to figure out. You may have to wait. We have to leave soon, and I still haven't told my crew about him."

Perwaty's face fell. "How soon?" He looked worried again, and frightened.

"Tomorrow. First we want to check out Radersent's ship, and we'd like him to come along. Can you tell him that?"

"Uh, sure!" Perwaty darted to his workbench and started tapping at the modified scanner at the end of the long cable. "You're gonna come back for it–for us, right?"

"Yes." Ennis replied immediately.

Moire nodded. "You can come with us now, if you want."

Perwaty's face worked, and he looked at the crab and then away. "I better stay with him," he said quietly. "Guess I can wait a little longer. Least I get ta go home." He glanced at the scanner. "He says he'll go with us. How we getting there, Captain? I suppose you don't want us going through the ship you're working on, if your crew don't know about him yet."

Moire nodded. "Is there another exit on this ship, maybe up top? I'll need to bring the scout in to pick you up, and there's not enough room at this level."

"Not that he can get to. His one arm doesn't work, see. But there's a main hatch on the other side that's clear."

"OK, we'll meet you there."

"Do you have something like that for when you're outside?" Ennis asked, pointing at the communication system.

Perwaty shook his head. "No, and I've tried. Just can't get the transmission protocols figured out. Mostly we talk before we go someplace, or just wave our hands or...or whatever."

Moire rolled her eyes and sighed. "This is going to be an interesting trip."

Ennis adjusted the scope, scanning for any loose debris as well as the hatch where Perwaty and the crab were waiting. "There they are. Watch out for that beam, it's right above the hatch."

The scout slowly drifted toward the hatch. Moire had a frown on her face. "I don't trust that hatch for docking, there's damage around it. Open the airlock and throw them a line."

Ennis got up and cycled through the scout's airlock. The ship was very close, close enough to not really need a line, but he tossed them one anyway. Radersent came first. Ennis felt a chill seeing the alien so close, without any barrier between them. The crab version of a spacesuit looked like a collapsed, leathery balloon that folded about his body. It didn't seem to have a separate helmet, unless the smoother, top part had that function. Three long, ropy extensions on either side of the head must match the crab's tendrils, although he was fairly certain Radersent had more than that. Maybe this wasn't his original suit.

The tendrils grasped the line, and the crab pulled himself into the airlock. Perwaty followed with the line itself. Ennis cycled them through to the ship. In gravity, the crab moved with a bobbing gait using his one working forelimb in rhythm with his hind legs. The crab was big—twice as wide as a human, and as tall when he had all his limbs on the ground.

"I don't think we can strap him in anywhere," Ennis said, watching the crab move cautiously into the scout. Moire nodded, her eyes on Radersent.

"He'll just have to hunker down. I'll hold off on the acrobatics."

"Very considerate of you," Ennis said dryly. "I doubt he wants any more injuries."

"Yeah." She looked thoughtful. "We can't do anything to help him either, poor bastard. Unless he can translate one of their medical texts for us."

She turned back to the pilot's compartment. Ennis started to follow, but saw her twitch toward the passenger section and understood. *Watch them.*

It would be a good test of Radersent's intentions, seeing how he behaved in his own ship. If he was going to try to trick them, it would be there.

"We're coming up now," Moire's voice came through on his suit comm. "See if you can get him to show you where a hatch is."

With Perwaty's assistance and some hand-waving at the scout's airlock, the crab eventually understood what they were asking. One suit tendril extended to indicate an indentation on the crab ship's hull.

"Looks like that big dent on the side, about a third of the way down."

"I see it. Stand by, I'm going to turn the ship." The scout rotated gently, then drifted closer to the crab ship. "Why don't you guys get in the airlock and tell me what's there?"

He'd never been so close to a crab ship, even in combat. It seemed denser than a human ship somehow, the hull surface more like a rock than something made artificially. The entry was deeply recessed in the surface like a small tunnel.

"You can come in about three meters, but that's it," Ennis said, carefully checking the position of the scout.

"Three meters, OK. Can you get in?"

"Yeah, with a jump. I think we'll..." He turned his head, seeing the crab move. Radersent stretched himself impossibly long, his suit stretching with him. He extended his one working forelimb to reach the deck of the crab ship and then folded his body to follow. His suit compressed to its original size again. "He's on the ship! What's he doing?" Ennis swung his weapon around, glimpsing Alan already taking aim from the cover of the outer airlock door.

But Radersent did not go any farther into the ship. With slow, careful movements, he bent his forelimb around what appeared to be an undulating fold in the wall of the tunnel. It pulled free, and as Radersent's tendrils moved over its surface, it became long and pliable, like a cable. The crab pulled it forward, toward the scout, until the end floated in front of Ennis. Then he just stood there, waiting. Maybe it wasn't an attack.

"What's going on? Everything OK?" Moire's voice was worried.

Ennis took a deep breath. "I'm not sure, but I think he's just throwing us a line." He reached out and grasped the cable, nearly dropping it when he felt it start to curve around his hand. A dark shape moved to take the cable–Radersent had come back. He seemed to be waiting for Ennis to do something. He thought for a moment. If it was a line, then it needed to be tied to the scout somewhere.

Ennis pointed to the cleat on the hull outside the airlock, and Radersent curved the cable around it. The tip of the cable kept moving after the crab had let go, winding tightly around the cleat and the cable itself.

"We seem to be attached," he said finally. "I sure hope we can get this thing off again, though." Ennis looked at the end of the tunnel. Some kind of structure was there, but he could only see it faintly. "We're going to need some lights."

A floodlight switched on overhead. "How's that?"

He grinned. "Better. I think we're ready to go in." He felt his heartbeat accelerate.

"Be careful, dammit. And keep talking," Moire snapped.

"Yes, sir. Reporting in every three minutes, sir."

"Smart-ass."

"What a quaint, old-fashioned term," he said, trying not to laugh. He grasped the strange cable and pulled himself across to the crab ship. The tunnel surface under his boots felt grainy, like sand over stone. Then he noticed he wasn't floating. "This ship has gravity," he said slowly. "Feels a little bit less than standard. Are you getting the vid feed?" They'd rigged up a transmitting vid that also had storage. It wasn't designed for vacuum use, though, and he was carrying it uncomfortably inside his helmet, tucked beside his jaw. One corner was starting to poke him in the ear.

"Yeah, I'm getting it. Make sure Alan stays behind you, OK?"

Alan had already followed him across, and he was staring wide-eyed at the tunnel wall.

Ennis waved him over and pointed to the wall surface "This is the stuff I saw on *Helios*. Remember the door?" Alan frowned, then nodded. "That's crab material. What they make their ships of. I saw it on a human ship, so I knew something was wrong. Only a crab would have put it there."

"He can't use our handles very well," Perwaty said, coming up next to them. "So he added the extra piece."

Ennis indicated the end of the tunnel. "Can he open this?"

Radersent undulated to the hatch, a tall oval in the side of the ship. It had a green, prismatic sheen with faint ridges. A projecting hub with spines was placed off-center on the oval, with a matching arrangement of struts on the hull. He wrapped his tendrils over the hub and twisted to use his good forelimb on the struts.

The oval shivered, and the faint veins thickened as the surface thinned and disappeared. The web of veins then collapsed to the edges of the hatch. Ennis stared, then shook himself, his mind numb. This was their hatch technology? How had Fleet managed to survive this long fighting them? What else could they do?

The space inside had more struts and spines; he assumed for more functions like opening the hatch. He turned slowly to capture it all on the vid. There were devices high up on the wall, and he wondered if Radersent was a small crab, or if they were special things rarely used.

"OK, let's go inside," he said, when he had seen everything. Perwaty pointed to the second oval, which was not on the facing wall, but at an angle to the one they had entered from.

The same action by Radersent to the new set of controls produced a slow compression Ennis could feel on the surface of his suit. The atmosphere seemed slightly cloudy to him now. He checked his readout and raised a surprised eyebrow. More than an atmosphere pressure, and the red pinlight suggested he didn't want to breathe whatever gases were out there. It was warm, too.

The inner hatch turned to web and then nothing. He took a deep breath and stepped inside the ship.

It's like a cave. Not like the big, open cave on Sequoyah, but like the vids he had seen of underground caves on Earth. Pillars descended from above, ending over their heads. Openings like tunnels started halfway up the curving walls and continued on. They looked like corridors, but how did the crabs get to them? It was empty, too. Just as Perwaty had said.

"What a weird ship!" Moire's voice was hushed and amazed. "Right out of an Escher drawing."

Ennis froze. The timbre of the sound was different, as if it was coming from a suit comm and not from the bridge of the scout. He turned slowly.

Moire was standing behind him, her head tilted to one side and an amused gleam in her eye. She backed up a step when she saw his expression of fury.

"You. You said..." He'd been so distracted he'd never noticed her following them through the hatch.

"Absolutely nothing about staying on the ship. You are out of your mind if you think I'd miss this. I don't see a single flat surface anywhere, do you? I wonder how they make these things."

"Will you please go back, now that you've gotten what you wanted?" he gritted out.

"I can't operate the hatch; can you? Might as well stay for the grand tour." She paused, and her cheerful expression became more serious. "I didn't join the exploration team just to find planets. I've waited all my life for this."

Ennis barely restrained himself from pointing out it could be the end of waiting for anything if something went wrong. She was inside and he couldn't get her out again without Radersent's cooperation. He'd just have to hope their trust was not misplaced.

Radersent was standing nearby, patient and motionless. Moire walked up to him, and he tilted his head back as she approached. Ennis reached to pull her back. They didn't know what that posture meant to a crab; maybe he was going to attack.

She pointed at one of the openings in the wall. Radersent turned and moved away in the direction she had indicated. When he reached the point where the curving wall met the floor, he kept going on the wall itself. Moire gasped, then ran after him.

"Moire! Wait!" Ennis yelled, running in turn. She didn't stop, and when she reached the edge jumped and stood on the wall, turning around in amazement.

"Hot damn. Look what they can do with gravitics!" She chewed her lip, gazing at the other end of the wall. "I wonder if I can stand on the ceiling?"

"I don't want you to stand on the ceiling!" Alan said loudly, sounding frightened.

Moire turned quickly and stepped back off the wall. "It's OK, the gravity is different in this ship. I won't fall." She walked over to him, looking about.

Ennis swallowed and tried to slow his hammering heart. He was going to have to talk to Alan and convince him to help. Moire actually listened to him.

It was a very strange ship. The faint mist obscured things at a distance, making it even more mysterious. He hoped the vid was picking up enough to be useful.

"What should we look at next?" Ennis asked. What would a crab control room look like? Did they even have a bridge?

"Hmm. That corridor is larger, maybe it's..."

"*Raven*. Come in, *Raven*."

The signal had an undercurrent of noise. Ennis glanced at Moire. She was looking startled and worried.

"That's Kilberton. What the hell is he doing here now?" she said.

"*Raven*, please respond. This is *Dunkirk*."

Moire made some adjustments to her communications controls on her suit. "*Dunkirk*, this is Roberts. What's going on?"

"We've got problems, Captain." Kilberton sounded relieved to hear her, but still worried. "McNaulty's crew boss has some questions he wants to ask you before he'll start the job."

Moire was looking very annoyed now. "Are you saying you brought him *here*?"

"There's more, but we need to show you. It's not good, Captain. I don't think you can return Commander Ennis as you planned."

She swore and changed her comm again. Now he couldn't hear the conversation, but he could tell it was not a happy one. Then she waved her arm in the direction of the entry and headed there herself.

"What's going on?" Perwaty asked, puzzled.

"Looks like we're heading back," Ennis said. "Something's come up she needs to deal with."

Radersent operated the hatch controls, and soon they were back in the scout. Moire wasted no time getting underway.

"Problems?" Ennis ventured, looking at her set face.

"If Kilberton can't handle it himself, it can't be good," she said, without elaborating. "We'll have to drop those two off before going to *Dunkirk*. Did you get enough from the ship?"

"Enough? No, but it's more than we had before. You could just leave us and come back later," Ennis suggested.

Moire snorted. "Now who's taking dangerous risks? We're split up enough as it is. Hopefully this won't take too long."

"What's wrong?"

Moire let out a breath, flexing her fingers on the controls. "Besides the fact that calm, collected Kilberton comes barging back a week early yelling that we've got more problems? Problems involving getting you back to Fleet? Isn't that enough?"

Ennis sighed. "I might be able to help, if you tell me what's going on. Or do you want to do everything yourself?"

"It's not about you," Moire said slowly, lowering her voice. "OK, maybe it is. There are some things we're doing a Fleet officer probably doesn't want to hear about. You've got enough with...I don't want to give you any more potential conflicts of loyalty."

"I see." His voice was as low as hers, and he was aware of the growing tension in his body. "That's my problem." It was kind of her, but too late. The conflict she was referring to was already there, and growing stronger every second he was with her. Every time he remembered how, when he had held her, the pain had stopped.

She turned to look at him. "Is it? If Fleet asks you about me, about our operations, how much will you tell them? If it was just my secrets I wouldn't care so much, but a lot of people are trusting me to keep them alive."

He saw the looming shape of *Helios* and the other ships coming close with relief. This was becoming a dangerous conversation. What would he tell Fleet? He should tell them everything, but he already knew he wasn't going to. He said nothing more until after Perwaty and the crab were dropped off and Moire headed to dock with *Dunkirk*.

"Do you want me to stay on the scout?" he asked quietly.

Moire shook her head. "That won't be necessary." She switched the comm to *Dunkirk*'s channel. "Kilberton. I have Commander Ennis with me. Can one of you tell him what's going on while I talk to our guest?"

Ennis followed Alan to the bridge, where the pilot, Kilberton, and Yolanda Menehune were waiting. They turned quickly to face the door when he entered. Kilberton's face was troubled.

"You must understand, we don't believe it is true. But others..."

"Let 'em see what we're talking about first," Yolanda interrupted. "I overheard some talk when we were on station. Found this marvelsheet going around, got a copy to bring back. Take a look."

She handed him a textsheet. It had a screaming yellow border and a morphing, mildly obscene titleplate at the top, and Ennis recognized it as one of the wilder circulars, "Hick's Picks and Probes."

"I like 'Tom-Tom's Tell-All' better," he commented, scanning down the content list. "If Hick's ever tells the truth, it's by accident."

Kilberton's eyes were wide with amazement. "You *read* these things?"

"See? Some people like 'em," Yolanda said, giving him a shove. "Open your mind a little, goodguy."

The listing was fairly standard stuff Ennis had seen before, in one circular or another. Deranged gestation facility worker switches tank IDs. Psychic predicts crab attacks on Earth. Secret colony hides supersoldier genetic engineering lab. Pirate gang terrorizes Fringe.

"Which one?" he asked finally, distracted. Yolanda peered over his shoulder and pointed to an article that had not caught his attention at all, it seemed so ordinary. *Ghastly murder on station one of many.*

He pulled up the article. As soon as he saw the station identified as Jessack he felt a chill. All the details were there, except the Toren agent was referred to as a "young Fleet technician on her first posting." A still of her in uniform, smiling and eager, was included. There were stills of him, too.

Lots of them, from all angles. The article went on to mention the attack on *Canaveral*, now inflated to two murders, and that he had escaped from the notorious prison colony Fimbul.

"Very convincing," Ennis said, taking a deep breath. "If it appeared anywhere else, I'd believe it myself."

"They don' have to believe anything but the reward," Yolanda said, her hands on her hips. "That part's true enough. Checked it myself."

At the end of the article. *For capture or confirmed death. 50,000 ED.* He whistled soundlessly. That was a hell of a lot of money, especially in the Fringe.

"Crew knows what really happened on Jessack; saw what you looked like when we found you. Probably can trust them," Yolanda said, looking doubtful. "Better not push your luck, though."

"Who would put such lies about?" Kilberton asked. "The risk they would be exposed..."

"Ah, but they were careful to include just enough truth," Ennis said softly. "I did come from Fimbul–but I wasn't a criminal. I was born there. There was a brutal attack while I was on *Canaveral*–but only one, and not a murder. I did kill Oberst. Toren shouldn't have mentioned what happened on *Canaveral*, though. That isn't widely known outside Fleet."

Yolanda narrowed her eyes. "I'm gettin' real tired of those jokers. Don't they have anything useful to do?"

Toren didn't want him getting back to Fleet. The reward was a very effective way of making sure he either stayed hidden or got killed. The kind of people who read and believed Hick's circular wouldn't be asking difficult questions, like why a Fleet technician was killed so far from the nearest Fleet post.

"I regret, Commander Ennis." Kilberton spread his hands. "Perhaps the captain will think of some other way for you to return safely."

Ennis stared at the textsheet without really seeing it. He had to make contact with Fleet; the information he had was too valuable. If Moire couldn't think of a way, he had to. Even if he didn't want to go.

CHAPTER 12
ODD JOBS

When Moire arrived there was only one person in the crew meeting area, a short, barrel-chested, powerful-looking man with rough black hair and an expression of suppressed fury on his face. His lips were moving, as if he were muttering curses to himself.

"Mr. Kostas?"

He turned his head to scowl at her. "You Roberts?"

She nodded. "What's the problem? If McNaulty didn't like the contract he should have said so earlier. I don't have time to waste." She was getting angry herself, just thinking about how much time it would take to find another contractor.

His face got darker. "Nobody showed me that contract. I'm the crew chief, and I'm responsible for their safety. No way in hell I'm gonna let them go off when you won't say where and you won't say what they're doing when they get there. I gotta sign off before we get the crew and the equipment, and I got nothing to evaluate. I–ain't–satisfied!" he said, stabbing a stubby finger closer and closer to her face with each word.

She resisted the urge to lean back, away from his anger. She needed to put him on the defensive instead. "McNaulty agreed to the secrecy. It's in the contract. If you don't like it, why are you even here?"

"I need the work. We all do," he growled. "People don't want to build much with the crab war going on, and when they do they don't hire the independent firms. Been real tough finding jobs. Bet you thought that would be enough, eh? But I got limits. I get real suspicious when somebody won't tell me things I need to know. Makes me think you got something to hide, maybe something I wouldn't go along with. You think just because I need work I'll do anything? Lots of us take our family on jobs, ya know. I don't risk my kids, or theirs. You don't like it, find another contractor."

This was going to take some work. Moire sat down at the long table, summoning up a calm, understanding face.

"I understand. *My* family's safety is involved here too." She could see she'd startled him, and he was listening intently. "That's why I need the secrecy. I have enemies that would love nothing better than to know where I am. I can't tell you that." Seeing his brows start to lower again, she added, "What would satisfy you? What do you really need to know?"

Kostas sat down opposite her, leaning back in his chair. "I wanna see the site, Roberts. We don't even got a survey to work off of. I wanna know what you want built there. I wanna see who's there and who I'll be dealing with. You don't want everybody knowin' where you are, I can understand with that. But I gotta know my crew won't get in trouble from this."

Trouble follows me like a dog. Moire sighed. It was risky, but not much more than bringing in contractors in the first place. Kostas wouldn't know the coordinates of Sequoyah or how to get there. The worst thing that could happen would be if he talked about the new Earthlike planet he'd been on and Toren found out. She'd just have to pound the need for secrecy into his head before sending him back. There wasn't much hope of keeping it quiet when the construction crew left, but by then they should have their defenses ready.

"OK, you can see the site. When you get there I think you'll understand why I'm so paranoid. If you still want the job, great, but understand the biggest danger to your crew is if they can't keep secrets. Not from me, but my enemies, you understand? If you don't like the risk, we'll take you back and find someone else." *Under a rock, maybe. We looked everywhere else.* She hoped her bluff wasn't showing. "If you agree, then we'll hand you the plans. You'll see my people there. Is that enough?"

Kostas shifted restlessly in his chair, drumming his fingers on the tabletop. "So how you payin' for all this? You got big plans but no budget, or what?"

"We salvage ships. That's why we're all the way out here."

He gave her a careful, thoughtful look through narrowed eyes. She noticed he wasn't revealing much, and he hadn't answered her question.

"So...you get a little impatient with the original crew, maybe helped them leave or somethin'?"

"We are not pirates, Mr. Kostas," Moire said with careful calm. "The ship had been drifting for years before we found it."

"That so." He gave her another shrewd look. "You been doing this for a while? Ever find any survivors?"

There was no reason not to answer his question truthfully. "Once. Two of them."

Kostas pursed his lips, then slapped both hands down on the table. "OK, deal. Show me the site, and we'll go from there."

Moire got up and extended her hand, and it was enveloped in a quick, powerful grip. "I'll make the arrangements. I hope we can do business, Mr. Kostas."

"Yeah, me too." He shook his head ruefully. "Guess we're both a little desperate, eh?"

Moire froze. "What do you mean?"

Kostas gave an offhand shrug. "You know we don't got a lot a work coming in. And you," he said with a bland face. "I hear you had a little trouble leaving Jessack. Didn't wait for the release, took some of the dock with you when you left."

I am never playing poker with this guy. I could lose a kidney. Kostas had a gleeful light in his eyes, watching her face.

"I don't like people tossing explosives at my hatch. Scratches the paint," she said, feeling reckless. Of course he knew. She should have thought of that. He would know everything that had happened there, including the chase and the shootout. No wonder he'd wanted to check her out. He knew he would be heading into trouble if he took the job on, but he still came. Very desperate, and willing to take a risk. Maybe this would work.

Kostas let loose a loud, sudden laugh, tilting his head back to enjoy it fully. "So it does. So it does," he said, wiping his eyes and still chuckling. "Though it makes me wonder what you want us to build for you, Captain."

"I think you'll figure it out when you get there," Moire said, escaping before he could ask her anything more.

Ennis could tell something had happened when Moire returned to the bridge. Menehune and Kilberton stopped their low-voiced argument to glance at her, and the tension in their faces relaxed when she nodded without saying anything. Alan looked up from the circular that he'd been trying without much success to understand. Ennis just hoped Alan wouldn't start asking for explanations, especially about what was going on in the titleplate.

Moire folded her arms and raised an eyebrow at them. "OK, now what?"

Ennis took the textsheet from Alan and handed it to her. "Somebody's been busy. I'm not going to be able to buy a ticket back and survive the trip."

"Damnation." She skimmed the textsheet, shaking her head, then handed it back to him. "Yep, that's Toren all right. Who else in the Fringe would have that kind of money? Or delicately insinuate that killing you would be a good thing?"

"What are we gonna do now?" Yolanda wanted to know. Moire collapsed in the realspace pilot's chair, hands steepled in front of her face.

"Got too many things going on at once. How the hell are we going to get you back to Fleet without getting either or both of us shot?" she asked, slanting a glance at him. "I'm running out of ideas."

"I think I may have one," Ennis said slowly, looking at the circular. The articles all had bylines. If he couldn't go himself he had to send a message. It would have to be carried by someone trusted, someone who could make sure it got to Pol Namur and Umbra without Toren hearing about it. Someone who wasn't Fleet, but who had access to the heart of Fleet

Intelligence. "If we can find Neville Harrington, he can tell them what's going on."

"The reporter?" Moire raised her eyebrows. "Why would they listen to him?"

"Fleet itself might not, but he knows someone in Fleet who will. Someone very, very interested in anything to do with the crabs." *And you,* he didn't add.

Moire frowned. "We still have the problem of finding *him*, also without getting shot. Do you know where he is?"

Ennis shook his head. "It's a gamble, but that's the only thing I can think of." He hoped he was right about Harrington and Namur. It would be awkward otherwise.

"What's this about crabs?" Yolanda said, straightening up and looking worried.

Moire sighed, closing her eyes. "We found a crab ship here. Oh yeah, and a crab survivor. Commander Ennis wants to get them both back to Fleet, for obvious reasons, and I said we'd help."

Yolanda and Kilberton were staring at her in horror. "Alive? Is it...restrained?" Kilberton asked faintly.

"Crab ship? What crab ship?" Yolanda said, hands on her hips. "When did that show up?" She glared at Moire.

Moire gave her a weak, unconvincing smile. "It was already here when *Ayesha* got pulled in. Hasn't moved since, so I thought it was dead like all the rest of the ships."

Yolanda's eyes narrowed. "Huh. Don't you think we'd want to know about a whole shipload of crabs in the area?"

"There's only one," Ennis said, and Yolanda Menehune's fierce gaze turned to him. "Something happened to the rest of the crew. We've been inside that ship. It's empty. Even the crab doesn't live in it."

"Where does it live, then?" Kilberton asked, eyes darting about nervously as if the crab would show up at any moment.

"In Perwaty's ship. Other survivor," Ennis added, seeing their confusion. "Human. According to Perwaty, the crab has been helping him. They have also figured out a way to communicate."

"I see." Kilberton swallowed hard. "That is very important. We must find a way for you to bring this information to Fleet."

"Is your comp scrambled?" Yolanda asked him, her voice shifting higher with emotion. "You forget about *that*?" She pointed at the textsheet on the console next to Moire.

"I have not forgotten," Kilberton said quietly. Yolanda subsided, her forehead starting to crinkle with worry as she looked at him. "We must find a way."

Moire stood up. "I suppose now is the time to tell the rest of the crew about it. We're going to need to split up three ways. Gren and his team have to figure out how we can tow the crab ship. One ship has to go take Kost...our guest to Sequoyah, and another needs to start looking for this reporter. *Dunkirk* has a dropship, right?"

Kilberton nodded, looking stunned.

"OK. Dock to *Raven*. We're going to have to figure out all the details. I just hope the crew doesn't have a fit about the crab."

"I'm going with you," Alan announced, reaching for the circular again. Moire sighed, and nodded.

Kilberton took his place at the realspace controls, a determined look in his eyes. Moire went over to the far end of the bridge, tilting her head at Ennis to follow. He noted with apprehension the bemused expression he'd seen when she came on the bridge had changed to a look similar to the one she'd had on the crab ship. Potential trouble.

"So. What makes you think finding this reporter will be worth it?"

"After the...incident on Kulvar," Ennis said, suddenly unable to meet her gaze. "When I reported in to Pol Namur in Intelligence, he already knew most of what had happened there. The only other person who knew, besides you, was Harrington. I don't know how he got that information to Namur, but he did. More importantly, I suspect this line of communication is not known by the rest of Fleet." Umbra was just enough outside Fleet hierarchy, and he knew Pol Namur was suspicious of Toren. It was the safest place they could send the information.

Moire rubbed her chin. "Hmm. We won't be able to search for him ourselves–too dangerous. If we dock anywhere to send a message, somebody will be looking for you or me, and then there's the chance of the message being intercepted. I suppose there's Redline, but..." Her eyes brightened. "Hey. I know someplace we can show up and nobody will know. Bone!"

"No detection systems to speak of, and we can land on the surface." Ennis nodded.

"It might be a bit slow, but it'll be safer than anything else. We can ask Lorai for help."

He smiled, remembering how suspicious the shuttle pilot had been when he and Harrington had been looking for Moire. "She'll help you, anyway. Do you think she would go herself? She'd recognize Harrington; he was with me there."

"I doubt it. She's pretty busy flying freight. She could tell us who we could send, though."

It was a good idea, and it would take time. He shouldn't be so glad.

"This Namur guy. He's the one who sent you to that outpost, isn't he? Because of me?" She was looking at him with a trace of sadness. "Hope he appreciates what you're doing now." She put one hand on his shoulder.

"I'm sorry it worked out like this."

He put his own over it, holding it even when she started to move away. "I'm not." He turned her hand over, tracing her palm, remembering the blood. How terrified he had been. He must have been in love with her even then and just hadn't known it

"No scars. You did a good job," Moire said softly. Her fingers curled about his.

"We are docked, Captain," Kilberton announced, and Moire turned away.

At first Lorai thought the sound she heard was the comm, and she drowsily waited for the automessager to come on. Then the insistent, shrill noise cut through her foggy mind. *That's not the comm*, Lorai realized, and woke up a little more. Now she could hear something pounding on a wall. Was somebody at the door?

It sounded like it was coming from the outside entrance. She was going to have to get up, then. Leaving people to freeze just wasn't done on Bone. Muttering curses, she shoved open the bed door, swearing with energy when the cold air hit her face. "I'm gonna charge 'em for this. Waking people up at this hour ain't kind or decent," she said to herself sourly.

She pulled her work coat over her sleep gear and shuffled out of the office area to the hanger. The knocking was louder. "I'm coming, I'm coming!" she said under her breath. They weren't in immediate danger of dying if they had enough energy to pound like that. "Don't knock the place down."

An unsuspected strut intercepted her shin, and she swore. She should turn the lights on, but then she'd see the stripped shell of the Beast lying there like a skeleton, and it was too damn depressing. Why didn't these idiots use the comm in the doorway to call for help?

She frowned. Now that she thought about it, wasn't that the broken comm she hadn't bothered to fix because nobody ever used it?

Light shone through the viewpanel of the door. She peered through blearily, just to be on the safe side. She didn't have much to steal now, but it would be real annoying to get shot.

There were two people in the space between the inside and outside doors. When they saw her, one of them pulled off her hood.

"Ohmygosh. Ren Roberts!"

Lorai fumbled with the door lock and latch, yanking it open.

"Come in already! Geez, give me a little warning next time, huh? How are ya, Alan?"

"I'm not Alan," the man said, and pulled off his hood. Lorai stopped reaching for him and blinked. It was the guy who'd been looking for Ren last, the one who'd tricked the Toren ship into leaving.

"Looks like you found her," Lorai observed, suddenly unsure what was going on and playing for time. Where had she put her gun?

He shook his head. "She found me."

Roberts gripped her shoulder. "I'm sorry to wake you up like this, but we need your help. Hope you don't have an early flight tomorrow."

If only... "Nope, it's all good. Come in and tell me all about it. How'd you get here? MagneTech ship?" Lorai asked, closing the door.

Ren tilted her head. "Got my own. Outside. We don't want anybody to know we're on Bone, which is why we waited until the middle of the night to knock on your door." She smiled, but it was a tired smile.

"I think this calls for the *good* booze," Lorai said cheerily, waving them into the office and slapping the heat sensor until it clicked on. Something wasn't right. Ren looked stretched tight, strain in her eyes. But the guy...what was his name again? He didn't look much happier.

She retrieved the good booze—what was left of it—from the data cabinet drawer it was hidden in and found three reasonably clean containers to drink it from. She shoved the pile of old textsheets, oily parts, and food wrappers on her desk unceremoniously to the floor. She could sort it out later—right now she had guests.

"So where is Alan, then?" she asked, pouring out.

Ren jerked her thumb upward. "In orbit. He wasn't happy about being left; wanted to say hello." She took a sip from her mug and coughed. "How is everybody?" she wheezed, eyes watering.

Lorai leaned her elbows on the desk, looking down at her own drink. So much for a nice happy chat. "Not so good. Guess you might not know about MagneTech coming in, huh? They found some big deposits near the Crystal Maze about a year ago—just after you left, in fact. Big enough MagneTech was interested, and once they got here they started taking in everything. Hardly any of the independent operations left any more. It's not even like they're trying to wipe us out; decent folks most of 'em. But they got their own shuttles, see? They run ships pretty regular to pick up the processed ore, and they ship what they need that way. *Ayesha* was the only ship that came regular before, and now...folks can order through them, too. Mammachandra ain't selling much these days, at least not from the store. Some of the freelance miners already left Bone, or joined MagneTech. Hell, even old Gip Farouz can't get much work. Got their own techs for that."

Ren was looking miserable. "I'm sorry. I didn't think, when *Ayesha* got wrecked. You guys depended on that, and I..."

"Ah, hell. We all knew that piece of crap was going to blow up some day and not come back. Nobody's fault. MagneTech is the big change. If they weren't here some other ship would've picked up the route, and we'd be fine." Lorai took a gulp, almost draining her cup, and let the alcohol warm her brain. Damn, but this was a depressing story. "Nobody's fault, but we're still in trouble. If I hadn't gotten some makework with the researchers in the Belt I would have gone out of business weeks ago."

Ren looked up, suddenly intent. "Ever think about working off Bone?" she asked.

Lorai snorted. "Been thinking about nothing else, but if I did I'd be starting over from zero. All my money's in those shuttles. Beast don't even fly anymore. Can't afford to fix it–in fact, been taking parts to fix the other one."

"This would be temporary. You could come back if you want to, but I have another idea that might work. We need your help, Lorai."

We? "Yeah, right. What can I do you can't?"

"Find someone without being noticed," the man said promptly.

"Ennis needs to get a message out," Ren said, indicating him. "Toren's hunting him too, now. Neither of us can go looking for this guy without attracting a lot of the wrong kind of attention."

Lorai snorted, trying to disguise her sudden spurt of interest. "I ain't a special agent. Who'd I be looking for? And how'd he know me from a used gasket?"

"You've met him," Ennis said, with a quick, flashing grin. "He was with me."

"What, that scruffy Englishman? The one with the nose?"

Ennis choked, covering his mouth with one hand. "His name is Neville Harrington, and he's a wireservice reporter," he said, when he could talk again. "I see you remember what he looks like. All you have to do is find him and give him a message." He reached into an inside pocket and pulled out a datatab folder. "He'll take care of the rest."

It wasn't like she had any other good choices, and now she was all curious. How could she resist? "Sounds like fun. I suppose you want him found soonest."

"As soon as you can without detection." Ennis hesitated. "This isn't without risk, you understand. Toren has spread the report I'm a rampaging murderer, so don't mention my name where people can hear."

Lorai widened her eyes. He didn't look like a rampaging murderer, and she didn't think Ren would have him around if he was. "Don't mean to be nosy, but where'd that come from?"

"I killed one of their agents," Ennis said, looking grim. "The agent was planning to kill me, so I don't have any regrets. That's when she found me," he said, pointing to Ren.

They *had* warned her, but it was still a shock. What was going on worth killing about? "What happens after I find this guy?" Lorai asked.

Ren smiled mysteriously. "I just happen to be in need of a shuttle pilot, especially one with her own shuttles. Of course, we're pretty much guaranteed to be in the middle of a shooting war sometime soon, so you may not want the job." She got up, fishing out a handful of credit chips and putting them on the desk.

Lorai picked one up and sucked in a deep breath. It was enough to fix the Beast and keep her fed and warm for over a month. Ennis handed her the folder and another, separate datatab.

"That has all the information I could think of that might help you find Harrington. Don't let anybody get that folder." He followed Ren out of the office.

"So where's this war gonna take place?" Lorai asked, all innocent.

Ren looked amused. "That's what the war's about. I'll tell you this much. You won't have to change the name," she said, tilting her head at the shuttle. "If you can, get out of Waylands without letting anybody know you're leaving Bone."

"How'm I gonna tell you I found Harrington?" Lorai asked when they reached the door.

Ren hesitated. "He'll tell us. I'll come back in a month or two and see if you still want the job." She looked at Lorai and smiled. "I hope you do. It's good to see you again."

Lorai saw them out into the bitter cold outside and watched them run out to the shadow just visible in the darkness. She looked back at her shuttle and the lettering on the side that said "All-Planet Delivery." The lettering she wouldn't have to change. She was starting to get an idea what all the fuss was about.

Now there was a patch of light in the darkness. She went to the outside door viewport and scrubbed at the frost on the surface. There they were, in the cockpit of their ship. She could see their faces. Ennis was saying something to Ren. Ren leaned over him, smiling, and he tilted his head up to meet her kiss.

Lorai took a deep breath and backed away from the door. *I dunno what was going on before, but looks like they got an understanding now.* She grinned. "Glory hallelujah. All this and a war too. I can't wait."

⚓

There were puddles of water on the cave floor when Moire landed the scout, and traces of windblown debris. She didn't see any obvious signs of damage to the gear or supplies stacked in the cave, so maybe they'd been lucky. Yet another reason to start building as soon as possible.

"Guess this planet has weather after all. I was beginning to wonder," Moire commented, unstrapping.

"What's weather?" Alan wanted to know.

Ennis grimaced. "In this case, lots of water falling from the sky." He was waiting for her to leave the cockpit, glancing up and then away. She still wasn't sure how to deal with what was happening to them, and it looked like he didn't know either. Better not to push it. Especially with Alan around to take notes.

"How did the water get up there?"

Moire grinned and left the scout. Smart as he was, she suspected Ennis would run out of answers quicker than Alan would run out of questions.

The cave seemed unusually empty of people, with most of the crew still out in the sargasso. Where were all the Created? She frowned, looking around. After a search she found Harvey Felden toward the back of the cave, muttering as he disemboweled a crate of small components, scattering packing material everywhere.

"Why in the name of humanity couldn't you take the time to list what *kind* of communication equipment you put in here, Menehune? Twenty-five, twenty-six..."

"Where is everybody?"

Harvey jerked upright. "Captain! You're back! I thought that was Kilberton coming in." He stood stiffly, grimacing. "They're out at one of the islands, mostly. Madele is here, with the injured and the ones who can't walk yet."

Moire closed her eyes, hoping there was a nice, reasonable explanation. "Injured?"

"One broken leg, couple sets of cracked ribs, a dislocated elbow, concussions here and there, and an assortment of sprains, bruises, and lacerations," Harvey recited, looking down his nose disapprovingly.

"What the hell have you been doing?" Moire asked, stunned. "Did the Created act up or something?"

"We were doing just fine until Kilberton showed up with George and his group. Seemed kinda anxious to get them off the ship, which should have made me suspicious. Aren't on the ground five minutes before they convince the rest of the kids to play something they call Hunt the Pirates in and around the supply crates. We don't have them latched down or anything here."

"I get the picture. Somebody knocked some crates over." Moire sighed. "Could have been worse. At least they didn't have their weapons."

"You gave them *weapons*?" Harvey shrieked. "Are you crazy?"

Probably, but it seems to work. "It made sense at the time. Did Kilberton tell you what happened at the sargasso?"

Harvey shook his head. "Didn't have time to tell me much. Soon as he dropped he started flying this Kostas guy around."

"Right." Moire glanced about, making sure nobody else was in earshot. "We found survivors this trip. Two of them. One of them isn't human." Harvey's face went slack with astonishment, and she nodded. "Exactly. That's just for you to know right now. Rest of the salvage crew knows, but they're still at the sargasso. George and company were there—we tried to keep it quiet, but you know how they are. I doubt they understand what the crabs are anyway, so that should be OK. But nobody else, got that?"

He moistened his lips. "Got it," he said in a hoarse voice. "Captain, what are you gonna do with, uh, with whatever?"

"Hand him over to Fleet, like a good citizen. And his ship. We're working on that. Where's Kostas?"

"He wanted to get a better look at the geology around here, so I found him something he could use as a ground scanner. Didn't know about handing him a gun, so I made George go with him instead."

Moire frowned. "Did you at least give him a commlink?"

"Sure. Restricted, though."

She scanned the code listing on her commlink, finding the only restricted code and selecting it.

"Kostas here," came the gruff voice.

"It's Roberts. Where are you?"

"Out by the cliff. I've got some questions for you. I'm coming back." The connection closed.

Moire raised her eyebrows. He sounded remarkably curt. What had set him off this time? *I hope George didn't try to blow him up or anything.* "The other Created...where are they again?"

Harvey shrugged his thin shoulders. "Loaded them up and took them to one of the islands. At least they're away from the equipment."

She should have thought about that before someone had gotten hurt. What was she going to do with them? They needed teachers, people to take care of them. Moire walked to the mouth of the cave, feeling depressed. Not long after, Kostas came stomping up the trail, followed by a sorrowful George.

"Guess I can see why you want to keep this quiet," Kostas said, waving a hand at the bay with the pseudotrees. "Worth its weight in gold, you might say." He gave a tight grin. It was so unlike him Moire started to worry. Then she noticed his hands. They were badly scratched, dried blood around the nails.

"What happened to you?" Moire asked, pointing.

He looked down at his hands. "I got mad," he said slowly. "Didn't take me too long to figure out something wasn't right with some of your people. Acting funny, you know?"

Oh yes. I know.

"They seem scared of people. Don't want to talk, most of them. George isn't so bad. Asks lots of questions about what I'm doing, and thinks about it. So it's not that they're stupid, right? Then I start asking *him* questions." The muscles in his jaw tightened, and his eyes narrowed. "What he tells me, somebody been doin' horrible things to him and the rest. Not too clear on the details about who and where and why, but it's enough. I got so mad I went out in the storm and all and just bashed a rock against a boulder until

I couldn't lift it anymore."

Kostas leaned closer. "He wouldn't tell me much, but he told me you got them out. So you tell me. Who are these goddamned bastards, so's I can rip their heads off? And what did they do to these people, that they got to have their names on tags around their necks so they can remember 'em?"

George clutched his nametag, eyes wide, and edged away from Kostas's red-faced fury.

"They remember their names just fine, now that they have them," Moire said finally. "They're the other reason I need your help. The people I rescued them from will be looking for me. That's why I want the facilities underground or hidden as much as possible. You did get the plans, right?"

Kostas nodded, looking bewildered. "But what's *wrong* with them?"

"Nothing's wrong with them, they just look older than they are. George, here, we think he's around seven."

Color drained from Kostas's horrified face. "How?"

Moire took a deep breath. "We're not exactly sure how they did it. But they did it to get a lot of compliant workers as fast as possible."

"They still doing it?"

"They only had one facility that we know of, and we took care of it. Permanently."

"Good." His face was savage. "Now tell me..."

The sound of running footsteps made Moire turn. Alan was coming directly for them, looking frightened. "Madele says come help. She's crying and yelling!"

There was a lot of noise coming from the back of the cave, now that she noticed. Standing next to an irate Kostas it had just blended in. "What's wrong? Is she hurt?"

"I think maybe she fell. Madele was helping her walk."

Moire's internal disaster meter dropped a tick. *Madele* wasn't hurt, but one of her charges was.

The impromptu medical ward was the center of the storm. Madele was trying to subdue a crying, flailing Created lying on the floor. Moire felt cold, watching what looked exactly like a full-grown woman act like a newborn infant. It was all there, just in the wrong shape. The awkward flailing movements, the endless, wordless cry of pain and confusion, the helplessness.

"We need to get her calmed down, or she's going to hurt herself," Madele gasped, grabbing an arm before it hit her in the face.

"You tried talking?" Kostas said bluntly.

"We rescued some when they were just...finished," Moire said quietly. "She's only a few months old. She doesn't understand words."

She watched him carefully, wary of his sudden temper. Kostas looked at the Created, his face working with some strong emotion. He turned suddenly to George, standing behind Moire.

"Get me a blanket. Quickly." George darted away and returned, holding a blanket at the end of an outstretched arm.

Moving with steady assurance, Kostas nudged Madele away and scooped up the Created in his powerful arms, wrapped in the blanket. The Created struggled and cried even more, but he ignored her, making soothing sounds and gently rocking her in his arms.

Moire was impressed. He didn't seem any more inconvenienced than if she had been a regular size baby. The Created stared at Kostas with wide eyes as he made nonsense noises in a gentle voice at odds with his size and strength.

Eventually the crying slowed and stopped. "So what you looking at, huh?" Kostas said softly, glancing at their gaping faces. "You long-haul spacers got some gaps in your education, looks like."

"We'd appreciate any advice you can give us," Moire said dryly. "You seem to have experience. Have you made your decision?"

"Hell yes, I made my decision." The Created made a small noise, and he lowered his voice. "Get me back so we can get the crew and start digging. You'll need some weapons platforms, you know. We can't get you the guns, but we can build everything else."

Moire did a quick scan. Ennis was nowhere in sight. "I'll get the guns." Somehow.

CHAPTER 13
FROM THE OTHER SIDE

Lorai shook her head. She hadn't seen so many people in one place in a long time. Standing around gawking wasn't going to impress anybody, and it sure wasn't going to find the person she was looking for. And how was she going to do that here? Not like she could go to Mammachandra's and ask.

"You are deciding where to start making trouble, no?" One of the crew of the ship that had given her a lift from Bone was grinning at her. "You better be good with that gun, you play cards here like you did with us."

"I took you like you tried to take me, ya leaky gasket. Stop pissing air. Hey, Piotr. How'dya find somebody in this place? Guy says meet him at this station but he didn't say where," Lorai said, starting early on her lying practice.

"He is nice, honest with no angry peoples looking for him, he might be in dock register. But why you want to see such a boring person?"

"'Cause he tries *so hard* to reform me," she said with a slow grin to encourage the wrong assumptions. "Really puts his back into it, ya know?"

Piotr opened his eyes wide. "For you, there is no hope. Send him to me, eh? I am very much in need of such reformation."

"Too true. I'll tell him you're available, when I'm done with him. Where's this dock register hide out?"

Following Piotr's directions, she plowed her way through the crowd. How did station people stand it? There was hardly room to move.

She wasn't really expecting Harrington to be listed in the crew or passenger lists that were in the register, and he wasn't. But close to the bottom of the screen listing innumerable Hernandezes and Iversons was a name she recognized. Henri Ibakate, captain of *Kolari*. She'd dealt with him several times over the years dropping cargo on Bone.

It might be worth checking him out. Henri wasn't a chatty person, but he was honest and wouldn't spread the word she'd been asking questions. He might even be willing to ask questions for her, if she made nice.

She noted down the dock and level on an old pennable textsheet, called up the station level directory, headed for the main sector of the station, then turned back to the kiosk and pulled up the directory again so she could find out what level she was on now. It was so much simpler dirtside–she could *see* where she wanted to go.

She had to push her way through the streams of people to get to the docking area. Everybody seemed to be going the other way. She saw one person with a thick reconstructive bandage on his arm, then two more injured people. When she really started looking, at least a third of the crowd had something patched up or traces of bloodglue visible, and everybody looked as limp as a used filter wipe.

Two of *Kolari*'s crew were standing outside the dock hatch, carefully watching the people standing about.

"No transit or crew openings," one said when she walked up, like he'd been saying it a lot and getting real tired of it.

"Don't want any," Lorai said. "Is Captain Ibakate around?"

"Waddya want him for?" the crewman asked skeptically.

"Need to ask him something. Name's Lorai Grimaldi; I flew freight for him couple times at Bone. If he's busy, I can leave a message."

He gave her a dubious look, not saying anything for a minute. "I'll check," he said grudgingly, and went back to the wall comm. After a brief discussion, he jerked his thumb at the door. He looked sour.

As she followed the signs to the bridge, Lorai wondered how she was going to ask for the information she needed without leaving tracks that could be followed. She needed a believable story; one with just a few lies she could keep straight.

"Lorai! I would not have expected to see you here." Henri Ibakate was just like she'd remembered him—tall, thin, and black as night. He had an air of dignity, too, more like an Inner Systems captain than a real Fringer. She was startled when he called her by her first name. He must be pleased to see her. "What are they doing without you on Bone?" A gesture invited her to take a seat in his office. Too clean and neat, but that was Ibakate for you.

She shrugged. "Things have changed. Not much cargo for me to run. Don't worry, I'm not asking you for a job," she said quickly, seeing his face close up. "I gotta find one eventually, but right now I'm looking for somebody." And why did she need to find this person? "I owe him money, see, and he thinks I'm still on Bone. Don't want him going there and finding me gone."

"I see." He looked worried. "That could be difficult right now. Everything here is in a state of confusion."

"Yeah, what's going on? You got guards at your hatch, people wandering around looking like practice day at Medtech Central..."

Ibakate's lips thinned. His air of tense worry increased, and that was something new. He didn't get worked up for nothing. "Criminy station was attacked," Ibakate said with careful precision. "It was damaged so badly they are evacuating everyone. No one knows if the crabs will return there, or attack this station next. Many of the refugees were brought here. My ship carried several hundred of them."

That certainly put her problems in perspective good and hard. She might have been close to freezing and/or starving on Bone, but no alien nasties were trying to blow her up.

He sighed. "I am also trying to find someone. My cousin was on that station but I was not able to find her there. No one I have contacted here knows of her. And I cannot return to Criminy, endangering my crew and ship, only to look for her."

"Thought you said everybody's out. Maybe the ship she's on went somewhere else?"

"Some emergency personnel stayed—and some others, to help. There was talk of attempting repairs. My cousin is with the local defense force, so she might still be there."

Lorai shifted in her chair, uncomfortable. "I am real sorry to be bothering you with all this going on. I didn't know. Just got off a ship today. If there's anything I can do..."

"Thank you. Palmer is going back, and he promised to make inquiries there. Who are you looking for?"

"Name's Neville Harrington. Just let him know I'm looking for him to give him his money back, since I'm not on Bone anymore."

Ibakate inclined his head. "I shall spread the word."

Lorai rose and shook his hand. "Much obliged. I hope you find your cousin."

Back on the docking level, Lorai couldn't keep the forced cheerfulness in her face from draining out. She should never have taken the job, that was the painful truth. Damn guy could be anywhere. He could be right on this station and she wouldn't be able to find him because she was just a dirtside shuttle pilot who had learned everything she knew about spy stuff from old trid episodes of *Star Hunter*.

She wanted a drink. No, bad idea. She'd promised Ren she'd do the job, and she was going to do it. She'd get drunk afterward. OK, so she was just a dumb shuttle pilot. What would she do if she needed a shuttle part? Find the company that made it, of course. So reporters had to...report to somebody, right?

It was easier going back to the central area of the station. She wasn't fighting the flow of traffic, and it had thinned out a little. Or maybe she was getting used to it, a disturbing idea. On her way yet again to the kiosk, the metallic blue holosign of an InfoService store got her attention. Maybe she could ask them. They delivered all sorts of data, and sometimes even small items.

"Now this is interesting. You are the second person today to ask about sending to wireservices," mused the guy at the counter. He had an amazing mustache, long and luxurious. Lorai had to force her attention away from wondering why he had grown it. "Wireservice posts aren't common out here. Unless you are thinking of the circulars? They take regular mail, most of them."

"No, this would be a wireservice. What do wireservice reporters do if they need to send something and they don't have one of these post things?"

"Well, this guy—the one who wanted to know how to contact the wireservice? He used our secure data package. Verified ID both ends, source and destination info coded and confidential." He looked at her expectantly. Something told her a secure data package wasn't cheap.

Lorai felt her pulse jump. "This other person you mentioned—he was a wireservice reporter?"

The counter guy shook his head. "Nah, one of the people off of Criminy."

So much for that idea. Lorai blinked, following a new train of thought. "So why did he want to send something to a wireservice?"

"Said the reporter wanted it sent right away. Smart thing to do, I suppose, though I wouldn't stay around Criminy myself hoping for more." The counter guy shook his head, making the mustache bob. Lorai tore her gaze away with an effort. What a weird thing to have on your face. How did he eat?

She should pay attention. The InfoService guy had said the reporter sent the message ahead, because... "You mean the reporter is still on Criminy?" Lorai asked, incredulous. She was starting to get a funny feeling about this.

"That's what the man said. Crazy, huh? I'd be on the first ship out."

"Yeah, me too." Lorai waved vaguely at him, backing out of the store. The *Star Hunter* people might know how to deal with confidential and coded data, but if it didn't involve a wrench she was better off trying something else.

It made sense. Ennis had mentioned in the datatab that Harrington tended to show up in dangerous places other people avoided. A recently attacked station would be perfect for him. And how many other wireservice reporters would be out in the Fringe?

Looked like Criminy was her next stop, assuming she could get there. She tried to ignore the sinking feeling in her gut. She didn't have much choice. She had to find Harrington, and if he was in a war zone she'd just have to go there. Maybe the crabs wouldn't come back.

What had Ibakate said? Palmer's ship was going to Criminy. She hoped it hadn't left yet.

✶

Ennis watched Moire pour the coffee. It was a different galley, but it was the same pot, the same chipped mugs she'd used to trick him all those months ago. Things were different now. She wasn't pretending she would go back with him.

"No, Penderhest could read just fine. He wanted me to learn how to speak correctly. Reading aloud was good practice."

"How very English." Moire grinned at him. When she finished pouring, he took the mugs and switched them, and her grin widened. It wouldn't help if she had drugged the coffee again, but it was the thought that counted.

"Yes, he was." Ennis shrugged. "It made a difference later. At least I didn't sound like a criminal every time I spoke. Didn't you say your mother made you do something like that?"

She made a face. "Nah, that was just a literary competition. First and last time I did it. Poor Mom. She was so sure if I just made an effort I would write something famous." Moire laughed. "Guess I did, at that. Trouble is, writing a hacking program tends to make you *infamous*, if people find out about it. Besides, it wasn't something she could really brag about."

"Translate 'hacking,' please." He was developing quite an archaic vocabulary, but she still came up with terms that confused him.

"Deliberate, unauthorized entry and rummaging around in a computer network. Got me where I am today." She raised her mug in a salute, and he did the same. Then they both drank. The coffee drinking was a tradition now. With every repetition the remembered pain lessened, replaced by something different, if no less painful.

"How so?"

She leaned back, tilting her head to one side. "I got caught. Trouble was, I only got caught because I found evidence of some other hackers in that computer, and I could tell they were up to something nasty. Government computer, too. Tried to let the owners know something was up, and that's how they found me. They didn't want any of the details out in a public trial, and I *had* stopped the bad guys, so...deals were made. I went to the Air Force, with strict rules about using their computers, and it was all downhill from there."

He could see the boundaries of painful memories ahead if he pursued the subject, so he refrained from asking any more questions despite his curiosity. It bothered him when he saw her remembering, and he always tried to steer the conversation away from anything that might bring bad times to mind.

He usually saw her only at meals, in company with the crew. He wasn't sure if this was deliberate on her part. He wasn't sure if he was glad. But sometimes they drank coffee together and talked, and it was a small comfort.

The shipboard routine would change now they were back at the sargasso, though. *Dunkirk* had made one brief stop to drop off Moire's mysterious guest after leaving Sequoyah, and then they had come here. At least this time there were two pilots aboard and Moire didn't look like a walking corpse.

He heard stomping feet go past the galley. "Sounds like Gren is ready to go," Ennis commented. "What can I do to help?"

Moire gave him a thoughtful look. "We're finishing the ship we worked on last time. Shouldn't take long, then we'll go back and see if Harrington's sent the message. We'll need to know what the crab needs if he's coming with us, though. Why don't you talk to him?" She grinned. "I hear crab translators have good job security."

"At least until the war ends," he couldn't help saying.

"Yeah. When the war ends." Moire grimaced. "While you're at it, ask him why we're fighting in the first place."

It was a good question, and one he'd wondered about before. As he suited up and traversed the carefully arranged wreckage between the salvage ship and *Helios*, the question echoed in another context. He wasn't fighting Moire any more, but they didn't really have peace, either. More of a strange cease-fire. How was he going to change that when she was constantly occupied with her crew and mysterious plans she wouldn't tell him about?

He'd practice on the crab. Maybe he'd get some ideas of what to do.

Perwaty met him at the hatch. "Your captain called ahead to say you were coming," he said, dogging the door shut again.

"Not my captain," Ennis said, feeling his face warm. "I'm...on loan." He loosened the front of the suit so his uniform was visible, angry with himself. He belonged to Fleet, and he shouldn't feel glad that someone had thought differently.

Perwaty just stood and blinked for a moment. "Don't think for a minute I'm complaining, because I was getting desperate enough to welcome being rescued by pirates, but you people are the strangest lot of humanity ever to share breathing space. You really are Fleet?" Ennis nodded. "And your...the captain, the others are too? She said she'd fought crabs."

"The captain has fought with Fleet, but she's...an independent."

Perwaty snorted. "Ain't that the truth. So what's her plan?"

"They want to fix some quarters for Radersent. I'm here to find out what he needs."

"He can do it himself better than he can explain it," Perwaty said, leading the way. "That's what happened here, anyway."

"How long did it take, though?" Ennis asked skeptically. "He doesn't look completely healthy, and we've got a schedule." Of sorts. At least, a schedule that would not permit three months for a wounded crab to do a cabin retrofit.

"Something like four weeks, maybe. Mostly because it took so damn long moving things from his ship. I helped, of course. We got a lot of the words worked out then," Perwaty said, sitting down at his workbench and pulling the reworked device toward him. "You know, things like 'move it this way' and 'don't drop it on my foot'?"

The crab was already visible in the viewport window. Radersent was moving in a slow and gentle way, as if he were floating in moving water. Even the tendrils were in motion. It felt strange to Ennis how familiar the crab looked to him now.

"He's sure glad to see you."

Ennis glanced at Perwaty. "How can you tell?"

"See what he's doin' there? I call it 'happydancing.' If he's moving around like that, he's in a good mood." Perwaty looked up. "So what you want to say to him?"

Using the limited vocabulary at their disposal, they managed to get the crab to understand they were going to move him to a different human ship, and that Radersent should tell them what he needed.

"Now he's getting cryptic on me," Perwaty complained. "What's '[QUERY]SHIP' supposed to mean? He knows he's going on a ship. We just explained that."

"Maybe he wants to know which one," Ennis suggested after mulling it over. "If it's just to another wrecked ship, he might wonder why he should bother moving."

"Could be." Perwaty bent over the modified scanner, tapping out the stored codes that would be understood by the crab. Nothing complex, of course. Simple, concrete nouns and verbs. Philosophical discussions would have to wait for the linguists.

Ennis peered over Perwaty's shoulder to see what he had entered. The screen displayed RADERSENT GO ROBERTS SHIP.

Almost immediately a reply came back. [QUERY]RADERSENT GO SHIP SMALL SHE. [QUERY](MOVE, STAY) RADERSENT SLEEPING-PLACE SHIP SMALL SHE.

He was beginning to see how the communications were structured. "May I give it a try?"

"Oh, sure! Just tap here for a list of terms to select, and you have to hit 'Test Pulse' to send your message."

Ennis sat down at the bench, feeling the muscles in his back tense. He was getting a bad feeling that needed to be dealt with before they went any farther.

[QUERY]SMALL SHE=ROBERTS

YES

If the crab considered Moire to be less dangerous because of her size, it might think it could succeed in attacking her. Radersent hadn't shown any aggression at all, to anyone, but that could change. He needed to make the crab respect her.

What could he tell him? The crab already knew she'd fought and killed crabs. Maybe he could tell him about the carrier. That should make an impression, one human destroying an immense crab ship by herself. He could hardly believe it himself sometimes, and he had been there when it happened.

ROBERTS NOT SMALL DAMAGE. [PAST]ROBERTS DEAD BIG CRAB SHIP CONTAIN SMALL SHIP.

That seemed to make an impression. At least, the crab wasn't happydancing any more. He moved his tendrils slowly over his own communication device.

[QUERY][PAST]WAIT.

"What does that mean?" Ennis asked, pointing to the screen.

Perwaty's eyebrows went up. "That usually means how long until I get back, something like that. He's asking for a time, but not in the future. How long ago, I guess."

Had the crab understood what he had said? Why was he asking how long ago it had happened? How long had it been? With a shock, he realized it had been over a year.

"How do you do time, then?"

"That's a bit of a problem. We only got one unit of time figured out, something around twenty minutes for us. How long do you want to say?"

"Fifteen months."

Perwaty mumbled under his breath as he made the calculations, then tapped in the equivalent number and timecode to the scanner.

The effect was immediate. Radersent froze. Even his tendrils remained exactly in the same position they had been when the message was sent, immobile as stone.

"What happened? Is he all right?" Ennis took a deep breath, hoping he hadn't gone too far in frightening the crab. They still needed to talk to him. Maybe he was sick.

"Well, ya know I was sayin' the happydance meant he was feeling good? I'm guessing this means he ain't happy at all." Perwaty glared at Ennis. "What the hell you been telling him?"

"Just the details of what the captain did, fighting crabs. He already knows that!"

"Maybe he didn't really understand, then." Perwaty went over to the window, placing his hands on the surface and staring at the unmoving crab. Slowly the tendrils started to move again, and the long head turned toward the window. The sight of Perwaty seemed to reassure the crab, or maybe it was that he couldn't see Ennis.

Radersent reached slowly for the device again. Ennis waited impatiently for the message, hoping he would understand what the problem was.

[QUERY]BIG CRAB SHIP=SHIP HERE x 5. [QUERY]SMALL CRAB SHIP=900.

Ennis blinked. Radersent wanted the specs on the crab carrier? This was getting very strange. Even stranger, he was right. The size, the number of fighters it carried, they all matched.

YES.

A hooting sound came from the crab that he could hear through the window, but Radersent didn't freeze this time.

[QUERY]CHILD ROBERTS DEAD CRAB SHIP.

Ennis quickly selected the terms to tell Radersent Moire had done it alone. To make sure it was clear, he added more text to indicate Alan had not been with her.

Radersent seemed to think this over for a few minutes. It was hard to tell, but it almost looked like the ends of his tendrils were swaying.

[QUERY][PAST]ROBERTS SEARCH CHILD ROBERTS.

How the hell had Radersent known to ask that, and why was he asking? Maybe war was a family event for crabs, and he thought Alan should have been there. He puzzled over the implications until another message flashed.

MORE SEND.

The crab really wanted to know. He couldn't think of any reason not to tell him.

YES.

It wasn't his imagination. The tendrils really were moving. Somehow that answer made the crab happy.

"What was that all about?" Perwaty asked.

"I'm not sure," Ennis said slowly. "You said you've been stuck here three years, right? How long has he been here?" If the crab knew about the destruction of the carrier...

"A year, maybe."

"Not more than a year? Are you sure?"

Perwaty nodded. "I'd been to pretty much every ship I could reach in the cluster, looking for what I needed. His ship wasn't there a year ago."

That was better. The news must have spread among the crabs, including Radersent, before his ship was wrecked.

His comm bleeped.

"How's it going?" Moire asked. He smiled in relief, hearing her voice.

"It's been interesting. Radersent knew about the carrier you got."

It took her a moment to understand. "He *what?* Are you sure?"

"Sure enough. I'm not sure how he thinks of you right now. I hope you're planning some security features for his section," Ennis said, his paranoia picking up speed. What if Radersent suddenly decided to avenge the destruction of the carrier?

"You bet I am, especially after that bit of news. We need to talk about that. Gren's almost finished here, so we will have some crew freed up. Why don't you come back now, if you think he understands what we're going to do. The sooner we get his quarters set up the sooner we can go back to his ship and start loading supplies."

Wratursent pondered the words he was given
Words simply spoken by the dark-headed human
Now he knew fully the dangerous honor
Granted to him by the small human queen.

Driven by fear, his queen had sought danger
Left by the Breakers when they fought the Hsurwyn
Though the histories warned of their subtle deceptions
Their creations remembered the undying hatred
Through cycles of stars. Wratursent, obedient,
Heeded his queen, waited and watched
Ready to aid at the first sign of need.
Soon was he called, he and his comrades
Quickly they came and the same fate awaited
The evil had found them and would not be stayed
Fire and destruction, Wratursent alone
Survived the great blow. Unthinking in terror,
He returned to the great-ship,
Left at a distance by caution's advice

Now empty and silent, how could he live?
Surrounded by wreckage, ships of the enemy,
No kin to give comfort or queen to obey
Death would come without glory before it
No ship-guide remaining, he could not go elsewhere.
No queen would welcome an ill-fated one
Had he returned. Wratursent the Lone
Waiting to die, vowed to warn strongly
Any who ventured of the danger within.

Out of the wreckage, small and quick-moving,
Wratursent saw as he watched in the star-cold
This stranger not Hsurwyn, and neither Life-Breaker
A third traveling people with ways in the void.
Joy to end loneliness, joy to now know
The Breakers still slept and had not returned
Fear of this enemy newly created
Hsurwyn had made with unknowing action!
Spurred by his solitude, Wratursent gave greeting
Aiding the stranger when need had arrived
Jheem was his name. His people then found him,

Humans not fearing, the leader they followed
A queen warlike and fearless, bringing him home.
Rather than loneness Wratursent dared speak,
Showing himself to the feared ship-breaker
Known to the War Sisters, begged this queen entry
Would he have dared, knowing her name?
Not only ship-killer, but queen of the Scattered
As in the old tales, the few still remembered
Before the Destruction. Her sisterings ended,
Her children all scattered, fighting alone at the end of the tale.
But now is the story with glory continued
The human queen honors the Hsurwyn vow.
Her home new defended, her children recaptured,
Glory and memory fully regained. How he is honored
Wratursent the Lone, he who was nothing
Will take part in glory, his name remembered
With the human war queen.

CHAPTER 14
SALVAGE JOB

As soon as Palmer dropped his ship back into realspace the barrage of signals was immediate. Lorai gaped at the communications console, trying to sort them out.

"Anybody still there?" Palmer shouted from the pilot's pit.

"Dunno, but they sure left their distress beacons on," Lorai said, her gaze snagging on the official station identifier code in the display. "Hold on, got the main office."

Either the person manning the station comm didn't know the correct procedure for ship hailing or they didn't care anymore. Lorai heard panic underneath the carefully delivered message. She relayed the information to Palmer.

"The main section is losing pressure. Shipsuits mandatory if we leave the ship. They want to know how much room you have for passengers."

Palmer swore under his breath, then hauled himself out of the pit without bothering with the stairs. His battered face showed concern. "Ask 'em where the hell *Boniface* is. They got cargo space enough to put the whole damn station in."

Lorai relayed the message, feeling the tension knotting her stomach go up a notch when she heard the reply. "They say *Boniface* who? You're the first ship to show up after the evacuation order. Oh, and don't try any of the cargo berths—stay topside. Reactor's having problems."

Palmer ran his stubby fingers through his stiff hair, making it look even wilder. "How'm I supposed to get any salvage if I fill my holds with people? Stop looking like that. Ya really think I'm gonna leave these poor slobs to freeze-dry? Guess the warm fuzzy feeling of a good deed well done will console me when I'm an itinerant dockworker who has to save up for a liter of Pain-Away." He shifted his gaze to the pit, grimacing. "I'd sure like to know where Tran Huong got to. *Boniface* left ten hours before I did."

He leaned over the console and toggled the comm to general pickup. "Hey, station. How many passengers we talkin' about?"

The woman at the station comm was prompt. "Twenty-seven. We're the last. Is anybody coming after you?"

Palmer shrugged. "Maybe. I wouldn't count on it, though. I can fit you guys in somewhere, but you can't take a lot with you. You'll need your own supplies, too. I don't have much."

"Can do," replied the station. "Most of us are on Level Two. Pick any dock you like, we should have one still undamaged."

"This just gets better by the minute," Lorai commented. "I wonder if the station will stay in one piece long enough for us to get docked. Want me to watch the screens for you?"

Palmer grinned, a scar on his face pulling the smile slightly askew. "Good idea. You'd think they'd been in a war or somethin', all this debris floating around. Good thing I don't keep *Lady* for looks 'cause she's gonna get a crater or two."

Palmer ran *Lady of Leisure* on the ragged edge, sometimes by himself but more usually with one or two additional crew. Nobody else was willing to go back to Criminy with him, so he'd been very glad when Lorai showed up. She'd learned a lot about him on the way out. He took dangerous jobs, scavenged anything that wasn't welded or bolted in place, and didn't always check if it already had an owner. When on station he liked to relax by getting into fights, which was why his face looked like a topographic map. The ship had gotten its name, he claimed, because "that's the only way I'm gonna get either one."

Between Lorai's careful watching and Palmer's skillful handling, *Lady* made it to a Level Two dock with only a few minor dings. Lorai did a quick check of her shipsuit seals as Palmer finished running the interlocks. She'd been wearing it constantly after seeing how Palmer liked to run his ship. She didn't think the station was making people wear them for fun, either.

At first glance Level Two looked like any ordinary, non-disintegrating station level, if you ignored the group of frightened people impatiently waiting for the hatch to open. Then she saw people lying on pallets farther down and beyond that, closed pressure doors. Everybody knew stations had them; they were part of the safety system and were tested regularly. Seeing them actually in use made Lorai very uncomfortable.

"Where'd they come from?" Palmer said suddenly, jerking a thumb at the pallets. "I thought they got the wounded out first thing."

"We found them in a section that had been cut off," a man in a grimy uniform said. "A day ago, or is it two now? The ship they evacuated everybody but us on—pilot warmed up the gravitics too close. Part of the station got caught in the field. Already structurally damaged, and that was all it took. Fortunately there was a large air pocket, and then the survivors got clever and found a way to signal us. But they aren't in good shape. Lost one already, and some are getting worse."

"OK, let's get some mass moving," Palmer said, waving his arms about. "Get them in, get your stuff and some food, and we'll get the hell out of here. I'll getcha back quick as *Lady* can run."

Lorai breathed deeply, wondering if she would be able to tell when the pressure dropped. Concentrate on surviving; concentrate on getting these poor folks somewhere safe. Then she could worry about what she was going to do next to find Harrington, because if he'd been here he'd left on that last ship. She didn't see anybody who looked like him here, and that nose would be hard to hide.

While Palmer started the able-bodied moving supplies, Lorai headed for the wounded, wondering where they could stow them. They were still wearing their station uniforms: stained, burned, and torn. She glanced about for something to move them on but didn't see anything. They might have to do it by hand.

"Got to go back…" moaned a woman slathered in burn gel. "Please, somebody go…still alive, I saw…" She tried to sit up, whimpering with pain.

"What's she talking about?" Lorai asked.

"She thinks she saw somebody still back there, where we got trapped," said a man with bloodglue smeared on his scalp in a blue mess. His face was tight with pain. "Give it up! It doesn't matter; there's nothing we can do!" He pushed the burned woman back on her pallet.

"Didn't anyone check?" Lorai asked. If Palmer's was the last ship, somebody ought to try. There was also the tiny, niggling thought that Harrington might be there. She had to make sure. Ren was counting on her.

"When the beam broke and the hull went we were on the station side," said a man with a suit nametag that said D'Este. His words had the slow, measured sound of someone talking through pain meds. "It's vacuum now. Not sure if anything could trap air on the other side. We were there a long time…"

"There may be some people still trapped," Lorai explained when Palmer came to see what was going on. "Let's take a look, at least."

Palmer rubbed one ear. "Well, um, that might be a problem." He didn't look at her.

"Why?"

"All we've got for air gear is this," he said, tapping his shipsuit collar. "They were just asking me if I had anything more. We don't have any way to get to 'em. I know it's rough, but those are the facts."

Lorai snorted. "Yeah? So how do you get all that scrap metal in your holds, then? Wishing real hard?"

His face was red now, making the scars even more visible. "Servo arms and a couple welder bots I fixed up," he mumbled. "Don't like vac."

She sagged in disbelief. A hard-core spacer who was afraid of suiting up. Palmer, of all people. She could see he was afraid, and ashamed of it.

"Where I come from we don't just leave people to die without at least *trying* to get 'em out. What about moving *Lady*?"

He shook his head. "Too many big pieces out there. Take the hull out if I tried."

"Dammit, I'm going to do *something*."

"What are you going to do for air?" Palmer said sarcastically. "Wish real hard?"

Lorai unsealed the tiny front pocket of her shipsuit and pulled out the spare oxygen capsule. Only one, since they were expensive. She wished she had ten now. "One will give me fifteen minutes. I have the one in the collar and this. At least I can look, all right?"

"Which level, Captain?"

That was Kilberton, on the salvaged ship. Moire studied the station plan, chewing her lip. It was like the opening move of chess, a game she'd always been lousy at.

"You go in on three. We'll be on four. Stay on board until we come for you, OK?" She thought for a moment. "Is Menehune there?"

A small click, and Yolanda's voice came over the link. "Got somethin' for me, huh?"

Moire grimaced. "Yep. I want you to check the situation on the station. If it seems safe, get the latest versions of the three main circulars and meet us at our dock. If not, scoot back to Kilberton and give me a call."

"It would be better if I were to go with her, if it is dangero—"

"No!" Kilberton meant well, but he couldn't help looking like the law-abiding citizen he was. On the lower levels of Kulvar that was a very dangerous thing. He knew it, too. So why had he volunteered?

"Yolanda can move around without attracting notice much easier without you. She'll be careful. Right?"

"Damnall sure I will. Mammababy gonna die of old age if she can."

Kilberton's only response was a sigh of resignation.

"Is there trouble?"

Moire started. Ennis was standing next to the pilot's chair. He had spoken softly enough that he would not have been overheard by anyone else on the bridge.

"Last time any of us was here, it looked like there was going to be a major shakeup. Everybody was carrying and nervous, so you can imagine what it was like."

"I know what it was like." His voice was curt. He shook his head sharply. "Fimbul was like that all the time."

Oops. And here she was making him remember his wonderful, happy childhood all over again. "Whatever was going to happen has probably happened, but I want to be sure before we wander in like a bunch of tourists."

"Good idea." He glanced at her. "Do you really need to sell the ship? It could tie you down until you find a buyer."

Moire leaned back in her chair. "I pay my crew well, and they stay loyal.

Payroll is a huge chunk of my budget." That was true, but not the real reason. They had enough from the previous sales for that and a good bit over. What she really wanted was enough cash to get some weapons and cover the construction, which was bound to be more than the initial estimate. That much would never change in the entire history of the universe. She was sure even the crabs had this problem.

Which reminded her...she flicked one of the viewers to the vid in Radersent's quarters. The crab was hunkered at his workstation, tendrils manipulating the device on his end of the communication link. She switched to Perwaty's side of the secure area and saw Perwaty surrounded by all the Created, including her son. They appeared to be having an intense discussion concerning what they were going to show the crab on the new display system that had been installed to help with the language lessons. She punched the comm.

"We're docking in a few minutes, Perwaty. I'll need you to close things down and lock up on your end, OK? Kids, you need to leave."

A chorus of protest erupted from the Created. "But why? We were being quiet and everything!" George sputtered. "We're *helping*."

She saw Ennis grinning from the corner of her eye. "I'm sure you are, but remember, we have to keep Radersent a secret so he'll be safe."

Perwaty got up, wiping his hands on his coverall. "I'd really like to...I mean, my family–they think I'm dead. I just want to let them know that– could I please send a message?"

"Of course you can." Moire hesitated. "Kulvar's a rough place, though, and we're docking in the bad section. If you really want to send it yourself keep that in mind."

"I can write it up on a tab for one of you to take. Don't worry, I won't tell them about you or anything. I don't suppose you know how long you'll be needing me?" Perwaty had agreed to help them with Radersent at least until Fleet had been contacted. She had the feeling he was doing it more for Radersent's sake than theirs. It was hard for Moire to ask him, knowing how much he missed his family, but they desperately needed his experience.

"Sorry, that's still up in the air." A puzzled pause told her that once again she had slipped into anachronism. "We don't know yet. I'll let you know when we do."

"Why can't we stay with Radersent?" George said stubbornly. "Jim gets to stay."

"Jim stays because Radersent is afraid of being alone, but I need you to guard the ship. What if somebody got in and tried to hurt him?" Moire babbled, improvising wildly. "You can't see out of the secure section, so you need to be outside. Don't go out the hatch, though."

She saw Hideo shaking his head sharply on the vid, alarm visible on his face, and the other Created sobered up as well. They reluctantly started to leave.

"I wonder how long that will work," Moire said after closing the connection.

"The duration of this visit, maybe," Ennis said, looking skeptical. "I doubt it will go a second time."

Moire shook her head at him, knowing he was probably right. She sat back and switched to the realspace controls, patching the station connection to the captain's earring. The connection was so bad she couldn't hear the hail, and she yanked the thing free with a curse. "Do these things need batteries? I thought all gizmos nowadays had lifetime power supplies."

Ennis picked it up and turned it over. "It may have been damaged—you said they made some modifications, right? This is the one from *Ayesha*?"

"Yeah. Toss me that commlink, will you? I need to have a chat with the Bribery Department."

He handed it to her and took a seat on the pit stairs. "Is Kulvar so corrupt you can't even dock without bribing someone?"

"To dock on the levels we want, we do. If I wasn't on the hit list of two different armed factions I could go to the legal levels." Kulvar picked up then, and Moire focused on negotiating a reasonable payoff. Things had changed—she ended up paying more than she wanted to, but managed to get a dock on the main section of Level Four instead of one of the terminals. Harder to move the ship in, but much nicer in the event of a quick, unscheduled departure since it would be difficult for anybody to block access to their dock hatch.

She moved *Raven* in slowly and docked, hoping Kilberton was already in place. She didn't want to stay here any longer than she had to. "Think Harrington got the message yet?"

Ennis shifted on the stair. "I doubt it. Lorai would have to have found him days after we left."

"Yeah, I doubt it too. I wonder if she's had any luck." Moire picked up the comm again and set two of the crew to man their hatch. She'd issued weapons before they'd even dropped out of webspace. It took a few tries, but she managed to set up the vid feed from outside the hatch. Kulvar Lower assumed its visitors would be paranoid and usually tried to accommodate it.

"I hope Menehune didn't run into anything," Moire said, and chewed on her lip. She shouldn't panic. Yolanda was probably taking her time and being extra careful. Of course it would take longer.

"Assuming Harrington isn't here—and I doubt he is—what happens next?"

Moire spun her chair around to face Ennis. He didn't seem too upset about it. He was looking at her intently, and she only hoped her face did not reveal how much she was enjoying the view.

He was still looking at her patiently, but now with a hint of amusement. He'd asked her something, but what was it? Damn his distracting blue eyes. Then she remembered.

"Since you've started George and company on the path to perdition, you may as well finish the job and teach them the entire manual of arms. With special emphasis on not shooting unless your commanding officer and/or adoptive mother tells you to."

Ennis grinned. "I want hazardous duty pay and some good blast armor, then. No, I meant what you–your crew–will be doing."

Moire leaned forward, elbows on her knees, and stared at the decking. "Gren, Montero, and their assistants have been working all hours trying to figure out how to tow that crab ship. They think we can use this big ore ship that's out there; one that saved us the first time, as a matter of fact. It's one of those surface landers, for asteroids and rock planets, so it has a bigger power plant than most ships." She glanced up at Ennis. "What if we can't find him?"

He grimaced. "Yes, we should plan for that. I don't know. The big problem is communication."

Moire thought for a moment. "How about towing it somewhere Fleet will find it? Maybe with a beacon or something."

Ennis shook his head. "If they aren't expecting it, they'll assume it's a trap and blow it up. You haven't been in the thick of it for a while now. We aren't doing well, and Fleet won't take a chance. Not like that. Even the beacon they'll think was stolen."

It made sense, unfortunately. So, they had to find a way to get a believable message back to Fleet, with or without Harrington. She couldn't do it, that was for sure. While Fleet wouldn't shoot any of her crew out of hand, they wouldn't listen to them either without proof, and if they tried that through regular channels Toren would find out. Which left Ennis. *No.*

Moire sat up with a jerk. It would happen even if they did get a message to Harrington. Ennis would return to Fleet, and she had a horrible feeling she knew what they would do.

"When you go back, are they going to send you off by yourself to some sheet-metal outpost on the edge of the Fringe so Toren can grab you again?"

He was still staring at her. "The ship would be a big...I don't know. Maybe they would." His expression was bleak.

Now she was getting angry. The kind of deep, cold anger that didn't fade or burn away.

"What's wrong?" He leaned closer, eyes searching her face. "Look, Fleet has bigger problems than me. As far as they're concerned, I'm expendable."

"You are not expendable to me." The edge in her voice surprised her. "If they think you are, I'm not sure I should let you go."

She was standing now, and so was he, confronting each other in the pilot's pit. She expected him to blow up at what she'd just said, but he didn't. He just stood there, his face working, and the pain in his eyes even stronger than before.

"I don't want to go," he said finally, in a rough voice. "But I have to. Do you understand?" He reached out and held her face in his hands. "Do you?"

"Sometimes." Her throat was so tight she could hardly speak. She pulled him closer and held him tightly, feeling his response, feeling his arms around her. He sighed and sank his face into her hair. She turned her head to whisper, "Right now, I don't understand at all."

He made a sound that was halfway between a laugh and a sob and started kissing her, kisses that increased in intensity and hunger. Moire did her best to satisfy him, with a gratifying degree of success. *Perhaps my office would be a better place for this...*

As if reading her mind, a comm signal bleeped. Reluctantly, Moire pulled one arm free and punched the button. "Roberts here."

"Captain! We tried your direct line but you didn't answer."

Moire grimaced. "Something's wrong with my earring."

"Menehune's here, and on her way."

"Right. Thanks." She closed the link, hoping her voice sounded normal. Turning her attention back to Ennis, she gave him a thorough, passionate kiss and then resolutely pushed him away.

"That's no way to dissuade me," he said, reaching for her again.

She put a finger to his lips. "Hold that thought. I just wanted to give you something to tide you over. Company's coming."

"So?"

"So Yolanda would probably give advice on technique, but Alan might come with her. If you want to explain this to him, good luck."

He let go. "Not without the blast armor, thank you."

When only Yolanda came through the door, Ennis gave Moire a look, which she ignored. Somebody needed to be cautious for both of them, especially since pretending the attraction wasn't there didn't work anymore.

Catching the speculative look on Yolanda's face when she glanced at them in turn, Moire spoke quickly to head off any embarrassing questions.

"How is it out there?"

Yolanda made a sort of balancing gesture. "Eh. It's pulling down."

Moire shook her head. "What does that mean?"

"The cut happened, but everybody's still trying to figure out how they stand, ya know? Some people don't like the new ceeyo, some people want the ceeyo to like them more than he does, everybody got somethin' making an itch. Think it will be better with this guy, though. Zandovar ain't crazy to kill, just wants money. We can work with that." She reached into an inner pocket of her jacket. "Got the circulars ya wanted."

Ennis took the textsheets silently and started scanning through them.

"Think it's safe for us to go out?" Moire asked.

Yolanda scratched her head. "If we're real careful and don't go too deep, yeah. See, they're still learning the new order and strangers make 'em nervous. I got an idea, though. If we get some kinda ship identification for everybody that goes out—you know, so they can tell we belong together? Then they start to see us around, know we aren't part of anything they care about."

"You mean like a uniform?"

"Nah, just some kinda mark."

Moire thought for a moment. It went against her instinct of not being noticed, but Yolanda's argument made sense. They had to be known here to be safe. "OK, do it."

Yolanda nodded, then pulled out a commlink. "I gotta call Kilberton first, though, or he'll think I'm dead already. And don't tell him I'm goin' out by myself again, OK?"

Now this was a change. Wondering what was going on, Moire made the merc handsign that meant "all clear." Yolanda grinned and activated her link as she left the bridge.

Moire looked over at Ennis. "Any messages?"

He shook his head. "Nothing." He looked like he would say more, but then Moire heard the sound of stumping feet coming toward the bridge.

Gren came in waving a datapad in his hand. "I think we figured out a way, but we'll need some specialized components I doubt we can find with salvage. They're pretty new."

"Great. You know we can't stay long here, and we have to put the salvage ship up for sale. How are we going to do this?"

Gren sat down heavily at the communications panel. His eyes were bloodshot and his shoulders sagged. Moire wondered how many hours of sleep he'd had recently and felt guilty about her objections. She couldn't afford to lose anybody, though, especially her chief engineer. He would insist on going himself, too.

She looked at his datapad, trying to come up with a solution. A few minutes later Yolanda entered the bridge, panting, and handed her a neat stack of floppy gray squares, each printed with a simple, stylized black line drawing of a bird and lettering that said "Raven" at the top.

"How the hell did you get that done so fast?" Moire said, astonished.

"Got a stand that does these patches and things real close to our dock. Saw 'em coming here; that's what gave me the idea. I paid her extra, and she said she'd tell her other customers the captain of *Raven* hired her to make stuff for the crew."

"That was real smart. Now we have to figure out how Gren can get his shopping done and I can get the salvage ship on market without staying here all day."

"I can go by myself," Gren said, sitting up straighter. "The tech end isn't as bad as the rest."

Yolanda shook her head sharply. "No comp, no data. It's bad everywhere now. Don't even think about it, Captain," she said, pointing her finger at Moire and scowling. "You'd go and say something antique like you do, or ask some hardbody what he meant when he says he got load."

Moire smiled weakly, remembering the incident. "Nobody got shot."

"That was before the cut. Wanna bet that hardbody don't remember you? You're eighty years out of date and it shows. Gotta watch you every minute, I do."

"OK, fine. You take Gren before he falls over and get his stuff. I'll just have to wait until you get back."

"I can go with you." Ennis came over to where they were standing.

"No." Moire paused and took a deep breath to calm herself. "They'll know who you are; that circular ad has been around the Fringe and back again by now." She wasn't going to make him go back to the criminal environment he'd worked so hard to avoid, even if it was safe for him.

He smiled crookedly. "You don't know those people. Being a confirmed killer is a mark of distinction. If they do recognize me, they'll just think I'm one of them."

"What makes you think you know anything about Kulvar Lower, huh?" Yolanda wanted to know. She shot him a challenging look. "Take my main line taglight way, yeshure. You menu allaround, random snap, read?" She looked him up and down, her lip curled.

"Mainline allaround, gita. Bag a count."

Yolanda gasped, shocked. Ennis's face had gone cold and hard, and he gave her back stare for stare.

Now would be a good time for the subtitles to appear. Then Yolanda cracked up.

"Right, you got load. Where'd you learn?" She chuckled again. "Haven't heard that last one for years."

"Ever hear of Fimbul? I grew up there."

She frowned. "But that was...I mean, plenty of bad types, but it was a prison, right?"

"It was supposed to be. Didn't always work out that way. I wouldn't be here otherwise. And when the blowup happened—there were no rules. The guards were the first to go."

Yolanda nodded slowly. "Right. OK, you can go with her. Don't let her talk to anybody if you can help it, though."

Moire blinked. "Excuse me? He's not going."

"I'll do my best, but you know what she's like," Ennis said, sighing.

"Yeah, we all do."

"Hello! This is your captain speaking! This is an unscheduled mutiny, I'll have you know."

"Come on Gren, let's move. Captain's in a big hurry." Yolanda tugged at Gren's arm.

Moire sighed and rubbed the bridge of her nose. "She's trying to help you," Ennis said quietly. "So am I."

She looked up at him, watching his expression carefully. "Are you sure you want to do this?"

He nodded. She didn't like it, but he knew what he'd be getting into better than she did. "Yolanda. Before you go, check in with Perwaty. He's got a message to send. Do it priority data, OK?"

"He got that kind of money?" Yolanda asked dubiously.

"We do, and we owe him." Moire glanced at Ennis. "You'd better change into something that doesn't look like a Fleet uniform, OK? I'll get us some guns. Got another message for you to send," she said in a lower voice to Yolanda as Ennis left the bridge. "To McNaulty. Tell them to meet us on Bone with all their people and gear. We'll provide transport out. That's a priority data too, and if you can convince the clerk to fudge the station of origin, do it."

"Is he going to still be with us?" Yolanda jerked a thumb at the direction of the door. Moire knew who she meant, and sighed. "We'll figure that out when we get there."

※

"I'm about ready to go out," Lorai said into her commlink. "I'll let you know if I find anything."

"Good luck," Palmer said. The signal was lousy. "Get moving."

Lorai closed the inner door of the airlock, wedged herself carefully around, and unsealed the heavy, clear hood of her shipsuit. She almost pressed the activator nub before she realized she hadn't attached the cable. Once it was firmly connected to her and the ship, she took a deep breath, sealed the hood, and opened the outer door.

Only when she'd carefully stepped out did she start the oxygen capsule going. Her hood was stiff now in vacuum. One quick glance to get her bearings, then she crouched huddled under her protective sheet of plastic, carefully skimming over the station surface. There was just enough residual gravity that she could get traction if she didn't push too hard or too fast, but it was difficult to remember that when all she wanted to do was haul back on the cable and get inside.

They'd figured any survivors would be in the section below. The only way to get there now was by going outside, and there were millions of shards of sharp metal debris–hence the sheet of plastic she was hauling to cover her back.

She reached the hatch sooner than she expected. It opened slowly when she worked the controls, and only cracked the seal. It had to be running on emergency power, then. Not a good sign. She'd used up ten minutes already. Then she realized there was no way to fasten the cable and cycle the airlock. She had to have the cable to get back, but she also had to be able to get inside.

She struggled to remove the piece of plastic without straining her shipsuit, feeling sweat bead on her face and not being able to wipe it off. "I sure hope this works," she muttered to herself, attaching the other end of the cable to the plastic and gently moving it in place, flat against the station hull. She watched for a few seconds, but it didn't budge, and she turned quickly back to the airlock and cycled through. She'd find out if she'd been living right or not when she got out again.

The interior was a shambles. Her hood was relaxed now, meaning there was some kind of pressure, but she didn't feel like taking it off. She had to move fast and look everywhere. Much of the interior had been wrenched away from the bulkheads and was strewn in piles, and a survivor could be under any of them.

Scanning quickly, her eyes wide to catch anything that looked like a body, she saw streaks of something dark on the floor. They ran between a closed emergency pressure door and another, regular door that was blocked by a fallen light array. Her pulse quickened when she saw the tan fabric of a station uniform, but then she saw that the chest was crushed. She glanced quickly at what she could see of the face, but there was nothing she recognized.

Something ahead...something that looked like a plastic tent. She doubted that had been there originally. Using a piece of strut to knock away the sharper pieces of the light array, she scrambled through the door. Another body on the floor, or pieces of it. She swallowed and looked quickly away. She *really* didn't want to get sick in her shipsuit.

There was someone in the tent. Someone moving. She rustled the fabric, and the shadow of an arm reached up and did something that opened a slit. She ducked inside. A man lay surrounded by canisters and other junk. He was filthy. His face was smeared with dust, blood, and some kind of dark oily fluid that also soaked one side of his tan uniform. One leg was bent at an unnatural angle.

He was looking up at her with bloodshot, desperate eyes. His mouth opened, but either her hood obscured the sound or he couldn't speak. Lorai pointed at him, and held up one finger. "Just you? Anybody else?" she shouted.

He pointed to himself, then shook his head. His shipsuit collar was dangling free, and her heart sank. There was no hope of getting a seal. Now what was she going to do? The only way out was through the airlock.

"Dammit, just when you think you've got it all figured out..." She bit her lip and knelt to examine his suit. Even the oxygen assembly had been damaged, so she couldn't use that. There were slashes in the fabric elsewhere, too. First things first. He needed to breathe. That meant oxygen, and something to hold it.

She unsealed the tent and dashed out. The two dead people—their shipsuits weren't usable, even assuming she could get him into a new one, but the oxygen assemblies were still there. One was damaged, but she managed to get the other, grimacing in distaste at the blood and matter still covering it.

He seemed to understand what she was doing when she came back. He had an extruder with a cartridge for sealant tape, and she cut off a chunk of the tent material to make a jury-rigged hood for him. She wasn't sure how they were going to get the sealant tape off of his skin afterward, but that was a minor problem.

She tucked the hood material carefully around the salvaged oxygen assembly, making sure she could reach it to activate it and that the edges of the plastic were completely sealed by tape. As she did she noticed the survivor had a rather prominent nose—almost Roman. This guy was wearing a station uniform, though. Didn't matter now. Harrington must be dead, or had left already. Time to save what she could.

She was starting to pant now. Her oxygen capsule had given out, and she still had to get him out to the hatch. She pulled out her spare capsule and shoved it in the backup slot in her collar, but didn't activate it.

The man had no strength to help her, and he couldn't even stand. She taped his hands together at the wrist and pulled them over her head, wincing at the burden as she stood up. She'd have to be careful not to fall, or they'd both be dead.

Long, too long, to get back to the hatch. Her vision was getting blurry. Inner door shut. She activated her capsule with relief, breathing the oxygen, then twisted and got the survivor's capsule going too. She opened the outer door, searching in a panic for her cable. For a terrifying moment she thought it was gone, but it had just drifted down. She could still reach it.

She bent. Her fingers grasped the plastic, pulled, then found the cable tied to it. Suddenly she was out of the airlock, drifting away, and she felt the man on her back twitch and kick in a futile attempt to grab anything that could save him.

She had the cable. She wrapped it quickly around her wrists so it could not pull loose. It was almost impossible to fight the instinct to pull, pull hard, but if she did it could snap the cable or make it come loose from its connection, with the extra mass now attached to it. She had to pull gently and not strain it, and they had to hope no fragments came their way, either. The shield would not cover them completely.

The cable went taut. Lorai took up the tension in her arms, then gently,

gently started to go hand over hand up the cable. Too slow and they'd both suffocate. Too fast and the cable would come loose. She tried not to think about that. There was nothing she could do if it did. Her commlink wouldn't be any use out here.

They started to drift back toward the station. Shaky with relief, Lorai kept going until she finally made it to the open airlock and was able to shut the door. A station tech was waiting for her when she cycled through.

"He's the only one," Lorai wheezed as soon as she got her hood open. "Let's get him on the ship—he's banged up pretty bad."

She wasn't sure if she could have gotten back without the tech's help, because she felt like nine days of misery. It took all her concentration to walk forward. The man was coughing now; deep, racking coughs.

Palmer was pacing in front of the ship hatch. As soon as he saw them he started shouting. "Come on, everything's loaded! Let's get the hell out of here!"

They stumbled in. Palmer dogged the hatch and sprinted for the bridge. Lorai and the tech dragged the wounded man through the corridors crowded with people and supplies, finally dumping him on top of a crate. He moaned when they moved his broken leg, trying to say something that was drowned out by coughing.

"Here's some water. Somebody's getting the medkit."

Lorai took the drink bulb and held it to the man's mouth. He drank greedily, draining it. He sighed.

The tech tried to wipe off some of the oily fluid from the man's face, but it didn't help. "What's your name?"

The man wheezed, coughed, then tried again. "Harrington."

CHAPTER 15
BECOMING HUMAN

Harrington stifled a groan as he shifted in his bunk. The next time—assuming there was a next time—he'd make sure to bring his own supply of pain medication. Between broken bones and bruises there was no comfortable position to sleep in, so he didn't. They didn't have enough meds on board even for the critically injured. He would simply have to develop a stoic mentality.

He'd been damned lucky, at that. There had been moments, trapped in the wreckage, when he'd wondered if he'd survive.

The door slid open, and his rescuer stepped in. He frowned in an effort of thought, trying to figure out why he felt a twinge of recognition.

"How ya doin'?" she inquired. Harrington firmly squelched an unworthy spurt of resentment at her cheery tone.

"Nothing has fallen off, so we continue to hope." He coughed and winced at the fresh twinges of pain. "Please tell me you've discovered a crate of medical supplies hidden in a corner."

She shook her head. "Sorry. But if you wanna build yourself a new leg, we got lots of mini-servos and some titanium rod." She sat down on the pile of padding that served as her bed and slumped against the wall. "Wish we had that crate, though. Lost another one. Woman who told us you were still back there—she was just burned too bad to last."

Harrington closed his eyes. "I regret I did not have the opportunity to thank her for saving my life. I did thank you, did I not? I can't remember. I'm Neville Harrington, by the way."

"Yeah, I know." She grinned. "Lorai Grimaldi. We met on Bone."

Of course. That was why she looked so familiar. He would not have thought she would be so glad to see him. "What a remarkable coincidence. The Fringe can seem quite small sometimes."

"Coincidence nothing. I was looking for you."

Damnation, his head hurt. "A fortunate circumstance, since otherwise I would still be on that station trying to perform illicit chemical reactions for oxygen."

Grimaldi gave him a look. "Before I got to Criminy, idiot. I heard there was a reporter staying on a shot-to-hell station and thought it might be you, so I got a berth on this ship. What were you doing in a station uniform, huh?"

Harrington winced again, from embarrassment. "I switched places—I thought temporarily–with a legitimate station worker for journalistic purposes."

"Nosing around, most people call it," Grimaldi commented.

"Very likely. In any event, the individual took advantage of his new appearance to escape on one of the civilian rescue ships, and by the time I, too, wished to leave, I was not permitted. There was nothing for it but to make the best of a bad situation." He coughed again, unable to stop. Grimaldi handed him a drink bulb, which helped. She was looking amused, and he supposed he could not blame her. "May I ask why you were looking for me in the middle of a war zone?"

"Remember when you were on Bone? Somebody with you?"

Harrington nodded, starting to worry. Had something happened to Ennis? He hadn't heard from him after he'd received a brief message indicating Ennis had arrived safely at his new post.

Grimaldi got up, opened the door to the tiny cabin, and looked up and down the corridor before closing it and sitting down again. Completely mystified, Harrington watched her take out a datatab folder from an inside pocket of her jacket. "You gotta be careful with this, OK? Seems to be one of those swallow-if-captured deals, to hear him talk about it."

"How intriguing. I have to ask–why are you helping Commander En–"

Her hand covered his mouth in a flash. "Shh!" She took her hand away. "Don't say his name, OK?"

He nodded, mystified. "As I was saying–I was under the impression that you were not terribly fond of either of us, so why are you helping our, er, mutual acquaintance?"

She shrugged. "Things have changed. Besides, Ren asked me to."

"Ren?"

"Ren Roberts. You know, person both of you were looking for?"

Harrington hesitated. "You are aware that is not her real name."

Grimaldi looked at him for a long moment. "So? She's probably got her reasons."

"And you will forgive my abominable curiosity, but why can't I say his name?"

She leaned closer again. "If he didn't put the details in that file, look in any cheap circular. Somebody's got a big reward with his name on it, sayin' he's a repeat murderer."

This was not good. What had Ennis gotten himself into now?

"Sure hope he doesn't need you for any heavy lifting, 'cause you need some repair work," she said, looking him over dispassionately.

"I'm in complete agreement," Harrington said. "Perhaps I should see what he has to say."

"Right." Lorai got to her feet, stretching with a groan. "Gotta get back to the others." She left, locking the door behind her.

Harrington pulled out the cheap little datapad he had used in his undercover persona, mourning the loss of his larger, custom-made model. Still, the cheap one had survived all his latest adventures in working order.

The first datatab was a shock. All vid stills, hundreds of them, which he tabbed through faster and faster as he realized what he was seeing. A crab ship. A huge crab ship, and yet there were suited human figures present at what appeared to be some sort of entrance. Where had Ennis found it? Had he gotten inside? Who were the people with him?

In his excitement he tried to sit up, but his injuries made themselves felt and he fell back with a groan. He had to find a medic as soon as the ship docked. This was too big to miss. What was in the other tabs? Harrington quickly switched the first one out. More stills, but this time on the surface of a planet he didn't recognize. He did recognize the woman in one of them, though. Moire Cameron, without a suit or helmet, shading her eyes from the sunlight while behind her was a view of water and green islands in the distance. The implications made his head hurt even more.

The last tab had some files and a recorded message from Ennis. He looked thinner than when Harrington had last seen him, and his uniform was the worse for wear. "I hope you got this, because I need your help. You've seen the stills–that's only the beginning." He never mentioned Toren by name, but implied they were behind the murder charges and reward. Harrington replayed the message, disturbed by Ennis's appearance and expression. He looked like he'd been through hell.

One file had instructions for contacting him by putting a certain ad in a circular. Harrington was then to show up on Kulvar three weeks after placing the ad.

That was good. He should be able to find enough medical attention to be fit and ready for the dangers of Kulvar by then. He'd send the ad in as soon as they docked. How he was going to survive the suspense until his questions were answered was another matter entirely.

Ennis walked quickly through the ship, glancing at the status readouts on the hold doors. All locked, so they couldn't be there. The holds were crammed with gear now, and Gren Forrest had expressed himself quite strongly on the subject of the Created clambering all over his crates of sensitive components. Keeping them occupied and out of trouble was Ennis's semi-official duty on *Raven*, and he hadn't seen them for a while. That was usually a sign of trouble.

He reached the door of Radersent's hold and opened it. The Created were all there, and he felt himself relax. They were always eager to spend time with the crab. They seemed to be trying to explain something using Alan's picture dictionary.

Seeing they were occupied for a while, he left. He needed to come up with something more for them, though. They had to learn how to interact with humans, too, especially if Moire was going to be spending any amount of time on Kulvar. Sooner or later they would lose their fear and find their way off the ship. The Created were almost as ignorant of the criminal underworld as Moire and much less quick to pick up hints.

Maybe she'd like to help out. Ennis went back through the ship, looking for her. It seemed strangely quiet. He frowned, glancing in the galley. There should be at least one or two of the off-duty crew there at this time; usually more. It was empty. Then he saw the meeting room beyond it appeared to be occupied.

He went in. It was crowded with excited, talking crewmembers, gathered before the long wall in back of the room. Sheets of hardcopy had been fastened up, covering a large section of it. When he was able to get close enough, he saw it was a printout of a topo scan of Sequoyah, with many of the islands and geographical features now labeled by hand with a fine-tipped paintpen that was being passed around.

"I got mine," Kwife Ivers, the assistant engineer, said with a grin. With neat, even lettering, he wrote "Bessel" next to a strange, symmetrically shaped island. "Looks just like a first order function, doesn't it?"

"I'll take your word for it," someone else said, snatching the pen. "Hey, looks like the first shift got the good ones. Who picked 'Game Place'? What's that?"

"Kids did that one." Menehune was watching, one shoulder against the wall. "It's where we dumped them to keep them out of trouble, remember?" She looked up and saw Ennis. "Hey, Commander. Picked what you're gonna name?"

"What's going on?" he asked, delaying a direct answer. He was an outsider here, too, even though nobody drew attention to it now.

"Captain decided we needed some names, and everybody gets to pick one. She did these." Menehune tapped the sheets of printout, and Ennis recognized the main island with the cave. The island was named D'accord and the cave was New Houston.

Menehune held out the paintpen to Ennis. He looked at it for a moment, then shook his head. "I think she intended for the crew to have the honor." It was a temptation, though. He could name something on a planet and it would stay, at least for a little while.

Menehune gave him a look of exasperation. "So? Not like there ain't enough to go 'round. Besides, you been working like crew."

"Yeah, go ahead, Commander. Nobody's even started on the northern islands yet," Ivers said with a friendly grin.

Ennis glanced around and only saw encouragement, but he still hesitated.

"Captain! Commander Ennis can name something, right?"

Ennis turned sharply. Moire Cameron was standing in the doorway, glancing around at the people and the wall of printout with a look of satisfaction.

"Of course he can." She nodded. "Good work, people. You even left some for the folks dirtside, when we get back there."

Ennis took the paintpen and turned back to the map, overwhelmed by the possibilities. The larger islands had already been named, and despite the hospitality of the crew he didn't want to risk resentment by picking anything major.

He looked more closely at the area around D'accord. It took him a moment to orient himself—if the cave was there, and the bay of giant trees *there*—then the cliff top had faced southwest. And there was the group of three small islands he had seen, with a fourth hidden in their midst. He wrote "Shangri-La" carefully to one side of the hidden island.

Moire was standing nearby, watching him.

"What brought this on?" Ennis asked.

"I got tired of saying that-place-over-there, you know? And it gives them something to do. Not much for the crew until we get back to the sargasso."

"It's a good idea." He handed the paintpen to the next person and stepped back. She'd made them all believe in Sequoyah, even him. Everybody on the ship was willing to fight for it. And everybody on the ship thought he was a part of it, just like they were. One of them.

They believed in her, but did they see the haunted look in her eyes? Did they know what she was thinking of, that she'd agreed to go back for trial? If they did, would they be so welcoming to him?

It didn't matter. He couldn't stay anyway. "When are we going back to Kulvar?"

Moire shrugged. "We'll get them started on the tow ship. Probably leave after a week or so, see if we need to get any additional supplies. Gren should have the plan all ready by now. I was looking for him when I came in here. Have you seen him?"

"No. Did you look in—"

He heard voices in the corridor, one that he recognized as Gren's. Gren stuck his head in, his shaggy eyebrows going up when he saw Moire.

"There you are. Did you know the commlink says you're off-ship?"

Her eyes widened, and she glanced down at the control bracelet on her wrist. "It must be that damn earring again. I'm going to have to carry a regular commlink instead. Do you have the plans?"

She went out the door with Gren.

"Why doesn't she replace it if it doesn't work anymore?" Ennis wondered.

Menehune snorted. "'Cause she's too busy getting stuff for the ship, or educational chi-cha for the kids, or medical supplies. If she ever gets reimbursed from the general ship fund *I* never seen it, and I do the books when Felden ain't here."

"She gave a fellow mercenary nearly everything she had, and she didn't even tell him she'd done it," Ennis said, remembering. "Sounds like she's doing it again."

Menehune put her hands on her hips and stuck out her chin. "Yeah, so we do it right back. Random, gites. Tell your watchmates, get me a list. Back on Kulvar we go shopping for the captain and nobody says a word, right?" She gave a challenging look around the assembled crew.

"Yeshure," Ennis said. Menehune grinned.

It had taken him time to find the information he could use; time and caution. Kolpe had begun to wonder if he had been mistaken in waiting, but then suddenly activity began to pick up at the construction firm. Workers were making arrangements, releasing housing, and stopping services. Members of the firm made repeated and frequent visits to the dock section.

Taking a calculated risk, he penetrated the records of the ship they had visited most often, a big freighter. It confirmed all his suspicions. The ship had been hired to take almost all the employees of the McNaulty construction company, and gear, to a Fringe planet named Bone.

He read over the shipping instructions for the equipment, frowning in puzzlement. The large-bore tunnel excavators he expected; those were used extensively in moon or asteroid site construction. But if the LBXs were there, why was there only one wall sealer? Why bore tunnels if they couldn't be pressurized?

It was possible his target had hired another construction firm elsewhere and they were bringing the sealers. It was not completely impossible that she had found her own, but he discarded the idea as soon as it occurred to him. Sealers were rare, expensive, and more importantly, only made in Inner Systems locations. He doubted very much that Cameron would have taken the risk to acquire something the firm already owned.

Cameron had been on Bone before. Kolpe had extensive data on the planet, including a recent hand-compiled map of settlements and stations. There had been something curious about the planet, he remembered. He read through his notes. Life forms. *Atmosphere.* Not quite enough to be truly Earthlike, but enough to make a suit unnecessary. Or tunnel sealers.

He wondered what she was planning. A base of operations, perhaps. That was the one piece of information Toren refused to give him—*why* they wanted her brought in. If she was planning to construct a base on Bone, she might be able to do it in secret. His information indicated planetary security was sparse, and mostly occupied with gun battles between various flavors of armed action committees. No controlled access points to the planet, like an orbital station. If she had a surface ship she could land anywhere on the planet.

There was very little tech infrastructure on Bone, which greatly hampered his effectiveness. He would have to deal with people, and with such a small population strangers would be noticed no matter what he did to disguise himself.

He thought, staring at his datapad's screen. He was absolutely certain that Moire Cameron would be on Bone to meet the construction people. If they were building something for her there, she would insist on it. Even if they were going somewhere else, information would be there. He had to get it, and he couldn't do it alone.

Very well. He had access to a vast amount of resources. Toren would send him anything he asked for if he told them Cameron would be there.

Moire scooted closer to the edge of the top bunk to watch the action below. Alan was definitely the best of them, but then he'd been out and interacting with real people longer. Still, George was not far behind, and the rest were learning fast.

"Let's try it again. This time you are by yourself. Ash, you go first." Ennis straightened and folded his arms, assuming his guard persona. Moire grinned. He was having far too much fun with the game playing.

The others whispered encouragement and hints to the reluctant Ash. She swallowed and did her best to hide her trepidation under a cold, stolid front. It was surprisingly effective, when she could hold it.

"Let me in," she demanded, and gulped.

Ennis looked down his nose at her. "Why should I, gita?"

Ash froze, her eyes wide.

"Ask him why not." Moire said. She was allowed to make suggestions, as long as they didn't look to her first.

"Why not?"

"I don't see nothin' for me," Ennis replied.

Ash glanced out of the corner of her eye at the top bunk, but Moire remained silent. Ash tilted her head, silent for a moment. "You could get in trouble if you don't," she said finally.

George cheered, then quickly covered his mouth with both hands as Alan and Hideo shushed him, horrified. Moire struggled to keep a straight face. It was a good reply, and even better, Ash had thought of it herself.

Ennis caught her eye, saw her amusement, and winked. He unfolded his arms, indicating the scenario was over. "Not bad, Ash. Remember not to show what you are thinking when—"

Moire's commlink chirped, and she picked it up from the bunk. "Yeah?"

"Captain. We are ten minutes from dropout."

"Close dropout?"

"Yes." She thought she could hear the sigh in Kilberton's voice. He didn't like it, but only the legit travelers to Kulvar–all three of them–ever dropped out at the regulation safe distance. The rest had too many enemies or too little trust to wander around in realspace that long, vulnerable to attack. If they were pretending to be Downunder players they had to act like it.

"We should be docked in less than half an hour," Moire told the others watching her, jumping down from the bunk. She looked at the commlink, grimaced, and put it back in her pocket. "I've got to get a replacement for that damn earring when we're there, too."

"But..."

Moire turned to look at Hideo, who had suddenly gone silent. She'd caught a glimpse of a fierce scowl on George, which might have something to do with it. Something was going on; the kids had been acting strangely ever since they'd left the sargasso. Maybe she should have made them stay there. No, the repair crew would have spent all their time keeping them out of trouble, and they had enough to do already. She'd just have to watch them carefully. What had she been getting into when she was their age? There was an incident with an unsanctioned pet frog, and redecorating the walls of her room with toothpaste, and...

"We'll go with you!" George said happily. "We know all about Outside now."

Moire was sure the stunned expression on Ennis's face mirrored her own. "Uh. Um, maybe you should get some more practice first?"

This unleashed a storm of protest from the Created, who indicated they had practiced more than enough. Moire ducked out of their cabin with mumbled excuses, heading in the direction of the bridge. Ennis was soon walking beside her. She was glad, as she was any time she could be with him without an audience. Then she saw his shoulders shaking and his eyes bright with amusement, and she narrowed her eyes.

"You've created a monster," she commented.

"You were the one who said keep them out of trouble."

She stopped and glared at him, hands on her hips. "Did that sound like staying out of trouble to you? Now they want to go and find it!"

Ennis held up his hands. "I know. Look, it might not be such a bad idea. They have to try it sometime. If you can dock in the safer area they can probably handle a quick trip."

Moire closed her eyes, taking a deep breath and trying to calm down. "It's not a good time."

Gentle fingertips stroked her face. "It's never a good time," Ennis said quietly. "This is their world. War without and enemies within." Something in his voice made her snap her eyes open. "I was only a few years older than they were when…Penderhest took me everywhere, even the worst places, because I had to know. If anything happened to him…I had to know how to survive."

He looked so bleak, his eyes full of memories. Moire held his face against hers, trying to warm away the remembered cold and fear. "You survived," she whispered. "It's OK, you got out…"

The itchy-bone feeling of the dropout washed through her. She had to dock, she had to plan, and why did this always happen just when they were getting comfortable? She stood back, and Ennis reluctantly let go. "Let's see what Yolanda says."

Yolanda thought it was a good idea. Moire got the impression she included Moire in the category of people needing practice, and the truth of it irritated her. It was also true they could contact the ship agent by comm when docked, and all the items Gren had asked them to get were routine, nonspecialized components they could simply have shipped to their holds. If Harrington's message showed up, they would have to get a passkey to the lower levels, but for everything else they could dock on Three. Moire just nodded without looking at them when they asked her.

Ennis left the bridge to get the Created. Slumped in the observation chair, Moire watched him leave, reflected in a display screen. When he walked by Yolanda he handed her something with a slight twitch of his hand, which she promptly pocketed in a smooth gesture while glancing Moire's direction. So it wasn't just the kids having some kind of secret plan. At least it wasn't something she had to worry about, if Yolanda and Alan and the rest of them were part of it. She hoped.

When she could forget how young the Created were, she had to admit they looked professional. Their bulk-bought clothing gave a uniformlike impression, and with the ship patches the effect was complete. As they went through the common areas of Kulvar's third level she watched them as carefully as she could without being obvious about it, and she knew Ennis and Menehune were doing the same. It was an effort for the kids not to stare at all the new things, but they did a good job. Maybe Ennis and Menehune had been right, after all.

She had Alan buy the circulars. Ennis scanned them as they walked on. The tiny crease at the corner of his eye deepened, then disappeared when he tucked the textsheets in his pocket. He glanced at Moire and shook his head, and she felt a surge of guilty relief. No word from Harrington. Not yet.

"Think you can handle things from here?" Yolanda stopped at the entrance to their dock row. "Got some errands to run, since it's quiet."

Moire glanced down the row. It looked safe and empty. "You have your commlink, right? Do you need to go far?"

"Nah, this ain't heavy load, don't have to go down." Yolanda patted her pockets, then pulled out the commlink and showed it to her. "Won't be long."

"OK, just be careful." Moire tried not to wonder about Menehune's errands. They depended heavily on her criminal information, and it was only fair they let her profit from it. Even if Moire wished she wouldn't.

She caught a flash of movement from the Created, and once again had the feeling she had just missed some silent communication. They seemed happy and excited, but maybe that was just the result of getting to go outside. Moire pulled out her own commlink.

"Hey, *Raven*."

"Yes, Captain?" Kilberton answered.

"Tell Pico to watch for us, OK? We're almost there."

A pause, then, "He is ready. He says no one has come by the hatch since you left."

"Good." Moire glanced along the row, observing the hatches on both sides. They weren't the only ship docked here; at least three other hatch lights were green. Shouldn't there have been other people around, or had Pico not been paying attention?

Raven's hatch opened and Pico's round, cheerful face peeked out. "Saw ya! So where'd Menehune get to?"

The first sound Moire heard was another hatch opening. She glanced over and saw movement on the other side of the row, toward the end. She looked away and heard a shot, followed by others that whined past them or flashed on the decking. Pico made a sound between a scream and a groan and slumped against the open door.

She had a gun. She had to use it, or they would die. People were pouring out of the end hatch now, all armed. She fired wildly, hoping to at least ruin their aim.

One of the attackers shouted, "Get the door!"

They were after the ship. Pico was holding the hatch door open, too badly injured to get inside, and they couldn't get to him. Pico must have heard with his last few seconds of consciousness, for he scrabbled with bloody hands until he had moved away enough for the automatic closure to take over.

Moire continued firing while they retreated until the door had shut. Alan was yelling hoarsely for her to run away, and she did. Out of the row, then where? Too much open space...

Beside her, Ash cried out and stumbled. Moire caught her arm and nearly stumbled herself when she was pulled off balance, but then Ennis was on the other side and they were all dashing for a narrow, dead-end hallway with doorways just indented enough to provide minimal cover.

The shooting had died away, and she felt a sudden spurt of fear. They were at the hatch, she just knew it. "Kilberton," she gasped into the comm.

"Kilberton, are you there?"

"Captain! What is—"

"Undock the ship. Get to departure range and get a lineup set, got that?"

"I can't leave you there!"

"Yes you can, and you will if you don't hear from me in three hours. Leave immediately if anybody comes after you. Remember the folks back home, dammit! Now get the hell away from this station!"

She didn't want to even hint about Radersent, but she knew he'd figure it out. And they really couldn't risk both pilots who knew the route to Sequoyah being captured.

"Yes, Captain! Undocking now..."

If she squinted, she could see *Raven*'s hatch, which did seem to have a number of people around it. She saw the light change from green to red with relief, then turned her attention to the people around her.

Ash was huddled in the corner of a doorway, her face contorted with pain and the effort to remain silent. Moire could see blood darkening the side of her leg. George was beside her. Hideo was sharing Moire's doorway, and Ennis and Alan were on opposite sides of the entrance.

Ennis glanced back. "We have a problem," he whispered. Moire rolled her eyes, and he shook his head sharply. "Ammunition."

Moire checked her magazine. It was empty. Hideo held up two fingers. Ash didn't even have her gun anymore. George had four left. A pity she hadn't planned for a firefight when they left the ship, and brought more ammo. At the time she was thinking of minimizing any damage the Created might do by accident. In addition, they had only handguns—again, for a lower profile. They couldn't even hit the bad guys unless they were obliging enough to come closer.

Time to yell for help. She should have told Kilberton...told him what? Call the cops? Everybody on Kulvar was bought, one way or the other. She didn't even know who they'd been attacked by, except she doubted it was Toren this time. She punched in Yolanda's comm code. The commlink searched, then stopped. She punched it in again, swearing.

"Ship isn't in the station network," Ennis said softly. "Kilberton might be able to send to you, but you can't get another commlink signal now."

"Terrific." She thought for a moment. "Assuming we survive and get out of this, how do we tell Kilberton?"

"Station signal. Somebody will have access, if we have money." Ennis stiffened, backing up just enough to stay out of sight. "They're coming this way."

He fired a single shot, then pointed at Alan. Alan took aim, going completely motionless before firing. His shot was followed by a cry from the row.

It seemed like hours. Moire heard their single shots, desperately trying to think of a way out as she cobbled a makeshift bandage for Ash's leg. The doors in the hallway were locked, and from the looks of things weren't even worth a bullet to open. She might do that if they had nothing else to try. If they waited long enough, would Yolanda come back, figure out something was wrong, and get help?

"Company," Ennis said suddenly, leaning back against the wall and wiping sweat from his face with his sleeve.

"Whose side are they on?" Moire asked.

"Not sure. Enemy doesn't look pleased to see them; they're moving back."

Moire darted across the hallway to stand next to him. Their attackers were not visible; still taking cover. The group Ennis was indicating were openly and heavily armed, and looked like they would be quite at home in the lower levels. Now a a third group was arriving, wearing uniforms. Station police. The first group of hardbodies eyed the station police with contemptuous amusement and walked up to them without fear. The two new groups were talking, but Moire couldn't make out what was being said. The station police left, slowly at first, but then with speed.

She glanced at Ennis's face, and it told her enough to realize they might be in even more danger now. "What do you think is going on?"

"Territory fight. Look out, they see us. Hold your fire!" This to Alan, who was ready to start shooting again. Moire nodded at him, and he looked at her uncertainly.

A handful of the heavily armed arrivals were now standing about the hallway entrance while the rest rounded up the attackers that were still alive. The goons that had attacked her ship were soon standing in the corridor with their hands in the air, looking desperate.

"You guys wanna tell us stories too?" said one of the toughs in charge, a lanky, youthful-looking man with dark skin and strange bodymods that pulled his skin into ridges and points.

"They attacked us," Moire said tightly. "No reason."

"Sure." He smiled and revealed pointed teeth. "Who needs a reason?"

Maybe she could shoot him and take his weapon. No, the others were too watchful.

"Let's go visitin'," the lanky man said, gesturing with his weapon. "Zandovar wants ta talk to ya."

There wasn't any choice. They had five rounds left between them. They walked carefully out of the hallway, hands raised.

CHAPTER 16
BLOOD PRICE

The new arrivals hadn't shot them yet. That was one positive sign, and Ennis tried desperately to think of others. Moire appeared to be unharmed. Hideo had taken a hit, but not a serious one. Ash was a problem.

"Drop the poppers," the leader said. His crew had their weapons trained on them and their attackers. Ennis slowly lowered his gun hand and tossed the weapon forward. Everybody else did the same, except Alan.

"You too, gito." Moire twitched a glance at her son, her eyes going wide with fear.

"Do it," she said shortly.

Alan's face went hard. "But they—"

"*Do it!*" Moire yelled. "That's an order!"

Alan flung the gun away, giving her a hurt and resentful look.

The leader grinned his sharp-toothed grin. At his signal his crew surrounded everybody involved in the fighting.

If he started thinking about what could happen, he'd be paralyzed by fear. He hoped the Created would remember what he and Menehune had drilled them on. This was a shakedown trial that hadn't been planned, but they were doing well.

Better than they should. Ash and Hideo should have been crying and frantic with pain—they hadn't had any experience with this kind of thing. A cold wave washed over him as he remembered some things Moire had told him. Perhaps they did have experience. They hadn't always been with people who tried to protect them.

Ash was stumbling between George and Hideo, who were half-carrying her between them. She looked bad.

"Will you let us do something for her?" Moire asked the leader, who looked Ash over with indifference.

"She'll last long enough," he said. Moire started to protest, and he snarled at her.

Last long enough for what? Memories of Fimbul came crowding back painfully. It wouldn't matter if these people knew the Created were children, either. Ennis looked away, fighting to keep his face from revealing anything. The first rule was never show fear.

The second rule was don't get involved. As they went through the corridors people they met turned away, vanished, or looked right through them as if nothing was there. Except one: a thin, silver-haired man inside a communications office who stared as they went by.

Ennis closed his eyes briefly, fear and hope and frustrated disappointment rushing through him in quick succession. Harrington. But there hadn't been any message in the circulars!

"Hold up," one of the toughs said. They had reached the area with the dropdowns. They couldn't all fit in the dropdown at the same time, so they went down in two groups.

Moire took advantage of the crosstalk involved in figuring this out to whisper, "What's wrong?"

He shook his head without saying anything, seeing the eye of the leader on them. The guards at the entrance to the fourth level stood aside as soon as they saw the leader. Inside was much as he expected, except for the occasional patches of black and pockmarks on the walls that told him just how nasty the change of power had been.

Then they were being herded into another bank of dropdowns. Moire lifted an eyebrow at him and he shook his head minutely, feeling even more worried. She had the same intent, focused look he'd seen on the salvage ship when they thought the crabs were invading, and her face was pale—too pale. She was terrified.

Fifth level was like nothing he'd ever seen. Fimbul had been violent, crude, and dangerous, but in a chaotic, survivalist way. This was all the sick, twisted things he'd ever heard of or seen, done because someone could make money from it.

He heard a stifled gasp from Moire when they passed a wall of clear, narrow, vertical boxes, each with a briefly clad man or woman inside. Flashing text scrolled over the surfaces, listing skills and vital statistics. Without needing to speak, they both shifted and nudged the Created between them, keeping them in the center of the group.

At first he thought the moaning was coming from Ash, but it didn't sound like pain. Then he saw the source, up ahead at the corner of a cross-corridor. A naked man hanging from a suspension harness, his skin painted with something pearlescent, strings of jewel-like decorations tied about his body.

He saw Alan glance up, his mouth trembling. "Don't look!" Ennis whispered harshly. He kept his eyes focused straight ahead, locked on the back of the tough walking ahead of him, but the writhing, contorted limbs were still on the edge of his vision. He could smell blood as they passed by; the man was going to die soon, die of ecstatic pleasure. It looked like he'd been overdosed with allacome, probably to serve as an advertisement for a sexshow.

When they stopped before a large, dark doorway it was almost a relief.

The leader spoke briefly at a wall comm, then went inside. A moment later he came back and gestured for them to follow.

The interior atrium was spotless and covered in dynamic film, even the floors, which gently pulsed and flowed with shaded color. He'd never seen it before, only heard of it. It was supposed to be very expensive. Across from the entry, a delicate porcelain vase stood on a polished wooden table. More money, and access to markets on Earth.

"Jonders. I understand you have found something that requires my attention." The voice was rich and smooth. Ennis turned his head slightly, saw the leader of the toughs step forward with a very different manner to stand before a man who looked completely out of place.

The ceeyo of Kulvar was tall, slender in an athletic way, and dressed like an Inner Systems business executive in full trousers of dark bronze silk and a long vest over a tight metallic top. The rich brown-and-gold brocade of the vest wasn't regulation business, nor the large, openly armed bodyguards. He had a finely chiseled brown face outlined by a narrow, carefully trimmed beard, and his dark eyes were looking them over without any evidence of interest.

The head tough cleared his throat. "Cordoba wants to know we doing action on three, says what 'bout this deal, hah? So I go, find these guys tossin' pops up there. Cordoba showed up too, but I said we gonna fix it and he left. He ain't happy, though."

"Cordoba's unhappiness will be temporary," Zandovar said in an absent manner, still looking them over. His gaze sharpened, and the ends of his mouth twitched slightly upward. "Merlliot. Why have you not come to see me earlier?" His voice had gone even softer, and Ennis felt his stomach tighten. Zandovar wouldn't have his people shoot them here; too much risk of damaging his expensive decor. Somebody was going to die soon, though. He was sure of it.

"Didn't think you'd want me down here." Merlliot was one of the attackers, and he looked nervous but not desperate. "Since I worked for Olvey, 'n all."

"I used to work for Olvey," Zandovar said gently. "So did Jonders, and many others. It is not a permanent condition." A long silence deepened. "Perhaps you can give me an explanation for why the station enforcers felt the need to leave their comfortable offices. Why my explicit commands were ignored."

"She gets it going soon as she sees us!" Merlliot said, pointing at Moire. "We didn't say nothin'!"

Zandovar thought for a moment, chin in hand, then turned a polite, inquiring gaze to Moire.

"They shot and killed one of my crew as he opened our hatch," she said in a tight, controlled voice. "We returned fire in self-defense."

A more military than criminal description of events, but that shouldn't be a problem. However, the more she talked the more Zandovar would know she wasn't fluent in the language of the underworld, and that would create a whole different set of problems.

"I have said the third level is to be kept quiet. Too much violence disturbs our...special equilibrium with the upper levels. I have said that *all* who break this rule will be punished."

Ennis tensed, frustration building as he desperately tried to think of a way out. He could see none.

Zandovar gestured. "However. This is a special situation, is it not, Merlliot? This is not the first time you have tried to rob a ship there. Work has been hard to find, hasn't it? Thought you could make Third your own? I've been looking for you." He smiled, showing white teeth. "Did you think I did not know?" he whispered.

Merlliot was sweating now, and one of his gang made a sudden dart for the door, only to be brought up short. A series of brief, unpleasant noises came from the knot of people around him. When they moved away he was lying on the floor, coughing up blood.

Zandovar made a grimace of distaste. "A waste of effort, and you've made a mess. Take them to see the view."

"No! No, it was them, they did it! They–" Merlliot yelled desperately as he was dragged out along with his gang. The door shut with a soft click, and Ennis heard nothing more.

A little better, but they still weren't out of it yet. What did Zandovar want? How could they negotiate with him? He was too hard to read, and Ennis hadn't heard much about him. Yolanda...did she know where they were? What could she do if she did?

"Which of you is in charge?" Zandovar asked, hands behind his back. Before Ennis could take the chance to deflect attention from Moire, Jonders pointed at her.

"She give orders, and they do it."

"Thank you. Is that true?"

Moire nodded, her jaw working. "If you're worried about a mess, she's bleeding all over your floor because those guys shot her," she said jerkily, indicating Ash. "Jonders was in too much of a hurry to let us fix her up. Can we at least get some bloodglue?"

Ennis tried to keep breathing. It might work, but it was a risk. He could see no hint of what Zandovar was thinking in his dark, cold eyes.

"I have not met you before, I think. What is your name?"

Moire gave him back stare for stare. "Ren Roberts. I've done business on Kulvar before."

He tilted his head slightly to one side. "And that business is...."

"I sell ships. Salvaged ships."

In the background an androgynous individual with long white hair, apparently an assistant, tapped at a datapad. After a brief moment, the assistant showed the datapad to Zandovar.

"I see. You have been very fortunate in finding these salvage ships, it appears. It does not take you long."

Moire smiled tightly. "No. It doesn't."

Zandovar looked at her for a moment, then glanced at Ennis. His eyes narrowed slightly.

"Jonders. Have them bring medical supplies to the greenhouse, and refreshment. Come, you will find this interesting."

Flanked by several armed guards, Zandovar led them along a side corridor and down a ramp. Metal doors in a flowing, ornate design opened to a large, high-ceilinged room with plants in containers and growing along the open beams. The air was damp and warm, and it smelled...it smelled like Sequoyah did. Alive.

"A garden." Alan said softly, looking about in wonder. His face lost some of the angry, sullen look.

"Is it secret?" George asked. Moire and Ennis both shushed them. Neither had spoken loudly, and Ennis hoped nobody had noticed. Ash was barely conscious, her head hanging down and her feet dragging as they carried her.

The greenhouse had cast metal benches along the sides, and they laid Ash down on one. Moire stripped off her jacket and put it under her head as Ennis tried to see how bad the injury was.

"I think the bullet is still in there," he said finally. "She needs a medic." One of Zandovar's guards came up and handed him a standard medical kit. He rifled through it, pulling out a packet of bloodglue, a fluid pack, and some painkillers.

Moire knelt down beside him, next to the bench. "What does he want?" she whispered, reaching for the bloodglue and cracking the packet open.

"Can't tell. I don't think he's planning to kill us." He didn't tell her that had him even more worried. There was no good reason for the main crime lord of Kulvar to give some unknown ship captain and her crew a tour of his home–he wanted something from her.

Ennis tore the leg of Ash's pants where the wound was, and Moire dabbed at the caked blood with a swab before squeezing the bloodglue in. The painkillers were already starting to take effect, and Ash had drifted off.

"When you are finished, come and join me," Zandovar said, seated at a wrought metal table in the center of the greenhouse.

"You do the talking," Moire whispered.

"I can't. He knows you're in charge, it will make him suspicious."

"What do I say?" She sounded on the verge of panic.

He briefly covered her hand with his own, under the guise of attaching the fluid pack. "He's motivated only by power and profit. Pretend you are too."

"Right." Moire nodded sharply, looking grim and determined, and stood up. She pointed at Alan, George, and Hideo. "You stay here with Ash. Don't talk."

Ennis followed her to the table. Moire took the chair opposite Zandovar and Ennis stood behind her and to one side, in his character of subordinate. On a large plate in the center of the table were several angular, crispy-brown objects. Smaller plates were before each chair.

"Merlliot was one of the last remaining toolers of the previous ceeyo," Zandovar said casually. "I knew he was trying something; I also knew someone was robbing ships without my permission. Until now I was not able to find him in the act. I appreciate your assistance in removing this final obstacle." He gestured at the plate. "Please, try one."

Moire leaned stiffly forward and took one of the strange, triangular things. She took a bite. "Interesting," she said, when a raised eyebrow seemed to make an inquiry.

"And this means..."

She licked her lips. "I've, ah, never had wings with that type of seasoning. It's good."

Wings?

Ennis thought he saw a flash of a bemused expression in Zandovar's face, and broke into a sweat. She took several more bites, then put the rest back on the small plate in front of her. Now it looked like a framework of rods. Bones. They were eating bone meat. Why wasn't she finishing it? Zandovar might be offended at the waste.

Before he could think of a way to warn her, the ceeyo spoke. "I wonder that I have not heard of you before," Zandovar said, sitting back after selecting one of the delicacies. "Given your...aggressive salvage business."

That had to be the most polite way to refer to piracy he'd ever heard.

"I prefer to keep a low profile," Moire said, with complete sincerity. "I find ships, I sell them. I hadn't heard you were interested in that line of business."

Zandovar looked at her coolly for a moment, then smiled. Ennis started to worry again. "I am always interested in discussing business. While it is true I do not deal with ships, I do have an interest in...crew. You could salvage them as well, you know."

Ennis saw Moire stiffen as his meaning became clear. Casually resting his hand against the back of her chair, he poked her with one finger as a warning.

"My salvage techniques are something I prefer to keep to myself. Witnesses are inconvenient," she said finally. That was good; she made it clear there were no survivors to be sold into slavery. He gave a gentler poke, and she continued. "If I can find a way around that problem I would be pleased to do business with you. Perhaps you could tell me what you are looking for?"

"Certainly. Contact me when you have something; I can make use of them all in some way." Ennis thought of the hanging man and suppressed a shudder.

Moire chose to interpret that as a dismissal and edged her chair back. "Thanks. I will."

Zandovar smiled slightly. "You are in a hurry to leave? I am told your ship is no longer docked."

"I don't want to waste your time. My ship will be returning soon."

Zandovar blinked, and again Ennis had the impression the crime lord was puzzled.

"So why did you order it to leave?"

"To give my people freedom of action." Moire was standing now, and Ennis could see her face wore an expression as enigmatic as Zandovar's.

"Your orders are carried out, I see. Does he follow your order to keep a low profile?" Zandovar asked, indicating Ennis. "That must be a difficult task for him, given his previous...proclivities."

"He's doing quite well," Moire said, glancing back at him and smiling. "Once I gave him a few hints."

Zandovar's eyes widened. "Indeed." He gestured, indicating they could leave. "You can see Jonders on your way out for a passkey."

Moire caught herself sagging and forced herself to stand upright. She was so tired...she looked at her chrono. Two and a half hours since the firefight, and the medtech wasn't finished with Ash. At least they were back on Level Three, where their lack of weapons wasn't as dangerous.

The passkey was an annoyance. They would need one eventually to get to the lower levels, but she'd been planning on a per-use one. Much, much cheaper than the fullsite Jonders sold her. Since the alternative was somebody getting killed and ruining what good impressions they had made on the ceeyo, she didn't complain.

Once they'd gotten to Three it wasn't so bad. After a brief but furious argument about who would go, which she lost, Ennis had left to send a signal to Kilberton. She didn't have a choice—they had little time before he was supposed to leave for good. She still didn't like sending Ennis off by himself, unarmed.

"I left you in an empty dock row!" Yolanda barged in the door of the medical office, pushing past a medtech that didn't get out of the way fast enough. She stopped where Ash was lying. "Ancestors preserve...what happened?"

"Ambush from another docked ship," Moire said wearily. "Pico's dead.

Ash got hit and lost a lot of blood. We had to go down to see the big boss before we could do anything about it."

"*Copra*. You mean...the ceeyo?" Her voice was hushed.

Moire nodded.

"All right, she'll do," the fierce little medtech said before Yolanda could say anything else. "Gotta rest though, OK? And get somma those regen fluid packs; that'll help with the blood loss. Leave that alone, it'll heal faster. Damn near like a little kid, you are."

Hideo stopped fiddling with the bandage on his arm, and Moire tried to stop her racing heart. The medtech had just been using a figure of speech; he didn't know anything. He couldn't.

"Yolanda. How did you find us?"

"Ennis told me. Said to tell you ship's coming in. Damn near gave me a seizure when I come up and the dock's empty, and I couldn't get Kilberton on the comm. I guess you had good reason."

"That'll be fifty ED," the little medtech said, glaring at them. He seemed to blame Moire for everything. Payment...she'd given everything she had left to Ennis to send the signal. Moire glanced at Yolanda, mouthing a question, and she rummaged through her pockets before pulling out a paychip. The medtech's mood seemed to improve with payment. "Rent ya a carry-cart for five," he said easily.

"That won't be necessary." Ennis was in the doorway. Then Moire saw he had a float pallet with him, and she felt giddy with relief. She knew that float-pallet. *Raven* was back.

"Come on, let's get out of here." She patted Alan on the shoulder. He shrugged away from her angrily. He'd been in a mood ever since the firefight. Well, on the ship they could sort things out. They'd have the long return trip to the sargasso to do it.

Ennis didn't say anything all the way back to the ship. She kept glancing at him from the corner of her eye, and came to the conclusion he was in some kind of mood too.

With the Created finally stashed safely in their cabin and the door shut, he turned to her. "Were you trying to get us killed?" he said finally.

"What? I didn't know those goons were going to be there!" Moire said, hurt and puzzled. "It was *not* my idea to go out, remember?"

He shook his head sharply. "No. In the greenhouse."

Moire sighed. "You're going to have to explain. Use small words, OK?"

"What were those things you and Zandovar were eating?"

The question didn't make sense at first. "Wings. Chicken wings. Snack food, you know?"

Yolanda was listening to all this with growing amazement and horror. "He let you have some?"

Some of the fierce intensity left Ennis's eyes as he searched Moire's face, seeming to pick up on her confusion. "The only chicken I've ever had has been grown in a vat, in nodules. No wings."

"Uh oh." Now she understood. Real chicken wings, meaning real chickens, meaning, here-and-now, lots and lots and *lots* of money. And she had mentioned how she liked the sauce. "That must be why he ate the bones." She shrugged at their stares. "Well, in my day you didn't."

Yolanda made a little whimpering noise. "You left yours?"

Ennis nodded, a small, wild grin on his face. "That is correct. The ceeyo of Kulvar was showing off his wealth and you didn't even notice. He's going to be very curious about you now."

Blast and damn. Zandovar looked like the type of guy who liked to indulge his curiosity, and had the means to do it.

"Yolanda!" Kilberton was half-running down the corridor, his eyes wide. "I heard you...you are all right? Commander Ennis said nothing about you and I worried."

"Yeah, I met up with him after he sent the message. I'm OK," she said, looking at her feet and scowling. "Better than Pico, anyway. Or Ash."

"I wanted to tell you, but I was afraid they'd notice a direct signal and perhaps locate you," Kilberton said, a worried expression on his face.

"Almost wish you had. Might've been able to help." Kilberton hung his head, and she hurriedly added, "Ya did good. You didn't know. Hey, Captain–I'll go see if we got any of those fluid packs the medtech said to use."

Moire nodded, and Kilberton and Yolanda turned to leave. "OK, and finish up any business we still have on station. We'll leave when you're done."

"No." Ennis held out a hand to stop her. He looked up, and his blue eyes were bright with some strong emotion. "I saw Harrington."

The news was like a jolt of cold water. "Are you sure?" she asked weakly. "The circulars...."

"I know! I saw him when they were taking us down. He saw us too, I'm certain."

"Great." Now they had to find him. That was the whole reason for being here, after all. She should be glad. "What do we do now?" Damn, her voice was rough. She needed sleep.

"He contacts us. There's a maildrop I set up earlier for this. I checked before I went back to the clinic. Nothing yet."

Yolanda came back down the corridor, carrying something in both hands. "We only got two more of these. You want I should buy more?" she asked, holding out the fluid pack. She handed Ennis a blue foil box with the other hand.

So Yolanda had been doing some shopping for Ennis? "Yeah. Order more. We have to stay a little longer, until we get a message." She tilted her head at Ennis and he gave Yolanda the maildrop code. "Let us know when something comes through."

The door to the Created's cabin opened, and Alan peeked out. When he saw them there he went to shut it, but Moire spoke first. Something was eating him and she should deal with it now, even if she felt like hell. "Come out, Alan. I want to talk to you."

He shuffled out reluctantly, refusing to look at her.

"I'll check on Ash," Ennis said, getting the hint. He took the fluid packs and went inside.

She looked at Alan for a moment, wondering how to handle the situation. What would her father have done?

"Come on. Bet you're as hungry as I am." He said nothing, but followed her to the galley. She grabbed a leftover fruit square and found some of the thick, sweet drink Alan liked. "Sit." He sat. She put the mug in front of him. He pushed it away.

She waited for a moment. "Are you hurt? Do you need to see the medic too?"

"No." A sullen, resentful answer, but with something else lurking in the background.

"Then what's wrong?" She put a hand under his chin and lifted until he was looking at her. He squeezed his eyes shut.

"I don't like you anymore!" he said finally, his voice catching. Tears started to well up and fall down his face. "You...you yell at me, and...and won't let me have a gun, and..."

OK. Now she had something to work with. "And what?"

He sobbed, unable to speak. Moire got up and found some dry-wipes, and gently dabbed at his face. He cried even harder, suddenly clutching at her and burying his face in her jacket. "Don't make me go away, don't!"

"I can't."

He looked up, gulping. "You want *him* to stay and not me!"

A very observant young man, Alan. She wondered how long he'd known.

She sat down next to Alan and put her arm around him. "If I tried to make you leave, Commander Ennis would be very angry with me. He wouldn't like me anymore."

He wasn't completely convinced, but now he was curious. "Why?"

Moire hesitated, trying to figure out how to explain without creating more confusion. "He grew up in a very bad place, with bad people. His mother and father died when he was much younger than you. Someone found him and took care of him, or he would have died too. You're too young to be out on your own, Alan," she said, brushing back the hair on his forehead. He was so miserable, and she had to make him understand. "You would get hurt. He wouldn't like that at all. And I would be very sad if you weren't here."

"You yelled at me. Loud, and your face was mad," Alan persisted, but he still held on to her. He was trying to understand.

Moire sighed. "Remember how many people were there? Remember their guns?"

"I could have shot them," he said doggedly.

"You could have shot *some* of them. We didn't have enough ammunition. We had to surrender to survive. I yelled at you to drop your gun," she said, holding his face in her hands, "because I was frightened. If you hadn't dropped it they would have killed you."

"They would?" he whispered. "How did you know?"

She hugged him, shaking her head. "That's one of the things you'll learn as you get older, OK? But meanwhile, you have to do what I tell you to."

He mumbled something in her shoulder that sounded like grudging agreement, and she leaned back against the bench, stroking his hair. She studied her half-eaten fruit square, too tired to finish it, and started to doze off.

Soft footsteps brought her back to alertness. Ennis was standing nearby. "I think you should check on the others. Our recent adventures seem to have upset them."

Alan stirred and blinked, rubbing his eyes, and Moire got up stiffly. "They scared the hell out of me, so I can't even imagine what they were thinking."

"They thought they were back at the Place," Alan said sleepily. He shuddered. "I thought I was, when I saw the man hanging."

Moire exchanged a horrified look with Ennis, fully awake now, and left the galley for the Created's cabin.

When she got there she could see he was right. They had pulled the pads from the bunks and piled them in the space between, and they were huddled together under their blankets—even Ash. They looked at her fearfully when she came in. They had done this before when they first started traveling on the ship, until they had been persuaded to leave the bunks intact.

"We'll...we should put them back?"

Did it really matter? "You can leave them there for now. But you need to be careful of Ash. That can't be comfortable for her." With Alan's help, she rearranged the pads and pillows so nobody was squishing Ash. Alan squirmed into the group, and they all seemed to relax now they were sure nobody was angry with them.

Moire sat down on the edge of the pads, and Ennis took a seat nearby. He was still carrying the blue foil box.

"Does this make you feel better?" she asked cautiously.

George turned his head to look at her. Ash's head was resting on his stomach. "All together is...we were allowed. They said not to touch, but sleeping time was different. It made the bad things stay away from remembering."

"Sometimes they would put you alone, and dark," Hideo said very quietly. "After they hurt you."

She would leave the light on.

"Do you think I should give this to her now?" Ennis asked the Created, holding up the box.

"Yeah!" George said, his face brightening. Ash made a protesting noise when he shifted. "Is it the one we said?" Hideo sat up, holding his blanket close around him.

Moire took the box. It was heavy, and it took her a moment to figure out how to open it. Inside was a broad, gold bracelet and a graceful carving of a dragon, curved back to reach for a dangling blood-red stone.

"You needed a new captain's earring," Ennis said, looking bland. "They thought it should be something like this."

The cool metal of the dragon fit easily about her ear. It was precisely balanced and even adjustable. Under the control bracelet was a datatab, presumably the instructions. Even it was ornate, the plastic cover washed in a rippled pattern of thin gold.

"Thanks, kids. This is great." She touched the bracelet lightly, starting when a display panel became visible. After a moment it faded and the bracelet looked uniformly metallic again.

"The rest is in your cabin," Ennis added. "The crew also had some ideas."

The rest? Her eyes stung, and she stared at the blue foil box completely unable to speak. It was fatigue, that's all. They'd planned this...Moire covered her eyes with her hands.

Someone was tugging gently at her arm. Hideo looked at her with concern and held up the corner of a blanket. "You could stay," he offered.

Murmurs of agreement came from the other Created. "You guys need to get some sleep," she said gruffly.

"I don't want to sleep," Ash said, her face twisting. "I'll see it again. I don't want to!" George tightened his arm about her.

"How about I read you a story?" Moire asked. "Then you could sleep thinking about that."

"OK, but you have to stay until we are all sleeping," Hideo said after a moment.

That sounded fair. Alan handed her his battered reader. She shifted closer, and they snuggled up. She shifted again, trying to find a comfortable position, and discovered Ennis accommodating her quite comfortably indeed. She started reading from *The Jungle Book*. After the first story she could see the Created start to breathe slower, and she gradually let her voice trail off midway through the second when she thought they were all asleep.

The Created had the right idea. This was very comfortable. She suspected Ennis was asleep too, even though he was still holding her. The Universe wouldn't let this last long, in her experience. Well, the Universe could just wait until it handed her the next emergency.

Yolanda would find her if anything went wrong. Very carefully, moving as slowly as she could to avoid waking anybody, she took out her commlink and turned the sound off.

CHAPTER 17
CONCERNING THE DANGERS OF PART-TIME JOBS

Undoubtedly it all made perfect sense from the correct perspective, Harrington mused. Good wine needed no bush, and a discreet, secure venue for meetings involving those with criminal tendencies would likewise have no need for something as mundane as a sign.

Since he was not a member of the criminal underclass—yet—he had some difficulty finding it. Really, a few minutes of time on Ennis's part giving at least the sector and level would have been appreciated. Perhaps that was not done on Kulvar.

"I am here for a meeting," Harrington said to the armed and armored guard standing before the entrance.

"Sure you are," she drawled with tolerant amusement. The other guards scattered about the corridor snickered. She beckoned to someone inside, in the shadows. "Think you can take Killer here in by yourself, or you need backup, eh?"

The summoned guard drew back his lips in a half snarl and jerked his head at Harrington to follow him. The darkness was sudden, and Harrington stumbled on some roughness on the floor before his eyes adapted.

"Scanner." His escort had stopped before a round platform, just large enough to stand on. It was lit from above. More guards were dimly visible ringing the room, weapons at the ready. Harrington took his place on the platform and waited, trying to not feel like a target.

He could hear sotto voce queries and puzzled answers, then silence. A young man with phosphorescent hair came out from behind a screened display and walked up to him. "You ain't got no weapons," he said, with an air of pointing out a potential embarrassment.

"Yes, I am aware," Harrington said.

His matter-of-fact reply seemed to disconcert the young man for a moment. "Sell ya one," he offered, looking concerned.

"I am sure the security here will be quite adequate for my needs," Harrington replied.

"That's if tha rules get broke," the young man said, looking shocked. "Ev'body gets one weapon. We tag it so's we knows who done what. You start it, you get banned. Got some nice hotshots, quick powerup and small grip."

"Thank you, but I believe my, er, colleagues will be able to provide what I need," he said firmly. Perhaps he was underdressed for the locale, but he was reluctant to purchase weapons from someone with no real interest in keeping him alive.

The glowing-haired man shrugged. "Gotcher code? Lookup's on the wall goin' in."

Harrington stepped off the platform in the direction indicated and found a long, narrow corridor with tubelights at the bottom of one wall and a series of alcoves with privacy screens along the other. Finding an empty alcove, he entered and tapped in the code Ennis's message had given him on the display. A number and a floor map flashed up, and after a moment disappeared.

He followed the indicated directions through more dimly lit corridors. The number that he had been given matched that on the door of a closed booth. He pressed the annunciator, and shortly the door clicked and slid open. Ennis was standing inside, out of immediate view. Once Harrington was inside and the door closed, Ennis turned up the lights.

"What happened to you?" Ennis gestured at his face.

"Oh, I had some difficulty leaving Criminy. For future reference, pressure door hydraulic fluid can irritate sensitive skin."

"I'll keep that in mind." Ennis grinned, and Harrington found himself startled into thinking Ennis had changed, but in a subtle way, difficult to pinpoint. It wasn't just the lack of uniform. Ennis was wearing ordinary ship-crew gear now. His jacket had a grey patch with what appeared to be an ink-and-brush symbol of a bird, with the name "Raven" at the top. "Help yourself," he said, waving at the small drink dispenser at the other end of the table. "You'll probably need it."

"You appear to be having some adventures of your own," Harrington said, selecting a short uxo. The one benefit of uxo was that it was not pretending to be anything else. Anyone who had ever had real brewed beer suffered in the Fringe. "Now tell me, what have you been doing to get a price on your head?"

Ennis leaned back in his seat. "You remember a certain large military and colony supply company that wanted to talk to me? They infiltrated the base I was posted to and kidnapped me. When I managed to get away, they had the brilliant idea of the reward. I have no idea if there really is a warrant out for me—out here it doesn't matter. The reward is real enough." He shrugged. "That's why you're here. I can't even get to Fleet to report in."

All very well, but it didn't quite add up. He took a sip of uxo. "You know, I have the impression the mail service is still working."

Ennis sighed. "Think it through, will you? They got to me *in a Fleet base.*

Their agent was posing as a Fleet technician. Somebody had a lot of inside help for that, and–"

A soft beep interrupted. Ennis stood and looked at a small viewer, then dimmed the lights and opened the door to admit someone. With the door closed and the lights back, Harrington found himself staring at Moire Cameron.

He'd expected her to be here, of course. It was just that the theoretical possibility had nowhere near the impact of the physical reality. She was wearing a dark red sheetleather jacket, and a red drop dangled from her left ear, forever beyond the grasp of the gold dragon that reached for it. She looked very much at home on Kulvar.

She tilted her head at him. "Mr. Harrington. A pleasure to see you again."

Especially when you aren't pointing a weapon at me, I'm sure. "Please call me Neville. It feels like we've been acquainted for a long time."

She smiled. "Centuries." She took a seat next to Ennis and handed him a datatab folder. He flipped it open, and taking out a small datapad, he inserted the first tab and tapped at the controls.

"While I am fully determined to report in as soon as I can, we have some important information to get back to Fleet immediately."

He had to listen, of course. His curiosity would permit nothing else. He had to find out what the two of them, together, thought was so important they sought him out to take it back. He also needed to know why they had specified him as the messenger.

Cameron was leaning back in her seat, watching Ennis with a faint smile. She glanced at Harrington. "Looks like Lorai had no trouble finding you. You got here quick."

"She is a most determined individual," Harrington replied, firmly repressing the rising memories of desperation and despair, hoping his handcrafted oxygen tent would work. "I had only just arrived, and was arranging the message you had requested when I saw you go by."

Ennis and Cameron had similar hardened expressions for a moment, then Ennis turned his datapad so Harrington could see the screen.

"We have a ship," he said simply.

Harrington had studied the stills Lorai Grimaldi had given him until he had them memorized. He knew they had found a crab ship. Now he was seeing that they had gone inside.

"I am fascinated, utterly fascinated. But how on earth do you suppose I can help you? With all due respect, the military is not exactly eager to spend time in the company of the press, and I..."

"...have done it before," Ennis interrupted. "You sent back word after our first visit here. It got to them before *I* did."

Oh dear. "I have no notion what gave you such a fantastic idea, but I do assure you I am not a clandestine member of the armed forces," Harrington said, trying to imbue his voice with polite scorn.

"Did I say you were?" Ennis was equally polite. He reached into his jacket pocket and brought something out. "To him, that might even be an advantage. He likes to work outside the rules." He held a small glowball between his fingers.

His reaction must have showed.

"Gotcha," breathed Cameron, her eyes narrowing, watching him from her deceptively relaxed position.

This was not going at all well. He took another, deeper drink of uxo. "Just supposing, for the sake of argument, that this incredible story were true–what would be so important for them to know? We have seen crab ships before, rather frequently, in fact. I don't wish to cast doubt on your veracity, but I haven't actually seen the thing myself, you know. They will...they might ask these questions, don't you think?"

"It's intact. Working," Cameron said. "I know that's not common."

"Any time we've gotten close, you-know-who steps in and grabs it," Ennis added grimly. "I don't understand how they get away with it."

"You aren't alone," Harrington said before he could stop himself. "I don't suppose I could see it?" he asked hopefully.

Cameron grinned. "It might be noticeable even here. Besides, we need you to–"

"Yes, yes, send a message. Which at this point will read something like, I saw some stills of what appears to be a crab ship, nothing else to report. Do I have that right? I'm sure that will receive immediate attention."

"Sounds like he wants something more," Ennis commented, looking at Cameron with an enigmatic expression.

"So we give it to him," she said.

They had planned this, he realized with astonishment. And they were enjoying it. They looked as satisfied as two wolves with a cornered rabbit. Well, at least he'd get to see the ship.

Cameron stood up. "Ready to leave? OK, wait here fifteen minutes or so after we go, then get your gear. Level Three, dock four ninety-two."

He followed these instructions, chafing at the delay. At least he didn't have much to pack–the only important item being his new high-capacity datapad. He found the dock without difficulty.

Cameron was waiting. "You see anybody else head for this hatch, yell," she instructed the armed crewman who let him in. "Don't take chances."

The man nodded, and Cameron indicated Harrington should follow her.

"You are expecting trouble, Captain?"

She looked grim. "I've already had plenty this trip." She went silent again. They were heading toward what should be the cargo area of the ship. Perhaps they had arranged extra bunk space there.

"How long will it take to get there?" Harrington asked.

A small smile twitched at the corner of her mouth. "It's at the end of this corridor."

She was not taking him to the ship. The wave of bitter disappointment was followed by a surge of annoyance. "Then what was all that show about? I had been under the impression that–"

"We'll bring the ship to you. It's a long way away, in a place I don't want to advertise. This is the other part of the message you need to deliver." She stopped at a door with a security scan. It clicked open for her, and she stepped inside, where Ennis and another man were waiting. "You'll understand we didn't even want to talk about him out there."

Harrington at first could make no sense of what he saw. They were in a furnished room, with a terminal, viewscreen, and a large display panel mounted next to a wide viewport. A viewport that showed another interior room on the other side, where a bulky, disturbing shape was...moving.

"What is that?" he asked, pleased that his voice remained even.

Ennis smiled, the resemblance to a wolf once again flitting across Harrington's mind. "Meet Radersent. That's his ship we have."

"Dear God." Without conscious thought he went to the viewport, drawn irresistibly. His eyes drank in every detail, every alien feature, wondering what the crab saw in turn. It appeared to be holding some kind of device.

"More send," a synthetic voice said, coming from a tangled mass of equipment on a bench.

"Guess he wants ta know who you are," a man with stiff dark hair said. "What's the name?"

"This is Jim Perwaty," Ennis said. "He and Radersent were shipwrecked in the same location."

Harrington put a hand against the wall to steady himself. They were talking to the crab. "Tell him my name is Harrington." Questions jostled in his mind. He couldn't decide which one to ask first.

"You the one who's gonna go tell Fleet?"

Perwaty's question released his paralysis. "Are you mad? How could I possibly leave now?"

Ennis turned on him, eyes blazing. "Because if you don't, the war could drag on until we're all dead of old age. Dammit, that's priceless information! He knows the ship and he's willing to talk to us. Fleet needs this, and you are the only means we have to get it to them."

"There must be another way." This was too cruel. What could be better than the chance to interview a crab? How could they even think of asking him to give that up?

Cameron stirred. "If I show up anywhere legal, Toren or Fleet will grab me and I have other responsibilities right now. Ennis just has Toren to worry about, but he can't go either. We need this to get to the right person the first time, because we might not get a second chance. This is too important to screw up."

The synthetic voice spoke again. "Query, where picture humans?"

Cameron gave Perwaty a quizzical look. "He means the kids," he explained. "They like using the display with him."

"They'll be back as soon as we leave," she said. "Which depends on Mr. Harrington."

He took a deep breath. "You have to understand, you are asking me to turn my back on the best story I have ever had. You'll hand him and the ship over to Fleet and they won't let me get near either of them again. I have wanted nothing more than this—and you want me to *leave*?"

"We don't have a choice," she said, a note of regret in her voice. She exchanged a look with Ennis. "And it's just the ship for now."

"Then I want to come back," he said forcefully. "If he's not going with the ship, I want to return and stay with you until he does leave. Fleet isn't the only one with a need for information. This is the first alien intelligence we've encountered, and the rest of humanity deserves to know what we've been facing all this time."

Ennis made a sharp, negating gesture. "That's not possible. Fleet—"

"Fleet will have plenty of time to figure out how to deal with Mr. Harrington's plans for publication," Cameron interrupted. "If he's on my ship he's not going to have much opportunity to spread the news."

Ennis stared at her, his jaw working, then threw up his hands. "They aren't going to like this."

"That's their problem. It sounds fair to me." The tone was one of finality.

"Right, then," Harrington said brightly into the brittle stillness between them. "What exactly am I supposed to tell them?"

Ennis hesitated, then took out the datatab folder he'd had at the meeting place, only now it had several more tabs. "There's a list of locations here," he said, tapping one with a blue border. "You have access to a data account with bounceback?"

"A limited one."

"It will do. Give us the address. We'll send you a message with the number of one location on that list. The ship will be there."

Very cautious. Quite proper, under the circumstances. He entered the address into Ennis's datapad.

"Query, Harrington child Roberts?" said the mechanical voice.

The crab was standing so close to the viewport he could see the tendrils on either side of his narrow head shifting among themselves, like restless snakes.

"It would appear something is being lost in translation," Harrington observed, after recovering from his surprise.

"He asks that about everybody," Perwaty said dismissively. "Never have figured out why."

"Everything ready?" Cameron asked. Ennis nodded, and she tapped at the broad gold bracelet on her wrist. "Ready, Kilberton?" She paused as the answer was relayed, then indicated the door. "OK, let's go. Sooner you leave the sooner you can come back," she said, looking at Harrington.

They both saw him out the hatch. He was aware of a tense feeling in the air, and they seemed hurried suddenly. The crewman was still on guard, weapon drawn. Harrington caught the glance between Cameron and the guard, a minute shake of the head that followed.

"Keep it safe," Ennis said softly.

"I give you my word," Harrington replied. The hatch opened.

He was not surprised when the dock indicator changed to red seconds after the hatch was closed.

It floated in the sargasso, starlight reflecting off beams that should never have been visible. *That has got to be the ugliest ship in creation.* Moire gave the viewscreen another glance, shuddered, and turned back to *Raven*'s realspace controls.

"Tell me more, Gren."

There was a pause. Gren was on board the modified ship, moving it into position.

"Main personnel hatch is standard, and a couple of emergency ones. Forward docking controls, too. Cargo hatches won't match anything. Got more space for cargo than *Raven*, but it's scattered all over. We can get the crab box in, though."

"Will it fly?" She couldn't help asking. Gren had a gift; she trusted his judgment implicitly. It was just *looking* at it. The front section, about a third of the ship, looked more or less intact. What had been the ore-hauler's main cargo area was gone. Only the outer structural ribs and the gravitational nodes remained. The back end was open. It looked like a skeletal fish.

"Everything tests out. I tuned it to balance with the crab ship inside, since we're going to do a slipstream tow."

She shuddered again. Well, no guts, no glory. That was the only way to get the ship out, unless they suddenly had a communication breakthrough and translated the crab pilot's manual.

"OK, we'll be there in a few minutes. Guess we'll give it a try."

Ennis had come on the bridge while she was talking, and his gaze strayed to the viewscreen. His eyes widened, and his face sagged with fascinated horror.

"Is that...?"

"Yup." Moire made a minor adjustment to the board. "Gren is proud as punch. That was not an easy order I gave him."

A grin flashed across his face. "I was just thinking...Wernicki at Lambert Station–I told you about her, right?"

Moire nodded. "If it wasn't in the manual, it didn't exist? She'd better not see this. She'd have a seizure."

"Exactly."

The skeletal ship occupied all of the forward screen now, and she started the docking procedure to the one functional hatch.

She took a breath and forced herself to speak. "Gren told me they found a ten-person escape pod, intact. Just needed some recharging and routine maintenance. He thinks there'll be no problem tucking it in that tunnel to the crab ship hatch for your quarters."

It was hard, watching his face change when he understood. For a moment he looked like the old Ennis, grim and joyless. She hated that.

"We should get Radersent to fix those melting doors of his so humans can open them. Won't do much good to hand off a working crab ship if they have to use a can opener to get in," she said, with a cheerfulness she did not feel. It worked; a reluctant smile crossed his face.

"You use the strangest expressions sometimes," he said, shaking his head. "I'm going to have to find a reference for all these archaic terms."

All the docking pinlights were green. She got up and stretched. "Better talk to Gren. We might not be able to get to the crab ship when we're in drive."

The interior of the tow ship was still littered with pieces of equipment and other gear. Gren listened to her question with his usual gloomy expression. As she had feared, the gravitational weirdnesses would cut off access to the crab ship.

"Anything that might disturb the field would be bad. If it was one of ours we might be able to do it, but..." Gren rubbed his chin. "It's risky."

"Yeah, we've got enough of that right now. Guess we'd better have Radersent get to work on the door controls while we get the ships lined up."

Gren grunted. "He'll have plenty of time, then."

He was right. It took over a day of careful, painful maneuvering to get the tow ship, now named *Frankenstein*, backed up to capture the crab ship. Gren had to turn off the gravity nodes until the ship was perfectly aligned, since otherwise the field would have pulled the crab ship in and damaged *Frankenstein*. Even with Kilberton in *Raven* and somebody else in the scout to help guide, it was a frustrating process, but finally everything was arranged to Gren's satisfaction and he slowly brought the nodes on line.

As soon as it was clear the crab ship was in place, Moire immediately went to sleep while Gren did his final alignment checks and rested up himself. He and the assistant engineer would be just as busy as Kilberton and herself once they started up, since the gravitics would need constant attention.

Then it was time.

"OK, folks, check your shipsuits. This is the real thing," Moire said over the general shipwide channel. "Drive will start up in three minutes." She powered up the realspace drives, taking both ships well away from the main area of the sargasso.

The ramp-up was agonizingly slow, but smoother than she had expected. Gren called out the field changes he was making as they went to full field. She had her lineup ready, fighting the growing influence of the anomaly that had caused the sargasso in the first place.

"Full field," Gren snapped. "Full field, uniform throughout."

"Acknowledge full field," she replied. "Drive engaging."

She knew something was horribly wrong the instant she hit the switch. She could *feel* the field shift, in that same bone-deep way she always felt the change from webspace to real. One hand slapped the emergency dropout as the other fought to keep the control on target, and she saw a flash of blinking red pinlights.

"Gren! Get that damn field stable!"

He didn't respond for a second, making her panic. "Field is stable–at least, it would be if we hadn't just lost two nodes. What happened?"

Moire glanced at the ship status board. "Looks like we took some damage. No hull breaks, though." She checked their position. Maybe if they had gotten away from the sargasso in that brief pulse, they could start up again and get away. "Somebody go out in the two-seater and check it out."

They were closer to the sargasso than when they started. That was impossible. She had a lineup; she'd done it many, many times before. The anomaly might be a pull on them, but it should have just slowed them down, not pulled them back.

She stared at the scanner, hoping for enlightenment. Maybe they'd have to take it out farther in realspace, then try it again. Farther from the center of the sargasso.

She leaned forward. The scanner was showing something there, and it wasn't a ship. At least, not a human one. It must be the oldest craft caught by the sargasso. A pity she'd have to wait to check it out.

A signal pinged for attention–the outside check. "Two of the ribs are damaged," a breathless voice announced. "Looks like the crab ship is getting loose."

They managed to get the crab ship sort of back in alignment, and Moire returned them to their original location, closer to the repair station. Gren stumped up to the bridge, angry that his careful work had been damaged.

"OK, something seems to have affected the crab ship," Moire said wearily after much discussion. "So lets ask the crab." She wondered how they were ever going to get something as abstract as a webspace gravitational anomaly across, but it turned out they didn't have to.

"Models?" Moire asked, looking at the roughly made objects her son handed her. She looked in the crab's quarters. The crab had an assortment of his own, much more finely made. Some seemed to represent human things, but with an alien cast.

"He made some, to help with words," Alan said. "We can say more now."

They also could feed in vid signal to the display. This didn't always work, and Moire suspected the crab didn't see the display like humans did. If it was a simple, black-and-white diagram, though, he could usually make it out. George had developed a real talent for translating vid stills into these diagrams. They made several attempts to explain the problem without success, until George drew the outside view of *Frankenstein* and the crab ship.

Radersent extended his head in the way they now knew indicated interest. "Query, go star-star ship break?" the synthetic voice Perwaty had added to the diagnostic scanner output said.

"That's web travel, we think," Perwaty explained. Moire nodded, and Perwaty sent the reply.

An absolute torrent of words spilled from the output. Moire blinked, stunned, and she could see from the reactions of the others they were equally astonished.

"Star-star crab ship near (undefined) break. Past, Radersent she and Radersent crab go. Past, (undefined) dead Radersent she and dead small-ship. (Undefined) dead crab. No see crab ship star-star (undefined) not break. Human ship not dead. Past, Past, (undefined) dead crab."

Radersent's head was pulled in now, and only his tendrils were moving on the communication device. He was very upset about something.

"Anybody have any idea what he just said?" Moire asked after trying unsuccessfully to puzzle it out.

"I'm guessing something like 'that won't work,' which we already know," Perwaty said dryly. "But he's saying something about *him* and not being able to go anywhere."

Moire frowned. "We already know the anomaly got him, too. He's saying something about it killing crabs, right? Maybe that's why he's all by himself. Still doesn't help us, though."

Perwaty nodded, and sent another message. Moire saw "[QUERY]FIX" flash across the screen.

Radersent responded immediately. His tendrils picked up a model of the crab ship. One set of tendrils held it in front of his long, bony face. The others opened up in a cone shape, very much like the ribs of *Frankenstein*. He held it so the crab model ship was just like George's diagram, then a twitch of the tendrils made it fly away.

"Break," said his synthetic voice.

Moire grinned. Radersent understood what had happened, all right. The crab went and got the model again. This time he held it so the tendrils enclosed the entire ship.

"No see crab ship," he said. "(undefined) no see. No dead crab ship. See human ship. Star-star yes."

Moire felt suddenly cold. Maybe this was just bad translation, but he seemed to be talking about something that deliberately attacked crab ships. When he talked about damage, he used the word "break". Now he was using the term that meant "kill".

"So we just need to extend the field, is what he's saying," Gren commented, breaking his long silence. "That makes sense."

"Yeah, yeah," Moire waved it away. "I got that. Do you hear what else he's saying?" She held out a hand for the scanner, and Perwaty let her take it. [QUERY]RADERSENT SHIP BREAK.

"No," said the voice. "Radersent ship dead."

MORE SEND. SHOW.

The crab started assembling his models and arranging them carefully on a flat surface.

"It's going to take at least two weeks to fix the damage and extend the nodes," Gren said while Radersent worked. "Is that going to..." he hesitated, glancing at Ennis.

"Yes." They were already dangerously close to the deadline when she would have to get to Bone to pick up the construction crew. Two weeks was well over the limit, and that assumed it would work the first time. "We're going to have to come back. Again," she said with a sigh. "Hey, what's Radersent doing now?"

The models were mixed in with a sea of bits of junk now. There was a pattern forming, confirmed when he began to name the models. "*Helios*," Radersent said, his one working forelimb indicating one. "Radersent ship."

It was the sargasso, at least this section. Then he put one silvery lump at the far end. "(Undefined). Past, dead Radersent ship. Past, past, dead crab ship. Bring human ship."

The location was near the center of the sargasso. Where she had seen the unrecognizable object at the edge of the scanner range. This made no sense. The sargasso existed because of a gravitational anomaly, and anomalies had no realspace presence at all. There was nothing to see. She didn't remember all the details; they knew more about the effects than the theory in her day. Which meant it might not be a real anomaly, but something very different.

[QUERY]MACHINE. She pointed at the silver lump on Radersent's display table

"Yes."

[QUERY]CRAB MACHINE.

"Machine yes. Crab machine no. Human machine no. Dead, dead, dead." One forelimb swiped suddenly at the silver lump, sending it off into the shadows. Whatever it was, Radersent didn't like it.

"Oh shit," Moire whispered. "More aliens."

Kolpe felt like he was going to explode. The Toren enforcer ship that had brought them to Bone was too small, especially when he had to share space with Plymson. Heyt, the commander of the ship and its complement of armed personnel, treated Kolpe and his mission as a minor annoyance, something not to be taken very seriously.

"Are you expecting me to attack that ship?" Heyt asked, pointing at the screen where the larger of the two ships that had arrived was picking up cargo containers from another ship, the one they had been tracking.

"No," Kolpe snapped. "The orders are to take the target *alive*. That is the highest priority, do you understand?"

Heyt's eyes narrowed. "I understand the target is on one of those ships. I understand nobody's left any of these ships to go dirtside. So you tell me how we get this target without taking direct, ship-to-ship action."

"We wait for the target to land." Kolpe turned back to his communication intercept equipment.

"Why can't we wait on the ground and get in position?"

He clenched his teeth, breathing deeply. "Because you would freeze in that position, if you didn't die of oxygen deprivation first. Wait at least until the target is on the ground. Once she is, we can keep her there."

Heyt gave a tight smile and left.

This was not going as he had planned. It was becoming clear Cameron was not staying on Bone as he had thought, so of course there was no need for her to go to the surface for anything. This was only a waystop. If so, it argued that the next location they were bound for was even more remote and sparsely populated than Bone–and thus he had to get her here.

He wasn't even sure which ship she was on, or that she was even...no, she *had* to be here. There was simply no other possibility.

The communication chatter was all about stowing equipment and cargo, mind-numbingly boring. Even though he had transcription and signal analysis going on all the live channels, he still sat and listened. Attention to detail was the key to success–and if he did not listen to the other ships, Plymson would talk to him.

His mind drifted, thinking of how he might tease out the secret of why Toren was so determined to capture Moire Cameron alive. It would be a long trip back to headquarters, and Heyt and his enforcers would be easy to distract. Cameron might know what he was after, though; she might even try to get information from him. He smiled. It would be very interesting.

An alert signal interrupted his musings. Signal from the main ground camp, Waylands. He switched to that channel.

...yeah, got back couple weeks ago.

You still want the job? Get that shuttle in gear, girl! We're leaving soon.

I ain't leavin' Beast behind now I just got it all fixed. Come and help? Just like old times.

The voice. He recognized that voice. He followed the conversation intently. Someone at Waylands wanted Cameron to come down there for some reason they both knew but weren't specifying. His muscles tensed in a futile effort to force her to overcome her reluctance.

OK, I'll be down in a bit. Better find Alan, he'll be real upset if I don't take him.

Kolpe snapped to his feet as soon as the signal cut off.

"Heyt! She's going down to the planet!"

The landing craft was even more crowded. To his disgust, he could not avoid occasionally touching Plymson.

"Deorbit as if you're going to the equatorial region," he said curtly to the pilot, who looked at Heyt for confirmation. He hated working with these people, who would listen to anyone but him. "There are action committees who try to land there unnoticed. It will not attract the target's attention. Follow the terrain as low as you can from there. Got it?" He couldn't help the trace of contempt.

Heyt nodded at the pilot, giving Kolpe a measuring stare. He ignored it. He was so close...nothing was going to be left to chance now. Even the enforcers. Toren hadn't needed to be told to send a ship without markings, and the crew was wearing plain black gear.

"If we keep anybody from sending a signal, they'll keep thinking we're an action committee," Heyt said, narrowing his eyes. "That will make cleanup a lot easier." He moved back from the pilot's section to where the enforcers and Plymson were seated and began giving them a briefing.

Kolpe followed. He didn't like Heyt's train of thought; he could see that violence was going to play a part in any plan Heyt was involved in. The best he could do was channel the violence so that it didn't interfere with his job.

When Heyt had finished, Kolpe spoke. "You have a set of vid stills. Study them carefully. You must not kill the target. You must not endanger the target. Is that clear?"

"Is there anything else you would like to tell us, Mr. Anders?" Heyt was almost vibrating with anger. "I've got my orders, and I intend to carry them out even if it means causing damage. We won't tag your target, but I can't promise that for anybody else."

Kolpe shrugged. "I don't care what you do with the others. But Cameron is *mine*."

CHAPTER 18
A DANGEROUS NEED

Alan was still bashfully recovering from one of Lorai's enthusiastic hugs when he finally understood why they were there. Moire thought he was about to bounce up and down like a real kid.

"You're coming *with* us?" he asked, face wide with astonishment and happy surprise. "To stay?"

"Yep, long as you guys need me," Lorai said, grinning at him.

"Are the others coming too? Jens and Mammachandra and...and everyone?"

"This is their home, Alan. I think they want to stay here," Moire said.

Lorai cleared her throat. She picked up a tool lying on a hydraulic housing and put it back down again. "Um, actually...I sorta asked around, you know, seeing what people were thinking? They, um, they want to talk to you." Lorai must have seen the shock and horror on her face, because she hurried on. "I didn't say nothin' specific-like! You didn't tell me much yourself, but I could guess you had a big project going on. Real big. Thought you might have room for 'em."

The laugh escaped her before she could stop it. Yes, they had room. They also had a desperate need of any willing volunteers. She still wished Lorai hadn't said anything.

Lorai took them to Mammachandra's. When Moire saw who was gathered at the restaurant she felt a little better. Not the hordes she had been fearing; just a handful of people, most of whom she knew. The restaurant itself was looking slightly shabby, and the store was dark and from what she could see, full of crates and boxes and not goods for sale. Munchausen the nerya, looking even more mangy and lumpy of fur, was undulating around the crates making muttering noises. It evidently did not approve of the rearrangements.

"We are anyhow determined to leave," Mammachandra said, dismissing Moire's first attempt to explain that this might not be a good idea. "See, what we have we can take is already packed. We would leave earlier but Lorai told us you might know of a place to go."

"Good places are wanting much," Jens explained. "We must pay for space for a shop, for working in—and still we would need to ship these things. They are too much money for us to give up, but where will we sell them?" There was no sign of his usual cheerfulness in his face, just despair.

Moire sighed. "Did Lorai mention this is...will be a dangerous place? Remote, primitive, bad mail service..."

"Indeed, you describe to us Bone," Gip Farouz, the ancient mineral analyst said in his gentle voice. His lined brown face was calm. "In my youth I came here for the danger, for the remoteness of this place. Now that I am old I cannot say I wish for danger, but I cannot stay here if there is no work for me to do. If I may earn my living in a dangerous place then I will go there."

It was said gently, but with resolution. Nobody else looked like they were planning to change their minds, either. At least she could offer them someplace warmer, with more oxygen.

"Let them make their own decisions," Ennis said quietly, as she hesitated. "They aren't your responsibility until they do."

She stared at him. His expression was serious. "Are you saying you'd take them, even with everything that will happen?"

"They're desperate," he said intently, his blue eyes never leaving her face. "You don't know their situation like they do. If they're willing to consider going with so little information, it must be bad. I've been that desperate." His voice wavered, then steadied. "Nothing out here is completely safe. They know that."

Hard to argue with that kind of experience. Moire didn't even try.

"Still got that comm setup in back?" she asked Jens. He nodded, and led the way. Kilberton wasn't on deck on *Dunkirk*, but Yolanda Menehune was. "How's the loading going?"

"Almost done," Yolanda said. "Maybe two, three hours. They got it all in but they gotta dog it down right and get it settled."

"Great. Can you send Ulrike down with the dropship? We have some more people and gear to take up."

"What, they left some down there?" Yolanda sounded annoyed.

"No, these are new people. Locals that want to come along."

"Really? Damn but yer quick, Captain. I'll send her down."

Moire closed the channel with a grin.

"I might as well take some up too, in the shuttles," Lorai said. "I know Mammachandra and Jens have got a full load between them."

"Yeah, start loading up. I know it's getting late local time but we can't stay too long." It was never a good idea to stay in one place, even if it was Bone.

"I'll get a pallet hauler." Lorai left the restaurant.

"You are having enough room for all this?" Mammachandra asked, sounding doubtful.

Moire looked around. Alan had discovered Munchausen and was playing with it. "How much gear do the rest of you have?" Moire asked. As she thought, except for some diagnostic gear belonging to Farouz, the rest was just personal belongings. "Look, we're going to be making room for the two shuttles no matter what. I think we can get you taken care of, and if–"

An alert shrilled in her ear. The signal came through immediately, meaning some kind of override, but from where? *Raven* and *Dunkirk* were too far away, and the scout didn't have anybody on board. She absently noted the sound of an incoming craft, but it sounded fast, too fast for landing.

"...being shot at! Mayday!...taken damage...help me!"

Ennis saw her reaction and instantly demanded, "What? What's wrong?"

"Ulrike is taking fire. Unknown ship. Jens! Send out a general warning!" She saw Jens heading for the communications room as she sprinted for the door. Ennis was right behind her. She had to get to the scout; it had measly guns but better than no guns at all.

She pulled up her oxygen booster as she ran out the main entrance of Waylands, heading for the cleared landing area where the scout was. A dark plume of smoke told her where the dropship was, still high and descending. So what ship had she heard earlier?

An explosion came from behind Waylands, then a ship streaked past her. It was dark and fast and looked loaded for bear. It was going to intercept Ulrike.

The scout. She had to get the scout up. Something slammed into her back and she landed hard on the frit-covered ground by another ship's landing gear, the cold sand and ice grinding in her face. Ennis was shouting in her ear.

"They're at the ship! Get back inside!"

Now she saw it. Dark figures by the scout, carrying rifles. What the hell was going on? She scrambled back to her feet, keeping in the cover of the ship. Maybe she could steal it...no, the door was locked.

A loud explosion jerked her head up. The dropship had taken a direct hit from the enemy ship and was cartwheeling down out of control, trailing smoke and flame. She felt the impact when it hit. Ulrike had never had a chance.

The lights of Waylands went out just when they got to the door. In the evening twilight the sudden contrast made it seem completely dark inside, but then the dim illumination of emergency lighting became visible.

"Who are they?" Ennis panted as they ran back down the main corridor. "They had a clear shot at both of us when we came out but they never fired."

Moire swore. "Then it's Toren. They want me alive, remember? With the oxygen boosters on, people all look the same."

She burst into the restaurant and recoiled at the smell of smoke and burning plastic. That first explosion must have been here. "Alan!" she screamed. "Where are you?"

"I'm here," he called. He didn't sound like he'd been hurt. Moire stumbled over something in the gloom and found him. He was kneeling by Jens, who was covered in blood and moaning.

"In the doorway he was standing when the explosion came," Mammachandra said, ripping open a med packet with shaking hands. "It was the communications tower, I am thinking."

Of course. Cut off any communication with possible help. That wouldn't last forever, but probably long enough for them to do what they wanted to.

"You have some weapons in those crates, right?"

Mammachandra nodded slowly, with unhappy eyes. "I do not remember where. We can look."

No. The goons would already be in Waylands by now; they didn't have time and it would make too much noise. At least she, Ennis, and Alan had their sidearms. "Get him hidden somewhere, and stay quiet. They've got people on the ground with rifles."

What were her options? Comms were out, so she couldn't get Kilberton—not that there was anything she could do except warn him. Maybe if they thought she was inside, they wouldn't be guarding the scout.

"How many do you think there are?" she asked Ennis.

He thought for a moment. "That looked like an armored orbit-to-ground transport. Carries about fifteen besides the pilot. But there could be more than one."

"Got...report," Jens whispered painfully. "One ship from orbit. To Belt. Today."

"They would be thinking it is one of the action committees. But they do not come here, it is the Belt they–"

"It's not an action committee," Moire said curtly. "Personal enemies." Who would have all kinds of gadgets and gizmos and, more importantly, ammunition. What did she have they didn't? She didn't have to worry about keeping any of the enemy alive. She knew Waylands. And she was probably the only person here who hadn't grown up in an enclosed environment.

"We're going outside. You still keep the heavy gear by the back door?" Mammachandra nodded. "If you're staying here, keep out of sight. Hide if you can. We'll try to draw them off."

"What's the plan?" Ennis asked quietly as she led the way back through the kitchen. Alan was following her closely.

It was very nice of him to assume she had one. "Let's say there was just one ship, since they only saw one deorbit. If there are only fifteen of them they can't keep a watch on all the outside doors. They saw us run in, and our ship is out front. They may watch the main doors but I'm betting most of them will be inside." She grabbed one of the heavy coats hanging by the back entrance.

Ennis nodded. "Take out the rear guard and go back in and clean up the rest. Probably the best we can do, unless we can get help."

They cautiously exited the building. Moire winced at how noisy the frit was underfoot. If she slid her feet, it was slower but a little quieter.

"Stay close to the building!" Ennis whispered. "It'll mask your heat signal."

There was also less frit. The quickest way to the scout was to go around Lorai's hangars. Moire hoped she was OK; they didn't have time to check. Two quick explosions coming from the front made her jump, and she pulled Alan flat against the wall as the attack ship flew slowly by. Damn, but that was a nice ship. Pity the bad guys had it.

As soon as she turned the corner around the hangar, she swore. Not only was the scout destroyed, the other ship beside it was too. "Great. Now we're really in trouble."

"Lorai has shuttles," Alan said, looking worried.

"That ship would shoot them down without even thinking about it. They're too slow." She stopped and pulled them both down with her in the hollow between the hangar and an abandoned engine casing. "We need to get that attack ship. There has to be another ship it came with; that thing isn't web-capable."

Ennis nodded. "Probably armed. Do you think it will attack our ships?"

"That would get noticed dirtside. They won't want to risk that unless they have to. If, for example, I manage to get out of here and up there." Moire sighed. "But how the hell do I get that ship? We don't have the weapons, and even if we did I want it intact. We have to take out the Toren ship if we're going to get out of here alive."

Ennis glanced at the main entrance, just visible around the corner from where they were. "I've got an idea. First we have to get the guards they left outside."

It made sense for him to take over for that part. He had training and experience, she didn't. She couldn't shoot for beans, so of course she got detailed to be the diversion. It was just lucky for Ennis that Alan didn't figure out what "diversion" meant until it was all over.

"Now what?" Moire asked, watching him and Alan drag the two bodies into the space between the two sets of the main entrance doors.

Ennis started to strip his gear off in the dim glow of the emergency lights. "We transform ourselves into Toren employees."

"But there are only two uniforms..." Moire stopped when she saw his amused look. "Oh. I get to imitate myself." She hoped the standing orders were to keep her uninjured, as well as alive. "I appreciate your attention to detail, but why are we doing this?"

"Their commander will have the commlink to the attack ship," Ennis said, sealing the front of the dark coverall. The blood was not even noticeable. "We just have to find and kill the commander."

Moire took off her oxygen booster hood and the heavy coat. No reason to let them suspect she'd ever been outside. Then she experimented with ways to hide her sidearm while pretending to have her hands tied behind her. Ennis and Alan left their hoods on, even though the light was probably bad enough to not be necessary.

"Grab her arm, like you have to pull her along," Ennis told Alan. Alan looked puzzled and worried.

"It's just another Game," Moire explained. "You're pretending to be one of the bad guys."

They moved through the doors. Halfway to the first cross-corridor they were hailed. "Is that her?" Ennis just nodded and walked forward. "Lemme find Heyt, and then we can get off this frozen–"

The man gasped and doubled up as Ennis drove the knife home.

"So. We're looking for someone named Heyt." His face was cold and remote as he watched the man collapse. Something had happened to him.

"Why don't you use your gun?" Alan asked as they continued.

"Too noisy. Don't talk now." Even his voice was flat and clipped.

They went all the way to the entrance to Lorai's hangars without finding anyone else.

"I'd better go first," Moire said. "She might shoot you if she knows what's going on and just sees the uniform."

Ennis nodded. She carefully opened one door and peered in. Everything looked normal, but she could smell something. Recent gunfire.

"Lorai!" she whispered. "Are you there?"

No answer. She slipped inside and stumbled on a body in dark overalls. "I'm guessing she knows, all right. She seems to be doing something about it, too." Moire commented.

"There's another one over here," Ennis added. "No commlinks."

Great. They'd have to go back the other direction.

They retraced their steps, back in captured prisoner mode. Moire sniffed the air. Not gunfire this time, but something burning. It seemed rather strong to just be from the explosion in the restaurant.

A body in the main corridor, but it wasn't one of the Toren troops. A local. They came to her old home corridor, but the smoke was so strong there they couldn't go any farther.

She frowned, trying to remember the station layout. "That's not good," Moire said softly. "I think Ulrike hit the power station when she crashed."

"So?"

"It's near the main oxygen condenser."

Ennis drew in a sharp breath, understanding. "We'd better get this finished quickly, then, before it decides to blow up."

Where were the rest of them? A sudden burst of shots came from the far end of the main corridor, beyond the restaurant. A pause, and then another burst. Ennis picked up his pace, and Moire and Alan followed. She checked that she could still grab her gun when needed.

She could hear voices now. Angry voices.

"We know she's here, so stop lying! Didn't do them any good, did it?"

They were in an empty bay that Moire vaguely recalled having been an equipment-rental store. The dark-coveralled Toren people were facing a group of frightened locals. Two crumpled bodies were lying on the floor beneath a blood-splattered wall.

"Wait for my signal!" Ennis hissed.

"Him next," one of the Toren people said. He pointed to Gip Farouz.

"I have nothing to tell you," Farouz said with dignity. He raised his chin.

"Heyt!" Ennis yelled. The man who had pointed turned his head sharply.

"Good work," Heyt said in a clipped, light voice. "Let's go." He waved the other Toren people out into the corridor. They went, but reluctantly. It didn't take much effort for Moire to act fearful as they moved toward her.

"What about them?" one asked, jerking a thumb back at the bay. "Shouldn't we take care of 'em now?"

Heyt glanced at Moire, then away, as if he didn't see what the big deal was. "We'll take care of them from the ship. They aren't going anywhere."

What was Ennis planning? Now they were surrounded by Toren troops, and it was only the smoke and dim light that kept them from discovery.

"Where the hell is that asswad Anders?" grumbled Heyt. "I'm not waiting for him or that randy guard of his." He pulled out a commlink.

Ah. The secret plan revealed.

"Gevorsian. Land at the front," Heyt ordered. "We have the target."

He put the commlink away just as they were passing the entrance to Mammachandra's. Ennis suddenly shoved Moire through the double doors, Alan stumbling with her, and opened fire on the surprised Toren troops in a furious blaze. Moire landed hard, scrambling to her feet to stop Alan from joining in.

She was too late, but the fight was over. Ennis had gotten them all, including the commander. He was staring down at Heyt when she came out. Ennis had taken off his hood, and he was gripping his rifle so tightly his knuckles were white.

"Let's check inside," Moire said, counting the bodies. "If they had their full complement of fifteen, we're missing some."

Ennis seemed to come back to the present with an effort. "He mentioned two that were missing," he said finally. He bent down and took the commlink from Heyt's body. "The pilot should signal when they land."

Moire cautiously opened the inner door, staying out of view. "Anybody in there?"

She heard running footsteps, and then Lorai poked her head out. "Damn but I'm glad to see you! We heard all that shooting and didn't know what to think."

"Everybody OK?"

Lorai grinned. "A few holes here and there. We'll survive. Except, of course, for the one the little guy got. I don't know how he did it. He could barely hold the gun. Guess they don't teach these mining officials everything."

Moire glanced around quickly. Everything was as Lorai said; a few holes that seemed to be patched already. A slight, terrified-looking man in rumpled clothes was clutching a mug of something like it was a safety line. His entire body was shaking.

"Hey, how'd you know something had gone wrong?"

"Mammachandra told me," Lorai said. "After you left, she took the chance and ran for it. We gathered up people on the way back."

Ennis had wandered over to the body lying in the middle area between the restaurant and the store. It was wearing a dark coverall.

"Shuttles OK?"

Lorai nodded. "No damage. You need 'em?"

"Need you to be ready. We have one last piece of unfinished business, and I want your help."

A beeping noise came from the commlink Ennis held, and he tilted his head toward the door. "One more time," he said, and tried to smile.

"W-wait! Are you l-leaving?" the little man said, panic in his eyes. "W-what if there are more of th-them?"

"You'll be safer without me," Moire said, her hand on the door. "Come on, Alan."

"I w-want to go with you," the little man said. He put his mug down and hurried to the entryway. He failed to notice the huddled lump of Munchausen on the floor, emerging from the crates, and stepped hard.

Munchausen erupted with a supersonic scream. The little man spun away with incredible speed, one hand reaching inside his jacket. Suddenly Ennis launched himself at the little man, grappling with him. A blast of energy made them both cry out, and the little man jumped back, looking very different and not at all afraid. Ennis had his weapon out.

"He's Toren!" he yelled. "Get away!"

Alan was suddenly in front of her. She saw the little man look at her with strange, empty brown eyes, then flick to Alan's face, and his expression changed to one of surprise. Ennis fired, and the man jerked, then ran for the door. Moire and Ennis ran after him.

"He went down that corridor!" she yelled, pointing. Ennis sprinted ahead in the direction she'd indicated.

An immense explosion shook the ground, and smoke poured from the corridor.

"That would be the oxygen condenser," Moire said, picking herself off the ground yet again. She was going to have a fine assortment of bruises, assuming she survived this. "Let's get that ship. He's gone."

Ennis pulled on his hood, and Alan did the same. Moire decided to leave hers off. It would only be for a few seconds, if it worked.

The attack ship was just outside the main entrance, sleek and beautiful. They ran out and the hatch door opened for them. The light was better in the ship and the pilot quickly realized something was wrong–but not quickly enough.

"OK, now it's time for *my* plan," Moire said, yanking the pilot's body out of the chair with a grunt. The trick was getting close enough to the Toren ship in orbit to fire without getting shot down herself. "You guys go back and find Lorai. We're going to do pretty much the same trick we pulled with those goons, only I'm going to be chasing her, got it? She has to make it look like she's trying to get away. Tell her to head close enough to the Toren ship I can make it look convincing, but not so close they can get a shot at her." She sat down in the chair and pulled down the scanner screen to find the Toren ship. "There. Got the coordinates?" Ennis nodded. "Good. Now get Alan back inside."

He looked at her for a long moment. "Is there any other way?"

She knew what he meant. She could tell how hard it was for him not to argue, to make her stay. "We have to get that ship before they realize something went wrong down here. I'm the only one who can do this. I'll be as careful as I can. And if I'm not..." she looked away. "Gren's in charge."

His face was so pale. Ennis nodded. Alan hadn't understood anything except he was supposed to leave, and didn't want to.

"I'll be back soon," Moire promised. Either under power or as re-entry fragments. "Now go help Lorai."

For a moment she thought Ennis was going to argue, seeing tightening muscles of his jaw, but then he kissed her, hard, and dragged Alan with him out of the ship. Alan was staring at Ennis with wide eyes, too shocked to resist.

She powered up the ship as soon as they were clear, drifting it around so the nose pointed at the shuttle hangar. It was just what she needed. She'd have to be careful not to overgun it.

Even though she'd reminded herself, she hit the throttle hard when the shuttle burst out of the hangar. Lorai was doing an excellent job of imitating a frantic, desperate escape, and she did her best to look like a not-very-good interceptor.

There it was. Glimmering on the scope. Almost close enough. A signal pinlight lit up.

"Gevorsian, stop playing with them! Heyt will skin you if he finds out."

Yes. Close enough. She broke away from chasing the shuttle, and now she did gun it. Full throttle, and she armed the main guns from the pilot console. For a moment she wondered if she could capture the Toren ship, but it was a reflex salvage thought and quickly discarded. She could not afford to make any mistakes.

"Gevorsian! Wake up, you idiot! Gevorsian!"

She had range. She fired. A hit, but not a good one.

"Gevorsian!" They were screaming now. "Wrong target!"

This is for Ulrike. "I'm not Gevorsian," Moire snarled. She fired again. There was a flash on her screen, and the voice went silent.

"I'm sure glad this is the last trip," Lorai commented, slowing the shuttle down and turning it to dock with *Raven*. "It's been fun and all, but it's time for a nap."

Ennis dragged his attention away from the view of the approaching ship. Almost there.

"Is everybody loaded?"

Lorai snorted. "Everybody who still wanted to come. Coupla faint hearts are thinking maybe Inner Systems aren't such a bad idea. Fine for them if they like living in a tiny metal box."

Moire was waiting for them when the hatch opened. She looked twitchy with fatigue and adrenaline, ready to react to anything, but he couldn't tell what she was thinking. Her face was closed.

"What did the police say?" she asked Lorai. They'd finally been able to get help once the shuttle got to *Dunkirk*, and the local enforcers were already at Waylands.

"Action committee, 'course. Nobody's saying anything to make them think different. Police *may* figure out they wanna talk to you, but I wouldn't count on it. Everything's a mess since they had to evacuate Waylands."

"Good." Moire scrubbed at her face with her hands. "Got somebody watching the scanners, dirtside as well as orbit. Nothing's showing that shouldn't be there. I hope that was the only one." She smiled wanly at Lorai. "Thanks for your help."

Lorai gave her a hearty hug, and a thump on the shoulder. "Any time." She grinned. "Better get some guns on my shuttles, if this is going to be a habit."

Moire didn't smile back. "I'll get you guns."

Ennis felt cold. He knew she was planning for an eventual attack on Sequoyah, but this made it too real. If it was like this fight, such a near-run thing...he closed his eyes briefly, trying to calm his mind.

Lorai gave her another thump, evidently to cheer her up, and left for the hatch. "See you there!" she waved.

"I won't…I've got another stop first," Moire called. Lorai turned back, looking puzzled. "It could take a while. Kilberton will have plenty of work for you, since Toren got the dropship. And Ulrike." Her face twisted. "He'll know if anybody else can run the other shuttle."

Lorai nodded. "Right. When are you leaving?"

"Soon as *Dunkirk* does. Kilberton said they had to rearrange some cargo to get your shuttles in, so a few hours."

Lorai waved again and shut the hatch. Moire glanced at the status indicators, then looked at him. There was a raw scrape on her forehead and a dark bruise on her jaw. All the things that could have gone wrong ran through his mind, one after the other, all ending with the one thing he feared most. He'd pushed the thought away before, unable to accept how very possible it was.

I could have lost her.

Terror closed his throat, froze his breath. He touched the bruise on her face with trembling fingers. Suddenly he was overwhelmed with the conviction that she was badly wounded, that she was concealing it, and he held her tightly, running his hands over her frantically, trying to find the injury. Convincing himself she was real, still alive.

He became aware Moire was doing much the same thing to him. Their mouths found each other hungrily, and slowly the terror died, replaced by a growing passion.

"Too close, too close," he whispered, seeing again the little man moving toward her in the restaurant. "He almost got you…" He shuddered and held her even more tightly.

"How did you know?" Moire asked, wondering. Her hazel eyes were full of light, and shades of color. They were deep, mesmerizing.

"I saw the gun. In his coat, when the creature startled him. The gun I used to have." He stroked her side where the ceramic needle had hit her, and she stiffened, shock in her face as she remembered. "It's a very distinctive weapon."

"That must be the best-traveled sidearm in the galaxy," she said with a shaky laugh.

"I should have tossed it down a disposal chute when I found it," Ennis said savagely.

Moire shook her head. "Without that, would you have even suspected him? I didn't. He looked so harmless, so frightened…"

He kissed her again, for comfort and to drive the image from his mind. He lost himself in her response, the increasing urgency overwhelming him. Now she was pulling him to follow her away from the hatch. Nothing could have stopped him, and he didn't want to stop. Still, at the door of her cabin he found himself saying, "We may regret this later."

Her lips moved, close enough to his ear he could feel it. "Maybe. But wouldn't you rather regret something you did than something you didn't do?"

His answer did not involve any words. He had no regrets, he realized, certainly not then. In that time, that place, with her, regret could not exist. Nor was anything like regret present when he drowsily drifted awake sometime later, spent but contented. There was something more, though, than simple physical satisfaction and love.

He could see Moire's face dimly in the red glow of the ship status indicators displayed on the wall of her bunk. He studied every feature, happy, and knowing his happiness was going to come to an end.

What had changed? She knew he loved her. He'd helped her fight her enemies, who were his enemies too. But he hadn't thought about that then. They had tried to hurt her and that was all that mattered. He hadn't thought of Fleet. He'd forgotten everything but the need to protect her, by any means.

He shifted to hold her closer. If he remembered everything, every detail, he would have that when she was gone. The scent of her skin, the feel of her hair, how her body had moved with his.

Maybe he would come back. Wouldn't Fleet want to send him to find her again, to get the crab, more valuable even than the ship? And if Fleet kicked him out, he could come back on his own. Free.

The sudden realization made him gasp, and Moire stirred and murmured in her sleep. He could come back, and she would welcome him. Her crew would welcome him. He had somewhere to go. The thing he'd been searching for all his life, without realizing it. He'd have to fight to keep it, but it was worth fighting for.

He leaned closer, careful not to wake her, and whispered, "I'm home." Her arm tightened around him reflexively for a moment, and he let himself drift back to sleep.

This time the ship pickup worked. Moire still had to fight *Frankenstein* free of the anomaly, or whatever it was in the center of the sargasso. The crab ship stayed in tow. Eventually she couldn't even feel the pull, but she still stayed on emergency watch on the bridge. The ship tow was too dicey to take chances with.

Ennis was with her constantly. He watched the indicators when she snatched a few hours of sleep, or just kept her awake by talking to her. Sometimes she wasn't sure she wanted him there, when all it did was remind her of passion she could no longer indulge in. The trip to the sargasso had not been nearly long enough for either of them, and now...now she had to keep her mind on her work.

"You already sent the message to Harrington about the dropoff location?" Ennis asked. He was sitting on the steps to the pilot's pit.

"Yep. It's the fifth on the list, so I told Kilberton to put the message 'Remember, remember the Fifth of November.'"

"'Gunpowder, treason, and plot.'" Ennis laughed. "How appropriate. He'll be surprised you know that. I used to think it was something Penderhest made up."

Moire hesitated. She'd have to tell him sometime, but it wasn't easy. "You may have a wait there. Kilberton has to unload all that gear at Sequoyah before he can deliver that message, and then it's however long it takes to get to Harrington and his invisible friends in Umbra."

Ennis raised an eyebrow. "They'll be expecting it. If he got to them, they'll be ready to go as soon as they know the location."

He didn't seem too worried about it. "Then you'll understand I can't stick around. I can't take the chance they want to talk to me, too." Again, no big surprise on his part. "What are they going to do with you?"

Ennis shrugged. "I'm not sure. Probably ask me lots of questions about Radersent. Perwaty is making me vids to take back, which will help."

"Make sure you tell them about what Radersent said about the sargasso anomaly," Moire said. "If there's somebody else out there who can make gravitic webspace mines...."

"Got it." Ennis looked grim. "All we've seen is the crabs so far. Maybe these others are on the other side of the galaxy. Still, something to watch out for." He paused. "What are you going to do next?" When she hesitated, he added, "That you can tell me about."

She felt bad about it still. It wasn't that she didn't trust him; she didn't trust the people he was going back to. She hoped he understood that.

"Got to get ready for Toren," Moire sighed. "It's just a matter of time now. They figured out we'd be at Bone without much trouble. I still don't know how. Lorai swears she didn't say anything until she got back, and there wouldn't have been enough time after that for the information to get to Toren before we arrived."

He got up and stood behind the pilot's chair, gently rubbing the back of her neck. "You have to be careful," he said quietly. "Even on Kulvar. They'll sell you out if the price is high enough. You're safe only as long as they don't know who to sell you to."

Moire leaned back, feeling the muscles in her neck go loose. Ennis had very strong hands. She was going to miss that. "I know."

"Did I tell you what Jens told me, before we left Bone?"

She shook her head. Jens had been pretty banged up by the explosion; she was surprised he'd been able to talk at all. At least he was going to survive.

"His wife left him alone in there when she went to get Lorai," he said. "Jens was there, hidden, when that Toren agent with the gun came in. He said the man came in with that enforcer he shot. He deliberately killed her, then changed his uniform and told the locals he was with the mining company." Ennis dropped down, his arms around her shoulders for a moment. They tightened. "Jens said...he enjoyed killing her. Please be careful," he said softly.

She put a hand on his arm, hearing the tremor in his voice. "That guy intercepted an exploding oxygen condenser plant," she said, trying to reassure him.

Ennis grabbed her shoulders and shook them. "There will be others." He sounded exasperated. "Professionals, like him. They might not remember Toren's orders to keep you alive."

What a cheerful thought. Maybe it was time to stop running away, waiting for Toren to find her. It had felt good when she blew up the Toren ship. Maybe she should give them something to worry about for a change.

"I'll keep it in mind," Moire said.

Gren pointed at the printout with a stubby finger, and Ennis tried to pay attention. It was important, even if all he really wanted to know was where Moire was. "Here's some diagrams of what Radersent did, or at least as much as I figured out. He did a good job. Both doors open just like they should; I tested them and so did some of the others. Your shelter takes up a lot of room in that tunnel, so we rigged ladders fore and aft so you can get over it. Menehune loaded plenty of supplies, so that's OK."

If Ennis had had any doubts about how the crew viewed him, they had vanished. Almost everyone on the ship had given him something to take with him. It was a good thing it was a ten-person shelter.

"Why do you have to leave?" Ash persisted. The Created had only recently found out he was leaving, and they were not pleased. "When are you coming back?"

It was a question he didn't like to hear. "I don't know," he snapped, then added in a more even tone. "As soon as I can. I have to take this ship to Fleet."

They had seen the crab ship, now free of the tow and positioned beside them. The Created thought this over for a minute, and apparently decided it might take him some time. Ash's face crumpled in misery.

He saw Moire standing in the doorway of the meeting room then, and a wave of cold washed over him. *No. Not now.* But he couldn't do what he wanted to do for her here. He had to go back to Fleet and convince them.

He didn't trust his voice right then, so he silently gathered up the printout and the other items and went out with her to the interceptor. The Toren attack ship had replaced the destroyed scout as their transfer vehicle.

"Your suit's inside," Moire said abruptly.

He nodded.

"Is there anything else you need?"

Just you.

The distance was hardly anything between *Frankenstein* and the crab ship. He barely had time to get his suit on. He snatched one last, bittersweet kiss before he sealed his faceplate. Her face was sad, and now tears were trickling down it.

"You tell them," she said roughly, "if they don't send you back I'll come and get you if I have to break into FarCom to do it. Got that?"

"Message received, Captain," he said, trying to smile. "I'll warn them."

Then he was alone in the airlock. Outside was the dark wall of the crab ship, with the bulky shelter looking strange in its new alien surroundings. He stepped into the tunnel entrance, turned, and waved at the viewport.

The interceptor pulled slowly away and returned to the tow ship. He stood and watched until he saw it start to leave, moving to engage the drive at a distance that would not affect the crab ship's position. Then he went inside the shelter. Gren had thoughtfully added a good scanner to the console, probably to help him when the Fleet showed up. He turned it on, watching the one bright spot on the screen move away. His heart. His home. It shimmered and disappeared as the ship went into drive.

The End

ABOUT THE AUTHOR

Sabrina Chase was originally trained as a Mad Scientist, but due to a tragic lack of available lairs at the time of graduation fell into low company and started working in the software industry. She lives in the Pacific Northwest and is owned by two cats.

Further sordid details may or may not be available at her website, chaseadventures.com